FINISTERRE

BY THE SAME AUTHOR

DI Joe Faraday Investigations

Turnstone
The Take
Angels Passing
Deadlight
Cut to Black
Blood and Honey
One Under
The Price of Darkness
No Lovelier Death
Beyond Reach
Borrowed Light
Happy Days

DS Jimmy Suttle Investigations

Western Approaches
Touching Distance
Sins of the Father
The Order of Things

Spoils of War

Finisterre
Aurore
Estocada
Raid 42
Last Flight to Stalingrad
Kyiv
Katastrophe

FICTION

Rules of Engagement
Reaper
The Devil's Breath
Thunder in the Blood
Sabbathman
The Perfect Soldier
Heaven's Light
Nocturne
Permissible Limits
The Chop
The Ghosts of 2012
Strictly No Flowers
Acts of Separation

NON-FICTION

Lucky Break
Airshow
Estuary
Backstory

Enora Andressen

Curtain Call
Sight Unseen
Off Script
Limelight
Intermission
Lights Down

FINISTERRE

GRAHAM HURLEY

HEAD of ZEUS

An Aries Book

First published in the UK in 2016 by Head of Zeus Ltd
Paperback edition first published in the UK in 2017 by Head of Zeus Ltd
This paperback edition first published in 2022 by Head of Zeus Ltd,
part of Bloomsbury Publishing Plc

9 7 5 3 1 2 4 6 8

A catalogue record for this book is available
from the British Library.

ISBN (PB): 9781800244887
ISBN (E): 9781784977801

Typeset by Ben Cracknell Studios

Printed and bound by CPI Group (UK) Ltd, Croydon, CR0 4YY

Head of Zeus Ltd
First Floor East
5–8 Hardwick Street
London EC1R 4RG

WWW.HEADOFZEUS.COM

For Brigitta

'Where there is fighting, there
is only victory or defeat.'
Joseph Goebbels

Finisterre

From the Latin *finis terrae*,
literally, 'the end of the earth'.

PART ONE

1

On 19 September 1944, the day the French port city of Brest fell to the Allied armies, a German submarine was limping south across the Bay of Biscay. *U-2553* had left Kiel nearly two weeks earlier, crossed the North Sea, rounded the Orkney Islands, then tracked south along the western edge of the minefields off the west coast of Scotland. A special voyage with a special significance, entrusted to one of the giants of the U-boat service.

Kapitän Stefan Portisch had been in submarines since the beginning of the war in 1939. He was tall, thin, blond, slightly stooped and looked much older than his twenty-four years. This was a new crew, the usual mix of seasoned veterans and young first-timers, but already Stefan had won their confidence.

They knew he'd had a hand in sinking hundreds of thousands of tons of enemy shipping. They admired the way he never boasted about the honours this combat record had brought him. And by watching him at the closest possible proximity, they sensed that command – the ability to coax the best out of men under conditions of extreme difficulty – was something he'd learned the hard way. In the game of war, as one of the veterans had put it, *Kapitän* Stefan Portisch was a lucky card to tuck in your pocket.

Stefan's latest promotion had taken him to one of the new *Elektro* boats, equipped with a *Schnorkel* to recharge the batteries without having to surface. Underwater, it could sustain five knots for sixty hours on a single charge. It was bigger than the old workhorse, the Type VII, which gave the crew extra room for a shower and even a freezer for fresh food. So far, so good. But this was the first time since the war began that Stefan Portisch had sailed without torpedoes.

Only one of the five strangers who'd joined the boat an hour before sailing had deigned to introduce himself. This was a thin, mirthless SS *Brigadeführer*. According to the orders from Berlin lodged with *Kapitän* Portisch, his name was Johann Huber. He had the senior SS look: dead eyes and an icy disdain for the small courtesies of life at sea. He was clearly on board to safeguard the other four passengers, and the pile of wooden crates so carefully stored for'ard in the torpedo compartment. So far, like them, he'd shown no interest in conversation or even the odd game of chess. This little group took their meals apart, raiding their kitbags for bottles of Gewürztraminer and tins of foie gras doubtless acquired from some Party hoard in Berlin.

The voyage was not going well. Stefan sensed at once that his crew resented the presence of these strangers. Above and below the waves, seamen were deeply superstitious. They had to rely on each other with a degree of trust more absolute than most marriages. These interlopers in their borrowed fatigues and fancy food had brought with them a strong whiff of the decay and corruption that seemed to be eating at the heart of the Fatherland. Somehow, they'd acquired a passage out of the ruined *Heimat*. Money? Power? Influence? No one knew. Except that *U-2553* was heading for Lisbon. And from

Lisbon these men could be in South America in no time at all.

Two days into the voyage, Stefan's second-in-command, a taciturn *Oberleutnant* from Bremerhaven three years older than himself, had put it best of all. These people are rats, he said. They're abandoning the Reich. They're spreading disease. They're a health hazard. They have no place here.

Stefan made his way to the tiny cubby hole where he marked up his charts. With five extra bodies aboard, space was precious. True, these new boats had slightly bigger latrines but one of them was now crammed with the personal luggage these people were taking with them. Back in Kiel, Stefan had watched the heavy suitcases passing from hand to hand. The latrine full, Huber had told Stefan to lock it. Then he demanded the key and slipped it into his pocket. My boat, those eyes were saying. My rules. My voyage.

Stefan was as curious as the rest of the crew to know what was inside those suitcases, and why the wooden crates in the torpedo compartment were so important, but just now his finger was tracing the pencilled line that tracked the progress of *U-2553* across the Bay of Biscay. A little over an hour ago they'd been five miles due north of Finisterre, the topmost corner of Spain jutting out into the Atlantic. Eight days earlier, hugging the continental shelf off the west coast of Ireland, they'd been located by an enemy destroyer and depth-charged.

The attack had lasted more than an hour, the crew at action stations braced for yet another volley of explosions as the thrum-thrum of the approaching destroyer grew and grew until you could taste nothing but fear in the dryness of your mouth. No matter how long you'd served, these terrifying moments tested the strongest nerves.

The strangers from Kiel had gathered in the clutter of the for'ard sleeping compartment, their faces already the colour of death in the dim light. After the first attack, all five of them had struggled into the standard-issue life jackets. As the jaws of yet another blast closed around the hull, Stefan watched them trying to steady themselves. The boat bucked and groaned. Lights flickered and died. Steam blew from ruptured valves. Then, at last, the attack was over. The destroyer had either run out of depth charges or simply lost interest.

Minutes later, the Chief Engineer had reported serious damage to the port prop shaft. He said his men were doing their best to effect repairs but he wasn't optimistic. With Lisbon more than a thousand miles away, *U-2553* was down to just three knots.

Since then it had got worse. Everyone knew these new war-winning subs were shit. They'd been thrown together from huge prefabricated sections. Back home, with the shipyards short of proper expertise, much of the work had been done by forced labour from POWs and concentration camps. Berlin still boasted about war-winning technology and record-breaking construction times but the new *Elektro* boats were plagued by faults. Of the eight so far launched, just two had made it into active service.

Stefan had met a fellow *Kapitän* from one of these crews in Lorient. He'd just returned from a lone-wolf bid to ambush a huge Allied convoy inbound from North America. Everyone aboard knew that the assignment was suicidal – too many escorts, too many aircraft – but a failure in the main propulsion unit only hours out from Lorient had spared them an ugly death. Thank God for lousy engineering, the *Kapitän* had muttered. So much for the wonder boat.

A shadow fell over the chart. It was the Chief Engineer with more bad news. In a whispered conversation, he told Stefan that the drive-coupling in the starboard prop shaft had developed a problem. Worse still, an intermittent malfunction with the float that protected the *Schnorkel* was threatening to get worse.

Stefan raised an eyebrow. The *Schnorkel* was a mast-like tube that slid up from the conning tower and sucked in fresh air to feed the diesel engines. For some reason the float at the mouth of the tube was getting stuck, cutting off the air supply. Without fresh air, the diesels wouldn't work, and without the diesels there was no way of recharging the batteries without surfacing.

'You want us to surface?'

'Yes, sir. And I'll have to close down the prop shaft before we can make any kind of repair.'

Stefan's eye had returned to the chart. On the surface, the diesels could recharge the batteries without turning the prop shaft. Already up top it was twilight. This close to the shore of a neutral country, the only real danger would be the odd fishing boat. Stefan glanced up at the engineer.

'How much time will you need?'

'Hard to say. Two hours? Three? Depends.'

Stefan nodded. The most recent weather forecast had warned of an approaching storm. Winds from the north-west gusting at eighty knots. Waves cresting at twenty metres. At normal cruise depth, the boat was immune from bad weather but the need to recharge the batteries through the *Schnorkel* had taken them to within touching distance of the surface. Already he could hear the hull beginning to groan as the boat wallowed along. Offering themselves to a storm of this magnitude would be suicidal.

'You think we have a choice?'

'No, sir.' The engineer's eyes had strayed to the chart. 'We could lose the prop shaft completely. This close in, no engines, no power, no steerage way, would you really want that?'

Stefan gazed at him a moment. The law of diminishing options, he thought. This whole bloody war captured in a single question. Robbed of choice, he mustered a tired shrug.

'Fine,' he said. 'Then we surface.'

*

Los Alamos is in New Mexico. The same morning found Hector Gómez sitting at his desk on the sprawling site the Americans dubbed the Hill. Gómez was a huge man, Hispanic in girth, Mexican by origin, impressively ugly. He'd joined US Army Intelligence after years of front-line service with the FBI and just now he was contemplating a drive to Santa Fe when his phone rang. It was a glorious morning up here on the mesa and after a leisurely breakfast in the commissary, Gómez had dropped into his office in the Admin Building to check on his mail before heading out. He hadn't had a day off in weeks.

'Gómez.' He bent to the phone.

For a moment, he couldn't place the woman's voice. Foreign. German, maybe. Or one of those fussy, neurotic Hungarian women who seem standard issue if you happen to be a refugee genius in the field of nuclear physics. Either way, the lady at the end of the phone was seriously distressed.

'It's my husband,' she kept saying. 'Sol.'

'Sol?'

'He's here. I'm looking at him. He's shot dead.'

'*Dead?* You're serious?'

'*Ja.* There's blood everywhere. Please come. Please help.'

Gómez reached for a chair and settled behind the desk. He'd recalled the name at last. Sol Fiedler. Nice old man with thinning grey hair and a lovely smile, probably chasing fifty. Checking his watch, Gómez dallied briefly with passing the call on to the colleague who was supposed to be covering for him but then had second thoughts. Nothing seriously interesting had come his way for months. Just the endless daily chore of security checks and queries from the mail censor that fell to Army Intelligence. Santa Fe could wait.

'I'm there,' he said. 'Don't touch a thing.'

Marta Fiedler lived on the bottom floor of one of the Morgan two-storey duplexes on the outer fringes of the sprawling complex. Her front door was open and Gómez could hear the blare of a radio.

He stepped into the apartment from the blaze of sunshine and for a moment his world went inky black. He was wearing a light windcheater over his regulation shirt and tie and he drew his gun. In his FBI days he'd lost count of fellow agents maimed or worse for stepping into an ambush.

He called Mrs Fiedler's name, heard nothing. He tried again and finally stirred a response, a small animal wail of acute distress. Making his way to one of the bedrooms at the back of the apartment, he found her curled beside her husband.

Sol Fiedler's body lay diagonally across the bed. The embroidered counterpane was the colour of curd cheese except where blood and gobbets of brain had exploded through the

9

side of his skull. His eyes were open, the lightest blue. Beside his outstretched hand was an Army-issue Browning automatic and the acrid stench of a recently expended shell hung in the chill of the air-conditioning.

Gómez reached down. Fiedler's body was still warm but there was no sign of a pulse. The neatness of the entry wound was circled with powder burns and Gómez cursed himself for having left his camera in the office. He'd drive back to fetch it when he was through here but first he needed to know a great deal more.

Marta stared up at him. She and Gómez had met a couple of times before on cookouts and other social events. On the last occasion, less than a month ago, they'd talked about a bunch of ancient Indian ruins in the Bandelier National Monument, a favourite destination for weekend excursions among the Hill-folk. He remembered her telling him how hard it was to prise Sol away from his work. The Gadget, she'd said, had taken over both their lives.

'He left a note.' She nodded at a neatly folded sheet of paper on the carpet. Her years in America had done nothing to soften her accent.

Gómez picked it up. He'd remembered something else about this couple. They had no children. Quickly, he scanned the note.

Mein Liebling, it began. *Ich kann nicht mehr. Die Arbeit ist übel. Vor mir ist Blut und noch mehr Blut. Ich will nichts mehr damit zu tun haben. Du weisst das. Ich liebe dich für immer und ewig. Nichts kann das ändern. Das ist die einzige Lösung. Your ever-loving Sol.*

Everything typed, Hector thought. Nothing handwritten, not even the guy's name at the end.

'What does it say?' He finally looked up.

'It says. . .' She fumbled for her glasses and then reached for the note. 'My darling. I can't take this any more. The work is evil. All I see ahead is blood and more blood. I can't be part of this. You know that. . .' She broke off for a moment, shaking her head. Then she swallowed hard and resumed. '. . . I'll love you for ever. Nothing will ever change that. This is the only way. Your ever-loving Sol.'

Gómez said nothing. Then he asked for the note back and pressed her for more details. When exactly had she found him?

'Just now. When I came back. I'd been up at the PX. There was a delivery of salt beef yesterday. Sol loves salt beef.'

She took her glasses off and began to cry again, hopelessly confused by what had happened. Gómez put the note carefully to one side. He found a handkerchief in a drawer and gave it to her. She wiped her eyes, then blew her nose. Gómez noticed an English/German dictionary on the bedside table and a copy of an Armed Forces paperback western. Cheap Indian rugs on the floor.

'Was Sol here when you left?'

'*Nein*. He was at work in the Tech Area.'

'Have you phoned them? Talked to his supervisor?'

'No. Only you.'

She stared at her husband's body, shaking her head in disbelief, and Gómez extended a meaty hand, pulling her gently upright on the bed. He was thinking maybe a shot or two of bourbon but something told him that neither of them drank hard liquor. In the kitchen he killed the radio and put the kettle on the stove. Marta perched herself on a stool beside the window, bird-like, a small, fragile creature who'd just fallen out of the nest. She'd still got the handkerchief and turned her head away.

'That note.' She blew her nose again. 'It's just all wrong.'

'Why?'

'Because Sol always called me *Spatzling* when he wrote to me.'

'*Spatzling?*'

'It means "little sparrow" in German. Her never called me *Liebling*. Never. And something else.' She nodded back towards the bedroom. 'He never used a typewriter. He never knew how. My husband was a genius. But he couldn't work a typewriter.'

'Do you have a typewriter in the house?'

'No.'

Gómez nodded, making a mental note. Check the typing against machines in Fiedler's lab. Anyone can type if they have to.

'What about the weapon? Do you recognise the gun?'

'Never. Sol hated guns. Any kind of violence. In Germany you saw things all the time, horrible things. Guns were everywhere.' She shook her head, emphatic now. 'Never again. No guns.'

'This country is full of guns,' Gómez pointed out.

'I know. But this country is different. You use guns to defend yourself.' She was staring through the open door towards the bedroom. 'Not for something like this.'

Sol loved America, she said, especially up here on the mesa. It gave him space. It gave him peace of mind. It gave him a chance to answer back. From the moment they'd got off the train at Santa Fe he couldn't wait to get up to the Hill and join the other scientists on the Tamper Group. After the nightmare years in Germany, she said, he'd at last found a centre – a meaning – to his life. Now this.

Gómez nodded. A lot of this stuff would be on record in the Personnel Department. The small print could wait. While the body was still warm you stuck to the obvious.

'Had he been depressed recently? Anything you might have noticed?'

'Nothing. Sol was a child at heart. Kids don't get depressed. Not Sol's kind of kids.'

'You're sure about that? He wasn't hiding anything?'

'Never.' She shook her head, a first hint of resentment. 'I'd have known. I'd have sensed it. I knew that man inside out. I knew every particle of him, every nook, every cranny. He could hide nothing. Because there was nothing to hide.'

'He ever upset anyone?'

'No one. Everyone loved him. Just ask. Ask anyone.'

'No . . .' Gómez frowned, looking for the coffee, '. . . lady friends?'

'I just told you.'

'Tell me again.'

'He was happy. We were happy. Why would he need anyone else?'

The coffee was in a cupboard over the sink. Gómez dropped a spoonful into a cup and added hot water.

'You take sugar?'

Marta wasn't listening. She wanted to know who'd do such a thing, who'd steal the man she'd loved.

'You're telling me someone killed him?'

'I'm telling you he'd never do such a thing himself.'

'How can you be sure?'

'Because we lived in a world without secrets.' She was staring out of the window, her eyes still bright with tears. 'Even here.'

*

It was dark by the time the storm hit. It came blasting out of the north-west, huge cresting waves, curtains of flying spume. The tiny huddle of men in the conning tower of the U-boat were wearing harnesses attached to the superstructure but even so they battled to keep their feet. All three of them were wearing layer after layer of wet-weather gear, hunched figures bent against the fury of the heaving sea. Stefan Portisch was one of them. He bent to the speaking tube as the bow reared up yet again and a wall of water came thundering out of the darkness.

Instinctively the men ducked. The Chief Engineer was still down aft in the engine room, supervising work on the failed coupling. In a couple of minutes, he said it might be worth slipping the prop shaft back into gear. Not before time, Stefan thought.

He grunted an acknowledgement and gestured for the other two men to go below. The wind was howling now but in tiny moments when the storm paused for breath he told himself he could hear the roar of surf away to port. In that direction lay the rocky foreshore of Galicia.

Stefan had never been to northern Spain but a year or so back he'd had a brief encounter with a French woman in Lorient. She knew the area well. She'd talked of the impact the cliffs had made on her – their sheer size, their sheer scale – and she'd described the emptiness of the beaches. This was a landscape, she'd said, that didn't need people. It felt prehistoric, unforgiving, majestic, pitiless. Over a carafe or two of thin red wine, Stefan had been impressed. Now he wasn't so sure. If the prop shaft held out they might be able to submerge and claw their way seawards. Otherwise, the game was probably up.

Down below, the storm had turned everything upside down. In the glimmer of the emergency lighting, sodden clothing and personal belongings had spilled from bunks. The deck plates were a mess of cables, ducts and broken glass. Tins of food were rolling around as the boat pitched. Crewmen, tight-lipped in the roar of the storm, were ankle-deep in water. For two weeks, as ever, these men had lived with nothing but the stench of diesel oil, rotting food, sweat and excrement, a fug that was the price of staying alive. Now, Stefan thought he could detect a new odour: fear.

The Chief Engineer struggled forward from the diesel compartment. He hadn't slept for days and it showed. A single upturned thumb spared Stefan the effort of asking the obvious question. The prop shaft was ready. Let's give it a shot.

'And the *Schnorkel*?'

The Chief shrugged, then crossed two pairs of fingers. The broken teeth of nearby Spain might yet tear them to pieces. *Que sera sera.*

Stefan ordered the hatch on the conning tower to be closed. The engineer wedged himself at the controls and fired up the prop shaft. Stefan heard a low whine as the recharged electric motor engaged then felt the boat shake itself like a dog. Anything to get away from the feral monster that called itself a storm. Anything for the comforts of deeper water.

'Flood buoyancy tanks two and three. Prepare to dive.'

The Chief reached for the big valves and the boat nosed down. Stefan stole a glance at the strangers in the for'ard compartment. Like the rest of the crew, they'd scented danger and they were back in their life jackets. As Stefan watched, Huber muttered something to the SS colleague at his side and then stepped across to the locked latrine. He fumbled for the key and opened the door. The jigsaw of carefully stowed suitcases had shifted during the voyage and three of them tumbled out. Huber bent quickly to the smallest and snapped the catches.

By now the boat was at thirty metres with the seabed rapidly approaching. The fury of the storm had given way to an eerie silence, punctuated by the rumble of the prop shaft and the steady drip-drip of dozens of leaks. Then, abruptly, came a harsh, metallic jolt, followed by the stripping of a million gears.

The Chief was staring at the control panel.

'It's gone,' he said bitterly. 'It's finished.'

Stefan turned back to him. Huber was rummaging for something in the suitcase.

'What about the other prop shaft?'

The Chief looked round. There was something crazy in his eyes.

'Why not?' He extended a weary arm. '*Heil Hitler.*'

He tripped a couple of switches then reached for a lever recessed into the control desk. The other prop shaft, already damaged, began to turn. Then he stiffened, his attention caught by another gauge. A key component on the batteries was already overheating. Carrying on would risk a fire or even an explosion. Only diesel power could carry the boat to safety.

Stefan nodded. In six years at sea, he told himself, he'd encountered far worse crises than this. Staring death in the face had become an occupational hazard. Rule one? Never lose your nerve.

He ordered the boat to surface again. The Chief blew the buoyancy tanks, watching the tiny gestures Stefan was making in the half-darkness to slow the climb before breaking surface. Stefan's hands lifted and fell, lifted and fell, orchestrating the ascent. He'd become the conductor of this mad symphony that threatened, at any moment, to become a full-blown requiem. Compressed air was still emptying the tanks. At a depth of four metres, Stefan levelled out. Fresh air sucked in through the *Schnorkel* had given him one last option.

'Go to diesels,' he said.

The Chief was ahead of him. The big diesels coughed into action and the damaged prop shaft began to turn again. Crew close to the command consoles were staring at the gauges. The one on the right recorded forward speed. The compass lay beneath it. Five knots on a bearing of 345. Enough to take them back to the open sea. Just.

For minutes on end the crew stood motionless. You could hear the storm again and the boat was heaving beneath their feet. Then the steady clatter of the diesels suddenly died and – throughout the boat – men were gasping for air, their chests tight, their eyes bulging. Stefan could feel it himself, a terrifying pressure in the throat and lungs, and he knew at once what had happened. The bloody float in the *Schnorkel* had got stuck again, cutting off the air supply. The diesels had sucked what remained of the good air from the hull and now there was nothing left but a vacuum. In minutes, everyone aboard would suffocate.

The Chief was already expelling the last of the water from the buoyancy tanks. As the boat surfaced, men were thrown everywhere by the violence of the storm. Stefan fought his way across the control space, struggled up the ladder into the conning tower and released the hatch. A torrent of water flooded into the hull.

Men crowded forward, desperate for the sweetness of fresh air blasting in through the open hatch. Among them was SS *Brigadeführer* Huber. He was clutching a small leather wallet. He was trying to scale the ladder , determined to be the first to get out. Stefan met him at the foot of the ladder and shoved him roughly back. The moment he lost control of this situation, the moment the crew panicked, would be the moment they'd all die.

Huber drew a handgun, a standard-issue Luger. Stefan stared at it. The dull gleam of the barrel was inches from his forehead. The boat was wallowing savagely, out of control, broadside on to the storm. Stefan tried to steady himself, still blocking the way to the steel ladder that led up to the conning tower. Huber's finger had tightened on the trigger. Why not now, Stefan thought. Why not here? Why not spare yourself the miseries of the minutes and maybe hours to come?

Then the hull shuddered beneath a huge wave, more water pouring in through the open hatch, and for the first time he heard the hollow metallic clang as the helpless submarine hit something solid. Rocks, Stefan thought. Then came another clang, a second death knell, as the granite reefs tore into the fragile hull.

Huber knew exactly what was happening. There was fear in his eyes. He pushed hard against Stefan, reaching for the ladder, but Stefan caught him off balance and managed to knock the gun aside. At the same time, the Chief stepped out of the shadows. He had a heavy spanner and he brought it crashing down on the side of Huber's skull. The man crumpled with a soft gasp – partly surprise, partly pain – and joined the rest of the debris swilling across the deck plates.

The watching crewmen raised a cheer as Stefan bent to retrieve the pistol and the leather wallet. In the roar of the storm, fresh blood was already pinking the water at his feet. One of the other SS men stepped forward. He had a gun in his hand.

Stefan studied him for a moment.

'You want to kill me? Like your *Brigadeführer* wanted to kill me?'

The SS man was staring at the inert body at Stefan's feet. The submarine steadied itself. Then, from nowhere, came a collective roar from the rest of the crew. They wanted these men gone. They wanted them out of the submarine. Or they wanted them dead before the storm claimed them.

A young radio operator from Kiel got to the gunman first. He had him by the throat, pinned against the bulkhead. The pistol had disappeared. More crew lunged forward, fighting the submarine's next wild lurch, then threw themselves at the other SS men. Stefan took a tiny step back. These men were brothers, *Kameraden*. They were also out of control but it was hard not to be proud of them, impossible not to sympathise with years of bottled up-anger: how they'd been lied to, manipulated, offered up as a sacrifice as the prospects of victory disappeared.

Two weeks earlier they'd put to sea in the dying embers of a war they sensed they couldn't possibly win. Cherbourg had gone. St Malo had gone. And now Brest, home to countless of their *Kameraden*, was in the hands of the Americans. And so what was left? Would Lorient be next, with its huge U-boat pens? And then St Nazaire? Of course they would. And so all that remained was this pitiful bid to spirit a handful of dead-eyed

Untermensch to a bright new future their crippled homeland could only dream about. That made no sense. That made the crew of *U-2553* accomplices in the shoddiest of exits.

Worse, in the face of an ugly death, it was an insult. After two weeks of quiet speculation about the contents of the torpedo compartment, about the grotesque fantasy of a Thousand Year Reich, the time had come for a reckoning.

This was civil war, and Stefan knew it. The SS men had gone down under the sheer weight of numbers. Stefan pointed Huber's pistol into nowhere and pulled the trigger. The fighting stopped.

For a moment there was nothing but the roar of the storm. Gouts of water were still cascading in through the open hatch. The SS gunman was the first to struggle to his feet. The other three, ignoring the body of their *Brigadeführer*, formed a protective barrier against the press of the crew. The smallest of them, an infant from Bavaria, was the only one with whom Stefan had formed any kind of relationship. He was bleeding from a gash on his lip. He looked pale and frightened.

'What now, *Herr Kapitän*?'

Stefan nodded at the ladder. 'You go first,' he said. 'All of you. When you get to the top, you jump.'

'What about the *Brigadeführer*?'

Stefan shot a glance at the body at his feet. His eyes were open and he appeared to be breathing. Then Stefan's gaze returned to the SS men.

'If he's not dead, he soon will be. There's no way we can get him out. You either take the ladder or my men will kill you.' Stefan braced against a savage roll to starboard. 'Your choice.'

*

Hector Gómez reported to a full colonel in the Los Alamos security organisation, a career soldier called Arthur Whyte. Gómez had been uneasy about the relationship for the year and a half he'd been down in New Mexico. Los Alamos was run by the Army. Whyte was a manager, not an investigator, and it showed. His loyalty was to the Project. The program had to stay on schedule, had to deliver the Gadget to the tightest of deadlines. The fact that no one except a tiny handful in Washington knew what the deadline was simply added to the pressure. You did your job. You asked no questions. As far as the rest of the world was concerned you'd become part of an army of busy ghosts: scientists, engineers and support staff who'd quietly shipped in from labs and institutions across Europe and the States. Up here on the mesa even the site itself didn't have a proper name. PO Box 1663, Santa Fe.

Whyte had an office in the same dull green Army-issue building as Gómez: top floor, better view, blessed with a water cooler that never broke down. He was a lean man, watchful. He had buffed nails and a complexion he was careful to hide from the sun. Before coming to the Hill, he'd run security at a big Army base in the Midwest. For a career soldier the Los Alamos posting was the chance of a lifetime, and Whyte knew it. There were twenty-eight men in Army Intel under his command plus seven civilians. Word on the Hill had Whyte eyeballing a promotion to a one-star brigadier.

'So where are we going with this thing?' he asked. 'The guy shoots himself. He's pissed with himself. It happens. It ain't gonna make anyone's day, least of all his, but we move on. Am I missing something here?'

Gómez didn't bother to go through it all again. Whyte was an intelligent guy. He'd understood the significance of the typed note, of the gun that had come from nowhere, of the lack – in Marta Fiedler's view – of any reason for her husband to put a bullet through his head. But that wasn't the point. It was Whyte's job to protect the racing heartbeat of the Los Alamos machine. He was the most loyal of soldiers. Absolutely nothing, in his view, should interrupt the heads-down dash to turn the Gadget into the biggest bang the world had ever seen. Least of all the suicide of just one of the thousand-plus scientists on site.

'And if it's not suicide?'

'You can't prove that.'

'Not now, I can't. You know I can't. But that's not how investigation works.'

Gómez went no further but he knew he didn't have to. This wasn't a conversation about a crime scene but a brisk reminder that life on the Hill was governed by a different set of priorities. Nonetheless, Whyte had a nose for trouble. Gómez knew his trade. And Gómez, irked, could be trouble of the worst sort.

'How much time would you need?'

'To do a proper job? A coupla weeks. Minimum. With more on the back end if the story develops.'

Impassive as ever, Whyte consulted his calendar. Today was Tuesday.

'You've got until the end of the week.' He looked up. 'Keep me briefed, yeah?'

Back in his own office, Gómez settled briefly behind his desk. He'd already established that the apartment above the Fiedlers' place had been empty for nearly a week, awaiting the arrival of new tenants. Neighbouring apartments housed single men sharing accommodation, all of whom had been in the Technical Area at the time of the incident. In terms of witnesses, Sol Fiedler had therefore died alone. Unless, of course, someone else had pulled the trigger.

The Browning automatic, bagged and tagged, lay on Gómez's desk. He was thinking about the shot itself, the sound of the explosion. In most places that would have attracted attention, maybe brought people running, but once again the Hill was different. Explosions were part of the soundtrack of life up here on the mesa. There was a special facility – the S-1 site – tucked up one of the more remote canyons where the metallurgists and the engineers conducted their experiments. Some days scarcely an hour went by without the boom of high explosive or the sharper crack of a bullet rolling over the landscape. People got used to it, even the birds, so the sound of the Browning automatic – a single shot – would have stirred no interest.

Upstairs, under pressure, Whyte had agreed to second another pair of hands to the investigation and Gómez had asked for a younger guy he'd come to trust. His name was Carl Merricks and, like Gómez, he came from Chicago. Picking up his detective skills in the lap of the US Department of Defense, he lacked FBI experience but he was quick to learn and Gómez had never been shy about establishing exactly what he needed to extract from a crime scene. Merricks would be handling the forensics: fingerprints from the entire apartment plus full tests on the handgun. The latter would include a match on the recovered bullet. The scene suggested that the slug must have come from the Browning but Gómez had learned never to trust such an obvious linkage. Something told him Fiedler's death was a set-up. Maybe the bullet came from another weapon.

Motive? Here, Gómez was in the dark. Ahead lay countless interviews with Fiedler's friends and colleagues. Marta had her husband down as Mr Nice, Mr Popular, Mr Happy, but Marta's stake in a relationship she'd turned into an entire life made her an unreliable witness. Maybe Fiedler had upset someone. Maybe, without even realising it, he'd pushed too hard on someone's door with consequences he'd never be able to imagine.

Scientific genius, as Gómez was beginning to understand, marched in lockstep with acute instabilities on the emotional side. A lot of these guys were like kids: vulnerable, easily upset, ticking bombs when it came to getting on with each other. A difference of opinion about some technical detail? Resentment about lab status or data access? A quarrel over a woman? Some tribal difference buried deep in a shared European past? The pressures up on the Hill were brutal and Gómez had no problem imagining circumstances that might have led to the shooting. Engaged in a race to blow up half the world, the death of a fortysomething nuclear physicist would have the lightness of a feather, and pretty much everyone knew it. Bang. Gone. Dead. Was that the way it had been? A moment of extreme violence to make some guy with a grudge against Sol Fiedler feel better about himself?

Gómez contemplated the proposition, knowing it was unlikely. Unless Sol Fiedler had been a stranger to his wife, unless he'd really taken his own life, then this thing had been planned by someone else. Poorly thought-out but planned nonetheless. Gómez knew from Marta Fiedler that Tuesdays, after her visit to the PX, she always went over to the school to help with the kids. That was her routine. It never varied. Except that this morning she'd not felt great and hadn't wanted to spread her germs around. Plus Sol, too, was feeling lousy. Hence his early return from the Tech Area, sent home by a supervisor anxious to avoid the bug spreading to any other of his precious scientists.

So who else might have known about Sol's presence back in the house? A rich opportunity if you wanted to kill the man and dress it up as some kind of suicide? Gómez pulled his notepad towards him, flipped to a new page and made a list of the obvious suspects. Working colleagues in the Tech Area. Close friends he might have seen over the weekend. Folks, in short, who knew he had a bug that would likely bring him back home. Alone.

Each of these people would have to account for their movements this morning. They'd need an alibi, corroboration, a cast-iron reason for Gómez to strike their names from the list. Only this way could he start to tease investigative sense into Fiedler's death. He leaned back, the beginnings of a smile ghosting across his face as he imagined the news bursting out of Fiedler's metallurgy lab and spreading like a prairie fire across the Tech Area: not only had the guy died but there appeared to be grounds to believe that someone had *killed* him. No wonder Arthur Whyte wanted Sol Fiedler put quietly to rest, a suicide accepted at face value. What was a single death in the fortunes of the nation, in the balance of history, when these people were scheming to incinerate millions?

Gómez checked his watch. Marta Fiedler had already moved out of the apartment to stay with friends. Tomorrow, once he'd taken a look at Sol's personal file, he'd make time for a much longer interview. Merricks, meanwhile, had sealed off the apartment and would be supervising the forensics. The body, already photographed, had been removed to the hospital morgue. The autopsy would be handled by a suitably qualified doctor on site. The phrase had been Arthur Whyte's. 'Suitably qualified' didn't begin to measure up to Gómez's evidential standards but for once he had to accept that access to Los Alamos was heavily restricted. No way was news of Fiedler's death going to leak further than strictly necessary. At least not for now.

Gómez was at the door when his phone began to ring. It was a voice he recognised at once. Agard Beaman. The rookie campaigner he'd looked after a couple of years back in Detroit. The guy who'd nearly taken a bullet from a hit man after upsetting the wrong people during the mid-term elections.

Gómez didn't bother with the normal courtesies. He didn't have to. Beaman was in a state of some excitement. Gómez could hear it in his voice.

'I'm in Santa Fe tomorrow,' he said. 'Tell me you're not busy.'

Gómez was staring down at his notepad. The to-do list, mostly minor stuff, filled three pages.

'I'm not busy,' he said. 'Tell me where and when.'

*

It took longer than Stefan expected to get the crew out of the stricken submarine. One by one, in the gloom of the emergency lighting, they fought their way towards the conning tower, scaled the ladder on the heels of the SS men and disappeared into the roaring darkness above. The *Oberleutnant* and a couple of sailors had done their best to break out the emergency rubber dinghies from their compartment on the heaving deck but they'd both been washed away. Each of the crewmen knew that their only hope lay in jumping overboard and hoping to God they caught the lucky wave that would lift them shorewards, avoiding the rocks that exploded around them, huge gouts of wind-torn spray, white against the blackness of the night.

Speared on the jagged rocks, U-2553 was already breaking up, her buoyancy tanks ruptured, her bow a tangle of iron plates, the remains of her hull shuddering under the impact of the waves. Alone in the control room with the SS *Brigadeführer* Stefan was only too aware his time was limited. He'd counted his men out and he knew he had at best minutes to make it up the ladder before the storm laid the boat on its side and beat it to death.

Huber was conscious again. Water was flooding into the hull, already knee-deep, slopping from compartment to compartment. Stefan had helped the SS officer to his feet and now he was clinging to one of the big stanchions, his face pale, blood still trickling from the gash in his scalp. Stefan told him that the rest of his men had left the submarine but he didn't seem to understand. I don't want to drown, he kept saying. You have to help me.

Stefan knew that getting Huber's body up to the conning tower would probably kill them both, and he could see in his eyes that he understood this. The end had come. But, please God, not by drowning.

Stefan still had the wallet and the Luger. He'd slipped the wallet into a pocket of his long grey leather coat but he'd kept the gun in his hand.

Huber was looking at it. Then he whispered something Stefan didn't at first catch.

Stefan bent low, asked him to repeat it.

'Shoot me.' He nodded at the gun. 'That's an order.'

Stefan stared at him. Since the U-boat war began, he must have killed hundreds of people. But not like this. So close. So intimate. So personal.

'No,' he shook his head. 'I can't. I won't.'

'Please.'

'No. I said no.'

'Then let me do it.'

The gun again. Huber couldn't take his eyes off it. Death by execution, Stefan thought. The fanatic's best friend. Live by the bullet, die by the bullet.

'You want me to give you the gun?'

'Yes.'

'So you kill me, too?'

'No.'

'You're crazy. Why should I believe you?'

'You needn't. Just shoot me. Just kill me. It's a small thing. Just do it.'

A small thing? Another huge wave lifted the boat. When it settled again, the hull buckling against the rocks, the list to starboard was more acute. Fighting gravity, Stefan could barely stand up. The water was rising fast and he could feel the iciness spreading up beyond his knees. Now or never, he thought. Him or me.

Huber hadn't taken his eyes off Stefan's face. Then a hand went to the pocket of his greatcoat and he produced a fistful of coins. Even in the dimness of the hull, they glittered.

'Polish gold.' He thrust the coins towards Stefan. 'They're yours. Here. Take them.'

Stefan didn't move. Loot, he thought.

'I said take them.'

Stefan shook his head. He wanted nothing to do with this man's booty, with this man's war.

Huber stepped closer. His breath clouded on the cold air.

'Yes? You'll do it?' He nodded down at the gun.

Stefan was looking up at the conning tower. For the first time, he realised the obvious.

'You can't swim?'

'No.'

Stefan nodded, at last beginning to understand. Huber's hand was reaching for Stefan's coat. Even now, even here, he needed to be obeyed. Over the roar of the storm, Stefan caught the jingle of coins as the gold settled in his pocket.

'OK, then.' Stefan shrugged, took a tiny step away, and then cocked the Luger. 'It's your choice.'

The *Brigadeführer*'s eyes should have been shut. In movies they'd have been shut. In books they'd have been shut. But they weren't. Huber was staring at Stefan, daring him, taunting him, *shaming* him into pulling the trigger. Even now, a breath away from oblivion, he'd maintained the pecking order. The SS were the true believers. The *Schutzstaffel* were still on top of the pile, surveying the wreckage of the Thousand Year Reich. *Treu. Tapfer. Gehorsam.* Loyal. Valiant. Obedient.

'*Heil Hitler*,' Huber said softly. 'Prove yourself a man.'

2

Santa Fe had two decent hotels. The crowd from the Hill met, drank, gossiped and occasionally stayed over at La Fonda. Visiting businessmen, physicists and commissioned officers above a certain rank favoured the Rancho Encantado. Gómez found Agard Beaman at La Luna. It was in the wrong part of town. The building had once served as an abattoir. Thirty rooms were shoehorned into two storeys. The air-con was little more than a promise. You'd be wise to avoid what passed as the restaurant. But it was cheap.

Beaman occupied a room on the second floor. When Gómez arrived, pulling his Lincoln into the dusty parking lot across the street, Beaman was hanging out of his open window, yelling at a couple of Indian kids in the street below. The moment he saw Gómez, he broke off the exchange.

'Come up, man,' he said. 'Room 207.'

Gómez crossed the street. The kids were young, no more than ten, both boys. One of them was swinging a tattered length of rope. The other glanced up at the open window then rolled his eyes and drilled his forefinger into his temple. The gringo? Nuts.

Beaman was sprawled on the bed when Gómez pushed at the door and stepped in. This was an imp of a man, barely five six, still young. Fiercely intelligent, he had limitless energy and a voice that came from a much bigger body. He was wearing patched shorts and a bleached white T-shirt in the late-summer heat.

The room was tiny and smelled bad. Beaman's bag lay open on the floor, books and clothes spilling on to the carpet. The carpet was as cheap as everything else, cratered with cigarette burns.

'What's with the kids?' Gómez nodded towards the window.

'They had a dog. A mutt. They had it on some kind of leash. That age you get bored. But there are limits, *comprende*?'

Comprende was new. Gómez had spent the best part of three weeks with Beaman in Detroit during the mid-terms back in '42, hired by the Democrats to protect their fiery young campaigner, but he'd never talked like this before. He used the word playfully but with a certain authority. Something's happened, Gómez thought. The boy seems to have grown up.

Gómez eyed the single chair, doubting it would take his weight. Beaman made space on the bed. Gómez shook his head.

'There's a bar on the next block,' he said. 'You need to get out of this shithole.'

The bar was called El Aero. It was clean and way off the main drag. Gómez used it most times he came into town. He liked the owner, a wizened old guy called Artie who'd once flown stunt planes at Kansas country fairs, and he appreciated the fact that no one he knew would ever set foot in the place. Privacy mattered to Gómez and Artie had the age and the tact to understand that.

The two men exchanged handshakes. Artie brought two beers to a table in the corner. Beaman liked the place on sight.

31

'They do food here?'

'Sure. Mainly Mexican. You hungry?'

Beaman ordered a plate of enchiladas. Since Detroit, Gómez thought, the guy's got even thinner.

'Good to see you.' He reached for his beer. 'So tell me . . .'

'Tell you what?'

'Everything.'

Beaman looked blank for a moment and then grinned. The grin was as boyish as ever, totally without guile, and Gómez was suddenly back in the sweaty half-darkness of the Detroit community hall as the elections came to the boil, watching Beaman on the tiny stage out front. The boy's sympathies were with the Congressional District's black population and they'd been there in their hundreds to listen. Agard Beaman had the gift of tongues, the talents of a preacher and memories of the way he'd played his audience that night had never left Gómez. Having beliefs so powerfully held was one thing. Gómez liked that, appreciated it. But being able to share those views, being able to bring four hundred people to their feet with a single gesture of that flappy little hand, was quite another.

'Your guy win? Up there in Detroit?'

'Yeah. It was close, closer than we ever expected, but we made it. Just. Fifteen hundred votes.'

'Important, then.'

'What?'

'The black vote. All those women.'

'Sure.'

'And I expect the candidate was truly grateful.'

'Me, too,' Beaman said. 'You saved my fucking life that night. Which I guess is kinda the point. I want to say thank you.'

Gómez held his gaze, watching the thin hand crab across the table towards his. Two guys on a motorbike had ambushed them as they drove away from the meeting. In the gunfight that followed, Gómez had shot them both to death.

'No problem,' he said. 'It's what I do.'

'Kill people?'

'Defend democracy. That's a joke, by the way. They'd have shot me, too.'

'You think so?'

'I know so. The Bureau ran checks afterwards. They were both crims, hit men, decent records, knew what they were doing. They ran with a local mobster. The issue was the money, who exactly was paying for the hit, and we never got to the bottom of that. I'd have phoned and explained it all but you were gone.'

'You, too. You just disappeared. I never understood that.'

'The Agency stood me down. By the next day I was on a train to Chicago. They had a guy in the morgue and not too many witnesses and they needed to wrap the whole thing up. I got a month's paid furlough. Plus there was no paperwork. I wasn't complaining.'

'And now?'

'Now is different.'

'How?'

Gómez studied him for a long moment, then shook his head. Beaman's hand had settled softly on his. Gómez, with some gentleness, removed it.

'Thank you is all I ever need,' he said. 'Tell me what happened afterwards.'

Beaman was still looking at Gómez's hand. Then he permitted himself a tiny frown of disappointment and shrugged. Life, he said, had been more than kind to him. The Democratic Congressman for Detroit's 13th District, safely back in the House, had spread the word about his efforts. Here was a young white activist who had won the trust – and the votes – of an ever-swelling black population. He had stamina and guts and a preparedness to go anywhere in the Union to continue the fight. The latter had caught the attention of a left-wing group in Washington with access to funding. The social revolution sparked by the war effort was flooding across the country, not least because the arsenal of democracy needed all the labour – black, white – it could lay its hands on.

Gómez nodded. A couple of years back, a leading black activist had organised a Negro March on Washington to demand equal opportunities in the workplace. Gómez had been part of an FBI operation to run checks on some of the campaigners' associates.

'Hoover assumed they were all Commies,' Gómez said. 'Turned out he was wrong though the Boss never wanted to believe it.'

'You've met Hoover? You know him?' J. Edgar Hoover was Director of the Federal Bureau of Investigation.

'Once. I'd just come out of the Marines. It happened Hoover loved Marines which I guess was just as well because he sure didn't love Hispanics like me. Or blacks. Or women.'

'So what's he like?'

'Tiny guy. Wears lift heels. Keeps strange company.'

Beaman laughed. In the end the march on Washington had never happened but the threat alone had pressured President Roosevelt into conceding equal opportunities legislation.

Artie had appeared and Beaman was making space on the table for an enormous plate of enchiladas. Gómez wanted to know whether he'd been involved in planning for the march.

'Somewhat.' Beaman was gazing at the enchiladas. 'If you want anything to change in this country you have to go to Washington. You have to get to know people. Then you can state your case. I guess if you're lucky you make an impression.'

'And you?'

'I made an impression.'

Artie returned to the table with a bottle of chilli sauce and a jug of iced water. Beaman made a start on the wraps of glistening chicken. He ate slowly, pausing between mouthfuls to edge the story forward. A couple of months after the congressional elections he'd been sent south. The battle for workplace rights was – in theory at least – over but blacks in the military faced all kinds of discrimination.

He mentioned an Army airfield. Carlsbad.

'That's New Mexico.' Gómez recognised the name. 'That's near here. Less than two hours.'

'You're right. Jim Crow country. This stuff is beyond belief. We're fighting a war. Men are dying. Blood is blood. You need every man you can find. You need to train him, motivate him, point him in the right direction. You ever heard of the 349th Aviation Squadron?'

'Never.'

'Here's a bunch of black guys, loyal Americans. There are lots of them. They're keen, they're brave, they can't wait to get into combat. But you know where the real war happens? Right there on the base. Take the theatre. A thousand seats. Maybe more than that. You know how many are reserved for our negro friends? Twenty. In the last row. At the very back. Same deal on the buses into town. You sit where you're told to sit while the whiteys enjoy the view.' He paused a moment, forking at the enchilada, then looked up again. 'You're black and hungry out there on the base? Forget it. No way are you allowed to eat in the canteen.'

'So what happened? What did you do about it?'

'Me personally?'

'You personally.'

'I talked to some friends in Washington. Applied a little pressure.'

Pressure, Beaman said, was the key. The White House would do anything to keep the tanks and airplanes rolling off the assembly lines. Black anger had a habit of spilling back into the workplace and so the War Department was directed to clean up bases like Carlsbad, forbidding segregation.

'And you were really part of that?' Gómez was impressed.

'I was. And I am. I was in Carlsbad yesterday, checking the base out. Full compliance. In this game you settle for nothing less.'

'And that's why you're down here? That's how come you made the call?'

'Sure.' He nodded and reached for his glass. 'They think I'm the man from Big Government.'

Gómez watched him attacking the enchiladas again. Then he leaned forward over the table, his voice low.

'So how did you know I was working at Los Alamos? This stuff's supposed to be beyond secret.'

'I asked one of my Washington friends.'

'How would he know?'

'She.'

'Really? She has pull, this woman? Contacts?'

'Yes.'

'Like where?'

'Like in the government.'

'She knows where to go? Who to ask?'

'She went to the top. She always goes to the top. Attorney General. Never fails.'

'Right.' Gómez had the feeling he was getting out of his depth. 'She has a name, this friend of yours?'

'Of course. Everyone has a name.'

'You gonna tell me?'

'Sure. Eleanor Roosevelt.'

'The President's wife?'

Gómez stared at him. Was Beaman kidding? Or did he really have the ear of America's First Lady?

'She's a friend. I just told you.'

Gómez was still absorbing the news. In some respects it made sense. Eleanor Roosevelt was famous for wandering off the reservation, for poking her nose into other people's business, for making a nuisance of herself. She was a believer in good causes, in dressing some of the country's self-inflicted wounds. Her column, read by millions, was syndicated from coast to coast. She was tall and somewhat gawky and outspoken but undeniably brave. People loved her for that and in the light of this conversation the title of her column said it all. 'My Way'.

'She's slipped the leash,' Gómez grunted. 'Am I right?'

'One hundred per cent. A fine lady.'

'You know the President, too?'

'Never had the pleasure. Mrs Roosevelt has an apartment

in New York. Washington Square. We meet there most times though I've been up to Hyde Park as well.'

Gómez nodded. Hyde Park was the Roosevelt family spread, hundreds of acres overlooking the Hudson in upstate New York.

'She has a cottage in the grounds,' Beaman said. 'Place called Val-Kill. Beautiful. I stayed over one night. She talked me to death.'

Gómez was inclined to believe him. This was beyond impressive. How come this skinny guy, toast of the Detroit slums, had made it to such elevated company? And why on earth was he wasting his precious time in a rundown New Mexico diner with a guy he barely knew?

'You saved my life,' Beaman said. 'I appreciate that.'

'Sure. But there has to be more.'

'You sound like a cop.'

'I am a cop. Sort of.'

'So trust me. You made a judgement back in Detroit. I know you did. I could see it on your face. You liked me. I intrigued you. Why? Because I was different. Because I cared. And because I knew how to work a bunch of women who deserved a bigger voice. Tell me I'm wrong.'

'You're not.'

'Good. Because I have a proposition.'

Gómez held his gaze. He half guessed what was coming.

'You think I'm a faggot?'

'Sadly not. Ever change your mind, just let me know.'

'So what is it?'

'I need protection. I needed it then and I need it now. None of this stuff is risk-free. A whole lot of people want to hurt me. Some of them would like me dead.'

'You know that?'

'Yes.'

'We're talking specific threats?'

'Sure.'

'Then take it to the authorities. To the police. To the FBI. To the Justice Department. Talk to your friend.'

'I did.'

'And?'

'She knows what I know. I'm in deep with the negroes. I want us all to be equal. I want us all to be friends. Since when have the FBI been interested in any of that?'

Gómez smiled. Well put, he thought. Beaman was right. Hoover loathed the President's wife, called her 'the old hoot owl', kept a vast file on her and her so-called Commie friends.

Beaman still wanted an answer. Gómez had already saved his life. He could do with more of that.

'I have a job already,' Gómez pointed out.

'I know. You'll be well paid. Better than now.'

'Your friend again?'

'The money will come from a friend of my friend but this conversation was Mrs Roosevelt's idea. She knows about Detroit. I told her. She was impressed.' He nodded. 'Are you telling me no?'

'I'm telling you things aren't quite as simple as you might think.'

'I don't understand.'

'Good. Because you don't need to.'

Beaman studied him for a moment. Then he wiped his mouth on the back of his hand.

'You left the FBI to work with the military. Am I right?'

'You are. Security on the base is handled by the military. My boss is an Army colonel.'

'So how come the decision? Why quit the Agency in the first place?'

Gómez held his gaze, then shook his head. No way.

'You're not going to tell me?'

'No.'

'But the move is permanent?'

'I didn't say that.'

'So you might . . .' The grin again. '. . . consider my proposition?'

'I didn't say that either.'

Artie was approaching. He collected Beaman's empty plate and asked whether they needed more drinks. Gómez shook his head. He had a job to get back to. He was done. A couple of dollars would cover the bill. He got out his wallet but Beaman was already on his feet. He handed Artie a five-dollar note, told him to keep the change. Fabulous enchiladas. His buddy here had been right. Great place to eat.

Artie left with a nod and a smile. Gómez sat back in the chair and emptied his glass.

'You needn't have done that,' he said.

'Pleasure. My friend insisted on paying.' Beaman looked down, extending a bony hand. 'One day you'll get to meet her.'

3

A piercing shaft of sunshine roused Stefan Portisch. He tried to struggle upright, failed. He felt a mattress of straw beneath him. He could smell cow shit. The sagging roof above his head was chequered with startling daubs of blue, smudged with racing clouds. The wind was still blowing hard, shaking the heavy clay tiles.

He closed his eyes. Still wet through, he was trembling with cold. He let his hands fumble with the buttons on his leather greatcoat and explore further. He felt disembodied, utterly helpless, bludgeoned half to death by a series of events he had trouble piecing together. He remembered struggling up the ladder as the submarine rolled and bucked in the storm. Then the sheer power of the huge waves rearing out of the darkness came back to him. The crew had gone. He was by himself. Another wave would toss the U-boat on to its side. After which, he was dead.

His fingers, numb with cold, found a deep wound in his lower leg. He withdrew them, held them out against the light. Fresh blood. His whole leg was throbbing and when he tried to straighten it he yelped with pain. Something nearby stirred. He could move his head just enough to locate the noise. The cow was only feet away, the huge brown eyes unblinking.

He'd jumped from the conning tower. He knew that. He'd waited for the next wave, judged the moment and launched himself into the boiling sea. He remembered letting the wave lift him clear of the reef, a small act of surrender, and then came the thunder that engulfed him as the roller broke on the other side. He'd braced for the inevitable impact as he hit the rocky shore, doing his best to protect his head, then reaching out for anything firm, anything solid, as the wave withdrew. Still mobile, he'd done his best to scramble up towards the dark mass of the looming cliff but then had come another wave, even bigger, determined to reclaim him. Underwater again, a plaything of the storm, he'd tumbled over and over, desperate to regain his footing. Had the miracle happened? Had he made it? The answer, self-evidently, was yes. So how come the wound in his leg? And the fact that, even now, breathing was so painful? His hands were exploring the ribs beneath his woollen shirt. Even a fingertip touch brought tears to his eyes. *Scheisse*.

He tried to roll over but it was hopeless. Getting off the rocky foreshore, scaling the cliffs, finding this tiny scrap of shelter, was a mystery, hours of agonising effort that seemed to have wiped all trace from his memory. He lay back, concentrating again on the submarine that had nearly killed him, on *U-2553*, wondering exactly what had happened to the rest of the crew. Some, like himself, might have survived. Others probably hadn't. Where had they gone? What had happened to Hans, the Chief Engineer, to fat old Wolfgang the cook, to the nervous young ensign from Glücksburg with the shaved head and the out-of-tune fiddle? What lay in wait for these precious *Kameraden* on this unforgiving corner of neutral Spain? He shook his head. He didn't know. Another chill gust of hopelessness.

Then came a new image, as bright as the slants of sunshine through the wreckage of the roof. Last night he'd killed a man. He could see Huber's face, almost touch it. He could sense his terror of drowning, and he could remember the terse resignation in his voice as he ordered his own death. Shoot me. Now.

Stefan was looking at his hands again. They were shaking with cold. He raised one to his nose, sniffed it. Somehow expecting the bitter tang of cordite, he could smell nothing. He'd shot the *Brigadeführer* three times, once through the left eye and twice through the chest as he fell backwards into the rising water. Three bullets. Bang, bang, bang. Sharp little cracks above the clamour of the storm before he'd tossed the gun aside, disgusted with himself. As a sailor and a patriot, he'd never had any time for the zealots of the SS. They were an aberration, a cancer, a vile growth deep in the body of the *Heimat*. Shipping these people south, having them aboard, being aware of their constant presence, he'd felt tainted, physically dirtied. But even so, last night had been unforgiveable, a memory he could never erase. Maybe, against huge odds, he should have tried to save this man's life. Instead, at point-blank range, he'd killed him.

The cow was stirring again. Stefan closed his eyes. Everything hurt. Nothing made sense any more. Dear God, he thought. Let there be an end to this madness.

The cow heard the approaching footsteps before he did. Time had moved on. Sunshine was hitting a different wall. The animal had struggled to its feet and was lumbering clumsily towards the muddy entrance. Stefan, blinking, gazed at the door. He must have pulled it shut last night, dropping the big wooden latch. Another mystery. The footsteps paused outside. A woman's voice. Old. Out of tune. Singing.

Stefan lay back, aware of his helplessness. He'd been dreaming about his grandparents. Their names were Berthold and Edith. They were simple people, not rich, not ambitious, not highly educated. Berthold, like his own father before him, had been a farmer. Home was up near the Kiel Canal, an hour's drive from Hamburg, on the flat, rich soil of Schleswig-Holstein. As a kid, with his brother Werner, Stefan would spend whole summers there. He remembered the weird sight of ships, big ships, slipping past on the skyline, strangers in the vastness of this landscape, and he remembered helping his grandparents out in the fields, lifting beets scabbed with wet earth and dropping them in his own tiny bucket. They'd had cattle, too. Black and white. Holstein Friesians, as he'd later learn to call them. Huge. Docile. Smelly. Dreamtime, he told himself. Another world.

The woman was kicking at the door. Finally the latch gave way and the gloom was bathed in sunshine. Silhouetted against the brightness of the morning, she stood motionless, talking to the cow. Spanish, Stefan thought. He spoke barely a word.

The woman abandoned the cow and bent to examine the latch. Watching her from the straw, Stefan knew he had a decision to make. There was no way he could get himself out of this place, not without help. Some of his ribs were probably broken. His leg, at the very least, needed stitching. Maybe that was broken, too. Either way, he needed help. Better this woman than a younger man with a reputation to make.

The woman looked about a hundred years old. She was wearing a smock that might have been made of sackcloth and a pair of wooden clogs. With the flower she'd tucked behind one ear, she could have stepped out of a medieval painting.

Stefan stirred. He liked the flower.

'Help me,' he said softly in German. 'Please.'

The woman stiffened, peering past the cow. Then came a tiny gasp and a volley of Spanish and moments later she was bending over him, the seamed old face full of concern. At the very least, she now understood about the door.

Stefan gestured at his leg, at his ribs. When she tried to haul him to his feet, he had to fight her off. She was much stronger than she looked but he knew she would have collapsed under his weight. What he wanted was a doctor, or maybe a nurse. Someone who could clean him up and sort out his wounds. He voiced the thought in German, getting nowhere. Then he tried sign language, gesturing at his leg. She stared down at him, alarmed. Then backed away, crossing herself.

Christ, Stefan thought. She thinks I need a priest.

He shook his head, extending a hand, knowing that somehow he had to get back on his feet. She gave him a look, still uncertain, then stepped forward and tried again to haul him upright. It didn't work. The pain was unbearable. White-faced, Stefan collapsed back on to the wetness of the straw. He shut his eyes, fighting the urge to vomit. Then he remembered the coins. Mercifully they were there, still in his pocket. He produced a couple, held them out. They were bigger than he remembered, strangely heavy. The old woman was staring at them.

'Take them,' Stefan said in German. 'Find me a doctor.'

She nodded, her eyes back on Stefan's face. She seemed to understand the word *Doktor*. Then she backed away, ignoring the proffered coins, and Stefan heard the scrape of the door closing and she was gone.

She returned within the hour. The man at her side might have been her husband. Same age, same weather-roughened face, but a smile this time and a bottle in his hand that turned out to be half full of plum brandy.

Between them, the old couple got Stefan to his feet. Outside, in the sunshine, a donkey stood between the shafts of a wooden cart. The back of the cart lay open. The old man forked straw on to the cart and then returned to the shed to fetch a box. The box formed a step. At the old man's insistence, Stefan took a pull at the bottle before they struggled to hoist him backwards on to the step. The harshness of the spirit burned his throat and lungs. Fighting for balance, his face contorted with pain, Stefan could feel the edge of the cart against the back of his thighs.

The old man was smiling again. His hands were huge. He put one of them against Stefan's chest and gently pushed. Stefan tottered and then collapsed backwards. The straw softened the impact but the searing wave of pain from his ribs drained the colour from the landscape. For a second or two he thought he was going to faint but moments later the old man was stirring the donkey into action. Bumping away down the track from the cowshed, every jolt bringing fresh agony, Stefan could see nothing but the scurry of clouds against the blueness of the sky. There was warmth in the sun, balm for his broken body, and far away he thought he could hear the rasp of surf. Rocks, he thought, and my poor bloody crew.

After a while, Stefan didn't know how long, the rattle and squeak of the wooden wheels on the rutted track gave way to a new surface, kinder, gentler, smoother. The donkey picked up speed and soon they were in the outskirts of a village. Looking up, Stefan could see wooden buildings crowding in from either side: rotting window frames, pitted mud walls, peeling plaster. Then came the rumble of cobblestones beneath the wheels of the cart and there was suddenly a line of washing stretched across the street, undergarments and towels and a sheet blowing in the wind. Some of the clothes were tiny. Kids, Stefan thought. Real life. Normality. Bustle. Conversation. The prospect brought a smile to his face. It felt like a kind of deliverance.

After the washing, the sky was suddenly full of swallows. He watched them darting hither and thither, enjoying the craziness of their flight. He knew they were after insects, that they needed to feed, that there was a logic in this madness, but here and now he wanted nothing more than to share their freedom. Left. Right. Up. Down. Perfect.

The cart had come to a halt. He heard the old man's footsteps, the clump of his boots on the cobblestones, then a rap-rap as he paused before a door. The door opened and there came another voice, male, light. The conversation was brief. Stefan didn't understand a word but suddenly he was looking at two faces peering down at him. One was the old farmer. He'd removed his hat. The other was a much younger man. He was wearing a collarless white shirt and a scrap of red handkerchief knotted at his throat.

'*Habla español?*'

Stefan shook his head.

'English?'

'A little.'

'Me, too. A little.' The man's smile was infectious. There was kindness in his eyes. Stefan smiled back, accepting his handshake.

'Agustín.' The man introduced himself. 'Tell me what hurts.'

Stefan touched his chest on both sides, and then his right leg beneath the knee.

'Bad?'

'Yes.'

'Very bad?'

'Yes.'

'OK.' He frowned. 'You're German?'

'Yes.'

'You came from the submarine? Last night?'

'Yes.'

'You're a lucky man.'

Stefan stared up at him.

'You know about the submarine?'

'Of course. Everyone knows about the submarine. Fishermen from the village tried to help. Everyone tried to help.'

'And?'

Agustín studied him for a moment, then gave his hand a squeeze and shook his head.

'I'm sorry,' he said.

Stefan wanted to know more. He wanted to know who had survived, how they were, where he might find them, but Agustín had disappeared. He was back with the old man. Stefan tried to concentrate, tried to disentangle some clues from the torrent of Spanish from the kerbside. He thought he caught a name a couple of times – Eva? – but he couldn't be sure. Then, without warning, the cart was on the move again.

The journey was brief this time. Was this a big village? Were they still on the coast? Was there a harbour? Access to the sea? Stefan searched in vain for answers. He thought he could hear seagulls but there was no sign of them overhead. Then the cart came to a halt. Another door. Another conversation. Three voices this time, all men.

Stefan tried to prop himself up on one elbow but failed completely. Then the cart swayed under the weight of one of the men. He was young, broad-shouldered. His face was nut-brown and he badly needed a shave but his grin was warm. Stefan looked at the hand thrust down towards him. It was huge.

'Enrico,' the man said.

Stefan shook the hand then shut his eyes as the man hauled him to his feet but the pain wasn't as bad as he expected. Somehow, with Stefan folded over his shoulder, Enrico made it off the back of the cart. Another man was waiting at the roadside. Stefan put his arms around their shoulders, allowing them to take his weight. The door of the house in front of him was already open. Upstairs, in one of the windows, he caught the briefest glimpse of a woman's face. She had a fall of jet-black hair. Her eyes met Stefan's for no more than an instant, then she stepped away. There were flowers in a jam jar on the windowsill and white lace curtains, carefully gathered back with twists of scarlet ribbon.

'*Señor?*'

It was the old man. He was still holding his hat. The other hand was extended, palm up, in a gesture of expectation.

Stefan stared at it a moment, not understanding. Then he remembered the coins. He nodded down at the pocket of his greatcoat. Help yourself. The old man needed no encouragement. His hand dug deep in the pocket and emerged with five gold coins. They shone in the bright sunshine. The old man was about to take the lot but Enrico stopped him. His voice was harsh.

'*Uno*,' he said. '*Solamente uno.*'

The old man began to protest but Enrico settled the argument by returning four of the coins to Stefan's pocket. Stefan was still trying to read the expression on the old man's face. It might have been disappointment at the trick fate had just played on him. It might have been anger. Either way, he didn't know, didn't care. He was alive. The old man had been well rewarded. And the nearness of the open door held the promise – however brief – of peace.

He did his best to thank the old man and then, remembering the face at the window, he looked up again but there was nothing but the flowers in the jar.

*

Mid-afternoon, after calling at the Project Office in East Palace Street, Gómez headed back from Santa Fe to the Hill. He rode the switchback stretches along the valley of the Rio Grande and then gunned the tan Army-issue Lincoln up the washboard zigzags that led to the *mesa*. On one of the tightest corners near the top of the climb, his windshield was suddenly full of a huge construction truck, the driver wrestling with the wheel, his hand on the horn. Gómez missed him by inches. Brake problems, he thought, as the truck swept past. The guy at the wheel was still fighting for control as the vehicle veered towards the drop-off and the desert floor below. This was a bony, naked landscape, unforgiving, and as the truck disappeared from his rear-view mirror Gómez pulled over to check the driver made it safely down.

The weather, unusually, was overcast and cool for September. The plume of dust dragged by the truck slowly diminished but in the stillness Gómez could still hear the gear box shredding cogs as the driver dropped the big engine down through the box before yet another hairpin bend. Finally he made it to the valley floor, a tiny speck crawling towards the distant frieze of the Sangre de Cristo Mountains. These shadowless desert spaces had always reminded Gómez of the moon, except they were the colour of blood instead of the pewter colour of death, and he remained at the roadside for a moment or two, still shaken by the near miss with the truck.

The pace the Army set on the Hill was beyond reasonable. The scientists, many of them, were working fifteen-hour days and everyone else struggled to keep up. Corners cut. Meals missed. Brakes left unchecked. Anything to keep the program on schedule. Gómez shook his head. As a peacetime Marine, and later in the FBI, he'd eyeballed serious injury or worse on a number of occasions, but every time it happened he'd had that split second to scope the odds and emerge intact. That's what training gave you. That was the way to survive. But the older, wiser guys knew better. The one that kills you, they always said, is the one you never expect, never anticipate, never even fucking *see* coming. The driver's boot pumping the brake pedal. The smell of charring asbestos from the linings. The blare of the horn. And Gómez suddenly helpless in the face of certain death. Shit, he thought. What a place to die.

Half an hour later, safely back on the Hill, he found his new partner sitting at the desk they shared in the Admin Building that housed the security organisation. Carl Merricks was a small guy, fit, watchful, content to keep his own company. He was a decade younger than Gómez and his enemies, who were many, called him Jinx. Gómez didn't care about the scuttlebutt. They'd worked a couple of jobs together and Merricks had never let him down. He was thorough, deeply private and immune to pressure from above. For the latter reason alone, Gómez deeply approved of the man.

A long list of names, some ticked, lay at his elbow. He'd spent part of the day interviewing Fiedler's colleagues from the Tamper Group. When Gómez enquired about meaningful leads he shook his head. Fiedler, he said, had been well respected and popular. No one had a bad word to say about the man and no one had the first idea why he'd take his own life. He'd seemed so content, so pleased to be up on the Hill, so proud to be part of the Project.

'You know how old the guy was?' Merricks glanced up.

'Thirty-eight,' Gómez said. 'Looked fifty, easy. Maybe older. Marta blames the hours the guy worked, and all the other pressures. Insane.'

Gómez wanted to know about alibis. Where had all these guys been when Fiedler died?

'Across there in the Tech Area. I checked everyone out. They were all at work. Every single one.'

'The guy had enemies?'

'Not that anyone's saying.' Merricks' eyes went down to the list again, then he shrugged and gestured at the phone. 'The Bureau came through. Guy wants you to call back.'

'Name?'

'O'Flaherty.'

'Did it sound urgent?'

'Everything sounds urgent to these people. Where were they when God invented manners?'

Gómez smiled. It was true. Most of his ex-buddies had raised impatience to an art form. Talk fast. Never apologise. Just like Mr Hoover.

Gómez shed his jacket. He'd deal with O'Flaherty later.

'So where exactly are we?'

Merricks tossed his pencil on to the stack of paperwork at his elbow and leaned back in the chair. He was up for the calisthenics session every morning at half six and Gómez knew he punished himself in the gym last thing most evenings. That way, you kept your body in reasonable working order but even so the sheer grind of keeping the security lid on a frontier town like this – a teeming settlement that wasn't even supposed to *exist* – was starting to show on his face. He looked older than his years. Not a compliment.

'You want the good news?'

'Try me.'

'I got us another desk.'

'Great, so where do we put it?'

'I got us another office, too.' He nodded at the door. 'Just down the hall there. Twice the size.'

Gómez was impressed. Working space on the Hill was more precious than water. So how come Merricks had managed to pull off a miracle like this?

'I asked nicely. Never underestimate the power of surprise.'

Gómez was still trying to work it out.

'There's a WAC called Jennifer in charge of this stuff,' he said. 'Answers to Whyte.'

'You're right.'

'She's ugly as hell.'

'Right again.' Merricks grinned. 'On the outside.'

'Meaning?'

'We got the office.'

Gómez smiled. Merricks had a kill rate on the Hill that would have been the envy of any combat pilot. Women loved the fact that he wasn't as loud and showy as many of the enlisted men, and they liked to believe that Jinx – with his sleepy eyes and his long silences – was a bit of a thinker. The latter assumption happened to be true. Another reason Gómez was happy to have him on the team.

'What else?' he asked.

Merricks reached for Sol Fiedler's security file. The dead metallurgist, he said, had left Germany in December '38. He and his wife had been living in Berlin for several years, with Fiedler working at the KWI.

'KWI?'

'Kaiser Wilhelm Institute. You're supposed to know this stuff.'

'Sure. Tell me more.'

Merricks returned to the file. According to Fiedler's immigration records, both he and Marta had been disturbed by what the Nazis were up to with the Jews and one night in late November, when the hard men went to town on the synagogues and Jewish businesses, they decided to get out while they still could.

'So where did they go?'

'England. He ended up in a government lab in Manchester working way below his pay grade. Marta hated England. When it came to Jews she thought some of the Brits were as bad as the Nazis and so she began to hassle him for another move.'

'Here?'

Merricks nodded. Fiedler's reputation in the field of metallurgy had evidently gone before him – a sheaf of important papers published in leading scientific journals – and within weeks he and Marta plus a whole bunch of guys from the Tube Alloys group were on a boat to Canada.

'Tube Alloys? You want me to explain?'

Gómez shook his head. Tube Alloys was the Brit code name for the atomic bomb programme. Even he knew that.

Merricks masked a smile. From Montreal, he said, the Fiedlers had gone down to Chicago where Sol got a job in something called the Metallurgical Laboratory run at the university by an Italian physicist, Enrico Fermi.

'Fermi's the guy who was figuring out ways to split the atom. Don't ask me about the science but he built himself a big pile of graphite blocks under a squash court right there in Chicago. No one thought it would work but apparently Fiedler was a believer. Turned out Fermi was right. The thing went critical at the end of '42 and a couple of years later here we are.'

'With a bigger office.'

'Sure. And if you want the truth a bunch of coupons helped.'

Gómez didn't enquire further. Among the G-2 crowd, the guys from Army Intel, Jinx was also known as 'Mr Coupon'. He always seemed to have an inexhaustible supply – for gas, for clothing, even for food – and they greased the wheels when he wanted a favour.

Gómez wanted to know exactly how long Fiedler had been up on the Hill. He thought he remembered the name from the early days but he couldn't be sure.

'You were here in the early days?' Merricks looked surprised.

'Two months after it opened. June '43.'

'I didn't know that. What was it like?'

'Mud and dust and not much to do except work,' Gómez said. 'There was an old school and a few buildings in the Tech

Area but that was pretty much it. Think the Wild West. Think Tombstone without the laughs.'

'You're telling me it's changed?'

'Big time. Back then there was nothing. You slept in a dormitory with sixty men. You want to watch a movie? Little frame hall with wooden benches and a big old pot-belly stove outside for when your beer froze. You want to make a phone call? One line out – and that belonged to the Forest Service. They called it the most secret place on earth and that's probably right. No one in his right mind would want to come anywhere near it.'

Gómez shook his head at the memory. Fifteen months later the Hill – though still top secret – was unrecognisable. Without doubt, the most secret place on earth. And probably the busiest.

Merricks was back with Fiedler's file. The couple had been childless. Once the Corps of Engineers had got properly organised, they moved into the modest ground-floor duplex that became their home.

'Where they stayed?'

'Yep.'

'Same neighbours?'

'Pretty much. The couple upstairs moved out last week. I also talked to the people next door.'

'And?'

'Same story. Nice guy. Shy. Devoted to his wife. Eccentric around figures. Clever like they don't make clever any more.'

Gómez didn't understand. The Hill was bursting with mega-brains, guys who understood the dark magic of quantum physics and were working flat out to blow up half the world.

'Fiedler was different. He went one step further. He had a party piece. Apparently saved him from too much conversation.'

'Like how?'

'Like he'd multiply two numbers – five-figure numbers – and do the math in his head. Moms loved it, especially the ones with older kids. They'd toss Fiedler the numbers and he'd calculate it right out, there and then, just using that big old brain of his, and come up with a result in no time at all. Took the kids hours to check if he was right. If they caught up with him he gave them candy bars. Made them savvy without ever knowing it. Education without tears.'

'Any of these women ever fall for him?'

'Not that anyone's saying. He doesn't seem to have been that kind of guy. Like I say, shy.'

'How about her?'

'Devoted. You can see it now. The rest of her life? She doesn't want to know. By all accounts she loved the man to death.'

'Interesting phrase,' Gómez said.

Merricks glanced up and then returned to the file. 'Fiedler made a couple of trips over the past year or so. Chicago one time. Caltech the other. Both on business. Took the train on both occasions. On the Chicago outing he was Saul Fernstein. In California he carried ID in the name of Sidney Freid.'

Gómez nodded. It was standard procedure for Los Alamos scientists to travel under false names, part of the blanket of mystifying security measures that had descended on the army of scientists living and working on the Hill. Most of these people were young and treated the code names and security drills as a joke but Fiedler, fresh from the darkness of the Third Reich, may have been different.

'You're telling me he was some kind of security risk?'

'Hard to say. There's nothing on his file. He was checked on entry to the States and checked again when he went into the program up in Chicago. Clean both times.'

'Meaning what?'

Merricks shot Gómez a look, then shrugged. They both knew that Army security, when it came to deep background, was a joke. Mr Hoover knew it, too. He'd grabbed as much turf for the FBI as he could when it came to hunting down Commie spies and told anyone who cared to listen that the Army people had never got past first base.

'Was Fiedler under surveillance on those trips?' Gómez asked.

'No. No one saw the need. According to his wife, when they were still in Berlin he gave money to the Republican fundraisers during the fighting in Spain but that just puts him alongside most of the other guys in the Tech Area. These people are bright. They also have a conscience. That doesn't make Fiedler a spy.'

'But he could have met someone? Is that what you're saying?'

'It's possible.' His eyes returned to the file. 'He was four days in Chicago, a couple of days longer on the West Coast. All it takes is a single meeting. On the street. A package left in a bar. Whatever.'

'So what would he have known? What would he have passed on?'

'He worked in the Tamper Group. He was a metallurgist first, nuclear physicist second. That's what took him to Chicago.'

'So what would he have known?'

Merricks held his gaze. This was a difficult area. All information on the Hill – indeed, on the Project – was strictly rationed. You knew what you had to know. Not a jot more.

Even the counter-intel people – folks like Gómez and Merricks – were hog-tied by the same rules. In theory.

'So what would he have known?' Gómez asked for the third time.

'He was working on the design of the high-explosive lenses that surround the plutonium core on Fat Man.'

Gómez nodded. Fat Man was lab-speak for one of the bombs under construction. Allegedly there was another. Little Boy? He didn't know. Either way, even these tiny nuggets of information were north of Top Secret.

'Who told you?'

'Guy I've gotten to know.'

'You trust him? Believe him?'

'Totally. We work out together. It's a pain thing. After that we speak truth to each other. He's the one with the stuff that matters. Me? I listen.'

Gómez rarely laughed but now was different. The moment he'd arrived on the Hill he'd sensed a deep divide, a yawning canyon, between the scientists and the military. The grown-ups were the guys in uniform. They were the ones who insisted on what they called compartmentalisation. Broadly that meant need-to-know. More than 120,000 were working on the Project nationwide and apparently less than a dozen knew anything approaching the whole story.

That was fine. That made perfect sense if you happened to be a soldier, or a politician, or any kind of official keeping this monstrous secret out of the laps of the Soviets. But the scientists, the techie guys, thought different. According to Mr Oppenheimer, their Director, the only guarantee of progress, of hitting the delivery date, was to keep everyone in the big picture.

Hence the weekly meetings behind the barbed wire over in the Tech Area. Without the constant exchange of ideas, sparks of genius in the surrounding darkness, the Project would stall. It might even wither on the vine and tumble into oblivion, ground to dust on the desert floor. Oppenheimer didn't want that to happen. Which was why his scientists – the people the military called 'the children' – refused to take their vows of silence.

Gómez had met Oppenheimer a couple of times. He didn't much like the man, and he certainly didn't trust him, but he had a sneaking regard for the six languages he spoke, and the ever-present cigarette, and the pork-pie hat, and the way the guy danced towards a handshake on the balls of his feet. Oppie, as he was known, also owned a Buick convertible, a beautiful car. It was black and lustrous and he tooled around the Hill driving himself from meeting to meeting, constantly on the move. That was stylish. That won Gómez's gruff nod of approval.

His military counterpart, effectively his boss, was a big, husky bear of a man, obsessively vain, General Groves. Groves – known as 'GG' – worked out of DC. His track record in the Corps of Engineers included building the Pentagon and everyone – including Oppenheimer – agreed that was seriously big potatoes. Compartmentalisation was also Groves' baby, another claim to the nation's gratitude, and he appeared from time to time on the Hill to confer intensely with Oppie. None of these get-togethers – unwitnessed, unminuted – appeared to make the slightest difference to the way the scientists behaved, which – as far as Gómez was concerned – made Oppenheimer a negotiator of genius. No one on earth stood up to Groves. Except Oppie.

'So Fiedler knew a lot. Like they all know a lot.'

'I guess so.' Merricks nodded.

'OK. So two questions. Would he pass this stuff on? And if he did, would that be enough to get him killed?'

'Or take his own life.'

'Sure. That's a possibility. He passes stuff on. He thinks he's close to being caught, to being arrested.'

'Or he just dies of shame. Like it says in the letter.'

'Right.' Gómez was frowning. 'So he's guilty as fuck. He gets a weapon from somewhere. He really does shoot himself to death. Is that the way it goes? No third party? Just him and his loyal wife and the pain inside he calls a conscience? Living with all that knowledge? Imagining all those deaths to come? Is that what you think happened?'

Merricks still had his finger anchored in Sol Fiedler's file. He glanced down for a moment, then looked up again and shook his head.

'No way,' he said. 'Not a chance.'

'How come?'

'Guy called Milos Schiff. I chased him down after you'd gone this morning.' He glanced at his watch. 'The guy takes a break in an hour or so. You need to meet him.'

4

Stefan Portisch lay on the bed, waiting for Agustín's return, staring up at the ceiling. Agustín was the doctor. That much he'd gathered from Enrico. He didn't have the language to find out whether he was the only doctor in the village but in a way it didn't matter. He obviously won Enrico's approval and that, for the time being, was good enough for Stefan.

He'd never been in a house like this – not in Germany, not in France. It was so small, so cramped, and yet so bare. Narrow stairs led up here, to the first floor. Enrico and his mate had wrestled Stefan from step to step, one in front, one pushing hard from behind, every lift, every shove, every chance collision with a doorknob or the edge of the hand rail a fresh jolt of pain.

Finally, they'd made it to the room at the end of the tiny corridor. The wooden floorboards seemed freshly polished. They gleamed in the wash of sunshine through the open window. The bed, mercifully, was high, the mattress perched on an iron frame. The straight bars at the head and the foot of the bed were topped with silver balls, a rare concession to something more frivolous than mere utility, and they jingled as footsteps criss-crossed the room. A black electric cable snaked across the wall and then ended in a brown Bakelite switch above the bed. Beside the bed was a tiny cupboard made of pine on which stood a light and a small plaster Madonna. The only other piece of furniture in the room was a table, also pine, pushed against the far wall. Above it, hung from a nail, was a black crucifix.

Agustín arrived within the hour. He was shorter than Stefan had expected. He wore black trousers that hadn't seen an iron for weeks, and the same collarless white shirt, though the scrap of red at his throat had gone. His feet were bare in a pair of ancient sandals and he carried a battered leather case he deposited carefully on the pine table.

Enrico had managed to remove most of Stefan's sodden clothing, taking it downstairs with a departing nod. Good luck, he seemed to be saying. Don't get cold. Semi-naked under the thin blankets, Stefan waited for Agustín's verdict. The doctor folded the blanket back and took a long look at his body. Then his hands were busy, mapping the livid bruising on both sides of his rib cage. Does this hurt? This? And this? Stefan greeted every question with a nod, then watched Agustín manoeuvre himself around the bed, bending to inspect the yawning wound in Stefan's lower leg in the light from the window.

The gash was deep, the work of rocks probably, or a sharp edge of the reef as he'd plunged towards the foreshore. The surrounding flesh was swollen and bruised a deep purple, while the lips of the wound had opened outwards, revealing layers of muscle and tissue deep inside. The wound was still weeping, leaving thin, pink stains on the single sheet.

Agustín nodded to himself and then left the room. From somewhere downstairs, Stefan caught a muffled conversation. A woman's voice, he thought. Then came the fall of water into a metal container and within moments Agustín was back with an enamel bowl and what looked like a length of cotton torn from someone's shirt.

The water was hot. Steam curled towards the still-open door, carried by the draught through the window. Stefan could hear the clatter of hooves from the street below and the yelp of kids playing. Agustín produced a bottle of yellowish liquid from his case. He gave it a shake and then glanced in Stefan's direction.

'Iodine,' he said. 'You're lucky I still have some.'

Stefan wondered whether he was angling for payment, whether word had gone round the village about the coins, then dismissed the thought. Lucky was probably right. He sensed these people would share their last everything.

'We had iodine on the boat,' he said in English. 'It's good.'

Agustín nodded, said nothing. He dipped a cup into the bowl of water and then added a slug of iodine, soaking the rag as he did so. The rag dripped hot water across Stefan's flesh as he bent to the wound.

'This will hurt,' he said, 'but we have to save the leg.'

'*Save* it?' Amputation had never occurred to Stefan.

'*Sí.*' He produced a cork from his pocket, blew on it, then slipped it into Stefan's mouth.

'Bite,' he said. 'Hard as you can.'

Stefan did his bidding. Liquid from the cup had transferred to Agustín's fingers, and thus to the cork. Pain tasted of iodine.

Agustín was swabbing the wound, using lots of the mixture from the cup. Stefan didn't know whether to look but decided not to. At last, with a grunt of satisfaction, the doctor finished.

'See?' he said. 'Not so bad.'

'The wound?'

'The pain.' He smiled down at Stefan and squeezed his hand.

'The wound will settle. There's no smell. I see no infection. It needs to be dry. Tomorrow I come back to close it.' He mimed a line of stitches.

'You have anaesthetic?'

'No. But I have another cork.' He gave his hand a pat and returned to the case for a roll of bandage which he wound lightly around Stefan's leg.

Stefan asked him about the house. Who did it belong to? Who should he thank?

'The man's name is Tomaso. He is a patient also.'

'Of yours?'

'*Sí*.' His hand made a brief flutter above Stefan's chest. 'He has the smoking disease. He can't breathe properly. One day it will kill him.'

Stefan nodded. He'd heard a cough from downstairs earlier, heavy and viscous, the rattle of gravel in his lungs.

'Tell me about my boat, my submarine.'

'You mean your crew.'

'Of course.'

'You were the Captain?'

'Yes.'

'The last off the boat?'

'Yes.'

Agustín nodded. He'd found a towel from somewhere to dry his hands. He tied a final knot in the bandage and laid the sheet carefully on top. Then came the blankets, one after the other. Stefan realised the wound had ceased to throb.

'My crew?' he asked again.

'All dead that we know about. Drowned. It would have been quick.'

'You think so?'

'Maybe.' He shrugged. 'I hope so.'

'How many bodies?'

'Twenty-eight by this morning. How many men on board?'

'Forty-four.' Stefan paused. Wrong, he thought, remembering the passengers who'd embarked at Kiel. 'Forty-nine.'

'More will come ashore. The women are on the clifftops. The fishermen are back at sea. A storm like that could take a body anywhere.'

'So maybe some survived.'

'Like you?' The smile again, with what felt like a hint of pride. 'I think not.'

Stefan nodded, trying to absorb the news. Crews changed all the time. That was the nature of the service. Men came and went. Some, transferred to other boats, died. Others won promotion, made their name, became famous back home. But what all these men shared was the feeling of being part of something small and important and intensely personal. You said your farewells. You sailed away. You hunted the enemy, and laid your plans, and spent a tense hour or two lurking in the heart of a convoy, and, fifty days later, if you were lucky, you returned to flowers, and a band, and a hug from the uniformed *Mädchen* at the jetty. He stared up at the ceiling, swamped by the memories. The Happy Time, when they were sending dozens of Allied ships to the bottom. The moment in the bright Breton sunshine when you felt the Commandant's fingertips pinning a medal to your chest. Your first step ashore after weeks at sea, and the days and nights that followed.

Deep down, he'd always accepted that there'd be a price to pay for memories like these but now that moment had arrived and he didn't know how to cope. War was supposed to harden you. War was supposed to shield you from grief. But the only survivor? The only man alive? All those faces, all that laughter, all that courage? Gone? He shook his head. Impossible.

Agustín was standing at the bedside. He said there was a possibility the lower leg was broken. There was a big hospital in Coruña with X-rays. Soon, tomorrow or the next day, he'd arrange for Stefan to be taken there.

Stefan stared up at him. Then he shook his head.

'No,' he said.

'No?' Agustín looked briefly confused. 'Why not?'

'Because I want to stay here.'

'Why?'

Stefan hadn't thought this through, not properly. All he knew was that his crew was probably dead and that his role in the war was over. He'd had enough. He was of no use any more. The moment he made an appearance in public – at the hospital, for instance – he'd be arrested and interned. Spain was still a neutral country but the government's sympathies were with the Reich. In theory, he'd spend the rest of the war in some prison camp. In practice, because he knew so much, because he'd *done* so much, he suspected he'd be quietly returned to the *Heimat*. The hero of *U-2553*. One of Admiral Doenitz's top commanders. Safe back home.

'I want to stay here,' he said again.

'That may be difficult.' Agustín glanced towards the door.

'Because of Tomaso?'

'Not just Tomaso.'

'There's someone else lives here?'

'Of course. Her name's Eva. She's Tomaso's daughter. She looks after him. She's been in England. She speaks the language. That's why I brought you here.'

Stefan nodded. The face at the window. The fall of black hair.

'And you think . . .?'

'I don't know.' He shrugged. 'She said OK for a couple of days. No longer.'

Stefan nodded. He thought he understood. His next question was all too obvious.

'She doesn't like Germans?'

'She hates Germans.'

Stefan nodded. Just like the rest of the world, he thought. He gazed up at Agustín, struck by another thought.

'Do *you* hate Germans? Tell me the truth.'

'I'm a doctor. I treat everyone.'

'That wasn't my question.'

'Then I can't give you an answer.'

'Why not?'

'Because I don't know you.'

There was a long silence. A woman in the street below was yelling at the kids.

'I have money,' Stefan said at last. 'Gold.'

'You mean for Eva?'

'Yes.'

'That will only make it worse. She'll think you're trying to buy her.'

'She's right. I am.'

'Then don't. She has beliefs. Strong beliefs.'

He was frowning now, looking down at the bed. Then he

folded back the blanket and the single sheet and ran his fingers lightly down the length of Stefan's swollen calf.

'Does that hurt?'

'No.'

He did the same on his shin. Again Stefan shook his head.

It was a lie and Stefan could tell by the smile on his face that Agustín knew it.

He replaced the sheet and the blankets. He said the best he could do was talk to a carpenter from the village. He'd splint the leg, immobilise it. If the shin bone was fractured, it would heal of its own accord. If it was broken, which Agustín thought unlikely, he'd need further treatment. Either way, Stefan would have to spend weeks, maybe longer, in bed.

'That's what you'll tell Eva?'

'That's what I'll suggest.'

'But you think she'll agree? You think she'll say yes?'

Agustín fetched his bag from the table and returned to the bedside. Downstairs, Stefan could hear Tomaso coughing. Agustín smoothed a pleat on the top blanket. Then his eyes returned to Stefan.

'I've no idea, my friend,' he said. 'This war is the father of many children. One of them is surprise.'

*

Most of the scientists on the Hill were in their late twenties. A handful were even younger, one of the reasons the place had the feel of some surreal university campus, a bunch of America's brightest, heavily policed by the military. Milos Schiff, on the other hand, was old. Gómez judged him to be early fifties at least. Merricks had fetched him from the Tech Area. He was thin, almost cadaverous, with a gaunt smoker's face and skin the colour of yellowing parchment. He wore a full beard, heavily threaded with grey, which was unusual at Los Alamos. With his heavy boots, badly patched dungarees and rumpled T-shirt, he looked like a jobbing gardener but his eyes were alive in the deadness of his face. They were huge, the softest brown, alert, mobile, brimming with something Gómez took to be amusement.

He wanted to know what was going on. He took all this attention to be a compliment. Did they have proper coffee, by any chance? Out of a percolator?

Gómez ignored the question. Merricks had briefed him already about the link to Fiedler. For a start, these two guys had been the same age.

'He was a friend of yours? Sol?'

'Sure. Terrible thing to happen. Can't figure it out.'

'You know him before, at all? Before you came here?'

'Never. I'm Hungarian. Magyar. Sol was a Kraut.'

'Did that matter?'

'Not at all. Guys like us, we're Jewish first, German or whatever second. Helluva man to be with. A listener, you with me? A guy who *cared*.'

He said they used to play chess on Sundays, the one day you could more or less count on to find time of your own. Sol played a very aggressive game, took lots of handling.

'Big surprise, if you're asking. Way out of character. The guy was a pussy cat in the lab, had the nicest manners. Show him a chess board and you're looking at a tiger.'

'So who won?'

'You really want to know? I did. Why? Because after a couple of games, if you're good, you can start to work out where the guy's coming from. Sol? He had lots of anger. Crazy moves sometimes. Mad.'

'Anger about what?'

'I never knew. We never discussed it. It was a chess thing. But I swear to God that man way down was fighting for his fucking life.'

'That's a big thing to say.'

'So is killing yourself.'

'You think that's the way it happened?'

'I dunno.' He shrugged. 'I'd never have made Sol for something like that. He was never a quitter. But who knows?'

He dug in the breast pocket of his dungarees and produced a tin of tobacco. From another pocket, a thin packet of papers. Gómez watched him rolling the cigarette. He had the hands of a musician – long fingers, perfectly formed, yellow with nicotine. Thirty seconds and the cigarette was done.

Merricks found some matches. He wanted to know about Mrs Fiedler.

'Marta?' Schiff sucked smoke deep into his lungs. 'Wonderful woman. A Magyar like me. I love the lady. Always have. Nothing but kindness. Old-fashioned, knows how to look after a man. Sol was the living proof of that, no question.'

'Except he's dead.'

'Sure.'

'So how does that work? You think he was fighting devils. The word you used was tormented. So how come his wife knew nothing about that? How come all this is such a surprise to her?'

71

'Sol was a shy guy. No way would he have shared any of that stuff.'

'Not even with his wife?'

'*Especially* not with his wife. All his life he wanted to protect that woman. Mission number one. And you know what? He was damn good at it.'

'Fooled her?'

'Sure. And fooled her good.'

The cigarette was cupped in his hand, as if he was protecting it from a high wind. He took another drag, tipped his head back, expelled the smoke in a long blue plume.

'I understand you live alone.' Gómez this time.

'Sure. Is that indictable?'

'Not at all. Were you ever married?'

'Twice. Drew the wrong ticket both times.'

Gómez nodded. Merricks had shown him Schiff's file.

'Your first wife?' he asked.

'Greta. She died.'

'How?'

'Disappointment, I guess. Greta expected Clark Gable. What she got was me.'

'There was a police investigation. Care to tell us about that?'

'Sure. They were disappointed, too. Thought I'd poisoned her. Never buy a week-old chicken in Milwaukee. The poor woman died of salmonella. It was there in the autopsy report, plain as daylight.'

'And you? You ate the chicken, too?'

'I was a vegetarian. Still am. Think what you like but it probably saved my life.'

Gómez glanced at Merricks. This was going nowhere.

'You've been seeing a lot of Marta Fiedler.' Merricks glanced down at his pad. 'Trips down to Edith Warren's place? The tea room? Excursions out to the Canyon? Am I right?'

'Sure. So where does this stuff come from?'

Merricks wouldn't tell him. Just wanted to know how come.

'Because we click,' Schiff said. 'Because she gets lonesome sometimes. No kids. No pets. Sol working his ass off. A woman like Marta needs a little stimulation and company does that.' He took a last suck at the roll-up and pinched the end. Then he looked up at Merricks again. 'So where did you get all this bullshit?'

'That doesn't matter. I'm asking you whether it's true.'

'Of course it's true. I'm not denying it. And here's something else. You know who asked me to take care of Marta? To call by when I dropped a shift? To drive her round a little? Go down to Edith's place? Share a little of that fine apple strudel together? That was Sol. Sol's idea. Why? Because he loved the woman, wanted the best for her.'

'Meaning you?'

'Meaning a different face in her life. And maybe a little laughter.'

'You're telling us Sol was a depressive?'

'Sol took life seriously. Sol took everything seriously. That's why he was so easy to beat at chess. The guy thought too hard most times. Other times he didn't think at all. Queen to rook seven. And I'm *watching* him, I'm there, inside his head. Idiot move. *Insane* move. Bam.' He paused, his hand straying towards his breast pocket again. Then he changed his mind and sat back in the chair, eyeballing them both. 'Hey, guys, I just got it. You think I shot him, right? You think I'm in love with his wife and you think my life and maybe hers would be sweeter if old Sol wasn't around. Call me impulsive, call me what you like, but that's the way it sounds.'

Neither Gómez nor Merricks said a word. The accusation hung in the air. Schiff's huge eyes drifted from face to face.

'Well?' he said. 'Am I right? Am I halfway right? Is this why I don't get coffee? Only pretty soon I've got to be back with my buddies, saving the free world. Any clues, guys? Maybe just one?'

Gómez had been watching him closely. He detected no signs of guilt or anxiety or even irritation. Here was a man who was happy to acknowledge that he knew the Fiedlers well, even intimately, who understood their little foibles, their daily routines, the countless ways they'd developed to make it through their years on the Hill. That was important. That made him a key witness.

Gómez told Merricks to put the coffee on. Then he turned back to Schiff.

'There's a chance this thing isn't quite what it seems,' he said carefully.

'You mean Sol shooting himself?'

Gómez nodded. He wanted to know whether he'd ever talked to Fiedler about politics.

'Sure. All the time.'

'And?'

'The guy was bright. A thinker. Also a worrier.'

'About what?'

'About the Soviets mainly. Sol had a theory and he was probably right. He thought the Gadget wasn't for this war at all. He thought it was for the next one.'

'Against the Russians?'

'Sure.'

'And that worried him?'

'Not at all. He thought the Russians were trouble. He'd read a lot about what happened in Spain and he never bought the line about Stalin riding in to the rescue. His take on Stalin was simple. The guy was a gangster. The thought of world domination under the Commies bothered him somewhat. The word he used was evil. What we needed was a big stick and then the Gadget happened by.'

Merricks was back with three cups and a percolator full of hot coffee. Jennifer, Gómez thought. Mr Coupon knows no shame.

Merricks poured the coffee. They'd run out of milk but Schiff said it didn't matter. Gómez was happy to accept that Fiedler hadn't been running nuclear secrets to the Russians. Now he wanted to know how many other buddies he'd had in his life.

'None,' Schiff said.

'None at *all*?'

'Not that I know of. The guy was popular the way quiet guys can be. No trouble. Super-conscientious. Heap of stuff to do? Give it to Sol. Impossible deadline? Calcs that won't resolve? Sol knows a way. But buddies? Real buddies? Never.'

Gómez said nothing. Watched Schiff tip the mug to his lips, take a sip, then another, then wipe his mouth with the back of his hand.

'I forgot,' he said. 'There was one guy he did get on with. His name was Frank.'

'Frank who?' Gómez was reaching for a pen.

'I don't know. This wasn't a scientist, not a guy like us. He wasn't in the military, either. He drove a red truck. Beaten-up

75

old thing. He must have been some kind of contractor. I only met the man a couple of times but it struck me that Sol liked him.'

'How do you know?'

'The way they were together. Sol was a sports nut, believe it or not, crazy about football. Coming down from Chicago, he was a big Bears fan. Turned out Frank felt the same way. There's a quarterback, famous guy, Spud Murphy. Apparently Sol had a framed picture up in the bedroom. Marta told me about it. He must have shown Frank the picture one time because Frank made him an offer for it but Sol said no.'

'When was this?'

'Recently. Back in the summer.'

'So he saw this guy a lot?'

'I guess so.'

'But you don't know?'

'No.'

Gómez nodded and made a note. *Marta?* he wrote. *Frank??* When he looked up again, Schiff was on his feet. He drained the remains of the coffee and then checked his watch. There was a war on. He had to go. Gómez thanked him for his time and hoped not to bother him again. Schiff shrugged, said no problem. When he got a moment he'd call by Marta, check she was OK. Then he was gone.

Gómez glanced down at his notepad. These last few days Marta had been keeping herself to herself, entertaining few visitors, hiding her grief behind her friend's locked door. This afternoon, to the best of Gómez's knowledge, she intended to return home. If Schiff was right about Frank being a contractor then Gómez needed to narrow the field. There were hundreds of these guys on site every day, driving up from Santa Fe and

God knows where else. The man in the red truck, he suspected, might be one of them.

*

Stefan awoke with a start. It was pitch-black outside, not a hint of light. The window was creaking in the wind and from downstairs he could hear someone practising on a piano. It was the same phrase, over and over again, different speeds, different emphasis, few mistakes. Whoever was sitting at the keyboard – Tomaso? His daughter Eva? – was feeling for an interpretation, seeking a way into the music, looking for a particular door. It was a classical piece, Schubert or maybe Mozart, full of sadness and regret. If you were dying of emphysema, Stefan thought, this is exactly what you might play.

Both Stefan's parents had been musical. His father had been crazy about jazz, his mother less so. She'd sung in the choir in the Lutheran church a mile away towards the centre of Hamburg. She could read sheet music and she loved Brahms. Brahms came from the city and before the war, and the arrival of the English bombers, she'd taken her young sons to the house where the great man had been born.

All Stefan remembered from that afternoon was the patter of rain against the mullioned windows and sharp looks from a particularly fierce official when he reached to finger through one of Brahms' musical scores but later that same year an elderly couple had moved into the neighbouring flat. Their names were Anton and Gretel and they'd quickly become family treasures, not least because they were more than happy for Stefan's mother to use their piano. Brahms had long been her favourite composer and it was a rare afternoon not to return from the school along the street and hear chords of a capriccio or a sonata muffled by the intervening wall.

Werner, Stefan's older brother, had no time for Brahms. He thought all that stuff was old-fashioned and boring, but Stefan, to his slight embarrassment, had always understood why his mother had loved it so much. The music spoke to him, too. So wistful. Yet so strong.

Stefan shifted his weight in the bed. His ribs still hurt when he breathed and there was a dull ache from his leg but the sleep had done him good. Reaching up for the Bakelite switch, he turned on the light. The bulb was tiny, casting the dim shadows to the corners of the room, but there was something standing beside the light and when he inched himself upwards on his elbows he found himself looking at a bowl of coffee. There were sodden little shreds of bread in the coffee but when he touched the bowl with the back of his hand it was still warm.

Someone's been up here recently, he told himself. Someone's stood by the bed and maybe watched me for a moment or two. The thought intrigued him. Maybe it was Eva. If so, what did she make of this sudden presence in her house? Of this echo of a faraway war? Of one of the hated Germans who'd turned Europe upside down, sparing only the continent's remoter corners, too insignificant – or perhaps too difficult – to be worth conquering?

He lifted the bowl to his lips and sipped it. The coffee was sweet and under the gaze of the plaster Madonna on the pine table it felt a little like a taste of the Eucharist. He took another sip, and then a mouthful, realising how hungry he was. The last day or so seemed to have telescoped beneath the tumult in his head, a passage of time that no longer made any sense, and he couldn't remember when he'd last eaten. They'd grounded on the rocks late at night. Normally, the crew ate around half past six. Two weeks into the voyage, they'd have exhausted the fresh supplies and started on the tins of sauerkraut and the jars of pickled fish.

Had he and his officers gathered round the tiny table? Elbow to elbow? Glad of the sudden collective warmth? Had he eaten his fill? Washed it down with the malted milk the cook had mistakenly ordered instead of coffee? He didn't know, couldn't remember, but a sudden pressure at the very base of his belly told him that he needed to urinate.

The need was pressing. He began to panic, looking hopelessly around. He had no idea where he might find a toilet. Worse still, he doubted whether he could even get himself out of bed. The obvious thing to do was shout. But he was determined not to be a burden to these people.

Putting the bowl aside, he did his best. His good leg, mercifully, wasn't on the wall side of the bed. He pulled back the blankets and the sheet and extended the leg over the edge of the mattress, feeling for the floorboards with his toes. They were rougher than he remembered. Half out of bed, he tried to coax his other leg to follow but the suddenness of the pain swamped him and he collapsed backwards on to the pillow. *Scheisse*, he thought, bracing himself for another attempt.

This time, if anything, the pain was worse but he was determined to make it to the corridor. Inch by inch, he swung his bad leg out of the bed. Bending it was out of the question. The knee, he realised for the first time, had also seized up. What next?

He sat on the edge of the bed, eyeing the door. The door was half open. A single lunge and he'd have the support of the doorframe. Then he could plan his next move. He stared at the door. The pianist downstairs had moved on from the repeated phrase but had come unstuck several bars later. Whatever Tomaso lacked it wasn't patience. He backed away from the mistake and tried it again. And again. And again.

Staring at the door, listening to the same sequence of notes, Stefan was reminded of his last precious seconds on the submarine, clinging on to the rail in the conning tower, trying to judge the intervals between the cresting waves, when best to trust his judgement, when best to jump. Tomaso, at last, was riding the music to the end of the bar. Then came a tiny pause and the lightest rustle of paper before he started on the next page. Now, Stefan thought. Just do it.

He tried to make it to the door – and failed completely. His bad leg collapsed and he hit the floor sideways. He felt the floor shudder under the weight of his body and he heard a sharp gasp of pain which became, all too shamefully, a scream. Me, he thought.

The music had stopped. Then came footsteps on the stairs. Stefan shut his eyes.

'*Puta.*'

A woman's voice. Stefan groaned, partly pain, partly humiliation. He opened his eyes to find bare feet inches from his face. He did his best to look up. Looking up hurt.

'You speak English?'

'Yes.'

He managed to raise an arm, offered a hand for her to help him up. She didn't move. She asked him what had happened.

He gestured at his groin, doing his best to explain.

'You need the toilet?'

'Yes.'

'You need to piss?'

'Yes.'

'Why not shout?'

'Someone was busy down there. Playing the piano.'

'That was me.'

She was frowning. In a single movement, she scooped the dish from the top of the cupboard and stationed it beside him.

'In there.' She nodded at the dish. 'I come back.'

Then she was gone. Stefan stared at the door, trying to disentangle the jumble of images she'd left behind. The way her hair hung around her shoulders. The sharpness of her features. The wide, generous mouth. Her inexplicable pallor, after a summer of Spanish sunshine. And a silver ring on her left thumb.

There was still a dribble of coffee in the dish. Stefan stared at it then fumbled with his underpants. Rolling over to urinate hurt but there was no way he was going to ask for help. Not after an introduction like that. His bladder was bursting and he missed the dish completely. Cursing, he tried to reposition himself but there was piss everywhere. He could smell it, swelling rivulets heading for the open door. Everything in the house was built on the slant. At last the flow slackened enough to direct it into the bowl. A cupful at the very most. Pathetic.

He lay back, exhausted, trying to work out something to say, some clumsy apology that might repair the damage. Maybe he should make a joke of it, put the whole episode down to bad luck and over-ambition, but something in this woman's face told him it wouldn't work. The pallor and the silver ring were interesting and the music was further proof. Of what? Of the fact that she didn't really belong here? That she wasn't just another peasant – good-natured, generous, eking out a life from this savage landscape? He told himself he couldn't possibly know, and, worse still, that his days in this house were probably numbered. And then she was suddenly back.

She was carrying a cloth and something else. She moved the dish carefully to one side and on her hands and knees she began to mop the floorboards dry. Stefan, watching, caught the scent of lemons. Finished with the floorboards, she put the wet rag in the dish. The other object turned out to be a pair of underpants. They looked enormous.

'You're wet.' She nodded at his own pants. 'Take them off.'

'It's OK.' Stefan shook his head.

'I said take them off.'

'I can't.'

'I don't believe you.'

'It's true.' He shrugged. 'Just leave me alone. I'll be fine.'

She studied him for a long moment. Her face was in shadow but everything about her told Stefan that Agustín had been right. This woman hated Germans, and everything she most loathed about them had probably come true, right here, in her own house. Then, without warning, her hands were tugging at the waistband of his pants, pulling them down. She was deft and strong and she knew exactly what she was doing.

'You're a nurse?'

'Once. You can lift your body? Help me a little?'

Stefan did his best, grateful that she spoke such good English. Another gasp of pain. Then she was easing his pants down over his thighs and lower legs, taking care not to dislodge the bandage. Naked now, Stefan had never felt more helpless. Maybe surviving hadn't been such a great idea. The notion, for whatever reason, made him laugh.

'You think this is funny?' She was staring at him.

'I think I'm very lucky.'

'You're right. You are.'

His pants had joined the rag in the bowl. Now she was coaxing the replacement underpants up his bare legs. He managed to lift his bottom again while she pulled the garment into position. Then it was done. She got up and stepped back, examining her handiwork, and as she did so the throw of light settled on her face. Maybe, just maybe, she was tempted to smile.

'You look like my father,' she said. 'When he was much younger.'

'They're his?' Stefan nodded down at the huge underpants.

'Yes.'

'Tell him thank you. Tell him I'm grateful.'

She didn't reply. She was looking at the bed. Then, without a word, she stooped for the dish and disappeared. Moments later, Stefan heard the scrape of a door opening downstairs and footsteps vanishing into the night. Was there a policeman in the village? Had he worn this woman's patience out? He lay still, starting to shiver, wondering whether he dared to try and make it back to the bed by himself. Then the footsteps returned and the door to the street opened again and he found himself looking up at two faces. The woman – Eva? – and Enrico.

Between them they lifted him up and lay him carefully on to the mattress. They worked well together, no need for conversation, and Stefan guessed that this was the boyfriend.

Stefan's Spanish didn't extend beyond a couple of words but he lost count of the number of times he muttered *gracias*.

Enrico gave him a grin and a pat on the shoulder. *No importa* appeared to mean what it sounded like. Then he was gone.

'You're Eva?'

The woman nodded, said nothing. She rearranged the blankets and adjusted the pillow beneath Stefan's head. Then she turned to go. Only by the door did she pause and look back.

'Soon you will need the toilet again.' She nodded at Stefan's backside. 'This time you must tell me.'

*

Marta Fiedler was trying to make a cake when Gómez and Merricks knocked on her door. Her forearms white with flour, she led them into the kitchen. Dusk was falling earlier and earlier up here on the mesa and the kitchen at the back of the duplex was in semi-darkness. Only when Gómez switched on the light did he realise Marta had been crying.

He threw a look at the mixing bowl and the brown bags of ingredients scattered beside the sink.

'We intruding here?'

'*Nein.*' She shook her head.

'You're sure?'

'Of course.'

She was watching Merricks fill the kettle. Gómez marvelled at the boy's touch around women. Never made a fuss. Never showboated. Just came up with exactly the right gesture at exactly the right time.

Marta turned back to Gómez. She wanted to know why

84

he'd come. Did he have news? Or was this yet another of those interminable interviews?

'I've told you everything I know,' she said. 'Everything I can remember. There's nothing left.'

She began to cry again. Gómez told her the interview wouldn't take long. Then she could get back to cake-making.

'I don't want to make the damn cake,' she howled. 'Who's going to eat it? Me?'

Merricks said he loved cake. Smelled great already. If she was looking for a home for it, he was happy to help out.

'It's not even ready for the oven. It's not even mixed. You know how long I've been trying to figure this recipe out? Since lunchtime. Your brain goes. It's hopeless.'

She turned away, apologising for her outburst. Getting through this thing was hard, harder than anyone could possibly imagine. One of the reasons there'd never be another Sol was that she couldn't bear to part with him again. It was a pain she couldn't describe, a pain that never seemed to leave her.

Gómez settled himself on a stool. His years as a cop had taught him never to be distracted by grief. In the end you have to move on.

'There's a guy called Frank we think you might know,' he said.

Marta was standing by the window, staring out at the darkness stealing across the distant frieze of mountains.

'Frank Donovan,' she said at once. 'Nice fella. Very pleasant. Good to us, too.'

'Who is he?'

'He's the coyote man.' She turned round at last, wiping a tear from the corner of her eye.

'Coyote man?'

'*Ja*. He comes up to the Hill every week. His job is to shoot coyotes. They worry the women. Especially the ones with babies or pets. Frank gets rid of them.'

'He calls by? He knows you?'

'*Ja*.'

'How did that happen?'

The question put a frown of concentration on her face. Finally she said she thought it was way back last year. Frank had been working near the duplex. It was a Tuesday and for once Sol had been in the house.

'He had the flu,' she explained. 'He wasn't well.'

Gómez nodded. The first sign of the flu and a suspect was banished from the Tech Area. An epidemic could bring the Project to a halt.

'So what happened?'

'Sol heard gunfire, single shots, bang bang. He went out to take a look.'

Frank, she said, was working in the scrub a couple of hundred yards away. When his work was done, Sol invited him back to the house.

'I was at the school with the little ones on Tuesdays. When I got back they were talking football. Like I say, Frank was a very nice man, easy to talk to. He was good for Sol, too. Opened him up. That wasn't such an easy thing to do, believe me.'

The friendship, she said, had deepened. A couple of times on Tuesday evenings Frank would stay for a meal. He loved her pickled herrings with mashed potato, served Berlin-style. Another reason Sol had warmed to his presence.

'You know where this guy lives?'

'*Ja.*' She looked round, then left the room. When she came back, she was holding a scrap of paper. Gómez glanced at it.

'Albuquerque's a three-hour drive. At least.'

'I know.'

'He comes all that way? To shoot wild dogs?'

'*Ja.*'

'You know anything else about him? Is the guy married?'

'*Ja.* A lady called Francisca.'

'Kids?'

'Three. Two girls and a boy. He showed us pictures once. Lovely.'

'And this is his address?'

'*Ja.*'

'He gave it to you?'

'Sure. There's a photo of Sol's he wanted to buy. Some footballer. Sol always said no but now . . .' She shrugged, turning abruptly away.

Expecting more tears, Gómez tried to change the subject but she managed to control herself. She said she'd wrapped up the picture and once she found the energy she intended to give it to Frank as a present, or maybe a keepsake. Something to go with the photos he'd taken.

'Photos?'

'Frank took some photos once.'

'Of Sol?'

'Of both of us. He wanted to show his wife.' She tried to force a smile. 'Nice.'

'You were that close?'

'We were friends, good friends, especially Sol and Frank. Sol loved Tuesdays. Couldn't wait for another one to come round.'

Gómez stole a glance at Merricks. Merricks nodded. Sol Fiedler had died yesterday. And yesterday was a Tuesday.

Merricks broke the silence. He told Marta the coffee was ready. Did she take cream? Sugar?

'Neither, thank you.' She turned away. 'You mind if we skip the coffee?'

5

With dawn in Galicia came the sound of hammering. At this time of the morning the sun was low, emerging above the line of roofs across the street and washing the room with light. Stefan lay back, enjoying the warmth on his face. Someone was stirring downstairs – footsteps, the odd chink of china, the fall of water into a sink – and his eyes closed as the memories from the previous night came flooding back.

He'd been a stranger to shame for most of his life. As a kid, he'd largely avoided the humiliations of getting caught out in a prank or even a lie. At sea, the pressures of war – of simply staying alive – had levelled the ground between him and his men. But last night, broken and helpless, he'd truly earned this woman's anger. He imagined her now, downstairs, maybe in the kitchen. Brisk, neat movements. Hints of impatience. And somewhere nearby the slowly drying evidence of his vagabond bladder. As a good German, he'd invaded her territory. And as a Spaniard – passionate, proud – she wouldn't be in the business of forgiveness.

He awoke again hours later. The sun had left the bedroom but the hammering, if anything, had redoubled, a small army of men and maybe women busy on some collective task.

Eva appeared within minutes. She was carrying a glass of water.

'I make you *churros* later,' she said. 'Agustín wants you to drink the water.'

Stefan hadn't a clue about *churros*. He assumed it was food.

'He's here? Agustín?'

'Downstairs.' She nodded. 'He says eating is not good. Afterwards maybe but not now.' Her hand settled briefly on her stomach.

'He wants to stitch me?'

'*Sí.*'

'Soon?'

'Now.' There was something in her face that spoke of satisfaction. They think I might vomit from the pain, Stefan thought. And they're probably right. His eyes strayed to the open window.

'And the noise?'

'Coffins. Many coffins. For your crew.'

Stefan nodded. Obvious, he thought. A small place like this, safe in neutral Spain, would never expect so much death, so many bodies. Another thought occurred to him.

'Are there Germans here? Has anyone come from outside?'

'You have a small office in Coruña. It's by the harbour. The man in charge is called Otto. He says he's a diplomat but maybe he's a spy as well.'

'You've met him?'

'Once. He was here yesterday. He speaks English like you, like me. Not so good but enough. I make the translation for the *ayuntamiento* and for the priest.'

'Did you tell him about me?'

She looked down at him, giving nothing away. In a different mood, thought Stefan, this woman would be very beautiful. He asked the question again. What might have been a smile ghosted across her face.

'No,' she said.

'Why not?'

She ignored the question, holding out the glass, insisting he drank the water. Stefan struggled up on to one elbow, spilled most of it on the sheet. He felt the wetness spreading across his chest. Then Agustín appeared at the bedside. He wanted to know about the wound.

'It's good.' Stefan gulped the last of the water. '*Muchas gracias.*'

'*De nada.*'

Stefan returned the glass to Eva. Agustín's case was back on the pine table. When he returned to the bedside he laid a surgical needle and a length of thread on the whiteness of the sheet. Stefan stared at it. The needle looked huge. It was curved. It reminded him of a fish-hook, the curve slightly flattened after hours of struggle with some monster shark. He turned his head away. He'd always hated the attention of doctors or nurses. Their presence, in his experience, always guaranteed pain.

Agustín threaded the needle, holding it up against the light from the window. Eva folded back the blankets and the sheet, exposing Stefan's leg. She unknotted the bandage, and then stood back while Agustín scissored through the stained, crusted layers of thin gauze. He peered at the wound, muttered something to himself, then his fingertips were exploring the swollen flesh on either side. Stefan lay back, his head on the softness of the pillow, trying not to wince. There followed a brief conversation between the two of them before Eva obliged with a translation.

'I will hold the wound together.' She mimed the action with her thumb and forefinger. 'Agustín will do the stitches. Too much pain, you shout. *Comprende?*'

Stefan nodded. The implications were obvious. No shouting.

'We start, OK?' This from Agustín.

'OK.'

Stefan shut his eyes. He might have been back at sea, racing away after a successful attack, aware of enemy escorts in pursuit as he dived and fled, bracing himself for a volley of depth charges. The parallel was far from exact but there was solace in this thought because the reality was seldom as bad as you'd feared. Boats, like bodies, were stronger than you'd ever imagined.

Wrong.

Eva was pinching the wound together. The pain was indescribable. Stefan wanted to kick the leg free, roll over, scream, anything to make the pain stop. Instead he gritted his teeth, wondering what had happened to the corks.

'OK?' Agustín again. The first stitch was already in and knotted tight. Then came another one, and another. For some reason the pain seemed to have receded, just the way the thunder of prop shafts and engines from the sub hunter overhead would magically fade to a distant rumble.

Stefan had one hand tightly bunched around the top of the sheet. The other was out in thin air, clenching and unclenching, a gesture that came deep from nowhere. It meant get on with it. It meant close the wound. And then it meant leave me alone.

Minutes later, an eternity, it was done. Stefan was aware of the sweat beading on his forehead. His jaw ached. His leg was throbbing again but the scalding pain had gone. He let go of the sheet and wiped his face while his other arm dangled off the side of the bed. Then, from nowhere, came the soft touch of another hand in his. It was Eva. She was bending over him. She gave his hand a squeeze, mopped his forehead with a damp flannel.

'Good.' There was a hint of approval in her eyes. 'Brave.'

Later, after the hammering had stopped, Stefan received another visitor. He was sitting up by now, the blankets heaped around his neck. The sun had gone in completely and there was a chill in the draught through the still-open window. He'd thought of asking Eva to close it but had resisted the temptation. One step at a time, he told himself.

The stranger at his bedside was a man in his thirties, tall, well-built, with a mop of black curls and a three-day growth of beard. He was wearing an open leather gilet, much scuffed, and there were curls of wood shavings in the folds of the shirt beneath. He stared down at Stefan's legs, one huge hand cupping his chin, while Agustín described what he wanted done.

When Agustín had finished, the man nodded and left the room without saying a word.

'Ignacio,' Agustín said. 'A friend of Tomaso.'

'He makes the coffins?'

'Many. All day.' Agustín rubbed his finger and thumb together. Money, Stefan thought. Fat wads of *Reichsmarks* from the agent in Coruña.

'And now?'

'Now he makes a house for your leg.'

The thought put a smile on Stefan's face. He liked Agustín. He liked the sharpness of his wit and the way he never bothered to soften the truth.

'So how long do I stay here?'

'A month. At least. Probably more.'

'And Eva?'

'Eva will look after you.'

'And the lavatory?' Stefan gestured at his belly.

'Ignacio will take care of everything.'

'How?'

Agustín shook his head, wouldn't say. Then the carpenter was back, clumping noisily up the stairs. He brought with him two wooden trestles and went back downstairs for a saw and lengths of what looked like thick pine beading. He set up the trestles and then measured one of the lengths of beading against Stefan's injured leg, marking the wood with a stub of pencil.

Four sawn lengths of beading made the ribs of a cage to serve as a splint. At the open door, he shouted down to Eva. She appeared with a leather belt. He grunted something Stefan didn't catch, then wound the belt around the top of Stefan's thigh. Producing a knife, he cut the belt in unequal halves, then hooped it around the lengths of beading top and bottom, driving nails through the leather and into the wood beneath. Eva, still in the room, watched him without comment.

Ignacio took the whole contraption and, with Agustín's help, slid it beneath Stefan's leg before securing the leather straps. His hands were rough against Stefan's skin but the fit was perfect. Ignacio stood back, assessing his work. Then he nodded at Stefan's knee. He needed another belt for a third bracing.

Eva shook her head. She hadn't got one. Ignacio asked again, louder. This man has no patience, Stefan thought. No manners, either.

The two of them had locked eyes, Eva and Ignacio. Then Ignacio shrugged, his hands finding his own belt, loosening it from his trousers. Moments later, his knife had slashed through the leather, a gesture close to contempt, and he was measuring the shorter length against the purple flesh beneath Stefan's swollen knee. Again, perfect.

He was bent over the bed, tightening the leather straps, grunting as his fingers dug beneath Stefan's thigh. This close, Stefan could smell the man's sweat and the garlic on his breath. Then he stepped back and Stefan tried to thank him but he paid no attention, pursuing Eva as she left the room.

Agustín was carrying the trestles out into the corridor. When he came back Stefan asked about Ignacio's belt. He wanted to buy him another one.

'No need.'

'Why not?'

'You've paid him already.'

'How?'

'Eva gave him one of your coins. Solid gold? For a belt? And this thing?'

He stepped aside with a weary flourish, gesturing at the cage around Stefan's leg. Then Ignacio was back. This time he was carrying an old chair, the kind that belonged to a table. In place of the seat, crudely balanced on the rim of the chair, was a bowl. He put it in the very middle of the room and made a dismissive gesture with his hand as if he wanted nothing more to do with it.

Stefan stared at the chair, at the bowl, at the wisps of rush plaiting still hanging from the frame.

'I shit in that?'

'You do, my friend.' Agustín nodded. 'And if you are very lucky, Eva will take it away.'

*

Hector Gómez looked up to find Arthur Whyte at the door of his new office. The office was twice the size of the cubby hole that Gómez had called home for more than a year. There was comfortably room for two desks and a filing cabinet that looked almost brand new.

Despite his best efforts to pretend otherwise, Whyte was impressed. He nodded at the filing cabinet.

'Where did you get that?'

'No idea, sir. If you want one of your own ask Merricks.'

'Maybe I will.'

Whyte wanted to know about an FBI manager called O'Flaherty. He'd had the man on the phone first thing, yelling about a submission to the Bureau Crime Laboratory in Washington.

'That would be mine, sir.' Gómez was busy. He wanted Whyte gone.

'You sent them a single slug, according to O'Flaherty.'

'That's right. Plus the gun. You'll recall we dug the bullet out of Fiedler's brain during the autopsy. We need a match.'

'Why couldn't we do it here? Why involve the Bureau?'

'Because they do it quicker. And better. And because our guys have other things on their mind.'

'How much else did you tell O'Flaherty?'

'Enough to let his people do the job.' Gómez shrugged. 'Where it happened. Likely range. Not much else.'

'He wants more.'

'There is no more. It's a stand-up job. Did the slug come from that gun? Yes or no. This isn't quantum physics, sir. We're talking first grade.' He glanced at his watch. 'Did he have an answer, by any chance?'

'He did.'

'And?'

'They got a positive match. That bullet came from Fiedler's gun. Like you say, black and white. Case closed.'

Gómez held his gaze. He'd been half expecting this.

'Fiedler hated guns,' he said. 'He wouldn't have a gun in the house. Neither would his wife. So what's he suddenly doing with a Browning automatic?'

'God knows, Gómez. But that's not the point. The point is, we move on.'

'You gave me until the end of the week, sir. Last time I checked, it's only Thursday.'

'You're telling me this investigation is ongoing?'

'I'm telling you we're doing our job.'

'Like how? Like where is this thing taking you?'

Gómez wondered how long he wanted to play this game. Should he tell Whyte about the tests Merricks was doing on typewriters in the Tech Area? On the ever-expanding trawl for areas of interest in Fiedler's private life? On the interesting friendship Sol had struck up with a guy who shot coyotes for a living? The answer was obviously no. The head of G-2 had cracked the case already.

'The guy's tired,' Whyte was saying. 'He's disturbed. He's not even very well. There are pressures in that Tech Area like you wouldn't believe. So one day, for whatever reason, he decides to call it quits.'

'And kills himself.'

'Exactly. We call that suicide, Lieutenant Gómez. I'll even spell it for you if I have to.'

Gómez let the insult fizzle out.

'You used the word disturbed, sir,' he said softly. 'What exactly did you mean?'

'Emotionally unbalanced.'

'How? In what respect?'

Whyte stared at him. He wasn't used to questions like these.

'Are you serious?' he said at last.

'Always.'

'Fine.' He stood up. 'Then I suggest you talk to my wife.'

Gómez had met Whyte's wife on a number of occasions. Her name was Thelma. She was a tall woman, handsome, fit, with a mane of blonde hair and a raw, undisguised ambition on her husband's behalf. This was a second marriage for both of them. They had no children and to fill her spare time Thelma did shifts in the Hill's library. Along with a bunch of other amateur thespians, she also turned out for the Hill's drama group. Only a couple of months back she'd played Daisy Fay Buchanan in an adaptation of *The Great Gatsby*, a role – according to some – for which she needed few rehearsals. According to Merricks, who was doing his best to lay the eager young divorcee who looked after the library's sci-fi section, Thelma had her sights set on Arthur grabbing a big staff job in DC. She wanted a brownstone in Georgetown, a decent car out in the street, and – above all – a nicer class of acquaintance.

Gómez had phoned ahead. Thelma had been expecting the call. This time of the morning the library was busy so she'd commandeered a small, airless office behind the issuing desk. Among the cardboard boxes and stacks of books, there was barely room for a couple of chairs.

Thelma looked pleased with herself. The arrival of Gómez had triggered a ripple of excitement among the women who served as volunteers.

'You want to talk about Sol Fiedler? That's fine by me. One condition, though. You happy this goes no further?'

Gómez shook his head. It was a ludicrous question.

'I'm G-2,' he said. 'You know everything's on the record.'

'You mean that?'

'I do.'

She nodded, evidently surprised. She was wearing a thin cotton dress, cut low, and she had a habit of leaning forward in the chair to confirm the contents. It was the kind of dumb body language that Gómez would never have associated with a colonel's wife but he guessed that marrying a man like Arthur Whyte was equally revealing. There had to be better ways of getting to Washington.

'This isn't easy,' she said.

'You want me to go?'

'Not at all.'

'And this is about Fiedler?'

'Yes.'

'Then tell me what happened.'

She frowned, said nothing. Her eyes strayed briefly to the door. Gómez didn't move.

'You know Frijoles Canyon?' she asked.

'Everyone knows Frijoles Canyon.'

'We were out there a couple of weekends back, a bunch of us, including Sol.'

Gómez nodded. Frijoles Canyon was part of the Bandelier National Monument, an area barely four miles out beyond the main east gate. Way back in time the creek had cut a deep cleft in the rocks, exposing volcanic air pockets that the local Indians had converted into cliff dwellings. A path climbed up to the canyon rim before looping back down to the watercourse below. The circular walk, for someone as fit-looking as this woman, would have been a breeze.

'You walked the path?'

'We all did.'

'And?'

'I was at the back.'

'With Sol?'

'Yes.'

'You knew him already?'

'A little, yes. Recently he'd started coming here to the library. He was crazy about American history. I could help him with that.'

'You recommended stuff? Specific titles?'

'Sure. And I got in other books for him. Material he'd come up with himself.'

She mentioned a couple of books about Ulysses S. Grant. Gómez hadn't heard of either of them.

'So you're out in the canyon,' Gómez said. 'What then?'

'Sol isn't young any more. That day was real hot. He was suffering.'

'You fell behind?'

'We did.'

'And?'

'He kept wanting to stop. He said it was too hot. He wanted me to find shade, just to rest up a while.'

'In one of the caves?'

'Yep.'

'And?'

She frowned again, biting her lip. Gómez couldn't decide whether her hesitation was genuine or just a tease. Either way, he was certain that Fiedler wasn't going to come out well from the next couple of minutes.

'The cave was bigger than I expected,' she said at last. 'And really cool.'

'You had water?'

'Gone. He'd drunk the lot.'

She said they'd found a perch among the rocks inside. She remembered the dust leaving an ochre stain on her new shorts. Back of the cave, in the darkness, she thought there might have been bats. Tiny squealing noises, high-pitched. To her surprise, Sol had gone to investigate, picking his way among the rocks. After a while, worried in case he'd fallen, she'd followed. Then she realised she must have passed him in the dark.

'He called my name,' she said. 'He was very close.'

She'd turned round, felt her way towards him. Then he was there. Naked below the waist.

'He told me he loved me,' she said. 'He told me he was crazy about me. He said he'd been watching me for months, working out when I went to the library, fixing for little meets, telling me all this hoopla about the books he wanted me to find. Then he got hold of my hand. He wanted me to stroke it. He wanted me to make him hard. Can you believe that? Sol Fiedler? A man as bright as that? A man as *old* as that?'

Gómez was aware that Thelma was beginning to sweat. He wanted to know what happened next.

'I told him to put his pants back on.'

'And?'

'He started crying. He said he just wanted to kiss me, to hug me. He said that would be enough. Then he said something else.'

'What?'

'He said we could do it later. Back on the Hill. He said he knew a place we could go where no one would find us.'

'You mean have sex?'

'Sure.'

'So what did you say?'

'Nothing. I was too shocked. I just wanted to have us out of there, back in the sunshine, back with other people. Tell you the truth, it was beyond spooky. Until then I thought he was quite a sweet old guy. Turned out I was wrong.'

Gómez wanted to know about the rest of the day. She said they'd made it back to the path. At her insistence, he'd gone ahead. She didn't want him behind her, ogling her fanny. When they finally caught up with the rest of the group it was late and time to go back to the Hill.

'After that, it was easy. I just made sure we were never alone. I think he was ashamed of himself. He wouldn't look at me. He wouldn't meet my eyes.'

'And did you ever talk to him afterwards? Before he died?'

'Once. He never came to the library again, not when I was there, but there was a time I was walking along Trinity Avenue and he passed me in his car. He was going real slow and then he stopped completely, pulled in, waited for me.'

'What happened?'

'Nothing. He reached across and opened the door. He wanted me to get in. He said we had to talk. I said no way, not after what had happened. Then he said something else. He wanted me to make a promise.'

'About what?'

'About his wife. I wasn't to tell her. He said if that happened there'd be nothing left for him.'

'And what did you say?'

'You really want to know?'

'Yes.'

'I said he should have thought of that in the first place.'

'You *said* that?'

'I did. I was angry. And you know what? I meant it. You take care of someone out there in the sun. You try and make things better for them, easier for them, and look what happens. The guy jumped me. No one does that. Not without consequences.'

'So you told her? Mrs Fiedler?'

'Of course I didn't. It was just a way of getting my own back I guess, of punishing him. If I'd thought . . . you know . . . the guy had a gun . . .' She looked down, knotting her hands, then she began to cry. Gómez didn't move. At length her head came up. Her face was shiny with tears. 'You think I killed him? You think that was my doing? My fault? Be honest.'

Gómez studied her. He had another question in mind but now wasn't the time to put it. Instead he asked about her husband.

'You told him what happened?'

'Of course.'

'And what did he say?'

'He said he'd sleep on it.'

'Meaning?'

'He'd figure out what to do, I guess.'

'Like confront Fiedler?'

'Sure. Except it turned out he couldn't. Because it was too late.'

'So maybe he'd have a word with Marta?'

'I doubt it. Arthur's a kind man, believe it or not. There'd be no point.'

'Sure.' Gómez nodded. 'So what else could he do?'

Thelma had found a tissue from somewhere. She dabbed at her eyes, then tried to raise a smile.

'Nothing, I guess, but you know what? This has been real helpful.' She gestured at the space between them. 'Don't you think so?'

6

Gómez had always liked Albuquerque. He liked the whiteness of the newer government buildings, the way the craze for art nouveau had wrapped the mouldings around some of the fancier gas stations, the pretty little Catholic churches promising shelter from the broiling sun, plus the feeling that something new and exciting had arrived in this corner of the remote Southwest. He even found it in his heart to purchase the odd trinket from the bands of wandering Indian street people. This particular afternoon he bought a piece of stone carving the size of his hand to give to Marta. He wasn't sure which animal it represented but that wasn't the point. The Indian who pocketed his three bucks promised Gómez the carving would bring good fortune. With luck like hers, Marta deserved a break.

Frank Donovan lived in one of the new developments out towards the city's airport. It was a frame house, single-storey, with insect screens on both windows and a tall, oblong panel of the same stuff covering the front door. The door was open and Gómez could hear a baby crying inside. He knocked twice. No reply. He knocked again and then called Donovan's name. At length a woman appeared. She was young, early twenties max. Mexican blood showed in the flatness of her features and after a good night's sleep she would have turned any head. Nice legs. And hints of a superb body under the loose cotton shift.

'Frank Donovan live here?'

The woman looked Gómez up and down. The sight of an Army uniform didn't appear to alarm her.

'Why you asking?'

'Because he and I need to talk.' Gómez jerked a thumb over his shoulder. He'd already checked out Donovan's registered vehicle details. 'That's his pick-up out front? The red one? Am I right?'

He sensed the woman was about to deny all knowledge of Frank Donovan but there was a movement in the shadows behind her and a man stepped into the tiny hall. He looked like he'd just woken up. Tousled hair and sleepy eyes. At least a decade older than his companion.

'That's me you're talking about.' He was mopping his face with a towel. 'What do you want?'

The woman stepped aside. Donovan didn't bother with introductions but limped down the hall and led Gómez into a room at the back of the house. Two more kids, both older. Donovan shooed them into the garden and swept the litter of toys into a corner with the side of his foot. The door to the kitchen was open and whoever did the cooking needed to invest in a fresh bottle of oil.

Gómez looked round. Marta had been right about the guy being a sports nut. The photos on the wall hung above the chaos of the rest of the room. There were three of them, all close-ups, all carefully framed, all featuring the same footballer. He was huge, bulked out by padding, but there was something in the forward lean of his body and the thrust of his chin that promised serious violence. His eyes were tiny, no more than slits. Framed by the helmet, they glittered with something that spoke of both determination and rage.

'Spud Murphy?'

'Sure.' The grin transformed Donovan's face. 'You follow the guy?'

'No, but Fiedler does.'

'This is about Sol?'

'Yes.'

'You know him?'

'Not really.'

'But you work out on the Hill there?'

'I do.'

'Then give him my best, yeah? Next time you see him tell him Tuesday, for sure.'

There was something in Donovan's delivery that sounded a tiny alarm deep in Gómez's brain. Too easy, he thought. Like he'd been expecting a visit like this. Like he'd been practising.

'You saw him this last Tuesday? Day before yesterday?'

'Yeah. Poor guy wasn't too well. Normally I stay on in the evenings but he said there was no point. The way he was feeling I'm guessing he went to bed.'

'So how was he?'

'I just told you. The guy was sick, said he'd been throwing up half the night. I told him to take it easy. His time of life, you need to be careful. Sweet man, though. A joy to talk to. Never bad-mouthed anyone. Never complained. Some of those guys off the boat might have brains the size of the planet but they can be a pain in the ass. Not Sol. Never. A real gentleman. Pleasure to make his acquaintance.'

Gómez eyed the tiny space available on the two-seat sofa, decided to stay on his feet.

'Anything else you'd care to tell me?'

'About what?'

'About the way Sol was when you saw him last.'

'I'm not hearing you, buddy. I don't understand. Like I say, the guy was in bad shape. That's allowed. That happens. What else do you want to know?'

'Did he strike you as unhappy? Depressed?'

'Like he was tired of feeling bad? Sure. Who wouldn't be?'

Gómez held his gaze, then changed tack. The draft put most men of Donovan's age in uniform. How come he wasn't in Europe? Or island-hopping across the Pacific?

'I done my time,' he said at once. 'Took a bunch of shrapnel at Midway. Worst day of my life, if you're asking.'

'You were a Navy man?'

'Sure, and proud of it. I guess there are two kinds of wounds, one up here, one down there.' He tapped his head and then his right thigh. 'Some guys survive intact except they go crazy. Me? I'm too dumb for stuff like that but those Zeros make a hole you wouldn't believe. Honourable discharge. July the 28th 1942.'

'And now?'

'Now I shoot smaller animals. Mainly coyotes. Ask Sol.' He frowned suddenly. 'Is he OK? Or are you trying to tell me different?'

'He's dead, Mr Donovan.'

'Dead?' He looked blank. 'Sol?'

'I'm afraid so.'

'How come? Like he was *really* sick?'

'Like he shot himself to death.'

'No.'

'Yes.'

'Shit.' Donovan sat down. For a long moment he stared down at his hands. Then he looked up at Gómez. 'I gave him a gun Tuesday. Lent it to him.'

'What sort of gun?'

'A Browning automatic. You're not telling me . . .?'

'He asked you for that gun?'

'Sure. Last week. Said he wanted to trying nailing them coyotes himself. One had been bothering him some. He'd never mentioned it to Marta but the dog came calling late at night, looking for scraps I guess.'

'So he wanted to shoot it?'

'That's what he told me.'

'A man who hated guns?'

'He never told me that.'

'Are you sure?'

'Yeah. Matter of fact we never discussed guns. He was interested about what I was doing up on the Hill there, that's the way we got to meet, but pretty quickly it was other stuff, sports mainly, especially football.'

'Sure. So let me get this right. You called by his place on Tuesday at what time?'

Donovan frowned, trying to recall.

'Around nine,' he said. 'Real early. I was working the fence line beyond his place. That time in the morning folks have the coffee on.'

'How do you know he wasn't at work?'

'His car was out front. Sol never walked.'

'He was pleased to see you?'

'He was sick. I think I mentioned it.'

'How long did you stay?'

'Ten minutes.' He shrugged. 'Maybe less.'

'And did you see anyone else around?'

'Nope.'

'Did he mention expecting anyone else to call?'

'Nope.'

'Did you drive back past his place when you were done?'

'Nope. No need. There's a quicker way.'

'You booked out at the gate at twenty-four minutes past three.'

'Is that right?'

'That's what it says in the log.'

'Then I guess it must be true.'

'Normally you leave around five. So why go so early?'

The question threw Donovan. For a split second Gómez saw something close to panic in his eyes. Then he nodded at the door.

'The little one,' he said. 'Maria. She's been sick, too. Thought I might have to take her to the hospital. Turned out I was wrong.'

'What was the matter with her?'

'Coughing all night.' He patted his stomach. 'Sick, too.' He got to his feet. He wanted this interview over. 'You never said about the gun.'

'Your gun?'

'The Browning. Is that what Sol used to do it?'

'Yes.'

He nodded, looking like he was trying to absorb the news. 'What about Marta,' he said at last. 'She's taken it hard?'

'Very. As you'd expect.'

'Sure. They were a sweet old couple.'

The two men looked at each other. Then Donovan checked his watch. He had a fencing job to finish across town. Guy'd be waiting for him to turn up.

'Sure.' Gómez nodded. 'Do you have a typewriter, by any chance?'

'A what?'

'A typewriter? Or maybe access to a typewriter?'

'No.' That same blank look. 'Why would I need a typewriter?'

'Invoices, maybe? I guess you've got a bunch more clients than just us on the mesa.'

'Sure. But I handwrite everything. It's easier that way. And cheaper.'

'How about Francisca?' Gómez nodded at the door. 'Maybe she types.'

'No way, man. That woman has trouble reading.' He forced a grin. 'Nice thought though. Maybe I should get her one. Set her up. Teach her how to spell. Live on what she'd make us. Sure would beat shooting dogs.'

Gómez stayed impassive. No typewriter.

'Where's the bathroom?' he asked.

'Out there. Second door on the right. The flush doesn't work too good.'

Gómez left the room. Instead of the second door on the right he tried the first door on the left. More chaos. More toys. This was where the kids must sleep. The adjoining room was tidier: big double bed, unmade, plus a noisy fan to keep the air moving. About to back out and find the lavatory, Gómez noticed the open suitcases on the carpet beneath the window. One was full of clothes, some folded, some not, and someone

III

had made a start on the second case. He hung on a second longer, then gently shut the door.

Donovan was watching him from down the hall.

'Second on the right,' he said quietly. 'I guess you must have forgotten.'

The two men gazed at each other for a long moment. Then Donovan asked how come Gómez knew his wife's name.

'Marta told me.'

'What else she say?'

'Nothing much. Except you and Sol were buddies. Shame, eh? I guess you're gonna miss him.'

*

The new storm had been brewing all day. Stefan lay in bed, listening to the wind. He read the sky like any mariner. First the long horsetails of high cloud that rode ahead of the incoming front. Then the tell-tale halo round the sun, the temperature plunging, the light thickening, the last fragments of blue swamped by a thick grey blanket of lower cloud. Then came the prelude to the storm, diminuendo, the first stirrings of wind, wooden shutters banging along the street, the rasp of fallen leaves, the rattle of a loose tile above Stefan's head. Now, nearly dark, the wind was howling through the village, a marauding animal, a physical presence that stirred surprise, then wonder, then fear.

Stefan had lived with storms all his working life. He knew their power. He understood what you had to do to survive them. In the open ocean, safe in a U-boat, it was simple. You dived. But much earlier, as a young cadet aboard a square rigger called the *Horst Wessel*, he'd been caught in one of the sudden squalls that blew up in the Baltic. The sheer force of the wind had taken the *Kapitän* by surprise, too, and he'd sent the cadets scurrying aloft with orders to haul in the heavy sails.

His feet on the tautness of the line beneath the yardarm, his body bent over the gathered armfuls of soaking canvas, Stefan had fought for his young life as the ship bucked and heaved, trying to toss him into oblivion. Twice he'd nearly fallen, a sentence of death from the topgallant, and the memory of the sudden darkness that had enveloped the square rigger – the shriek of the wind in the rigging, the groan of the huge yardarm – had never left him. At seventeen he'd thought he was immortal. Barely eight years later, in the teeth of yet another storm, he knew he was anything but. All those *Kameraden*, he thought. All those faces. All that laughter. Gone.

Mid-evening, at the height of the storm, the window with the broken latch smashed back against the wall, shattering the glass, and the room was suddenly full of wind. Stefan had gathered the blankets around his chin, hunkering down, waiting for this savage animal to lose interest and slink away. For once in his life he could do nothing and the feeling of helplessness, of having been taken prisoner by events, left him profoundly depressed. With the wind had come blinding stabs of lightning, neon-white, and hammer blows of thunder that seemed ready to crush the entire village, and at one moment he'd glimpsed a face at the door. It was Eva. She was looking at him. Then she was gone.

The storm passed around midnight. After a while, Stefan heard voices in the street, men and women venturing out, tallying the damage, counting the cost. He tried to visualise what they'd find – fallen tiles, broken glass, signs ripped from their mountings – and he wondered what living on a coast like this, exposed to the full violence of the ocean, would do to your soul. Did you become hardened in some way? Impervious to nature in all its moods? Or did this wild corner of Europe breed something closer to resignation? Bad things happened and with luck you survived. Until the next storm. And maybe the one after that.

Eva again. Already, as he grew used to the slow rhythms of convalescence, she was playing an ever-larger part in his thoughts but he suspected that just now something had come between them. After regular visits over the course of the morning, she hadn't been upstairs for hours. As the wind began to rise he thought she must have left the house but then, above the gathering storm, he heard the piano.

At the time he'd thought of calling out and telling her about the window but he'd resisted the temptation. So far they hadn't risked anything as dangerous as a conversation but on her part he sensed, if nothing else, a curiosity about this stranger who'd so suddenly appeared in her life. Agustín had mentioned that she'd spent some time in England, hence her command of the language. He also said she'd been a photographer, still took pictures. Stefan had pressed him for more details but the doctor had shaken his head. Ask her yourself, he'd said with a smile.

Really? Would that ever be possible? Or was he doomed to remain at the very edges of her life, a bad smell washed up by a war he no longer wanted to fight? He didn't blame half of Europe for hating the Germans. Not in the least. Had he been born French, or Belgian, or Polish, or Czech, or – God help him – Russian, he'd have felt exactly the same. Being despised by people you'd invaded went, all too literally, with the territory. But what had Hitler ever done to the Spanish? To Adolf's Fascist friend General Franco? To these sturdy Galician fishermen mending their nets in the windy sunshine? He didn't know, couldn't fathom it, but drifting off to sleep at last he knew he'd need to summon help next morning. Would she be back again? The face in the darkness by the door? Or had she truly turned against him?

When he awoke, hours later, it was Agustín at his bedside. The doctor had come to check on his stitches. He folded back the blanket, took a hard look at his leg and pronounced himself satisfied. The wound was healing nicely. No sign of infection.

'This thing is comfortable?' He gestured down at the splint.

'No.'

'A pity, my friend. Patience, eh?'

Stefan nodded. He needed to get to his pot across the room. Agustín helped him out of bed then fetched a pair of battered espadrilles from downstairs. There were shards of glass all over the floor from the shattered window and Stefan could feel them crunching underfoot as he managed to shuffle the nine steps to the chair. Agustín left the room again while he squatted on the pot. When he came back he brought news.

'Your submarine has gone,' he said. 'Finished. *Kaput*.'

'*Gone?*' For a moment Stefan thought someone might have stolen it.

'Destroyed. Broken up by the storm. You can see what happened from the clifftop. Everywhere. In pieces. Many pieces.'

Stefan was thinking about the SS men. Four of them had got out. One hadn't.

'Are there more bodies?' he asked.

'No. I don't think so.'

'But lots of wreckage?'

'Yes. For now the waves are still very high, very big. The German is back from Coruña. He has police with him, *Guardia Civil*. The police are on the beach. No one is allowed there.'

For a moment Stefan couldn't imagine why. Then he remembered the torpedo compartment for'ard, and the jigsaw of wooden crates, and the second lavatory stacked high with these men's luggage: suitcases and kitbags carefully secured. SS loot, he thought. Probably a fortune in gold and other precious metals. Maybe paintings, too, and religious icons, anything to buy them a new life in the sunshine of Argentina and Brazil.

Agustín had found a broom from somewhere and was sweeping up the glass. Then he helped Stefan back to bed. When he'd finished rearranging the blankets, Stefan asked him about Eva.

'Is she out today?'

'*Sí*. She helps with the translation again. With the German.'

'You've seen her?'

'Yes.'

He was looking down at Stefan. He was very astute.

'She thinks you're SS,' he said quietly.

'Me?' Stefan was astonished. 'SS?'

'She found a wallet in your coat.' He sounded almost apologetic. 'She showed me the papers inside. Johann Huber? SS *Brigadeführer*? Is that who you really are?'

Dimly, Stefan remembered the *Brigadeführer*'s thick wallet. He'd pocketed it after the Engineer knocked the man briefly unconscious as the submarine drifted towards the rocks.

'My name is Stefan,' he said stiffly. 'Stefan Portisch. I was *Kapitän* on the U-boat. You know that. I told you.'

'And Huber?'

'Huber was a passenger. There were five of them. He was in charge.'

'He gave you his wallet?'

'Not exactly.'

Agustín nodded. Then he turned to contemplate the pile of glass. Stefan wanted to know whether he believed him. Did he look SS? Did he act like a man like Huber?

Agustín said nothing for a moment. Then he turned back to the bed.

'Me, my friend? I believe you. Eva?' He spread his hands wide. 'Who knows?'

*

The checkpoint that controlled access to the Hill was a mile short of the east gate in the perimeter fence. Gómez had already enquired about Donovan's recent movements before setting off to find him in Albuquerque. Now, on his return, he wanted to know a little more.

There were two guys on duty. In charge was a middle-aged lieutenant called Alessori. He came from the Bronx, NYC, an area Gómez happened to know well, and over the past year they'd struck up something of an acquaintance.

Alessori took Gómez into the room at the back of the hut and dug in the refrigerator for a bottle of chilled Mountain Dew. The room was papered with photos of nude women torn from the pages of men's magazines. Gómez was inspecting a

117

blonde who reminded him faintly of Arthur Whyte's wife when he felt a nudge in the ribs.

'You find the guy?' Alessori wanted to know about Donovan.

'Sure.' Gómez took a long pull at the bottle. He was parched.

'And?'

'We had a conversation. Donovan was in the Navy. Did he ever tell you about any of that?'

'Never.' He was frowning. 'My recollection was he served with the 101st Airborne.'

'Screaming Eagles? He told you that?'

'Can't swear he did. May have been someone else. He's been coming here awhiles, anyway. Never gave us any trouble. Regular guy . . .'

It sounded like a question. Gómez wasn't minded to answer. Instead he wanted to know about the procedure when Donovan arrived and left.

'Normally, someone new, they get the full search. That's after all the ID procedures. Someone like Frank . . .?' He shrugged. 'The guy's been tooling up regular, seven, eight in the morning, that old pick-up of his, whole bunch of Tuesdays, longer than I can remember.'

'He gets the search?'

'No.'

'You wave him through?'

'Yep.'

'The guy's carrying weapons, right?'

'Yep. Every one of them authorised. Never an issue. Not once. We saw the paperwork way back. After that he turns up, shoots them dogs, does whatever else he's paid for and drives off back home. Like I say, part of the scenery. You don't much like coyotes? You want them off the reservation? That's Frank you've got to thank. Guy renders a service as far as we're concerned. Just hope he gets well paid for it.'

Gómez wanted to be sure about last Tuesday.

'He left earlier than usual, right?'

'Sure.' He nodded towards the front desk where the log book was kept. 'You asked that same question this morning. Guy lit out for home around three, three thirty.'

'You talk to him at all?'

'Sure. Briefly. He barely even stopped.'

'Did he seem normal? Did he seem OK?'

'Sure.'

'Not flustered at all? A little nervous, maybe?'

'Not at all.'

'So what did you say?'

'I asked him how come the early out.'

'And?'

'He had to pick up a new tyre for the truck.'

'He said that?'

'For sure.' He laughed. 'You're telling me you're surprised? The state of that wreck he drives?'

The summons was awaiting Gómez the minute he got back in the office. It was late afternoon. Merricks was busy at his desk, bent over a report.

'Don't know what you've done, man.' He didn't look up.

'So tell me.'

'I've had Tightass in here all day. On the hour, every hour. Where is he? Where's he gone? When's he back?'

Tightass was Arthur Whyte. Merricks treated the colonel with a pleasing mix of derision and contempt.

'So what did you say?'

'I told him you'd left to make enquiries.'

'Just that?'

'Just that.'

'You mention Fiedler at all?'

'Nope.'

'So how come all the attention?'

'Could be any of these babies. Take your pick.' Merrick gestured at the slew of paperwork across his desk. Then he picked up the phone and dialled a number from memory. 'Groves is in town and so is Oppie. Tightass has probably died of excitement by now.' He held out the phone for Gómez. 'Good luck, man.'

The summons took Gómez across the bridge to the Tech Area. He showed his ID to the sentry at the gate. Oppenheimer had an office on the top floor of one of the wooden lab buildings that fronted Trinity Drive. Oppenheimer's secretary met Gómez in the corridor and showed him into an adjoining office that had once been a classroom. There was a conference table with chairs, a blackboard, and a desk in the corner piled high with books. Two narrow windows offered a view of Ashley Pond and even now, turning back from the window, Gómez fancied he could still smell chalk in the air.

After a while a door opened next door and three men appeared. One of them was Oppenheimer. Another was Arthur Whyte. The third, instantly recognisable from the photos Gómez had seen, was the guy who'd trashed the Washington bureaucracy, steered this crazy project through two difficult years and still had 125,000 people by the throat.

Gómez had never met General Leslie Groves. Since the President hit the 'Go' button, the man had become a legend, partly because of his talent for self-publicity and partly because he was a genuine phenomenon. Anyone who could hold together a program as complex and potentially explosive as this one had Gómez's undiluted respect. The man was a monster – abusive, short-tempered, unforgiving – but this came with the territory. Without him, the Manhattan Project would have died on its feet.

In the flesh he was a big, pale, bulky man. The AC was broken and the temperature in the room had to be in the high seventies, but there wasn't a hint of sweat on his huge face, and his uniform looked box-fresh. He sat at the head of the table with Oppenheimer on one side and Arthur Whyte on the other. Gómez snapped a salute which Groves didn't bother to acknowledge.

'Sit down, soldier.'

Gómez did what he was told. Trouble, he thought.

Groves steepled his thick fingers. Rumour on the Hill suggested that his memory for times, dates, places – all the stuff you needed to mount a decent ambush – was near-perfect. Not a sheet of paperwork in sight.

'This guy Sol Fiedler shot himself to death on Tuesday morning. Am I right?'

'Yes, sir. That's the way it looks.'

'He left a note, right?'

'Yes, sir.'

'Explained to his poor wife that he had some problems with where all this work of his was headed? Words to that effect?'

'Yes, sir.'

'So he shoots himself. Not good. Not from Mrs Fiedler's point of view. And certainly not from ours.'

'I agree, sir.'

'And now, according to Colonel Whyte here, we learn that poor Sol had another problem, maybe one that Mrs Fiedler never suspected, certainly one he never wanted to share with her.'

'So I understand, sir.'

'So you *understand*? What does that mean, soldier?'

Groves was eyeballing him. He'd heard from others on the Hill that this man ran the entire project from special suites on the railroad as he criss-crossed the country from meeting to meeting. Looking at the paleness of his face, Gómez could believe it.

'Colonel Whyte's wife told me what happened, sir. I've yet to check her account.'

'*Check* her account? What in God's name is there to check? She's an attractive woman. Fiedler jumps her. A serious error on his part but you're telling me that's some kind of surprise?'

'I'm telling you nothing, sir. In my line of work we check everything. That's what you pay us for.'

'Glad to hear it, soldier. Very noble. But let me tell you something else. Where I sit, we speak the language of priorities. Some things matter, some things matter less, and some things, believe it or not, don't matter at all. What we have here is a sad little story about a guy who couldn't get his pecker up. Not without a beautiful woman like Mrs Whyte to give him a hand. That was foolish on the part of Mr Fiedler, but you know something else? These guys aren't normal. Clever? Yes. Brilliant? Many of them, sure. But not normal. And you want to know something else while we're on the subject? They hate us. Why? Because we make life difficult for them. They dreamed this Gadget up. They did all the hard math, ran the calcs, played God with the physics, and now we've come along and taken this beautiful toy off them. They hate that. They hate that we're the ones gonna decide what to do with it, how many bombs to make, where to drop them. These people, bright as they are, have finally understood what lies down the road. What lies down the road is exceedingly ugly, soldier. What lies down the road is death in six-figure numbers. Carnage. Charred flesh. Blood so hot it boils. Does that realisation make these people feel guilty? Of course it does. Does it make them get round tables like this and give us a hard time? Why, yes. But do we still need them? You bet your sweet ass we need them. Else half a million of our men are gonna wake up one morning on the beaches of Japan. More death. More carnage. You want that, soldier? You want our guys washing around in the surf, screaming for their mothers? Is that what you want to happen?'

Groves was bent forward, letting the question hang in the air. Everything about his body language – the jut of the jaw, the gleam in his eyes – demanded an answer but Gómez was lost. Spud Murphy, he thought, head down, thighs pumping, ball clasped tight.

'I'm not sure I understand, sir,' he said at last. 'I'm an investigator. Like I say, I'm paid to try and figure out situations like these. It sure looks like a suicide. But maybe it's not.'

'It's a suicide, soldier.'

'Is that an order, sir? Or an opinion?'

Gómez saw Whyte close his eyes. Even Oppie winced. Expecting the general's wrath, Gómez was pleasantly surprised to see a rare smile warm his face.

'You got it, soldier. As it happens it's both. But you can take your choice. All I'm telling you is this. The case, if there ever was a case, is now closed. The program rolls on because the program has to. Else we're gonna be killing the enemy for the rest of our lives and that would be dull work as well as unnecessary. You're going to walk out of here hating me but that doesn't matter either. Being hated is what I get paid for and it happens I'm very good at it. Sol Fiedler is nothing, soldier. He's not even a footnote in this story of ours. Sol Fiedler is history. Because Sol Fiedler is dead, a decision we believe he took for himself.' He turned briefly to Oppenheimer. 'You agree, Oppie?'

Oppenheimer said nothing. He'd been smoking since Gómez entered the room and an ashtray at his elbow was brimming with butts from an earlier session. Now he took his time to light another.

'Colonel Whyte says you have leave owing.' He picked a curl of tobacco off his lower lip. 'At least a couple of weeks.'

Gómez did his best not to look surprised. First time he'd heard of it.

'You want me off the Hill?'

'We're suggesting you take that leave. These are testing times, Lieutenant. It pays to stay fresh.' He held Gómez's eyes for a long moment, then permitted himself the ghost of a smile. 'Do we hear a yes?'

*

It was nearly dark before Eva finally reappeared in Stefan's room. She paused beside the door, checking that he was awake, then stepped inside. She was wearing a pair of rumpled trousers and a thick grey pullover. The bottoms of the trousers were wet and she brought with her the smell of the ocean.

Stefan smiled up at her. She asked him whether he needed to use the toilet. He shook his head.

'Maybe later,' he said. 'If that's OK.'

'You're hungry? I bring you food.'

Stefan shook his head. That, too, could wait. What he wanted – needed – was a chance to clear the air, an opportunity to break the gathering silence and prove that he wasn't who she thought he was.

'You still think I'm SS?'

She stared down at him a moment, not answering. Then she frowned.

'You talked to Agustín?' she asked.

'Yes.'

'When?'

'This morning. You found the wallet in my coat, yes?'

'*Sí.*'

'And that's why you thought I was someone else?'

'I thought you were Huber, *sí.*'

'Say I was Huber. Say I was SS. Say I'd gone through this whole war in my black uniform, doing the things the SS do, would that have made a difference?'

'To what?'

'To this. To us. To me being here.'

'There is no difference.'

'Because I'm German?'

'Yes. And because you come from the war.'

Stefan nodded. Whatever brand of German he was, whatever he'd done in the chaos of this war, he was still unwelcome. He found the distinction difficult to understand but if nothing else he sensed that he had this one chance to try and change things.

'I'm a human being,' he said. It sounded pathetic.

'So is Huber.'

'Huber is a bad man. Was.'

'And you?'

'I'm not a bad man. Not like Huber.'

'What makes you so sure?'

'Because I haven't shot people for the sake of it. Because I don't believe I'm part of some master race. Because, if you want the truth, I don't believe in anything any more.'

'You don't?'

'No.'

'And is that why you're here? Are you hiding?'

'Yes.'

She gazed down at him, her expression giving nothing away. Then she moved the cage that was his leg very gently and sat down on the bed.

'This afternoon I was with the German again, the man from Coruña,' she said. 'His name is Otto. He's an OK guy.'

'I find that hard to believe.'

'Why?'

'Because he's a German.'

The way he said it, the resignation in his voice, sparked a smile. Then, as quickly as it happened, the smile was gone.

'You know what would happen if they found you here?'

'I've no idea. I expect they'd take me away and shoot me.'

'For what?'

'For desertion. For betraying the cause.'

'What is the cause?'

'Very good question. I used to think it was the Reich. Then that went sour. Then I thought it was the *Heimat*, the homeland, everything I've come from, everything I was, but that's all gone, destroyed, finished. So the cause?' He shrugged. 'You tell me.'

'Maybe the cause is more war.'

'You mean killing more people?'

'*Sí*. Because the killing never stops.'

'Then I don't want it.'

'What do you want?'

This was the question that went to the heart of everything and Stefan knew it. What did he want? Here and now? Lying immobile in a stranger's house on the furthest edge of Europe? No glass in the window and his prospects, his life, his very existence in the hands of a woman who loathed Germans?

'I want to get well,' he said at last. 'And I want to feel normal again.'

She nodded, fingering the corner of the blanket. Then she lifted her head and swept the curtain of hair from her face.

'I was on the beach with Otto,' she said. 'They found another body.'

'Did they?'

'*Sí*. And you know who it was?'

'Tell me. I knew them all. Every single one of them. They were like my children. Even the older men.'

'It was Huber.'

'How do you know?'

'Otto had photographs. It was the same man.'

'What was he like? What state was he in?' Stefan felt the first stirrings of alarm. Three days in the submarine, Huber's body would still be intact.

Eva took her time answering the question.

'He had been shot,' she said at last.

'How do you know?'

'He had a bullet hole here . . .' she touched her left eye, '. . . and there were more holes in his leather coat, just here.' Her chest this time.

'Did Otto see all this?'

'It was Otto who told me. The *Guardia* have taken the body to Coruña. Otto insisted.'

'For what?'

'For examination. And afterwards for burial.'

Stefan lay back, trying to absorb the implications. If they ever found him, if they ever came for him, if they ever worked out what had happened, he'd be facing a murder charge, as well as desertion. Eva was right. The killing would never stop.

He eyed her from the pillow. The closeness wasn't just physical. Some of her reticence, her apartness, had gone. She seemed to want to talk. He asked her about the submarine. What else had come ashore?

'Many boxes. Many tins. Food. Oil. Ammunition.'

'And wooden boxes? With padlocks on?'

'*Sí*. The *Guardia* have a truck. The back of the truck is full.'

'And did you mention me at all?' It was a question he had to ask.

'No.'

'So they think I'm dead? Like the others?'

'You're missing. There are now forty-seven bodies. They think the other two have gone. That includes you.'

Stefan nodded. 'Missing' was an interesting word. That's exactly what he felt. Dislocated. Lost. Missing.

He looked up at her again and then extended his hand.

'My real name is Stefan,' he said. 'Stefan Portisch.'

'I know. I asked that, too. Otto had a list. You were on it. *Kapitän* Stefan Portisch.' She stared down at him. Stefan withdrew his hand, glad at the very least that she no longer believed he was SS.

'I have a question, *Kapitän* Portisch. Do you mind?'

'Of course not. Go ahead.'

'Who shot Huber?'

Stefan held her gaze. Then, very slowly, he smiled and shook his head.

'I need to use the pot,' he said. 'Can you help me?'

7

Sol Fiedler was buried two days later after a service at a synagogue in Albuquerque. Dozens of his colleagues from the Tech Area formed a modest cortège for the three-hour drive from Los Alamos, and Oppie arranged for a bus to take a couple of dozen of Marta's friends, and for drinks and a buffet meal afterwards in a downtown hotel. After the fruit course, Oppie paid tribute to Fiedler's many achievements in the field of metallurgical research, a graceful speech which won applause from Sol's fellow scientists.

Before he sat down, Oppie acknowledged that the pressures on everyone on the Hill were many and various but that stress of the kind that must have led to Sol's death was mercifully rare. Watching the faces around the table, Gómez was aware of the men exchanging glances. By now it was obvious that they, like him, had profound doubts about what had really led to Fiedler's death. The guy was too strong-minded, they said. And aside from anything else, he loved his wife too much to be apart from her.

As for Marta herself, she weathered the flood of hugs and sympathy with some grace. Only once during the service, when the rabbi was approaching the end of the *Hesped*, did the sheer power of the eulogy appear to affect her. Sol Fiedler, the rabbi said, was a man of rare learning, of rare wisdom and of rare humanity. The memories he'd left would be as precious as his life. A man like Sol was like water in the desert. He'd brought flowers from dust, and hope from despair. The end of a thing, he said in echo of Ecclesiastes, is better than its beginning.

At this, Marta ducked her head and wiped a tear from the corner of her eye. Later, after the meal in the hotel, she thanked Gómez for his kindness and patience. Among her many regrets was the fact that he'd never been able to get to know her husband for himself.

'I did nothing,' he told her, only too aware that it was true.

From Albuquerque, Fiedler's body – with Marta in attendance – was taken by train for burial in Chicago. Oppie paid the costs. Gómez and Merricks climbed back into their Army Ford coupé for the drive back to Los Alamos. Minutes into the journey, Merricks questioned Gómez's choice of route.

'Why are we heading for the airport?' he asked.

Gómez didn't answer. Minutes later he pulled off the main road and drove into the development that housed Frank Donovan and his family. As he'd half expected, there was no sign of the red pick-up outside. Neither, when he parked and knocked at the door, was there any indication of life inside. No children. No radio. No conversation. Nothing.

Next door, the householder answered Gómez's knock.

'They went yesterday.' He jerked a thumb at the wilderness of garden out back. 'Good riddance.'

Two days later, mid-morning, the crew of *U-2553* were laid to rest. Eva had warned Stefan about the funeral the previous evening. The bodies, she said, had been embalmed and were lying in coffins on the floor in the local school. The school was closed until after the funeral, and Otto had somehow found forty-seven Nazi flags to drape across the coffins.

The route from the school to the village church went down the street past Eva's house and she asked Stefan whether he wanted to be discreetly at the window to pay his respects. Stefan said no. He'd already said his private farewells to these men and the last thing he wanted to take away from this village was the taint of forty-seven swastikas. They already belonged, he told himself, to another life.

Nonetheless there was no avoiding the funeral. The church bell began to toll at ten o'clock. Like the steady drip of water, it quickly became unbearable. It summoned too many memories, sparked hot waves of anguish and regret that felt – to Stefan – close to despair. Then came the sound of boots on the cobblestones beneath the window and he wondered how a village like this could muster enough men to carry all those coffins, all that collective weight. Maybe Coruña is full of Germans, he thought. Maybe they've been trucked in. Maybe there were dozens of his countrymen in the street below, immaculate in their uniforms, bidding *auf Wiedersehen* to the fallen.

Behind the procession of coffins, and hardest to bear of all, was some kind of choir. It sounded like children's voices, maybe from the school. They were singing a psalm in Latin and Stefan recognised the words. The chant of their infant voices swelled and then died as they passed beneath the window, and afterwards – in the gathering silence – Stefan wept.

> Support us, O Lord,
>> all the day long of this troublesome life,
>> until the shadows lengthen and the evening comes,
>> the busy world is hushed,
>> the fever of life is over
>> and our work is done.
> Then, Lord, in your mercy grant us a safe lodging,
>> a holy rest, and peace at the last
>> through Christ our Lord.
> Amen.

Later, it must have been early afternoon, Stefan awoke to find Eva at his bedside. She was wearing a black dress with a rose pinned to her breast. When Stefan asked about the rose she loosened the pin and laid it on his pillow. It was the deepest red.

'For you,' she said, reaching for his hand. 'I'm sorry.'

*

The following day, Gómez prepared to leave Los Alamos. Merricks was driving him to the station at Lamy, twenty miles south-east of Santa Fe. From here he would be taking the train north, like Sol Fiedler, to Chicago. There he had business to transact before moving on to Washington.

He'd phoned Agard Beaman a day or so ago, explaining about his sudden windfall vacation, and Beaman had insisted on him staying over. He had a really neat apartment in DC south of the river beyond the Navy Yard. It was up high, third floor, and there were glimpses of the Capitol from the main window. He had two bedrooms and Gómez's name was on one of them. No arguments. Just say yes. Gómez, oddly touched, had obliged. Give it a week, he said. Then I'll be with you.

Now, with Merricks eager to leave the Hill and hit the road, Gómez remembered the last check he had to make. The doctor who'd performed the autopsy on Sol Fiedler was based in the hospital, along from the Admin Building. His name was Bud Jackson and he came from a small lakeside town in Illinois that Gómez had known well as a kid.

Jackson, like Gómez, had been on the Hill from the start. Last time Gómez had seen him was months back at the height of summer when Gómez checked in with griping stomach pains Jackson blamed on algae in the water.

Today, Gómez had phoned ahead. The doctor looked up from a huge pile of paperwork as Gómez tapped on his door. He had a big open smile. He was pleased to see him.

'You OK?'

'Never better.'

'Glad to hear it.' He gestured at the mess of paperwork. 'We've got another virus on the reservation. I'm blaming the Commies.' He opened a drawer and slid out what looked like a report. He checked the front page and then offered it to Gómez.

'Is that the autopsy findings? On Sol Fiedler?' Gómez didn't move.

'Sure. It's a copy. I thought that's what you wanted.'

'I've got one already. No need.'

'But this is about Sol Fiedler?'

'It is.'

'So what do you want to know?' He glanced down at the report. 'You think I did a crummy job? Is that it? Only I never went near the Medical Examiner course. Carving up dead bodies? Never appealed.'

'You did a fine job. You did what you could. Guy got a bullet in his head. Point-blank range. Powder burns round the entry wound. No one walks away from that.'

'So what, exactly, do you want to know?'

Gómez took his time. This was going to be tricky and he knew it.

'You'll know Arthur Whyte,' he said slowly.

'Sure. I guess he's your boss.'

'You're right. He is. Did he attend the autopsy? His name's not on the list.'

'He didn't.'

'Has he spoken to you since?'

'Yes. In fact he came here a couple of days back. Just like you. Said he happened to be passing by.'

'And?'

'There was something he wanted to clear up. Tell you the truth, I never understood why.'

'He wanted to know something? Clarification?'

'Sure. Something I didn't include in the report.'

'Like what?'

Jackson hesitated. He didn't know where this was going. Finally he shrugged. He knew that Gómez was carrying the Fiedler file. What the hell.

'He asked me whether Fiedler was circumcised. He knew he was Jewish, he knew all that. He just needed to be sure.'

'And what did you say?'

'I told him he was.' He paused, bemused. 'Is that what you were after? Is that all?'

Gómez was already on his feet. He could see Merricks through the window at the wheel of the Ford. He extended a hand.

'That's plenty,' he said. 'I need to catch a train.'

PART TWO

PART TWO

8

It was an early autumn morning in Chicago. A blustery wind off the lake carried the first chill taste of the coming winter and an elderly caretaker in patched dungarees was doing his best to corral a heap of fallen leaves. Gómez watched him from his perch in the window of the diner across the street. O'Flaherty was late. He'd promised eleven o'clock. It was now twenty past.

He arrived minutes later, as voluble and unkempt as ever. At Hoover's insistence, the Bureau's G-men wore their hair short, their grey suits neatly pressed and their black shoes permanently buffed. Yet here was a guy who'd guarantee you crazy shirts, food stains and a wild tangle of greying hair that hadn't seen a comb in weeks. Gómez happened to know he had the ear of J. Edgar, reporting directly to the big office in DC where he served as a facilitator in business the great man preferred to keep in the shadows, but even so there were limits. Hoover had been known to sack guys whose tie he didn't like. So how come he cut this hobo so much slack?

O'Flaherty settled noisily on the stool next to Gómez. Not a word of apology for arriving late.

'Well?' he said. 'Why the meet?'

'I need a favour.'

'You got one, didn't you? We turned the slug around real quick. Got you the result you wanted. You want the weapon back? Is that it? Only we understood you Army people ain't so keen on judicial process.'

The thought of Fiedler's death leading to any form of trial lit a flicker of amusement in Gómez's eyes.

'You've been reading my reports?'

'Sure. Me and a handful of others.'

'Including the Boss?'

'Sure. To the best of my knowledge.'

'You still speak to him regularly?'

'Nice try. If you guessed yes you'd guess right.'

'So what does he think?'

'Mr Hoover?' O'Flaherty had half turned on the stool and was eyeing the display of pastries on the counter. Gómez remembered a wolfish appetite for anything sweet. 'Mr Hoover thinks what he always thought. He'd love a slice of the action down there. He's decided Groves is the main man just now and it pains Mr Hoover greatly that he can't lay a finger on him. He tries but he fails. Groves is Mr Clean. It's driving Mr Hoover nuts. He knows you guys are sitting on a big fat egg. That big fat egg is all our futures, which I guess gives the good general something of a monopoly. Groves has the ear of the President. Not a situation Mr Hoover is prepared to tolerate. Army security is shit. We hear it from all quarters, including you, buddy. In which regard Mr Hoover says thank you.'

'No problem. I thought we had a deal.'

'Sure do. Is that what this is about? You've come to renegotiate? Only that might be difficult. Mr Hoover appreciates the work you're doing down there. You keep us close to the action. It's one thing to suspect the place is crawling with fucking Commies, quite another to have it confirmed.'

'So what happens to the names I give you?'

'We put them through the wringer. Full service. Root canal stuff. We dig deep. Every goddam particle we can find on the guys. Then I guess the files go to Groves. But always via the President.'

'Hand-delivered?'

'Sure.'

'By the man himself?'

'Who else? Knowledge is power, buddy. Always has been, always will be. Even your Mr Oppenheimer accepts that. Assuming he doesn't blow us all up.'

Gómez nodded. O'Flaherty had abandoned the conversation and was piling pastries on to a plate at the counter. Gómez watched him emptying his pockets, looking for change. These last fifteen months, on maybe half a dozen occasions, Gómez had been quietly meeting with a retired agent who'd once run the Bureau field office in Albuquerque. The guy lived way out in the suburbs – wife dead, big dog called Clancy. The meets happened at a series of locations downtown, fleeting exchanges in case of Army surveillance. The material Gómez passed along had nothing to do with the Gadget but everything to do with some of the scientists who were going to make the thing work.

It was Gómez's belief that these guys – maybe a handful, maybe more – were seriously flaky. Secrets were leaking to the Soviets but such were the pressures on the program that nobody was paying the right kind of attention. One day, in his view, he'd open the paper to find New York or DC a pile of ashes and he didn't want that to happen. Intel about intel, he thought. The spycatcher turned spy. Not the least of the ironies that stitched through his life.

O'Flaherty was back on his stool, licking sugar from his fingertips. He was never less than blunt.

'You've come a hell of a way,' he said. 'For what?'

'Another favour.'

'Name it.'

Gómez slipped an envelope out of his jacket. Gave it to O'Flaherty.

'The guy's name is Frank Donovan,' he said. 'He's a contractor onsite at Los Alamos. All the details on our file are in there.'

'So what else do you need?'

'Whatever you can give me. Guy claims he was in the Navy. That might not be true.'

'And you can't find out for yourself? You're telling me the Navy doesn't keep records? Isn't that why Groves built the fucking Pentagon?'

'The Navy people are pissed with Groves. He keeps them out of the loop exactly the same way he deals with everyone else. Like I say . . .' Gómez nodded down at the envelope, '. . . anything you've got.'

O'Flaherty had a mouth full of pastry. Then he wanted to know more about Donovan.

'Why's he so hot, this guy? You wanna give me a clue?'

Gómez shook his head. Private business, he said.

'And that's all? Two days on a train for that?'

'No.'

'You mean there's more?'

'Yeah.' Gómez nodded at the envelope. 'There's an address in there, the place Donovan has been living. He left in a hurry a couple of days back. I want it sealed off. I want your guys down there to go through it.'

'What are they looking for?'

'Paperwork, mainly. Bank statements. Letters. Plus any kind of lead on where he might have gone. There's a woman he lives with, too. Name of Francisca. Plus three kids. If they've all lit out he'll need a different vehicle. The guy's been driving a red Ford pick-up. He may have part-exed it. I need the details of whatever he's driving now.' He paused. 'You wanna write this down?'

'No.' O'Flaherty tapped his head. 'It's in here.'

'You're sure?'

'Yeah. Anything else we can help you with?'

Gómez asked O'Flaherty about the Immigration people. Were the channels still open?

'You mean frontier control?'

'Yes.'

'Anywhere particular in mind, *amigo*?'

'Guess.'

'*All* of them?' O'Flaherty couldn't believe it. There were dozens of crossing points into Mexico.

'Start with the closest. If the guy's heading south in a hurry, I'm thinking El Paso or maybe Route 11 down to Columbus. Either way he thinks he's gonna end up safe.'

'From what?'

'From us.'

'You gonna tell me why?'

For a moment Gómez toyed with sharing his suspicions about Donovan but then shook his head. Compartmentalisation, he thought. Need to know. If he was still carrying a Bureau badge, enquiries like these would come with the turf. As it was, working for Army Intel, he had no jurisdiction off-base. Hence the shopping list for O'Flaherty.

O'Flaherty wanted to know about Gómez's new bosses.

'They know you're here? Those dumb fuckers paying your wages?'

'They know I've got furlough.'

'And that's it? That's all I get?'

'Yeah. For now.'

O'Flaherty seemed to take the news personally. A couple of years back, the news that Army G-2 were quietly recruiting personnel with investigative experience for the Manhattan Project sites across the country had reached the ears of Mr Hoover. He and O'Flaherty had combed the ranks of front-line Bureau agents for likely applicants and one of them had been Gómez. He'd taken some notable scalps, chiefly in Chicago. His service record was second to none. His years in the Marine Corps would do him no harm in front of a Pentagon selection board. And so it had happened. Lieutenant Hector Gómez. En route to PO Box 1663, Santa Fe. Mr Hoover's canary in the Army's coal mine. Pulling not one salary but two.

O'Flaherty had always been Gómez's point of contact within the Bureau itself. Until recently, O'Flaherty had worked out of a small apartment that served as an office in DC, with Mr Hoover barely a couple of blocks away. In all truth, Gómez never even knew whether O'Flaherty was the guy's real name. Since the war started, even crime and justice had become a world of smoke and mirrors, nothing reflecting its true image.

Now Gómez wanted to know about Chicago.

'You're here for keeps?' he asked O'Flaherty.

'I doubt it. We've still got some problems in the munitions business. I thought my days running informants were over. How wrong can a man be?'

Gómez reached for his coffee. His own days in Detroit had taught him a great deal about how easy it was to disrupt the assembly lines.

'You still report to Mr H?'

'I do. And I've still got the place on M Street. This war will be over soon. Then I'm back in DC full time.'

Mention of DC brought Gómez's head up.

'One thing I forgot to mention. I need the stuff from Donovan's place shipped out. There's no way I can deal with it on the Hill.'

'Care to tell me where you'd like us to deliver?'

'DC.'

He wrote down the address of Agard Beaman's apartment. O'Flaherty barely spared it a glance. He'd yet to pick up the envelope.

'What if we say no to all this?' he said.

'Are you serious?'

'Yeah.'

'Then you find someone else to snitch on what's really going on down there. You wanna do that? Has Mr Hoover got another source at Los Alamos? Only now's the time to tell me.'

O'Flaherty didn't answer. Finally he picked up the envelope, slipped it into his pocket and then, with the ghost of a smile, he was gone.

*

Autumn came quickly to the bare, rock-strewn fields of Galicia. The harvest, such as it was, had been gathered weeks before, hand-cut fodder to keep the animals alive until spring, wooden carts piled high with potatoes and beets. The fishermen still put to sea from tiny harbours along the coast but always with one eye cocked at the sky. At this time of year, straddling the equinox, storm after storm swept in from the vastness of the Atlantic. One had already devoured a U-boat and its crew. No sane man would risk his life or his living in the face of such merciless violence.

Stefan, still bedbound, was getting better by the day. Eva paid him regular visits, bringing bowls of hot soup and rich golden tortillas spiced with chunks of chorizo sausage. During the afternoons, especially when the weather was fine and the room was striped with bars of sunlight, she'd linger at his bedside, making a space for herself among the tumble of blankets. After the thin-lipped silence of his first days in the house, she seemed to have come alive. Agustín had been right. She wasn't a peasant girl at all. Far from it.

One afternoon, Stefan asked her about the photography. By now, with some difficulty, he could make his way out of the room and limp carefully along the narrow corridor to the lavatory at the end. On one of these journeys he'd noticed the sharp tang of chemicals hanging in the air and when he'd enquired further, she'd confirmed that she had a darkroom downstairs where she developed her films.

The darkroom, Eva explained, had originally belonged to her father, Tomaso. He'd learned his photography skills at university in Oviedo and when he'd returned to teach at the local school he'd devoted his spare time to capturing moments of village life that would otherwise have gone unrecorded. Eva had scrapbooks of these photos and shared them with Stefan: an elderly peasant couple posing shyly in front of an old stone granary, set on pillars to keep the rats out; a gypsy violinist framed by a whirl of dancers at a street fiesta; a dog perched on a dry-stone wall, a loop of scallop shells hanging from its neck.

Stefan had been intrigued by the shells.

'It's a pilgrim dog,' Eva told him. 'Every year it walked with its master to Santiago de Compostela. My father said it lived to be twenty-seven years old. Everyone thought it was a miracle.'

Her father, she said, had taught her everything she knew about photography. She'd been a rebel at school but she loved languages. She'd learned first French and then English. She liked English a lot. It sat happily in her mouth. She liked the fact that it wasn't her native tongue. She liked the feeling that it turned her into somebody else. To speak another language, she said, you need to take off your old clothes and become a stranger to yourself. It was an arresting image, something that Stefan had never quite encountered before, not put this way, and he wanted to know more. Had she been bored with village life? Did she need to get away?

'*Sí.*'

Her father had given her an old camera for her twenty-first birthday. It was a good camera, a Leica, German. By now she'd become aware of the wider world beyond the village. She sensed that the country wasn't at ease with itself, that another Spain was stirring beyond the iron grip of Church and family. Then, the following year, the coal miners had gone on strike along the coast in neighbouring Asturias. She wanted to go there with her camera. She wanted to find out what was happening. Her father still had friends in Oviedo. She stayed with a family who lived in an apartment behind the railway station. The apartment was on the fourth floor. She described the day the striking miners arrived. They fought the government troops from the barracks along the road and then occupied the city. She'd watched the whole thing from the tiny balcony of the apartment. She said she'd never felt so alive.

'Alive?'

'*Sí.*'

'You mean excited?'

'No, I mean . . .' She touched the swell of her left breast. 'I loved these men. I loved what they were doing. They were fighting the Fascists. For me that was good.'

The government, she said, sent troops to punish the miners. Many of them came from Africa, from Spanish Morocco. They were organised by a general called Franco. They killed thousands of miners. They raped and looted and put men against the wall and shot them.

'You took photographs of all this?'

'Afterwards, yes. They left the bodies where they fell. They left the women, too. I took many pictures. Many. I gave them to the newspaper, to anyone who wanted to look, but then I realised that was what the Fascists wanted. They wanted everyone to see what they could do. They wanted everyone to know that they had the power. And so . . .' she shrugged, '. . . I stopped taking pictures.'

'And came home?'

'*Sí.* For nearly two years. I worked in the school like my

father. I took pictures of weddings and children and saints' days, just like him.'

'And then?'

'And then the war came. And so I left.'

'Where did you go?'

'Barcelona.'

Stefan tried to push her further, tried to find out what lay at the end of this long journey east. He'd met Germans, mainly pilots, who'd fought with the Condor Legion in the Spanish Civil War. They'd flown the new Me109s and they boasted about strafing the Republican trenches. They'd mocked the tiny stick figures trying to shoot them down with old rifles and they'd come back to the Fatherland knowing that command of the skies would beat any earthbound army. Stefan had known one of them from school in Hamburg. Dieter Merz had been four years older, something of a hero figure. He'd said that combat flying sometimes felt the same as playing God.

Stefan knew better than to risk a phrase like this on Eva. The last thing he wanted was for her to stop talking, to stop remembering, but however hard he tried she refused to take her story further.

'One day maybe,' she said, 'but not now. Not while the sun's still out.'

The following day, during the morning this time, she brought him photographs freshly developed from the darkroom downstairs. Her hands were still wet and the smell of the chemicals quickly filled the room. She spread the prints on the bed where Stefan could see them and then opened the window. There was glass in the window now and Ignacio had briefly returned to fix the catch.

Stefan was staring at the photos. They were taken from the clifftop and they showed the remains of something he didn't immediately recognise.

'It's your boat,' she said quietly. 'Your submarine.'

Slowly he made sense of the chaos of the wreckage scattered across the reef below. There was so little left of *U-2553*. It seemed to have exploded, torn apart by storm after storm. His eyes went from one print to another. He recognised the bare bones of the boat, the ribs that gave the submarine its strength, the battered remains of the conning tower. Then, in the last of the photos, he found himself looking at what must have been his control room, the pipework and the rows of gauges exposed and laid bare as if someone had taken a giant tin opener to the hull. He could even make out the tiny table where he'd lay his charts.

Eva, aware of his hovering finger, was barely inches away. He could feel the heat of her body in the chill of the morning air.

'I changed the lens,' she said. 'Eighty-five-millimetre. It's hard in the wind. You have to keep steady.'

'It's a fine shot. You did well.' He touched the very middle of the photo. 'That was my home. That was where I lived.'

'So small.'

'*Kleine*. Tiny. We lived like mice. And often we ate like mice, too. Cheese and stale bread.'

'You liked it? It was something special?'

'You want the truth?'

'*Sí.*'

'I loved it. Especially in the early days. It was all I knew. And I was very good at it.'

He glanced sideways at her, trying to gauge what kind of interest lay behind these questions. She had to be in her early thirties. Had her boundless curiosity survived the years since she'd left home for the Asturias? And then Barcelona? Or was he pushing at a door that would lead to something uglier? To recrimination, at the very least, and maybe to something far worse? He was still at her mercy. One misjudgement, one wrong turn in the road, and he might find the attaché from Coruña at the door. There's a German deserter upstairs, Herr Otto. Help yourself.

The thought alarmed Stefan. The penalty for desertion was death. The price he'd have to pay for killing a senior SS officer would be even worse. But that wasn't it. Just the thought of a return to a world of uniforms, of *Heil Hitler*s, of ludicrous posturing fantasies about winning the war, filled him with despair. He'd done his best for the Fatherland but the story was over. For reasons he couldn't fathom, he'd been spared by the storm and now – in Eva's phrase – it was time to make a new start.

He looked at her and smiled. She held his glance for a moment and then began to collect the photos. To his delight, she was blushing.

He said he wanted to ask her a favour.

'What is it?'

'I'd like you to teach me Spanish.'

She looked up at him, startled. Not embarrassed any more but surprised.

'Why? Why would you want to do that?'

'Because I believe you about languages,' he said. 'And because I want to become someone else.'

9

The Lakeview Sunshine Home lay four blocks inland from the road that skirted the grey waters of Lake Michigan. This was where the city began to peter out among the sprawl of the northern suburbs. The nursing home had neither a view of the lake nor a monopoly of sunshine but Gómez had chosen it on the basis of good advice and liked what he'd seen so far.

His father, Ricardo, occupied a room on the top floor. A series of strokes three years back had robbed him of pretty much everything Gómez had taken for granted in the looming, ever-present figure that had shaped his childhood and the years that followed. He could no longer walk properly. His long face, never pretty, sagged to the left. Bits of his long-term recall were OK but he had trouble remembering anything that had happened in the previous ten seconds. He was also given to sudden outbursts of unprovoked rage that could, if you didn't know this man, be seriously upsetting.

The nursing staff, thankfully, loved Ricardo Gómez. They'd learned to understand his frustrations and to live with his temper. They loved the way he tried to make up to them afterwards – the shakiness of his huge, gnarled hand on their forearms, the remorse filling his watery eyes – and on these occasions they were only too happy to feed his passion for Hershey Bars and maybe a mug of hot chocolate. For an old guy who'd made the long journey from the slums of Mexico City to a fine-paying job on the Chicago, Rock Island and Pacific Railroad, he'd won not just their approval but their respect. In so many ways, the grouchy, big-hearted occupant of Room 27 was the American Dream personified.

Gómez found him hunched in a recliner under a new-looking plaid blanket. By some miracle his hair, freshly combed, was still jet-black, a sure sign – in Gómez's view – that the family on his dad's side went way back to the Aztecs.

The old man peered up at him, one hand shading his eyes from the brightness of the afternoon sun. Then the seamed face broke into a beaming smile.

'Back already, son?'

Gómez stood over him, extending a hand. His dad had no grasp of time. He might have called by yesterday or last year. But that didn't matter. At least he still knew who Gómez was.

'How you keeping, Dad? Folks looking after you here? Still chasing all those pretty women?'

The old man nodded, not really understanding the questions but eager to keep the conversation going. He'd always liked company and, as a kid growing up on the city's South Side, Gómez remembered the house full of friends dropping by, mainly men. Like his dad, these guys worked on the railroad, first with the maintenance crews, then – when promotion beckoned – from the timetabling department. They called his dad 'Ricky' and after a while his mom had done the same.

Gómez stooped for the box of tissues beside the recliner and dabbed at the thin trickle of saliva that leaked from the corner of his father's mouth. The big old hand crabbed across and grabbed at his. Huge eyes, inches from Gómez's face.

'How's that wife of yours?'

'She's fine, Dad.'

'Tell her to call by and see me.' He gestured vaguely towards the door. 'Always welcome.'

Gómez hadn't seen his wife since way before the war. Her name was Pearl and after barely a year of marriage she'd gone off with a big Polish guy who worked in the construction industry. The marriage had been dead in the water for months by that time and Gómez, although he'd never admit it, had a sneaking regard for anyone in trousers who could put up with his wife's affectations. In the end they'd never even tried for kids, largely because Pearl didn't much like sex, leastways not with him, but at the time the divorce had upset Gómez's dad. He came from a Catholic family. You put up with what God gave you. Thank Christ the stroke had wiped the divorce from his memory.

Now he wanted to know whether Gómez was eating properly. Gómez, oddly touched by his dad's obvious concern, allowed himself a smile.

'I'm eating fine, Dad. Do I look hungry?'

'You always look hungry. That's why your mom buys you all that stuff for school. Boy can't get by on a bowl of flakes in the morning. Especially winter. Like now. Cold, is it? Out?'

'It's fine, Dad. Everything's fine.'

'Good. Glad to hear it.'

Gómez went to the window to check the radiators. They were both on. Keeping his dad here cost a fortune, one reason he'd taken the job on the Hill. The money the FBI were still paying him covered his dad's weekly bills at Lakeview but only just. Without two incomes, God knows what he'd do.

His dad wanted to know when the Krauts were coming to Comiskey Park. Comiskey Park was home to the Chicago White Sox. As long ago as Gómez could remember, his dad had always been mad about baseball.

'Krauts, Dad?'

'Them Germans. The Sox will whip their ass. Ol' Aches and Pains will hang 'em out to dry.'

Ol' Aches and Pains was a shortstop called Luke Appling, a White Sox legend for a whole generation from the South Side, and in the hospital after his father's first stroke Gómez had found a folded photo of the player in his dad's wallet. He'd returned the photo once he'd got out of hospital but when he realised his dad hadn't a clue who he was looking at he'd kept the shot himself as a reminder of the way his dad had once been.

His dad still wanted to know about the Krauts.

'What Krauts, Dad?'

'Them ones in the uniforms. Them ones giving us all such a hard time. You heard about them? They'll be playing the White Sox as soon as we can fix it. How else are we gonna win this damn war? You telling me you got a better idea?'

At last Gómez understood. His dad had reduced the last three years to a baseball game. A couple of home runs by the likes of Luke Appling and it would all be over. No more Nazis to bomb. No more Pacific islands to retake. No need for the Gadget, or even the Hill. Just a huge crowd at Comiskey Park and the home win on the scoreboard before the stadium began to empty. Maybe his dad was right. Turn three years of madness into a couple of hours of entertainment. Neat idea.

'The war's going good, Dad. Don't you worry about it. The White Sox, too. Anyone else come to see you recently?'

Gómez knew it was a question his dad couldn't possibly answer but he asked it anyway because it felt like ordinary conversation and that made his dad very happy.

'Sure,' he said, nodding. 'Sure I get visitors.'

'They bring stuff? Presents?'

'Sure.'

'Like books, maybe?'

'Sure, books. Lots of them.' The hand again, waving at some phantom bookshelf. 'When I get the time, I'll maybe get round to reading them. Nice, though.'

'What, Dad?'

'Books. Keep you company, you know what I mean? Keep the brain alive. The radio, too.'

Gómez spotted the Bakelite radio beside the bed. It was a Firestone, handy, portable.

'What are you listening to these days, Dad?'

'Listening?'

'The radio.' He nodded towards the bed.

The old man was looking confused. Gómez got up and switched the radio on. Classical music, he thought. Some symphony or other. Full orchestra. The works. He was astonished.

He rejoined his father, knelt beside the recliner.

'You're listening to all that old stuff now, Dad? Beethoven stuff? Mozart?'

The old man at last got the drift. His head went back and he closed his eyes. Then he smiled, and his hands started beating time with the music.

'"Sweet Lorraine",' he murmured. 'They don't write songs like that no more.'

The huge eyes opened and he reached up for his son.

'You staying over tonight, Hector?'

'Here, you mean?'

'Sure. Your mom bought chops specially. She'll do fries if we're real nice to her. And maybe even gravy.'

Gómez looked down at him, then shook his head. Mom. Another ghost his father still lived with.

'I'm off, Dad. Gotta war to fight.' He stooped to kiss his father's forehead. 'Back soon, eh?'

*

Stefan awoke to shouting from downstairs. Eva's voice he recognised. He'd never heard her so angry. The other voice was male, lower, with an edge of what Stefan took to be menace. He thought it might be Ignacio, the carpenter, but he couldn't be sure. After a while, a door slammed and then there was silence. Minutes later came the opening bars of a piece Stefan remembered from his childhood. Beethoven. 'Für Elise'. A sudden splash of sunshine after the storm. Upbeat. Fingers dancing through the melody. Then the key suddenly changing before the music came to an abrupt halt.

Stefan wondered whether to applaud. Then the door opened. It was Eva. She normally wore trousers. Today, a bright cotton skirt, cut an inch below her knee. Wonderful legs, lightly muscled, creamy white.

'I woke you up?'

'No. I loved the music.'

'Not the music. Not that. Before the music.'

'*No hay problema.*'

The phrase on his lips at last brought a smile to her face. She'd been teaching him the odd phrase for a couple of days now, just the essentials to get him through the most basic of conversations.

'You know who that was?' She nodded towards the open door.

'Ignacio?'

'*Sí.* And you know why he makes me so . . .' she frowned, '. . . crazy?'

Stefan shook his head. By now he knew better than to try and force the pace. Far better to let Eva stay in charge, take her time, decide exactly how much she wanted to confide.

She was standing by the window now. She opened it wide and peered out, up and down the street, both directions, then tossed her head. There was satisfaction in the gesture. Ignacio was evidently nowhere to be seen.

'You know about this man?' She was back in the middle of the room. 'He treats me like a dog. Because he thinks he owns me.'

Stefan wondered what to make of her choice of verb. Owns? *Besitzen?* Did she mean that? Were they together? The ill-mannered carpenter and this refugee from a different world? Were they a couple?

'I don't understand,' he said carefully.

'Not me, either. He comes here often. Sometimes my father has jobs for him. Jobs in the school. Jobs in the house. He gets well paid. But sometimes he just comes, and sits, and looks at me. Today especially. If a woman shows her legs in this village there are men who shout at her.'

158

'Men like Ignacio?'

'*Sí*.'

'He shouts at you? Because of the skirt?'

'*Sí*. And you know what he says? He says I shouldn't wear such a thing. He thinks I should cover myself. Like all the other women in his life.'

'He has that power?'

'Of course not.'

'So why does he say it?'

The question took her by surprise. Too direct, Stefan thought. After her time in Barcelona, this was another door he shouldn't open.

'He knows nothing about women, this man,' she said at last. 'And he knows nothing about the rest of Spain. All he knows is that I went away to Barcelona and came back somebody different. Different inside and different outside. I had no hair. And I wore skirts like these. I came back to look after my father and you know who told me how ill he was?'

'Agustín.'

'Ignacio. He told me my father was dying. And so I came home.'

'Your father was OK?'

'My father was sick. Ignacio was right. But he wasn't dying. Smoke all your life and one day it will kill you. For my father it's hard to breathe, hard to move. But he's not dead. Not the way Ignacio told me.'

'When was this?'

'Nineteen thirty-nine. Madrid had just fallen to the Fascists. I was on the road. I hadn't been home for three years. My father had a telephone. I made a call to tell him I was OK, that

I was alive. Ignacio answered the telephone. He was working in the house. My father was at the school. Ignacio told me to run back. Before it was too late. I believed him. That's why I came home.'

'And stayed?'

'No. Two months only. Then I went to England.'

'Leaving your father here? Alone?'

'My father gave me the money for the journey. He said to phone sometimes. If he got worse then maybe I come back. But he knew there was a war coming. And he wanted me to see England.'

She settled on the foot of the bed, her anger over Ignacio gone. She said she'd taken the train north into France, and then the ferry to Dover. She'd never been outside Spain. She'd never been to Paris. Paris was *maravillosa*. The summer was hot. People were happy. The day after she landed in England the Germans invaded Poland and the war began. Was it luck that she escaped the Germans? She thought so. Although nothing happened that winter. *Nada de nada*.

'You were disappointed?'

'Not at all. I'd seen too much killing. Too many deaths. The Spanish are good at many things but not at making war. The people of the left were like children. They died too easily. They put their brains on ice. They never really knew what to do. That's why the best matadors are always Fascist. Because Fascists know how to kill.'

Stefan was curious about England. How long had she stayed?

'Nearly a year. The bombers came to London in September. I found a job with a newspaper. I had my camera. I took many pictures.'

'You were under the bombs?'

'*Sí.*'

'German bombs?'

'*Sí.* The bombers came at night. They aimed for the docks. Many people lived there. Next morning I made photographs. Many bodies. Whole houses gone. For what? For your glorious Reich? So we could all learn German?'

'Is that why you hate us?'

'Of course.'

Stefan nodded. It seemed perfectly reasonable. Entire streets flattened. Families wiped out. The bodies of children tugged from the wreckage like broken dolls. Smoke everywhere. And, according to Eva, the foulest of smells from the broken sewers. She was staring at him, demanding some kind of response.

'I saw it myself,' he said quietly. 'In Hamburg. I was born there. I grew up there. It was my home. Then one night the bombers came, the English bombers, hundreds and hundreds of them, maybe a thousand, and they came the next night and maybe the night after that and afterwards there was nothing left.'

'You were there?'

'I was at sea. It was July. My mother had sent me a cake for my birthday. We got back to Lorient in August and the cake was waiting for me. It was in bits. Just like Hamburg.'

'You made a visit?'

'Of course. We all knew the bombing had been very bad but they never tell you the truth.'

'So how was it?'

'Terrible. The end of the world.'

'And your family?'

'Gone. Dead. Burned in the firestorm. Except my brother's wife. Her name was Angelika. She told me what happened, how it had been.'

'And?'

Stefan looked at her, then shook his head. How do you explain the loss of everything? How do you describe the moment when you realise your entire life has been erased? Wiped out? That you have literally nothing left? The images he'd seen that weekend in the ruins of the city he'd loved still haunted him. Even now, even here, he couldn't make sense of them.

Eva said nothing. There was nothing to say. Then she stirred.

'All the barbers in Barcelona were anarchists,' she said. 'One of them was called Juan. We were friends. He made me laugh. He made me dress in black. We went everywhere together. He was brave and often foolish. I loved that man.'

The early days of the revolution in Barcelona, she said, were like a fiesta. Everyone sharing everything. *Hola* instead of *Buenos días*. Flags everywhere, and posters and music and dancing. All the beggars gone. Then the people of the left began to quarrel and the fighting started in the streets and she and Juan went to Madrid where everyone said things were better organised.

'And were they?'

'Yes. The Communists are good at war. Very strict. They organised everyone. Even us. I went to the trenches to take photographs for the Communists. The Fascists were outside the city. They wanted to break us. They wanted to kill us all. The fighting never stopped. Also the bombing.'

'Germans?'

'*Sí.*'

Stefan nodded. The young pilots in the Condor Legion, he thought. School heroes like Dieter Merz. Playing God.

'The city fell,' he said. 'In the end.'

'*Sí.*'

'But you got out.'

'*Sí.*'

'And Juan?'

'Juan was arrested in the place where we were living. I wasn't there that night. They put him against a wall outside the flats. They shone lights from the headlights of the cars. Then they shot him.'

'You know that?'

'*Sí.* Next day I went to the place of the dead, the place where they kept the bodies. The robbers were there before me. They stole gold from the mouths of the dead. Someone had been messing with the bodies. Someone had put a *churro* in one mouth, a cigarette in another. There were old men in pyjamas, young men with no chest left where the bullets had taken them. One man still had his glasses on. I thought he was asleep.'

'And Juan?'

'I thought he was asleep, too. One shot. Through the back of his neck.' Her eyes began to fill at the memory but when Stefan leaned forward to try and comfort her she shook her head. This story had an ending and she was determined to share it.

'You know what's so crazy about war?' she said. 'It turns you into an animal. You learn tricks, you learn to survive because you have to, because there's no other way. You know the trick in Madrid? When we knew the Fascists were coming? When we knew it was the end? Every corner you went round, you raised your arms, just in case. Every corner, and the corner after that. A whole city with its arms in the air.' She paused for a moment, her hands knotting in her lap. Then her head came up again. 'You know what happened to us? In that war? The rest of Europe left us alone so we could carry on killing each other.' She closed her eyes. 'Madness.'

10

Hector Gómez spent another two days in Chicago, prowling the streets, peering into shop windows, drinking alone at a bar he'd often used near Soldier Field. The temptation was to look up old buddies, sink a beer or two, talk about the old times but he had no taste for any of that. The war had moved everyone on. Something this huge, that's what happened. You slipped your moorings. You drifted along with the tide and if you were lucky you washed up some place else and started another life.

He was staying in a cheap hotel he knew a couple of blocks from the stockyards, down in the southern reaches of the city. His dad had worked here in one of the abattoirs before he'd gotten that first job on the railroad. Gómez hadn't even been born then, but in the middle of the night – woken by the clank-clank of the incoming cattle wagons – he'd lain in the dark, trying to measure the lifetime's gap between the strapping young wetback he'd seen in the family album and the ruin of a man he'd just left at the Lakeview Sunshine Home. In ways he didn't fully understand, he loved both of them and the following day, after he'd bought flowers to lay on his mother's grave in the Catholic cemetery, he returned to the home.

He'd called at a kiosk by the tram stop to buy a bunch of comics. His dad was still in bed, trying to cope with the remains of his breakfast. He sat beside him, spooning the grits into the slackness of his mouth, and when his dad was done chewing he soaked a flannel in the washbasin in the corner and washed his face. The big rheumy eyes followed his every movement and afterwards, with the comics on the bedside table and Gómez ready to leave, his dad reached up and caught hold of his hand.

'Appreciate it, son.' The old man was close to tears. 'You better believe it.'

Gómez took the train to Washington. He slept fitfully during the night and awoke to the lush green spread of the Pennsylvania hills. The train was full of soldiers, officers mainly, and soon the compartment was blue with cigarette smoke. By lunchtime, they were easing into Union Station and Gómez stepped out into the crisp autumn air. On the phone, Agard Beaman had given him directions to his new apartment. Walk south towards the Anacostia River. Look for the Library of Congress, then the Marine Barracks, then the Navy Yard. Cross the river and you're nearly home.

It was a bright early afternoon and Gómez took his time. In his years in the FBI he must have visited this city maybe a dozen times but it never felt like he really knew it. The very middle, where the government camped, was like a film set: wide boulevards, handsome buildings, everything white. This, he told himself, was the beating heart of the free world, one of the few Allied capitals that remained physically untouched by the events of the last three years. It was from here that the nation was fighting not one but two wars, and the evidence was all around him.

Men in uniform striding briskly to their next conference. Typists and secretaries snatching a stand-up lunch in one of the diners along Massachusetts Avenue. Men in suits bent over payphones on the sidewalk. The arsenal of democracy was transacting its business as the conflict thundered to its end and Gómez fancied that many of these guys were starting to jostle for position. The taste of the coming peace was in the air. Eisenhower's armies were closing on the German border. Islands were falling like skittles across the Pacific Ocean. By next year, certainly, maybe even by Christmas, the fighting and the bloodshed would be over.

Really? Gómez wasn't so sure. From his perch on the Hill, plumb in the middle of the most secret place on earth, he'd spent the last fifteen months watching the comings and goings of these crazy young scientists. He had no detailed knowledge of what they were up to but he'd listened hard every time he could – at the commissary, at the weekend dances – and he sensed they were turning the language of science, the very composition of matter, on its head. Some strange new alchemy was happening right there on the Hill, right there in the Tech Area, and when some of them began to whisper of a twenty-kiloton bomb he had no choice but to believe them. He couldn't imagine an explosion that big but he knew that these guys were halfway round a very dangerous bend in the road and that nothing would be the same afterwards.

Twenty thousand tons of high explosive? He stood by the Anacostia River, looking back towards the heart of the city. Beside him was the industrial sprawl of the Navy Yard. Beyond, he could see the dome of the Capitol, bone-white in the sunshine, and the long stone finger of the Washington Monument. Drop a bomb like that on Union Station and it would turn the nation's heart to ashes. There'd be nothing left.

Beaman was living in a top-floor apartment half a mile south of the river. The area looked comfortable. There was shade from the trees at the roadside and kids were playing on a patch of grass beyond a timber fence. The houses were three-storey timber construction, white clapboard with overhanging eaves. Beaman's place badly needed a coat of paint.

Gómez let himself in and made his way up the stairs. The smell of charring meat hung in the air and on the landing at the top he disturbed a sleeping cat. It yawned and stared up at him, then went to sleep again. From somewhere close by, Gómez could hear the sound of a guitar, chords strummed at random, then the hint of a tune.

It was Beaman. He answered Gómez's knock, the guitar still in his hand. Jeans, grey T-shirt, bare feet. In another city he might have stepped off the beach. He was very pleased to see Gómez.

'Missed you,' he said simply, opening the door wider.

Gómez didn't know what there was to miss. When Beaman tried to give him a hug, he played along for a moment then stepped away.

'Enough,' he said.

Beaman had laid hands on a supply of coffee beans. The ancient grinder belonged in a museum. The percolator might have come from a war bonds sale. But the coffee, once it had brewed, was superb. Gómez, filling the tiny sofa, thought briefly of his dad back in Chicago.

'Appreciate it, son.' He nodded down at the mug. 'You're doing good.'

Beaman was full of news. Thanks to Mrs Roosevelt's helping hand, he'd established contact with black organisations across the country. In a couple of weeks' time, hundreds of delegates would be descending on Washington for a big pow-wow. The First Lady had fixed for a bunch of them to get to see the President. They wanted fresh guarantees of their status in the workplace and at the front line. They figured their time was coming and Beaman was so, so happy – and so, so proud – to be part of that revolution. He was one of many speakers who'd be talking to all these folks and tonight, as it happened, he'd be meeting with some of the movement's leaders in a white diner in Alexandria.

'These are black guys?'

'Sure. And one Hispanic.'

'Why Alexandria?'

'The government are putting up dwellings there, thousands of units. There are twenty thousand of our people living in alleys in this city. No running water. No sanitation. Squat all. So guess who gets to live in these new places?'

'Whiteys.'

Beaman nodded. Gómez took a sip of the coffee. An evening in Alexandria sounded a terrible idea.

'You want me to come?'

'Yes.'

'How many people?'

'No idea. Maybe a half dozen. Maybe more. This situation's very dynamic. Eleanor's favourite word.'

'She means dangerous.'

'She does. You've got a gun? Like last time?'

'I have.'

Beaman said nothing. He was on his feet, rummaging among a pile of paperwork on the Formica table beneath the window that served as a desk. When he found what he was after he turned round.

'Guy called O'Flaherty? He called this morning. He says he has something for you.' He nodded at the phone. 'Help yourself.'

Gómez took a cab back across the river. O'Flaherty occupied a single room in the bottom half of a neat, heavily secured FBI house on Q Street, north of the cathedral. Two agents sat outside in a plain black Chevvy and someone else was doubtless posted out back. Gómez paid off the cab, tucked his briefcase under his arm and approached the house. Unlike Beaman's place, the paintwork was immaculate. One of the agents got out of the Chevvy and demanded Gómez's name.

Gómez gave him his Army ID. One glance and the agent stood aside.

'Bottom bell,' he grunted. 'He's expecting you.'

O'Flaherty was on the phone. The cable stretched into the hall. Gómez followed him into the room at the front. There was a desk pushed against the back wall, a couple of filing cabinets, plus a two-seat sofa that might have come from a dentist's waiting room. On the beige carpet stood one of the grey metal boxes the Bureau used for shipping items around the country.

'Help yourself, buddy.' O'Flaherty had covered the mouthpiece with his hand. 'Came up this morning from Albuquerque.'

The conversation on the phone resumed. Gómez knelt beside the box. It was unlocked. Inside was an untidy mass of paperwork, a couple of road maps, a wall calendar, two bunches of keys and an unopened bottle of Jack Daniel's.

Item by item, Gómez began to sort through the paperwork. Most of it was routine stuff, the small print of Donovan's domestic life: a notification of forthcoming events from the neighbourhood school, a reminder that Francisca was due a dental check-up, a flyer for a war bond offer, a gimme from the local branch of the Salvation Army.

Only when he got towards the bottom of the pile did Gómez find what he was after. It was a letter from a local car dealership. It confirmed the sale of a Cadillac Stretch Limousine to Mr Frank Donovan. Paper-clipped to the letter was a colour photo of the Caddy. It was lime-green, encrusted with gleaming chrome. It had whitewall tyres, a black top and an impressive chrome décolletage. The photo bore an official stamp Gómez recognised. He was holding it up against the light when O'Flaherty came off the phone.

'Albuquerque field office,' he said. 'They interviewed the dealer. That's where the photo came from. Car used to belong to a buddy of his. Guy swears it was a steal.'

Gómez shook his head. No car was a bargain these days, not with the auto assembly lines given over to tanks and airplanes.

'How much?'

'Fifteen hundred. Plus that pick-up of his. The guy paid in cash.'

'Fifteen hundred? You're sure about that?'

'Yep.'

Gómez's eyes returned to the photo. Donovan shot vermin for a living. Where did he lay hands on fifteen hundred bucks?

'We've got a registration for the car?'

'On the back of the letter. Again, from the dealer.'

Gómez turned the letter over. New Mex plate.

'Did he talk to the dealer about any plans he might have? Donovan?'

'Not that the dealer's saying.'

'Never mentioned leaving town?'

'Nope.'

'What about the neighbours?'

'One side was empty. The other side never had much to do with Donovan. Didn't like the look of the man. Or the family.'

Gómez nodded. The neighbour he'd spoken with had told him exactly the same.

'Across the road maybe? Your guys try any more doors?'

'Sure. The guy right across the street didn't even know they'd gone. Seemed pleased, though. Never liked the truck.'

'Anyone else?'

'Yeah.' O'Flaherty went to his desk. 'The guys from the field office were shaking the place down when a guy came calling. Said he was a friend of Donovan, helped him out sometimes. Turns out Donovan did auto repairs, and home decorating, and pretty much whatever else he could turn his hand to. Guy was happy to lend a hand.'

'For money.'

'Of course. He said Donovan was real keen to get down over the border, see a little of Mexico. The guy was surprised because Donovan never seemed to have any money saved but that suddenly wasn't a problem.'

'So how did he get paid, this guy?'

'Cash. Always cash. Same-day payment. Donovan took the money off the client, split the proceeds.'

'No checking account?'

'Not that we can find.'

'Shame.'

Gómez returned to the box while O'Flaherty got back on the phone. Gómez was looking for evidence that Donovan had once been in the Navy. An honourable discharge after the wound he'd described would come with a pension, a money order delivered regularly through the mail.

At the bottom of the box he found an envelope. He fetched it out. The stamp was from abroad. Correos Mexico, orange, a shot of a steam train, ten centavos. The postmark was hard to make out. Gómez gave up for a moment and peered inside the envelope. Empty. He looked at the address again. It was typed. Mr Frank Donovan, 12 Yucca Street, Corrales, Albuquerque.

He put the envelope to one side, waiting for O'Flaherty to come off the phone. When he was through he asked him about the border police.

'Your people check?'

'Yeah.'

'And?'

'You were right. He took Route 10. Plumb south. Went over the El Paso crossing six days ago. Ten minutes to four in the afternoon.'

'How many of them?'

'Two adults. Three kids.'

'Destination?'

'Unknown. Seems like no one asked the question.'

'First place the other side?'

'Ciudad Juarez. Big city.'

Gómez nodded. He hadn't felt a rush like this for years. Not since his days in the Bureau.

'Take a look at the postmark.' He showed O'Flaherty the envelope with the Mexican stamp. 'What do you see?'

O'Flaherty studied the postmark, then grinned.

'You got it, buddy. Ciudad fucking Juarez.'

*

It was raining when Stefan eased himself out of bed. Eva had got hold of a pair of crude wooden crutches she borrowed from a neighbour down the street and after a painful rehearsal, slowly criss-crossing the room, Stefan had mastered the knack of throwing his injured leg out straight, while taking the weight of his body on the crutches and his other leg. Now, he manoeuvred himself through the narrow door and on to the landing. He could hear Tomaso down below, coughing his lungs out. The rasp went on, day and night, as he tried to hoist the balls of phlegm into his throat. Then, with a gasp, he'd spit the stuff out. Stefan tried not to imagine the bowl beside him, waiting to be emptied. Another chore for Eva.

He hadn't seen her all day and he realised he missed her badly. Not simply the conversations they were beginning to have, increasingly long, increasingly frank, but the knowledge that she was with him, a fellow presence in this house. The toilet was at the end of the corridor. He knew now that this arrangement was highly unusual in the village. According to Agustín, most houses had a toilet on the ground floor, making the pipe runs easier, but when Tomaso had first fallen ill he'd occupied the room where Stefan now lay and it had been Ignacio – at the old man's request – who'd installed the new toilet. Not that Stefan minded. Not in the least. Anything to avoid sharing the room with his own shit.

He began to shuffle down the corridor, then paused. There was another door across the corridor. It was always shut. For some two weeks now, lying alone through the long days and nights, he'd wondered exactly how this household worked. Tomaso slept somewhere downstairs. Of that he was sure. But where was Eva's bed? He'd never heard her footsteps outside his door but that meant nothing because the woman moved like a cat, barely stirring the air. Maybe this was the door to her bedroom.

He tried the handle. The door wasn't locked. He pushed at it very softly, praying he wouldn't find her inside. The door swung open and he found himself looking at a room the size of his own. The double bed hadn't been slept in for a while. The flowers in the vase on the windowsill were long dead. The tall doors of the wardrobe were shut and there was no sign whatsoever of occupation. The room smelled stale. No way would Eva be sleeping here.

About to close the door, he noticed the tiny framed photograph hanging on the wall above the bed. It was sepia. It showed a young girl. She was wearing a lacy white dress with a tiny silver crucifix around her neck. Gap-toothed, pleased with herself, head slightly cocked, she was smiling shyly at the camera. Even at this age – ten? Younger? – she was unmistakably Eva. The same eyes. The same tilt of the chin. The same fall of black hair. Her first communion, Stefan thought. Before real life took her somewhere rather different.

A little later, safely back in bed, Stefan heard male voices down below then footsteps on the stairs. It was Agustín. He'd come to check on Stefan's leg. He folded back the blankets and the top sheet and unrolled the bandage. Close inspection brought a smile to his face. The wound was healing beautifully.

'No need for another bandage,' he said. 'She must feed you very well.'

'She does. A fine hotel. No complaints.'

The smile widened. Agustín unbuckled the splint and then Stefan watched his fingertips dancing up and down his lower leg.

'That hurts?'

'Not at all.'

'Good.' His put his hand flat on the sole of Stefan's foot and asked him to push hard against it with his damaged leg.

'Well?'

'Good. It feels good.'

Agustín nodded. He asked Stefan to swing his legs out of bed then stood squarely in front of him, his hands extended.

'Grip hard,' he said. 'Trust me.'

'You want me to stand up?'

'Yes.'

'Both legs on the floor?'

'Yes.'

Stefan shrugged. Agustín, after all, was a doctor. Would he ask the cook to surface the submarine? No. Would he expect the navigating officer to make an omelette? *Nein*. So trust this man. All the same, he knew he felt nervous. His bad leg hadn't taken any weight for nearly a fortnight. The last thing he wanted was more pain.

He caught hold of Agustín's hands, then slowly he got to his feet. His lower leg hurt, no question, but it was completely bearable. Even his knee appeared to have returned to its normal size.

'You want me to try and walk?'

'No. You go back to bed. Tomorrow, maybe. But not now.'

'The leg's not broken?' Stefan pointed at his shin.

'No.'

'You're sure?'

'Yes. Badly bruised but no break.'

Secretly thankful not to try walking, Stefan sat down again, watching Agustín rearranging the blankets.

'No brace?'

'No brace. Just in case, we keep it. Maybe next week it goes on the fire.'

Stefan nodded. He'd always hated the device, not least because he didn't much like the man who'd made it. Ignacio, he thought. Telling Eva what not to wear.

Agustín asked whether he needed anything. Stefan shook his head. Then, when Agustín turned to go, he called him back.

'One thing,' he said. 'Do you mind?'

'Not at all.'

'Where does Eva sleep?'

'Sleep? Eva? With Enrico. Down the street.' The smile had returned. 'I leave you now. Back tomorrow.'

The rain got heavier. By seven, night had fallen. Stefan lay in the dark, trying yet again to get his bearings. He'd always assumed that Eva was living alone, unattached, either in the room along the corridor or somewhere downstairs. That was lazy thinking on Stefan's part and he knew it. This was a woman who'd seen a great deal. Who knew a great deal. Who had so much to offer. She was also beautiful. What man could resist all that? Especially in a village as remote and probably as backward as this one?

He lay back against the pillow. He didn't blame her. Not in the least. It was Enrico who'd helped him so willingly when

177

he'd arrived, who'd virtually carried him up to this little room. He was strong, and cheerful. He was a handsome man, and generous with his time. He'd also refused even to entertain the offer of any reward.

Alone, then. Marooned. Totally at sea. Stefan found the prospect profoundly depressing. There were, after all, only two people in this house, both men. One was dying. And the other, in ways too numerous to list, was probably already dead, if not in body then certainly in spirit.

Downstairs, Tomaso was coughing again. Stefan tried to blank out the noise, to pretend he was somewhere else, Germany maybe, where he spoke the language and knew the people and wouldn't be feeling quite so lost. But that, too, was a path that only led backwards, to countless images he was trying so hard to forget.

He shut his eyes, turned his head to the wall, tried to pretend he was physically exhausted, tried to trick himself into sleep. Sleep, at the very least, might give him an hour or two's grace before, awake again, he could summon whatever strength he had left and make some kind of peace with where he now found himself. But it was hopeless. The harder he tried, the more the memories crowded in.

He was back in Hamburg, months before the firestorm. It was a black time at sea, blacker if you happened to be with Rommel in North Africa or – God help you – on the Eastern Front. The Sixth Army had surrendered at Stalingrad, frozen half to death, starved of food, out of ammunition, fodder for the Russian guns. Nearly 100,000 men had surrendered. Countless more had been killed. And among those who had simply vanished was his own brother, Werner.

Werner, he thought. A year older. Always wiser. Always bolder. Always confident of victory. He'd been so, so wrong. Nineteen forty-three? Another year of seamless victories? *Nein*.

It was the same at sea. The years of German submarines feasting on poorly protected Allied convoys were over. The British and the Americans had learned how to find U-boats, and how to destroy them. The losses mounted and mounted until Admiral Doenitz had to withdraw the wolf packs altogether. Back at their base in Lorient, Stefan and his fellow *Kapitän*s sat around in the mess at Kernevel and licked their wounds. The unthinkable had happened. The Allies were everywhere. Putting to sea against odds like these was suicidal. And so Stefan applied for leave and took the train to Hamburg.

Listening to the rain and the sound of the old man downstairs, Stefan stared at the ghostly oblong of the window. His memories of that evening when he'd arrived at the *Hauptbahnhof* were all too clear. This was before the bombing. Hamburg was still intact but the people were like wraiths. They'd never much liked Hitler, never much trusted the upstart Austrian with his gangster cronies, but they'd buttoned their lips during the good times and worked hard to ensure a constant supply of new U-boats from the yards along the Elbe.

Now those times had gone. Stefan's mother had lost so much weight he scarcely recognised her. His father was finding it hard to get fuel for his motorbike. The winter had been bitterly cold and the flat was unheated. Most of the family's spare clothes had gone to the Winter Appeal for the boys in the east, and the rest were already at Stefan's grandparents, in case one day they had to abandon the city and head north. Only there, on the farm, did Stefan find any semblance of the life he'd left before the war started. Food on the table. Logs piled by the roaring fire. Just like the old days. Except his grandmother spent a great deal of time fussing around the POWs who'd been drafted into the countryside to help with the heavier work.

He nodded to himself, remembering the journey back to the city. It was May, late spring, and before returning to France he was staying one last night at the family apartment at Hammerbeck. His sister-in-law was living there with his mother and father. Angelika hadn't seen Werner since he'd left for Operation Barbarossa, the start of the push to the east. That was more than two years ago. She and Werner had married by telephone, one of thousands of such unions. She'd put her hand on a German helmet and sworn her oaths of undying affection and now she had no idea whether she was a widow or a wife.

That last evening in Hamburg, he and Angelika had talked long into the night. Stefan's father had left them a bottle of schnapps. Around three in the morning, with the bottle nearly empty, Angelika had asked whether the war was lost, whether it was all over for the Fatherland. Even then, deep in his heart, Stefan suspected the answer was yes but he remembered shaking his head, putting his arm round her, explaining that secret weapons were on their way, wonders of German design and engineering that would turn the tide of war and restore the Reich to its former glory.

'And Werner?' She'd been hopelessly drunk. 'You think he's alive?'

'I know he's alive. One day he will be back. I know Werner. Werner is a survivor. Like we all are.'

Really? In the darkness, for the first time, Stefan managed to turn over and lie on his side. On his good leg, admittedly, but it still felt comfortable. He pulled the blankets around him, trapping the warmth, shutting his eyes. He found himself in Hamburg again, but this time it was a very different city. It was August last year. He was standing in the rubble of Hammerbeck, wondering what was left of his life. The apartment block where he'd lived no longer existed. It was simply a gaunt ruin, black against the sky, eaten alive by the deluge of high explosive and incendiary bombs that had torched whole neighbourhoods. He couldn't believe it, couldn't fit the images together, couldn't tease any sense out of the desolation and the smell.

After days of wandering, of making enquiries, of begging for information, he'd found someone he knew, a teacher from the local school. She said she thought his parents and most of the neighbours had perished in the firestorm but she'd also heard a rumour that Angelika, his sister-in-law, had somehow made it out. Word was that she was badly injured but still alive.

It took a week to find her. She was at a sanatorium in the country run by nuns, one of dozens of badly injured refugees from the catastrophe that had laid waste to the city. The sister in charge of the ward took Stefan aside and warned him about what to expect. She'd touched Stefan's back between his shoulder blades. Her spinal cord is broken, she'd said. The nerves will never mend.

It was true. From the shoulders down, Angelika was paralysed. Stefan sat at her bedside for the rest of the afternoon. She couldn't move, couldn't feel a thing. The night of the biggest raids, she said, the sirens had gone off around midnight. She and Stefan's parents and the old couple from the next apartment had gone down to the communal shelter. The bunker was very crowded. When the bombs began to fall people held each other, especially the children, but there was no panic. The bombs kept falling, closer and closer, and then came the incendiaries and the gathering roar of scalding air that became the firestorm. It grew hotter and hotter. Smoke was curling into the bunker through every crack and the roar of the firestorm became something worse. It was an animal, she said. It wanted to devour us. You could hear the devil laughing.

Angelika was desperate to try and escape. Stefan's father said they had to stay for the sake of their elderly neighbours. When Angelika insisted, Stefan's father soaked a sheet in water from the fire bucket and wrapped it around her. She remembered a sea of white faces staring at her. The women were weeping. When she opened the big, heavy door, she could see nothing but flames. She took a step forward, blind panic, and heard the door clang shut behind her. Shielding her face, she plunged forward. The sheet acted like a sail. Buoyed by the firestorm, she found herself on a piece of open ground beside the Mittal Kanal. At her bedside, Stefan had nodded. He knew the Kanal. He'd played there as a kid. He asked her what happened.

'The roads were on fire. The asphalt. People were trapped. It was like treacle. They were burning to death.'

She found a way through. She threw herself into the water. Even the water was on fire, blobs of burning phosphorous and fuel oil, and people were dying just metres away.

'When you die,' she said, 'the sound is horrible. In the movies people are brave and die beautifully. When it happens for real it's different. At first you scream. And then you whimper. Then . . . *nichts*.'

Nichts. Nothing.

Angelika was lucky. At first. Her burns were superficial. Within days, she returned to Hammerbeck to see what was left. Even now, the rubble was still warm to the touch. Amid the ruins she worked out where she'd once lived, where the shelter might have been. The local wardens were trying to keep people away from the remains of the apartment blocks but Angelika managed to give them the slip. Determined to find the barest trace of her former life – *anything* – she began to poke through the wreckage. In so doing, she dislodged a heavy baulk of timber. Half buried by a sudden tumble of masonry, she tried to struggle free but her legs didn't work any more. And neither could she feel her arms.

Stefan remembered her face against the sheets, white and drawn, and the whisper of the nuns in an adjoining room.

'So . . .' she'd said, 'the war got me in the end.'

Stefan had taken her hand, not realising the futility of the gesture. The sister was right. Her back was broken. No sensation, no control. From the neck down, she could feel nothing. Not even Stefan's hand.

'And the shelter?' he'd managed at last.

'They got it open days later. Everyone was dead. Some of them had taken their clothes off. Their flesh was the colour of toast. *Bombenbrandschrumpfleischen*. They'd cooked to death.'

Now, in the darkness, Stefan heard a door open downstairs. He was on his back again, staring into nowhere. So much death. It was everywhere. It was a given. It was what you got used to. It was what happened. And the Germans, his fellow countrymen, even had a word for its latest party piece. *Bombenbrandschrumpfleischen*: the shrunken bodies of the firebombing. So precise. So matter-of-fact. So logical. The fate of an entire nation captured in a single phrase. Only the Germans, he thought. *Bombenbrandschrumpfleischen*. You reap what you sow.

After a while, there came the lightest of footsteps on the stairs, then a face at the door. Eva.

'You're asleep?'

Stefan turned his head away. He didn't know what to say. Eva stepped closer. He could feel her presence beside the bed. She reached down and touched his face.

'You're crying. What's the matter?'

'It's nothing.' He shook his head. He didn't want to meet her gaze.

'Agustín says you're nearly better.'

'He thinks so?' He managed what might have been a laugh. 'He thinks I'm *better*?'

'He does. He says tomorrow you will walk again.'

At last he turned his head. She was kneeling beside the bed now, her face inches from his. She looked pleased with him. She looked proud.

He reached out, touched her face.

'I didn't know about Enrico,' he said.

'Enrico?'

'Your boyfriend . . .' he shrugged, '. . . maybe your husband.'

She gazed at him. Then it was her turn to laugh.

'You think Enrico's my husband?'

'*Sí.*'

'Then you're wrong.' She caught his hand and kissed it. 'He's my brother.'

*

Gómez had trouble finding the rendezvous in Alexandria. The cab driver had never heard of the place and dropped Gómez off at the tram depot. Beaman had been right about the government building program. The area was a construction site: cranes everywhere and the potholed roads further ploughed by heavy trucks. Even now, mid-evening, work was continuing under the glare of the arc lights. Finally, a white woman with a couple of kids directed him to Rattlesnake Joe's.

The place looked new and trade was good: construction workers on stools at the bar, business types hunched over plates of steak and fries, couples studying the menu, not a black to be seen. At first Gómez thought he must have got the wrong diner but then he caught sight of Beaman. He was occupying a booth at the very back, alongside the washrooms. He was deep in conversation with the faces around the table, his skinny hand stabbing at the air as he made point after point. There were three other guys and a woman. All the guys were black and two of them wore suits.

The woman was Hispanic. She was getting to her feet as Gómez approached, and she was eyeing the door to the washrooms. She was tall, commanding. Gómez stared at her. She was wearing a fullish dress cut low round the neck. She had the chest of a diva and shoulders that might have belonged to Spud Murphy but the hands – already extended – were what really caught his eye. Beautiful hands, lacquered nails, and a thin silver chain looping around one wrist.

'I guess you have to be Hector.' Her smile was as big as the rest of her. 'Welcome.'

Gómez took her hands in his. He felt like he'd stepped into her house, like she'd flung open the door and welcomed him in. Life rarely took him by surprise but this was an exception.

'Hi,' he grunted. 'Pleasure to meet you.' He meant it.

She looked him up and down for a moment, not bothering to hide her interest. Gómez asked her name.

'Yolanda.' She nodded at the washroom door. 'I guess you'll have to excuse me.'

She was back within minutes. Gómez had settled at the table across from the space where she'd been sitting. He'd shaken hands with the other men, vaguely registering their names, content to settle back and await the woman's return while the conversation resumed. Beaman was trying to get some kind of commitment from these people about numbers. He wanted at least a thousand delegates showing up in DC. Anything less, he said, and no one would notice.

The washroom door opened. Gómez tried to disguise his interest behind the menu, aware of other eyes watching her from across the diner as she squeezed back behind the table. The guys at the bar had half turned. One nodded in Gómez's direction with a muttered comment to his buddy on the next stool. Pair of wetbacks with a bunch of niggers. Full house. His buddy laughed, said something else, and then came the audible clink of glasses.

Gómez ignored them. He wanted to know more about this woman but her interest was more pressing.

'Agard here says you're in the service, right?'

'Right.'

'Working in some top-secret outfit down south, yeah?'

'I wouldn't know about that.'

'Santa Fe?'

'Nice place. Especially this time of year.'

'Not gonna tell me more?'

'Nope.'

'Then I guess Agard has to be right.'

Her laugh was full, deep-throated. She had a warmth that was almost magnetic. Gómez felt himself being dragged in, like a ball of cosmic dust from deepest space. Not unpleasant. Not unpleasant at all.

He wanted to know about her, about what she was doing here in DC, about whatever set of circumstances had put Agard Beaman in her path. She glanced across at him with an almost motherly affection.

'That boy needs looking after,' she said. 'Which I guess is where we come in.'

'We?'

'Me and the guys here. We need Agard, no question. You'd know that. And Agard? He needs you.'

She began to discuss money. A 25 per cent raise on whatever Gómez was getting just now. The funds would be coming from a wealthy benefactor she knew back home in California, a white guy who was making a fortune in the fruit-growing business. Gómez, she hoped, would be pleased to know that folks like these existed.

Gómez didn't bother to hide his amusement. This woman didn't believe in foreplay. The offer was there on the table: a straight hike of 25 per cent. He wondered briefly whether to kid her along and get down to hard negotiations, but the last thing he needed just now was to turn this conversation into a business meet. There were other parts of her that were far more interesting.

'California?' he queried.

'San Diego. Beautiful city. Even nicer than Santa Fe.'

'You been there long?'

'Most of my life.'

'But not born there?'

'Ensenada. Just down the road. My folks headed north in the twenties.'

'Bad time to look for work.'

'Even worse in Mexico. Apples is apples. Melons is melons. Pick 'em north of the border and you get paid. Not well but better.'

'And that worked out for you all?'

'It worked out good. Six kids? We could strip an orchard in an afternoon.' She reached out and briefly covered his hand. 'That's a joke by the way. We went hungry, if you want the truth, just like everyone else. We went hungry and we didn't have no real place to live but you keep looking and I guess you keep picking and if you have my dad's luck you end up with a white guy who's at least one half decent and that makes every difference in the world.'

His name, she said, was Carlton Friedmann and she and her dad and her brothers and sister owed him everything.

'And you know why? Because the guy's Jewish. Because he has vision. Because he sees beyond all this . . .'

She nodded out towards the bar, towards the busy booths of mid-evening diners, towards the white faces that kept peering round in their direction.

'This bother you some?' asked Gómez.

'Not at all. Tell you the truth I'd be disappointed if it didn't happen. No cake rises without yeast. These people are yeast.'

'Nice, I like that.'

'My pleasure, Mr Gómez. They got little cages in this country where they put the people that make them feel uneasy. Ain't real cages with real bars. It's more a question of labels. But once you got a label, believe me, it sticks.'

'So what's yours?'

'Number one, I'm a union guy, I fight for the workers, just like our black friends here. Number two, I'm Mexican. Put those two together and what does that make me?'

'A Commie.'

'Hey . . .' She leaned across the table and kissed him on the lips. Pure delight. 'Since when did cops get to be so savvy?'

Gómez ducked the compliment. There was no sign of service. He realised he was starving.

'You guys ordered?'

'Still waiting.'

'You know what you want?'

She shook her head. Then she went from face to face around the table, asking what everyone was after. Gómez got to his feet. He'd place the order at the counter. She gazed up at him.

'You can remember all that?'

'Sure,' he smiled down at her. 'I'm a cop, remember?'

At the counter, Gómez waited for service. Both bartenders ignored him. The two guys who'd been looking at Yolanda were on his left. After a while, one of them glanced up at him.

'Why here, buddy?'

'Why not?'

'Don't think this place is for white folks?'

'The area or the diner?'

'Both. Decent people need a break. You want to eat with them negroes there are plenty of other places.'

'You're telling me to get out?'

'I'm saying you're not welcome.'

'You care to step outside and say that again?'

The guy on the stool looked him up and down, then shrugged and began to move. At the same time, Gómez felt a presence behind him. Yolanda.

'I'm breaking this up, guys. Love and peace, eh? Hate to disappoint you.'

She linked an arm though Gómez's and turned him away from the bar. She was even stronger than Gómez had expected. The black guys were on their feet, reaching for their coats. Beaman was still speaking at full throttle, finishing some point or other, oblivious to the small moment of drama at the bar. They made their way out through the restaurant, Yolanda pausing briefly at table after table, hoping the diners were enjoying their meal.

Out on the sidewalk Gómez wondered whether he was right to feel disappointment. In his world, you never caved in to pressures like these. On the contrary, you put your head down and kept swinging.

Yolanda was on the other side of the road, looking for a cab. When she found one, she yelled for everyone else to come over. The cab took all six of them. Just. Yolanda gave the driver the name of a motel a couple of miles out of town. The restaurant served until midnight. Their table was booked for nine o'clock.

Gómez stared at her.

'You're telling me back there was a set-up? We never meant to eat at all?'

'Sure.' The smile again. 'Welcome to our world, Hector. That's why we need you on board.'

11

Agustín arrived at dawn. Stefan was asleep when he stepped into the room and the village was silent beyond the half-open window. Eva was with Agustín. She crossed to the bed and gently shook Stefan awake. He peered up at the two faces. Knowing it was early, his blood turned to ice. Something's happened, he told himself. They've come to take me away.

Not so. Agustín was apologetic. He had to go to Coruña for the rest of the week. He had a lift with a fisherman taking his catch to market. He needed to be sure that Stefan's leg could carry his weight. Then Eva could supervise the list of exercises he'd written out.

Stefan nodded. The room was freezing, even colder when Eva folded back the blankets. Something was missing and he couldn't work out what it was. Then he had it. Not a single cough from downstairs. Not one.

'Your father's OK?'

'He's fine. He's asleep.'

She and Agustín stood in front of Stefan. Each took one of his hands. Agustín asked him to lean forward and then stand up, just the way he'd done it the day before. Stefan did as he was told. Teetering on his heels, he tried not to shiver.

'Your good leg,' Agustín said. 'Take a step forward.'

Stefan did so.

'Now the other one.'

Stefan nodded, knowing that this was the moment of truth, the moment when he'd know whether the bone in his lower leg was fractured or not. Very slowly, he stirred the leg into action, dragged it forward. The floorboards felt icy beneath his feet.

'Now stand on that leg. All your weight.'

Stefan was looking at Eva. She wanted this to work. He could see it on her face. Would this make it easier for her to say goodbye? To show him the door and the road to somewhere else? To rid her life of this sudden intrusion? He hoped not. He didn't want that.

'Your leg, Stefan.' It was the first time she'd called him by his Christian name. Before, he hadn't had a name at all.

'OK.'

His gaze went from face to face. Then he transferred his full weight on to the injured leg and at the same time tried to throw it forward. The jolt of pain made him gasp. It felt white-hot, as if the very bone itself was on fire. His grip tightened on Eva's hand. She stepped towards him but he shook his head. One more, he told himself. Just to make sure.

He tried it again, exactly the same movement, and this time the pain was even worse, a scalding wave that flooded down his leg and brought the taste of vomit to his throat.

Agustín and Eva helped him back to bed. Agustín said something Stefan didn't understand and she nodded and left the room. Stefan, the blankets heaped around his neck again, looked up at the doctor.

'I'm sorry,' he said. 'I tried.'

'*No hay problema*. You need time. Eva will look after you. I will be back in four days. Then we try again.'

Stefan nodded, grateful. He wanted to know about the Germans. Had they been back at all? Had he talked to them?

'Only the man Otto. He came to take pictures of the wreck.'

'He still thinks there are no survivors?'

'*Sí.*'

Eva was back. She was carrying the splint that Ignacio had made. Stefan stared at it. *Scheisse*. Between them, they slipped the contraption beneath Stefan's leg and Eva fastened the leather straps. With the splint and the crutches, Agustín explained, Stefan could still make it along the corridor to the lavatory. Stefan nodded. Wearing the splint was a return to the prison cell he thought he'd left behind.

Agustín hadn't finished. The villagers, he said, had decided to build a memorial to the men who had lost their lives on Stefan's submarine. Nothing extravagant, just a cairn of rocks and maybe a brass plaque recording the bare facts of the tragedy. The date. The designation of the U-boat. And the number of men who'd died. There was currently a debate about where the memorial should be. The fishermen wanted it on the clifftop, overlooking the reef. The village shopkeepers preferred a site near the harbour where it might attract visitors. Either way, the German attaché had promised to pay the costs.

'He needs to give us this money now.' Agustín was smiling. 'Because soon the war will be over.'

Stefan nodded. He said he hoped so. Then he was struck by another thought.

'So how many people will you say died? All of us? Including me?'

'Very good question. Maybe you think about it. And maybe then you tell Eva.'

Seconds later, he was gone. Stefan heard the low mutter of voices below as Eva let him out into the street, then she was back. For the second time in ten minutes, she rolled back the blankets.

'What are you doing?' Stefan couldn't understand.

For a moment she didn't answer. Then she stooped low and kissed him on the lips. Stefan stared up at her, astonished. Then he reached for her face, traced the curve of her mouth with his forefinger.

'Trust me,' she said. She was smiling.

She got him out of bed. Together, without the aid of the crutches, they somehow made it to the landing outside. Every step was an effort of will but something told Stefan to ignore the pain. The door of the other bedroom was already open. Candlelight flickered on the walls. Standing beside the bed, Stefan could see a hump beneath the blankets. Eva steadied him with one hand, pulled the sheets and blankets back with the other. The hump was a stone vessel filled with hot water.

'This is for me?' Stefan was staring down at the bed.

Eva shook her head. Then she went to the window and closed the wooden shutters. The shutters didn't fit properly but the room was still plunged into half-darkness. Against what was left of the light, she was nothing but a silhouette.

'No,' she seemed to have turned round. 'This is for us.'

*

For a moment, through a fog of last night's drinking, Gómez couldn't work out where he was. The ceiling overhead, like the walls, was made of cheap cedar board. The air in the room was heavy and smelled of several generations of smokers. A thin grey light seeped around the poorly hung drapes at the window. Gómez squeezed the throb of the hangover from his eyes and reached over, looking for clues. Huge double bed. And a naked body slumbering beside his own. He gazed at it for a moment, the memories slowly piecing themselves together. Yolanda, he thought. *Madre de Dios*.

They'd taken the cab back to the motel, a sprawl of units beside the big road south. The meal had been shit but none of these people seemed to expect anything better and afterwards he'd left Beaman and the black guys still talking around the single Formica table that passed for the restaurant while he and Yolanda took another cab to a liquor store he'd noticed on the drive out. He bought beers and a fifth of bourbon. Without anywhere else to go, they'd settled in Yolanda's room, sprawled on the bed, swapping life stories. By the time Gómez was done with the beers, Yolanda was close to halfway through the bourbon. She drank like a Pole, straight down, no chaser, yet when Gómez joined her for the home straight, the booze had barely touched her.

The room was hot – the big iron radiators were the sole feature that worked – and after a while she'd stripped to her bra and panties, not a trace of embarrassment. She was a big woman all over, extravagant curves, wonderful smell, and after Gómez had shed his trousers and shirt she'd said it was time to get to know each other properly. Seconds earlier they'd been talking about Pearl Harbor, about the way the Jap attack had changed everything in the space of a single Sunday morning, about the hundreds of Jap immigrants that had been rounded up in California and shipped to internment camps inland, and then suddenly she was all over him, two big people enjoying each other, total candour, total abandon, and the taste of bourbon on a stranger's breath.

Now, up on one elbow, he looked down at her and then traced the line of her shoulder down across her breasts, then lower still. She was naked on the bed. The room was still far too hot. They'd slept without sheets. She began to stir, trapped his hand, pulled it even lower. Then she rolled over and smiled and one eye opened.

'*Buenos días*,' she said.

They made love again, Gómez on top this time, their faces beaded with sweat, and afterwards Yolanda pronounced herself satisfied.

'Not bad,' she said. 'For a cop.'

Hector padded to the cracked sink in the cupboard that passed for a bathroom, and took the scrap of towel back to bed. He mopped her face, then her belly.

'I'm some kind of crime scene now?' she asked. 'Or you getting me ready for visitors? Only Agard promised to be back for breakfast. Not sure that's such a great idea. You see his face last night?'

Gómez shook his head. He reckoned he could manage it again if she was willing. The thought put a rare smile on his face.

'Beaman?' he said vaguely. 'You're telling me I missed something?'

'Sure. That boy's in love with you. He came to the room last night. Asked whether you were coming home. I told him you were drunk and in my charge. Disappointment doesn't cover it.'

Hector laughed out loud, opened his arms. He hadn't been with a woman since trying to coax his wife into bed. It felt like the first time all over again. He ducked his head between her legs. The sweetest, sweetest taste.

'You know the time, soldier?'

'Tell me.'

'Nearly half past nine.'

'Shit.'

'You told me last night——'

'I know, I know.' Gómez was already heading for the bathroom. 'Ten fifteen downtown.'

'You want me to get a cab?'

'I want you to stay right where you are.'

'I've got a life, soldier. You'd better believe it.'

Gómez was doing his best to soak himself while avoiding third-degree burns. The hot water was scalding. The cold tap didn't work. When he made it back to the bedroom Yolanda was on the phone calling the cab company. By the time she put the phone down he was nearly dressed. He lifted his jacket from the single chair and headed for the door.

'Gonna kiss me?'

'Always.'

'You want we do it again?'

'Tonight.'

'And skip the booze? Either way, I'm easy.' She fluttered a hand and told him good luck but Gómez was already gone. Traffic on the road into DC was backed up for half a mile after a dumpster truck hit a bridge. By the time Gómez made it to Q Street, he was half an hour late. A guy Gómez had never met before came to the door when he rang the bell. Tall, thin, wispy moustache, could have been a clerk. He mumbled a name Gómez didn't catch and led him into O'Flaherty's office. O'Flaherty, yet again, was on the phone. Gómez looked round for the box of goodies from Donovan's place but couldn't find it. The guy at the door had disappeared.

O'Flaherty was off the phone. When Gómez grunted an apology for being late he waved it away.

'You smell like a bar.' He waved his hand in front of his mouth. 'Ellis has gone to make coffee. Let's hope it makes a difference.'

'Who's Ellis?'

'Typewriting expert. Best we've got. Spent last night trying to match the envelope with the suicide note you gave me.'

'And?'

'He'll tell you. Meantime, I've been taking a little advice.'

'Who from?'

'Mother Tolson. The Boss is out of town. Tolson's in constant touch. Not perfect but next best.'

Gómez nodded. Clyde Tolson was Hoover's eyes and ears. Thanks to Hoover, he sat one level down in the Bureau's pecking order after a ballistic rise through the ranks. When they were both in DC, the two men ate lunch and dinner together, always the same restaurants, always the same tables. Rumour was the relationship went a great deal further but no one had yet produced the evidence.

'So what does Tolson say?'

'He thinks what we think.'

'And what do we think?'

'You kidding me? Fiedler has to have been a spy. Has to. Which means he was in deep with our Soviet friends.' O'Flaherty paused. 'I'm getting the impression Donovan has been around Los Alamos a while. Am I right?'

'Fifteen months. Since June last year.'

'And he buddied up with Fiedler? This relationship's been going on a while?'

'Yeah.'

'And I'm guessing the guy had a free pass out when he was done?'

'Yep. Every Tuesday. They never searched him. Happy not to.'

'Slam dunk, buddy. He can take whatever he chooses. Piles of the stuff. Wells Fargo. Every Tuesday. On the button.'

'You think so?'

'I do.' O'Flaherty crushed one cigarette and reached for another. 'So we have ourselves both motive and opportunity. Now we need to understand just how bad the damage could be.'

'Motive?' Gómez needed O'Flaherty to slow down a little.

'Sure. Plain as day. The guy's a Commie. Most of these Jewboy scientists are. They buy themselves out of Austria or Germany or wherever the hell they've been living and one of the things they bring with them is a bunch of screwball fantasies about socialism. These guys are born to the faith. It comes with their mothers' milk. One day, if you ever get the chance, ask Mr Hoover about Oppenheimer. Then stand well clear.'

'Another Commie?'

'Bet your sweet ass. And this is the guy in charge, am I right?'

Gómez nodded, said nothing. In truth he'd heard the rumour about Oppie from a thousand quarters but no one had ever come up with a shred of evidence that reading Marx and supporting the Reds in Spain meant you handed secrets to the Russians.

'Fiedler couldn't stand the Commies,' Gómez said. 'Everyone knew that.'

'Cover story. All these guys sing from the same fucking song sheet.' O'Flaherty waved a dismissive hand. Smoke curled in the air. 'So let's get down to the basics. What did the guy actually *know*?'

It was a question Gómez had often asked himself, about Fiedler most recently, but about one or two others as well. In theory, General Groves had locked individual scientists in discrete little compartments, restricting their view of the big picture, but science simply didn't progress that way, especially if you had to hit deadlines as tough as these.

'They talk a lot, people like Fiedler, people from the Tech Area. They meet every week. They compare notes. There are four divisions. Fiedler was a metallurgist.'

'Meaning?'

'He was working on one of the two bombs. You gotta think an orange in the middle. The orange is made of plutonium. This stuff makes a very big bang if you surround it with HE and get the trigger explosion just right. We're talking millionths of a second. And we're talking explosive lenses.'

'You know this stuff for sure?'

'I'm telling you what someone told me. Fiedler was in the Tamper Group. He was working on the lenses. Does that mean he knew a whole lot of other stuff about the plutonium itself? How it's made? How pure it has to be? I dunno. You need a proper scientist to tell you that but one thing I do know and that's this. These guys are making history and they know it. They call it the Dragon Experiment. The Dragon is the bomb, the Gadget. They're tickling the tail of the Dragon, seeing just how far they can go before the Dragon gets mad and blows us all up. They make it sound like a game, and I guess in a way that's what it is, but my point is this: if you're Fiedler you get to know a whole lot of stuff outside of the Metallurgy Lab without even being properly aware of it. Does that make sense?'

For Gómez, this had the makings of a speech. The effort of getting the right words in the right order had cleared his mind but he was still glad to see the coffee arrive.

O'Flaherty didn't bother with introductions. He wanted the answer to another question. Let's suppose Fiedler has been shipping secrets out of Los Alamos by the truckful. Let's agree that the Russians are clever enough to pick the stuff up. Let's get ourselves truly frightened and assume Fiedler has blown the whole damn project sky high. Why kill him?

Gómez admitted he didn't know, couldn't work it out. Unless Groves and Oppenheimer and Arthur Whyte were right. That Sol Fiedler really did shoot himself.

'Out of guilt?' O'Flaherty was pouring the coffee.

'Sure.' Gómez shrugged. 'Or despair.'

'He borrowed the gun you sent for analysis?'

'Yep.'

'From Donovan?'

'Yep. Donovan admitted it.'

'And then Fiedler blew his brains out?'

'Yep. And left a note. But the note's wrong. He never called his wife "Liebling". He called her "Spatzling". It means "little sparrow". These little details are important. According to Mr Hoover.'

O'Flaherty didn't acknowledge the joke. He wanted to pass on a little more intelligence.

'About?'

'Donovan. Was the guy ever in the Navy like he told you? No way. He never even passed the basic medic exam. Club foot from birth. The guy never wore a uniform in his life. Did he have a crime sheet? No. But word on the street has him running stolen autos up from Mexico after Pearl Harbor. That's when he wasn't shooting coyotes. The auto scam was never properly investigated. Nothing ever went to court. But we're looking at a dreamer here, a congenital liar, and I guess a man with a wife and three kids and no money in his pocket.'

'So he was in and out of Mexico?'

'Yep. Plus he had a Mexican wife.'

'I met her. Somewhat of a looker.' Gómez frowned. 'Exactly where in Mexico did these cars come from?'

'Where you'd expect. Ciudad Juarez. Right down the road there. Ellis? You wanna explain a coupla things to Mr Gómez here?'

Ellis had a briefcase. He took out a file and opened it, spreading the contents on the floor. Gómez recognised the typed letter from Fiedler he'd handed to O'Flaherty the previous day. Also the envelope with the Mexican stamp recovered from Donovan's house. Beside the envelope were a series of blow-ups.

'OK, so here's the story.' Ellis had a Southern accent. Georgia? Tennessee? Gómez couldn't be sure. 'I have the two exhibits. I'm looking for anomalies common to both, little quirks in the text, in individual letters. Could be damage to the key, to the carriage, could be any damn thing.'

Gómez nodded. He knew the science.

'And?'

203

'We got ourselves a match. Three examples. Capital "M", small "y", small "e". Blow these babies up and this is what you get.'

Gómez helped himself. Ellis was right. In every case, tiny nicks in the cast of the letters was duplicated across both documents.

'So what's the probability? Same machine? Both documents?' O'Flaherty was back in charge. He was looking at Ellis.

Ellis took his time, asked for the blow-ups back, peered at all three.

'Ninety-five per cent,' he said at last. 'And that's in a court of law.'

O'Flaherty was watching Gómez. He had something to add.

'Donovan had pecker trouble,' O'Flaherty said. 'Couldn't keep the fucking thing to himself. Guy I talked to in the Albuquerque office thinks he had another woman over the border.'

'Like where?'

'Guess.'

*

Eva came to bed mid-morning, the bedroom still curtained. She'd wheeled her father round to a friend's house further down the village and now she and Stefan had a couple of hours to themselves. She slipped in through the door, a bowl of water in her hands, and asked whether he was warm enough. He nodded, watching her take her clothes off in the half-darkness. He wasn't interested in what had led to this sudden reversal in his fortunes. Discovering why she'd so suddenly taken him into her bed could wait. All he wanted was her presence beside him, the touch of her naked skin, the chance to hold somebody else, to become – however briefly – part of something bigger than himself.

She was naked beside the bed. Stefan had spent a great deal of time over the past few days trying to imagine her body under the clothes she wore and he wasn't disappointed. Far from it. Full breasts, flat stomach and a habit of running her hands up and down her thighs. She wanted to know whether he wanted to get rid of the splint.

'Do you?' Stefan was grinning.

She nodded and laughed. Once, drunk in Madrid, she said that she and her anarchist boyfriend had made love after she'd bound his legs together with a couple of leather belts. They both had a passion for experimenting, for pushing the limits. Juan had always attached it to some aesthetic theory or other, a visionary, mould-breaking act that was going to free the middle classes of all their hang-ups and turn them into human beings, but Eva had preferred to settle for something simpler.

'Like what?'

'Like enjoying it more. Like making it last.'

'And did it?'

'No.' She giggled, her hand to her mouth. 'He exploded. Bang. Like a firework. He always said it was my fault.'

'I expect it was.'

'Why?'

'Because you're very beautiful.'

'And you?'

'I'm very broken.' He nodded down at his body. 'But I won't go bang.'

She unbuckled the splint and slipped the contraption off. Stefan heard it clatter to the floor. The bowl was on the sideboard beneath the window. She moistened her hands and returned to the bed, soaping his body very slowly, feet first, her fingers working between his toes, one after the other, then girdling his ankles, then up along the swelling line of his uninjured calf. Time and again she returned to the bowl for fresh water, more soap, until every inch of his body had been washed. Stefan had never felt so clean.

'Have you done this before?'

'Yes.'

'With Juan?'

'Many times.'

'And others?'

'Not so often.'

'I'd like to do it to you.'

'You can't,' she laughed. 'You have to trust me. And you have to wait.'

She was back with the scar on his thigh. Agustín's stitches were still in place, tiny black knots against the whiteness of his flesh. Eva plucked at one, a tiny delicate tug.

'You feel that?'

'Yes.'

'It hurts?'

'No.'

'Juan also had stitches. I took them out. We had no knife, no scissors. I used my teeth.'

'You want to do that to me?'

'And tell Agustín?' She laughed again. 'No.'

She fetched a towel from a drawer and dried him all over.

Then she slipped into the bed beside him and drew up the blankets. A perfect fit. She was up on one elbow, fingering his face, tracing the line of his mouth, testing the fullness of his beard.

'I can shave you. Would you like that?'

'Very much.'

'Maybe later. When we have more time.'

She wanted to know whether he shaved at sea. Every photo she'd ever seen of submariners, the men had beards.

'That's right. We never shave at sea.'

'Why not?'

'Water is too precious.'

'Of course.' Her hand was crabbing slowly across his belly. 'You know what we say in Spain? Clean on the outside, clean on the inside. You know what I used to say to Juan? To be clean is to be ready. You think you're ready?'

Stefan nodded, no longer ashamed of his helplessness. Then he reached down and caught her hand.

'You said later,' he murmured. 'Will there be a later?'

'I don't know.'

'Do you want there to be a later?'

'*Sí*.'

'Why?'

'Because you're a good man. Because of what you've seen, what you've felt.' She withdrew her hand and cupped it over one breast. 'Felt? You understand?'

'*Sí*.'

'War changes people. You think that?'

'War empties people.'

'Empties people? *Muy bueno*. I like that. Very much.'

'It emptied you?'

'It robbed me.'

'Of Juan?'

'*Sí*. And of many other things.' She glanced up at the first communion photo on the wall. 'You cannot go to war and come back like that.'

'Innocent?'

'*Exacto*. You go to war, you see many things, and afterwards you have to make yourself better. With small things.'

'Like this?'

'This isn't a small thing, Stefan. Not for me.' She straddled him, the long fall of black hair curtaining both their faces. Then she slowly worked him inside herself, tiny movements, spooning out their time together in the bareness of this room, and Stefan let himself drift away, protected at last from his memories, content to let her take control, deeply happy that they'd chosen to be so honest with each other and so reckless.

Much later, early afternoon, she stirred beside him. She had to fetch her father. His friend was very kind but Tomaso couldn't stand his wife's cooking.

'You want meat tonight? Sheep? Agustín says you must. To get better.'

Stefan said it didn't matter. Whatever Tomaso liked, he'd gladly eat. He gestured for her to come closer. He wanted to say thank you. And he wanted to know whether he could stay in this bed.

'You want to?'

'Not alone.'

'You think you have a choice?'

'I think *you* have a choice.'

'About what?'

'About later.' He looked up at her. 'You really want a later? Because now is the time to tell me.'

'*Sí.*' She nodded. 'A later? *Claro que sí.*'

12

J. Edgar Hoover was back in DC by mid-afternoon. His secretary had cleared a half-hour slot at four thirty and it was O'Flaherty who passed on the good news to Hector Gómez. They'd spent the day together running a variety of scenarios around Sol Fiedler's death and now had come the moment when they had to share their thinking with the Boss. FBI headquarters was several blocks away from Q Street. They walked.

Gómez had never met Hoover but like every agent he knew a great deal about the fussy little guy who'd seized the Bureau by the throat way back in the twenties and had never let go since. This was a man who understood that knowledge was the currency of power. This was the guy who'd painstakingly built huge files around anyone who could block his way or dilute his influence. In the early days they called him 'Speed' because he did everything – *everything* – at a thousand miles an hour. Since then, his nicknames had been less flattering.

Hoover's offices were on the sixth floor of the FBI building. The corridor from the bank of elevators was known informally as 'The Bridge of Sighs'. When the secretary tapped twice on the big oak door and then stood respectfully aside, O'Flaherty and Gómez found Hoover sitting behind a huge desk, pen in hand, reviewing a sheaf of documents. He glanced up, barely acknowledging their presence, then scribbled a couple of signatures.

'Take a seat,' he said at last. 'Tell me about Fiedler.' High voice, Gómez thought. Almost squeaky.

O'Flaherty launched into a brief. Sensibly he kept to the facts. At this stage, Hoover wanted the basics. Only later, according to O'Flaherty, would you be invited to sign up to whatever decision the great man had decided to take.

O'Flaherty had finished. Hoover was looking at Gómez. He wore a star sapphire ring on the little finger of his left hand and from time to time, like a nervous twitch, he'd play with it.

'So what's it like up there?'

'Where, sir?'

'Up on the Hill, among all those infant geniuses? I read a coupla your reports. I guess the Project keeps them busy.'

'Certainly does, sir.'

'History in the making? You get that feeling?'

'Not really. From where I'm sitting it's pretty much like any job. Except the place isn't supposed to exist.'

Hoover nodded and sat briefly back in his chair. The President had put Hoover in charge of all intelligence operations, leading the charge against foreign spies, and it rankled him that General Groves and a bunch of Jewboy scientists had managed to fence off dozens of sites across the nation from his prying eyes. Hence the bid to smuggle Gómez into the heart of the Project, the Bureau's eyes and ears on the Hill.

'You think he killed himself? This Sol Fiedler?'

'No, sir.'

'Care to tell me why?'

Gómez summed up his doubts in a couple of sentences. The typed letter. Calling his wife 'Liebling'. His hatred of guns. His passion for his wife. His commitment to the Project. The reputation he'd built among his buddies in the Tech Area. No one had a bad word to say about Sol Fiedler. Except he could come across as overly shy.

'No one else's wife involved?' Hoover's contempt for philandering was legendary. Men who stepped outside marriage he called 'double-yolkers'.

Gómez said he thought Fiedler was clean. Then he added a caveat. The wife of a senior officer on the Hill had made a private allegation about Fiedler exposing himself. Plus he'd wanted her to embark on some kind of affair.

'He's got a name, this officer guy?' Gómez had won Hoover's complete attention.

'Arthur Whyte, sir. Spelled with a "y".'

'And what's his role?'

'Head of G-2.'

'That's counter-intelligence.'

'Yes, sir.'

'Your boss.'

'Yes, sir.'

Hoover nodded, almost gleeful, making a note of the name.

'And you're thinking what, Mr Gómez?'

'I'm thinking the woman – the wife – made it up.'

'Evidence?'

Gómez described Whyte's visit to the doctor who'd performed the autopsy. He'd wanted to check that Fiedler had been circumcised. Why else would he need information like this except to stand up his wife's story?

212

'You think he put his wife up to this?' Hoover loved details like these.

'I think he's very ambitious, sir. And so is she. He knows the cards to play. The Project takes preference. In everything. Nothing stands in its way.'

'Not even this guy Fiedler? The fact that he might have been killed? The fact that he was shipping stuff out to the Russians?'

'The possibilities, sir. Nothing's proven.'

'So you've been warned off? Sent away? Is that what happened? Is that why you're here?'

'Yes, sir.'

'Thank Christ for that, soldier. At least someone in that goddam place understands his duty.'

Gómez acknowledged the compliment with a nod. 'Soldier' was the closest Hoover had come to irony.

'This man Donovan.' Hoover was looking at O'Flaherty. 'We're talking small-time criminal, right?'

'Yes, sir.'

'And you're telling me he's back over the border with his Mexican wife?'

'Yes, sir.'

'We know where they might be?'

'She has family in Guaymas. According to the immigration forms.'

Hoover brooded for a moment. Then his head came up. He was still talking to O'Flaherty. Mexico, he said, could be tricky. The FBI had no jurisdiction. The people down there could make life tough. The place was also full of Commies which was no surprise given what Donovan was obviously up to.

'We need to go after Donovan,' he said. 'But we need something else.'

'Sir?'

'Deniability. If the shit hits the fan it wasn't us.'

'Of course, sir. You're telling me we send someone down there?'

'Sure.' Hoover's gaze shifted to Gómez. 'You, my friend. I'm guessing you might speak the language. You certainly look the part. I want you over the border and then I want you up Donovan's ass. Find the guy. Sweat him a little. Worst case, you get a confession there and then. Best case, you bring him back. Anything happens, you're with the Army. Happens to be true. I like that. Anything else we can help you with?' He paused, fiddling with the sapphire ring, then offered Gómez the coldest smile. 'Soldier?'

Gómez was back at Beaman's place by early evening. The atmosphere was icy. Gómez was rarely in the business of apologising and saw no point in starting over. His free time was his own. He wasn't Beaman's property. If he chose to spend the night with a woman he'd just met then so be it. Consenting adults. So where's the harm?

'You think that helps the cause any?' Beaman was looking sulky.

'The cause?' Gómez couldn't believe his ears.

'The woman's married. She tell you that? Three kids? Husband? The whole shtick? She's a big part of what we do. She has connections on the West Coast you wouldn't believe. She has access to serious money. She knows some amazing people. We need stuff like that. Stuff like that is what's gonna make the difference.'

'She's also a great lay,' Gómez pointed out. 'Does that figure anywhere?'

Beaman stared at him for a moment, then stormed out of the room. Gómez heard the crash of cutlery in the tiny kitchen then the bellow of a radio, turned up to full volume. He'd never seen Beaman this way. The guy was like a child.

He stepped into the kitchen, his sheer bulk trapping Beaman against the corner where the fridge met the sink. Beaman spun round, staring up at him. So pale, Gómez thought. And so delicate. Beaman was expecting a slap. He could see it in his face. Maybe he even wanted to be hit, a fitting climax to this little tantrum. Instead, Gómez laid a huge hand on Beaman's arm. He could feel the boy shivering beneath his touch.

'I admire what you do,' Gómez said softly. 'I respect your sincerity. You have powerful gifts. You're gonna make a difference, and believe me that matters. No point winning a war if we lose the peace that's gonna follow. You agree with any of that?'

'You're too kind.' His lower lip was trembling. 'I just always thought . . .'

'No.' Gómez shook his head. 'You just always hoped.'

'Sure. Is that a sin?'

'Not in my book. And if you're asking for forgiveness, there's no need. I've been around a bit. I know the difference between a fake and the real thing. You're the real thing and you'd better believe it because one day your face is going to be all over *Time* magazine. You need to be ready for that. And to be ready you need to be a whole lot tougher.'

'I am tough. I'm tougher than you can ever believe. It's just that sometimes, not often, I need a little bit of something else. Don't tell me what it is but you've got it.'

'Protection?'

'Yeah. Sure. But protection I can buy. It's more than that.'

'Love?'

'Yeah. You got it. Love.'

'So what makes you think I don't love you? Not in that way. Not in the way you want. Not in the way you've maybe been counting on. But in other ways. You're an unusual guy. You're brave, maybe too brave. I can smell greatness on you. What we don't need is you smashing the crockery. We understand each other?'

Beaman gazed at him. His eyes were shiny with tears.

'Kiss me?' he whispered.

Gómez reached out, the gentlest punch on his upper arm, a gesture of affection. Then he shook his head.

'Dream on,' he said. 'I need to find that woman again.'

*

Waiting in vain for Eva, Stefan badly needed to get to the lavatory. Darkness had fallen. The splint was still on the floor where she'd abandoned it. Getting the thing on wouldn't be simple but he could see the outline of the crutches propped against the wall. With luck, he could make it from the bed. Then all he had to do was somehow get himself to the end of the corridor outside.

Easy. He lay still for a moment, listening to Tomaso coughing down below. He'd no idea whether Eva was with him but he'd heard no movement over the last hour or so and he guessed that the answer had to be no. Maybe she was back at Enrico's, he thought. Or maybe she was out buying food.

The village shop opened in the evening. She'd return any time.

He eyed the crutches again, then told himself his churning guts could wait. The candles had long died but the smell, the lightest scent of thyme, still hung in the air. Stefan shut his eyes. It was all too easy to imagine her back in bed, the shape of her body hanging over him, so deft, so gentle, so patient. He'd slept with a number of women in his life, a couple of them recently in France, and he'd enjoyed them all, but never had he experienced anything like this and what made it all the more puzzling were the odds they had to overcome.

He couldn't walk properly. Indeed, he could barely turn over. He belonged to a nation she despised. They didn't share a native language. They could manage in English but the real communication was by touch, and glance, and gesture. But none of these things – these restraints – mattered because what lay at the very heart of what they'd just experienced was something profoundly instinctive. Very dimly he understood that finding a relationship like this, a coming together, was extremely rare. If you were very, very lucky, it might happen once in a lifetime. If you were like the rest of the human race, it wouldn't happen at all.

Was that really luck? Or was there some cosmic force that – just occasionally – lent a hand in these matters? He lay still in the bed, chasing the possibilities around his head. Once or twice at sea, faced with a particularly well-organised attack, he remembered standing in the cramped semi-darkness of the control room, listening to the thrum-thrum of the enemy ships overhead. He'd known then that a single depth charge, tumbling down on a certain trajectory, could tear his world to pieces. Death would come slowly. Icy water gushing in through the broken hull, fountains of scalding oil from ruptured pipes, and the bursting pressure in your chest as the precious air they all depended on bubbled out into the icy darkness beyond.

On those occasions, like most of his crew, he'd prayed for deliverance and every time it had worked. They'd made it through the screen of corvettes. And weeks later, acknowledging the cheers from the welcoming committee at the quayside when they returned to Lorient, they'd made light of what had happened. Going to sea in submarines, you were always on nodding terms with an unspeakable death. There was no alternative. Except to trust in luck.

Was that why he'd survived the storm that had killed everyone else? Was that how he'd met Eva? Was it luck that had put her in his way? Was this the end of his journey? The moment when the rest of his life resolved itself into a single face? If raw need was any guide then the answer was yes. Need, and surprise, and a deep, deep yearning that was already beginning to alarm him. He was a rational man, partly because he'd always had to be, but this afternoon, and now, and the prospect of the times to follow, had pushed him beyond the reach of rationality. For any German, unconditional surrender had become an uncomfortable phrase. It meant the Fatherland in ruins. It meant total defeat. For Stefan, on the other hand, unconditional surrender was the perfect description of a place, a destination, a state of mind, he'd never dreamed existed.

He couldn't wait any longer. He pushed back the blankets and swung his legs out of bed. Two steps would take him to the crutches propped against the wall. For one of those steps he'd have to rely on his injured leg. He steeled himself, shut his mind to pain, took the first step. He could almost touch the nearest crutch. Almost. He steadied himself, then – with an effort of will – thrust his bad leg forwards. To his surprise and delight, it took his weight without protest.

He made his way out into the corridor, headed for the door at the end. His leg was moving well now. It was stiff, and every time it bore his weight he felt another little spasm, but the pain was nothing to his dawn efforts with Agustín and Eva. Whatever had happened since, he told himself, had worked a small miracle. He made it to the lavatory, abandoned the crutches and sank on to the pedestal. Moments later, he heard the door to the street open downstairs. Then came a woman's voice, calling Tomaso.

Eva, he thought. Deliverance.

*

Gómez met Yolanda in downtown DC. The after-work crowd at Danny G's had begun to thin and Yolanda grabbed a booth while Gómez made a call from the phone on the bar. By the time he rejoined her, she'd ordered a couple of beers.

'No bourbon?'

'Not yet.'

'Is that a promise?'

'Depends.'

'On what? On that husband of yours? On those three lovely kids?'

She was staring at him. Amusement gave way to irritation. Then anger.

'Mr Agard Beaman?' She'd lowered her voice. 'Is that where you got this horseshit?'

'Tell me he's wrong.'

'He's wrong. The man fantasises. Especially where you're concerned.'

'You're right. More right than you know.' He paused. 'Now's the time to straighten this thing out. You're not married. You have no kids.'

'I was married. Twice. I scared the shit out of both husbands and they moved on. One went back to Mexico. The other married someone a whole lot more dainty. Doesn't stop him lifting the phone, though. For old times' sake.'

'What's he missing?'

Yolanda eyed him again, more fondly this time. 'If that's a serious question, Mr Gómez, I could take offence. That was you last night? Emptying your balls all over me? Calling for your mother? I thought men only did that in battle? On the point of death?'

'Same thing.' Hector's hand covered hers. Just the sight of her fingers aroused him. 'Sorry about the third degree,' he said. 'Once a cop . . .'

'Sure. And you?'

'Me?'

'How many wives?'

'One. I sent her back. Never matched the picture in the catalogue.'

'That's plain nasty. Coming from you.'

'You think I'm ugly?'

'I know you're ugly. Ugly on the outside. Happens I like ugly.'

'And on the inside?'

'We'll see. Early days, Mr Gómez. Good start, though. Thank God I wasn't in the bedroom next door. I'd have died of envy.'

She lifted her glass, clinked it against his. While they were still sober, she wanted to get something else straight. She and her buddies were serious about Agard Beaman. The guy needed looking after by someone who knew what they were doing.

'Agard told us you saved his life once. In Detroit.'

'That's true. And something else.'

'What?'

'I knew what I was doing. You don't want the details and even if you did I'm not going to tell you but the point was I'd scoped the guy earlier. I knew what was going to happen down the road. How and when wasn't entirely clear but that didn't matter. Where I come from you get a feel for the obvious and the not so obvious. Men think they can hide. They can't. My way you get to stay ahead of the game. It's called survival.'

'And Agard?' Yolanda asked.

'Agard doesn't even know the game exists and that's partly because he's not interested. That guy lives in the moment. That's all that matters to him. He's got the best of intentions and he's Abe Lincoln on his feet and I guess from where you guys are sitting that makes him pretty important. But you're right. The boy needs looking after.'

'By you.' It was a statement, not a question.

'No way.' Gómez shook his head.

'Why not?'

'Because just now I have something else I have to take care of. But as it happens, we might manage a trade.'

'A trade? Between you and me?' Yolanda looked suddenly confused.

'Yeah. I guess this is a confession. Maybe not. Either way it's deeply shameful.'

'How come?'

'It's about last night. I remember most of it but not all of it.'

'You were good. The best.'

'Yeah. You, too. But something else. You've got a brother, right?'

'I got three brothers,' Yolanda said.

'But one still in Mexico.'

'All three are still there. That's the thing about boys. Lazy sons of bitches.'

'Right . . .' Gómez was trying to get to the point. 'So here's the thing. One of them – shit, maybe all three – are cops. Yes? No? Or did I imagine it?'

'One's a cop. The eldest. Diego. If you ever met him you'd laugh. Skinny as hell, unlike the rest of us. Never got his share of the family gene pool but that mother is the toughest guy you'll ever meet.'

'Is he honest?'

'Yeah. Which I guess is why he never got promotion. Still does six shifts a week, mainly nights. His choice. Are we getting the picture here?'

Gómez nodded, took another swallow of beer. He wanted to know where Diego lived.

'City called Ensenada. It's on the Baja, south of Tijuana.'

'You still talk to him?'

'All the time. We shared divorces. Shoulder? Weep? That boy opens up to no one on this planet. Except his kid sister.'

'You.'

'Me.' She was running her fingertip round the rim of her glass. The glass was still frosted from the chiller. She dipped her finger in the beer then reached for Gómez's mouth. Gómez trapped her hand in his. Business first.

'You think I can hire him?'

'Diego? You mean for money? Why would you want to do that?'

'Because I have some business to transact. Because I need someone who knows the territory.'

'This is private?'

'In a way, yes.'

'What kind of private? What are we talking here?'

Gómez toyed briefly with sharing some of the story from the Hill. Out of the question.

'You have to trust me,' he said finally.

'Big word.'

'I know.'

She was watching him carefully, making up her mind. This is a woman used to negotiations, Gómez told himself. Tread carefully.

'This is government business, right?' she said.

'Yeah.'

'Important?'

'Very.'

'You like this country? You like this country as much as I do? You want the best for it? After the war? After the fighting?'

'I do.' Gómez nodded. 'In fact I love this country.'

'Nothing you'd like to change?'

'I'd like to change plenty.'

'Are we talking last night? In that restaurant? Reptile Joe's?'

'Rattlesnake Joe's.' He nodded. 'We are.'

'Then we have a deal, Mr Gómez. Give me your hand.'

'Deal?'

'I talk to Diego. I tell him you're a good guy. I get him to say yes. You sort out the business end direct with him. And then, afterwards, you sign up with us to take care of Agard. How does that sound?'

Her hand was still extended across the table. Gómez stared at it. Beautiful. All his life he'd been careful to keep his options open and this inbred caution had served him well. He'd survived. He'd prospered. And now he was holding down not one but two jobs.

He was still gazing at the hand. The lacquered nails. The single silver ring. What the fuck.

'Deal,' he said.

*

This time Eva spent the whole night with Stefan. While she was undressing, he insisted on a cautious tour of the room, stark naked, the splint abandoned, the crutches wedged beneath his armpits, one foot in front of another, two complete laps. She watched him while she folded her clothes and when he was done, panting with effort beside the bed, she embraced him from behind, her body folded around his long back, her hands linked over the flatness of his stomach. A miracle, she agreed.

They made love again, quicker this time, more urgent, and afterwards, nose to nose in the darkness, he asked about her father.

'He's worried,' she said.

'About what?'

'I don't know. First I think it's here.' She touched Stefan's chest. 'Breathing is hard. Maybe he gets frightened. But maybe it's something else.'

'He knows about us?'

'No.' The thought alarmed her. He could see it in her eyes.

'Are you sure?'

'Yes.'

'So what about tonight? He must know you're sleeping here.'

'I said I'm sleeping here for him. Maybe he needs me. Then I come down.'

'And?'

'He likes that. In some ways he's a child. Alone he's frightened. I can make that better. You understand?'

'I do.' Stefan laughed. '*Totalmente.*'

'So I have two men? Two children? Is that what you mean?'

'Yes. A little.'

She kissed him. Her eyes were huge. She said she wanted to tell him something. She said it was a secret.

'You promise? Not to tell about this thing?'

'I do.'

'I talk with Agustín. Agustín thinks my father will need a hospital soon. Somewhere with oxygen. Somewhere with more doctors.'

'Where will that be?'

'Coruña.'

'When?'

'Soon.'

'And then?'

'And then the house will be empty.'

'You want to stay here?' Stefan asked.

'I want to know what you want.'

'I want to be with you.'

'*Verdaderamente?*' It was a whisper, her lips shaping the word in the darkness.

Stefan nodded. He'd learned the word only yesterday, from Agustín. It meant *truly.*

'Here or some other place,' he said. 'It doesn't matter.'

'Here will be dangerous.'

'Why?'

She shook her head, wouldn't say. Stefan asked again. He said it was important. He needed to know.

'This is a small place. People talk.'

'About us?'

'About you. It can't be a secret. Not here.'

'But the Germans have gone.'

'I know. But another place will be better. I will find somewhere. Maybe you have to be there by yourself. Until my father goes to hospital.'

'And then?'

'And then we go away. To where no one will find us.'

To where no one will find us. Stefan couldn't think of a brighter, sweeter future. Some place where they could put the war behind them, and the uniforms, and the killings, and Hitler's mad dreams of still finding victory under the ruins of the fallen Reich.

'That would be good,' he said. 'That would be wonderful.'

'*Maravilloso?*'

'*Sí.*'

'Then it will happen. You trust me? You'll wait for me?' She hugged him close, made him promise. Then she held him at arm's length in the darkness. 'Tomorrow,' she said. 'Tomorrow we find a place for you.'

The police came at four in the morning. The first Stefan heard was a thunderous hammering at the door. Eva was already out of bed. She wrapped a gown around herself and hurried downstairs. Stefan heard the door open. Then came voices, many voices, all male apart from Eva's. She was shouting at them in Spanish. Then he heard a slap and a scream. Eva, he thought, fighting to get himself out of bed, to get himself to the door, to offer some kind of resistance.

It was too late. The men were in uniform. There were three of them. *Guardia Civil*, he thought. They threw him back on to the bed. One of them wrapped a blanket around him, the roughness of his hands on Stefan's flesh. Then they half pushed, half carried him downstairs. Eva was standing in front of the room where her father slept, trying to protect him. Stefan could hear him shouting inside. Blood was pouring from a wound on the side of her face. Stefan swore at the men in German. He'd tried to struggle free but he knew it was hopeless. They were dragging him backwards towards the open door and the street beyond. It was freezing outside. His bare heels went clump-clump on the cobblestones, sending jolts of pain through his injured leg. Through the open door he could still see Eva. He wanted to yell at her, to tell her that one day he would be back, but a hand was clamped over his mouth and by the time they got to the van it was too late.

The van was parked on the other side of the street. The guards tossed him into the back. He could smell the sour tang of petrol and then came something else. A cigar, he thought. Two of the guards had clambered into the back. The third climbed behind the wheel and fired up the engine. As he did so, a shape beside him turned round. A face in the throw of light from Eva's house. The glow of a cigar between his fingers. And perfect German.

'*Guten Abend, Herr Kapitän*.' The man smiled. 'We have much to discuss.'

PART THREE

PART THREE

13

Gómez took the train to California. Yolanda was with him. They rode the southern route through New Orleans and Phoenix, a journey of two and a half days, and paused for an hour at El Paso for a change of locomotive. It was the middle of the night. Gómez walked up and down the platform, enjoying the warmth. Beyond the head of the train, at the very end of the platform, he peered into the darkness, wondering what lay in wait down the track. The knowledge that Hoover had cut him loose, that he had a couple of weeks to freelance the hunt for Donovan, was a big plus. Better still, Yolanda had volunteered – insisted – on accompanying him to Ensenada. She hadn't been back home for a while. Diego could be difficult. Best that she handled the introductions in person.

They arrived at Los Angeles towards the end of the following day and took another train down to San Diego. Yolanda had a modest, slightly dowdy apartment several blocks inland from the beach. To make up for the lack of a view, she'd brightened the place with native Indian carvings, faces mostly. They studied Gómez as he trekked from room to room. Yolanda had taste and a nice sense of colour. Her choice of rugs and wall hangings took him back to some of the cramped little apartments on the Hill, bright splashes of yellow and scarlet, local Navajo motifs.

Yolanda drove a battered old Chrysler. They sped down Route 1 and crossed the border at El Chaparral. Ensenada lay beyond the sprawl of Tijuana. Both cities, according to Yolanda, had been oases in the desert during the Prohibition years, drawing thirsty Americans down from the States. As much booze as your liver could take, and your choice of local *putas* afterwards. Yolanda had grown up in Ensenada and could remember the whores parading along the waterfront in the early evening under the watchful eyes of their pimps. Thirties Mexico, she said, was no place for a girl with ambition and any sense of justice. Gómez, unimpressed by what he was seeing, could only agree.

'That was your decision? Leaving?'

'Sure. My family still haven't forgiven me. A real Mexican doesn't live among the gringos. Some of these people would rather starve than cross the border.'

'And that includes your brother? The cop?'

'Afraid so.'

They'd agreed to meet Diego at a bar near the docks called El Pescador. The place was ten minutes from the police station and a chalked board on the sidewalk offered shrimp tacos at a handful of pesos a plate. Thanks to the traffic they were late and the moment they walked in from the brightness of high noon Gómez knew he had a job on his hands. The place was empty except for a dog asleep on the floor among the litter of cigarette ends. The air smelled bad: stale tobacco and cooking oil thinly laced with bleach. A songbird on its back in a cage near the window appeared to be dead.

Diego occupied a stool at the end of the counter, hunched over a plate of what might have been stew. When Yolanda tapped him on the shoulder and said hi, he barely acknowledged her presence. Brother and sister had, according to Yolanda, always been close but you'd never know it.

'You gonna put that spoon down a moment? This here is my good friend Hector.'

Diego eyed Gómez over the plate. A fall of lank black hair curtained the gauntness of his face. His eyes were sunken and a savage attack of teenage acne had cratered the pale flesh beneath the stubble. He was wearing jeans and a plain grey T-shirt and his scarred forearms were as pale and skinny as the rest of him. There was menace in his every movement, his every glance. If you'd just emerged from a night in the drunk tank, Gómez thought, and you had to account for your misdeeds, this man would scare the shit out of you. Good start.

'The name's Gómez. *Mucho gusto.*'

Diego ignored the proffered hand. He uncoiled from the stool and summoned the bartender. Gómez found himself looking at a glass of beer.

'Carta Blanca, *señor,*' the bartender said. 'The best.'

Diego muttered something Gómez didn't catch and the bartender disappeared. Yolanda asked whether Diego had talked to his bosses.

'*Sí.*'

'And?'

'They said no.'

'No leave?'

'No anything. They say no all the time. Am I surprised?' He shrugged. 'No.'

His voice was low, difficult to follow, as if he was talking to himself. Gómez had worked with cops like this before, hard men who'd taken a good look at the world around them and put up the shutters. They came across as losers but – in Gómez's experience – they were anything but.

Yolanda wanted to know what Diego was going to do about getting time off. On the phone, she reminded him, he'd told her *no importa*.

'I go sick,' he said.

'For how long?'

'A week. Maybe more.' His eyes found Hector. 'You have money?'

'Yeah.'

'I go sick, they don't pay me. I need thirty dollars a day. You also buy the food, a place to stay, everything. *Trato hecho?*'

'He wants to know if it's a deal,' said Yolanda.

Hector said nothing. Then he nodded at an empty table nearby.

'You mind?'

Without waiting for an answer, he collected his glass and led Yolanda to the table. Diego had returned to his stew. He swallowed a couple of spoonfuls, then checked his watch. He tossed a five-peso note on the bar, wiped his mouth on the back of his hand, and walked out.

Yolanda couldn't believe it. She was on her feet already, heading for the door. Gómez called her back.

'Leave it,' he told her. 'We'll talk later. He just needs to make a point or two.'

'And you?'

'Me?' He reached for his beer. 'I'm happy to oblige.'

They all met again in the early evening, different bar. Yolanda had shouted down the phone at Diego between equally difficult visits to a handful of her relatives. Deep down, concluded Gómez, families are all the same. Leaving is an insult. Leaving means turning the page. Best leave the early chapters well alone.

This time the place was better: a crowd of drinkers at the bar and live music in the shape of a gypsy-looking guitarist with a gaucho hat. Not a dead songbird in sight. Yolanda took charge, organising the drinks and ordering plates of black beans with corn and rice. Whatever she'd said to Diego on the phone appeared to have done the trick. He even offered a nod of thanks when she refilled his empty glass.

Gómez had no interest in small talk. He'd given Yolanda as much information as he could to pass on. Donovan was married to a woman called Francisca. She came from a city called Guaymas. According to the Bureau of Immigration, her family name was Muñoz. Donovan drove a lime-green Cadillac. He and Francisca and the three kids might have made an appearance recently. Yolanda had passed all this on to Diego and now Gómez wanted to know what he'd done about it.

'I made a call,' he said. 'I have a friend in Guaymas.'

'A cop?'

'*Sí*. We used to work together. Here in Ensenada. A good man. Tough.'

'And?'

'He makes enquiries. He may have found the family. Tomorrow we go down there and find out.'

He wanted to know about the money. Thirty bucks a day plus Gómez picking up all other expenses.

Gómez nodded. *Trato hecho.* Diego extended a hand. Gómez shook it.

'I meant the money.'

'You want it now?'

'*Sí.*'

'All of it?'

'*Sí.*'

Gómez began to shake his head. He was happy to pay half. Not a dollar more. Half now. Half at the end of the week. Diego shrugged, sitting back from the table, and Gómez waited for him to consult his watch. Yolanda stirred. She was sitting beside Gómez, squashed behind the table, and when her hand strayed towards her purse, Gómez shook his head. He didn't want her making any kind of peace here. This wasn't about money, about her making good the shortfall.

'Well?'

Diego was a hard man to pin down. His eyes roved around the bar, tallying faces, exchanging the odd nod of greeting, avoiding Gómez's gaze. Finally, he said he'd take half the money now, half later. Ninety dollars would buy Gómez three days of his time. Not a minute more.

'Three and a half days.'

'Three days.'

It was Gómez's turn to shrug. He reached for his glass, emptied it, then stood up.

'It's been a pleasure,' he said. '*Adiós.*'

They left for Guaymas at dawn next morning. The night's drinking lay heavily between them. Afterwards Yolanda had towed Gómez back to the cheap hotel where they were staying and after two hours' sleep he'd left her in bed while he went downstairs to wait for Diego in the street below. It was still dark. Diego was driving a black sedan, newer than Gómez had expected, and after the car had come to a halt outside the hotel he'd got in without a word. Diego looked as wrecked as ever. Gómez had never seen a man drink so much tequila and stay on his feet.

Guaymas was 160 miles away. The road skirted the coast. Inland were the mountains of the high sierra and the thin, grey light of dawn gave way to a spectacular sunrise over the topmost peaks. The potholed blacktop was barred with shadows from the spindly roadside trees and, apart from the odd truck, there was little traffic.

They hit Guaymas in time for a late breakfast. The city spread inland from a pretty bay, cupped by outcrops of unforgiving rock. The sea was an intense blue and Gómez could see warships moored alongside as they drove along the waterfront looking for somewhere to eat. Navy town, he thought. Probably rough.

They ate eggs and ham under the curious eye of the café's owner. Two strangers, largely silent, drinking one cup of coffee after another. Gómez settled the bill and after asking for directions Diego drove across town to the police station. There was a public telephone wired to a lamppost up the street and Diego parked alongside to make a call. A couple of minutes later, still parked up, Gómez watched a short, fat figure step out of the police station and waddle along the sidewalk towards them.

'Gonzalez.' Diego had seen him, too.

Gonzalez stopped beside the driver's door. He bent to the window and leaned in. The two men shook hands. There was a brief conversation, then Gonzalez passed Diego a scrap of paper and pointed a finger down the road.

There was an address on the paper. Diego had trouble reading it. Then he turned to Gómez.

'Ten dollars. For my friend here.'

Gómez extracted the note from his wallet and handed it across. Seconds later, Gonzalez had gone.

'Francisca?' Gómez was looking at the note.

'Gabriela. Her sister.'

Diego offered no other explanation. He started the car, the address on his lap, and drove back down towards the waterfront. Twice he stopped for directions, shading his eyes against the sun as strangers bent to inspect Gonzalez's scrawl. Then they were coasting down a narrow street in what looked like a slum area near the docks. Most of these houses had windows but no glass. Some of them had no doors either, just a yawning gap where the entrance should have been. In one, he saw a donkey tethered by a hank of rope. At the end of the street, a line of washing hung between the upper floors, grey-looking sheets and a woman's skirt that might once have been pretty.

Diego braked to a halt, peering at a door. The door was old, badly made, hanging from its hinges. The bottom half had been crudely braced where someone had tried to kick it in. The dusty outline of a number on the peeling stucco beside the frame.

'Here,' Diego grunted. '*Siete.*'

Diego opened the glove compartment. There was a handgun inside, a big automatic. He got out of the car and told Gómez to stay close. He paused in the sunshine to check the gun and then gave the door a kick. The door burst open and he stepped inside. Gómez followed. There were three rooms downstairs, squalid, empty. He could hear nothing but the buzzing of a million flies. Then came the steady trickle of water from the single tap in the room that served as a kitchen. The adjacent lavatory was thick with excrement. From the kitchen, wooden steps led to the upper floor. At the bottom of the stairs was a pair of man's trousers. Gómez paused to look at them. They'd been discarded in a hurry. He was beginning to get the picture.

At the top of the stairs, Diego paused. Two doors, one of them an inch or two open. He glanced back at Gómez, then nodded at the open door. Moments later, they were both inside the room, Diego's gun levelled at two figures on a mattress on the floor. The man, naked, was lying on his back. He was hairy and fat and the noises downstairs had done nothing for his erection. He stared up at Diego, at the gun. He wanted to be anywhere in the world but here. The other figure was a woman. Gómez judged her to be in her early thirties. Her body was going the same way as her client's but she had a fullness that some men found irresistible. Unlike her client, she showed no fear. Another shakedown. What a surprise.

Diego gave the man a kick, then jerked his thumb towards the door. Half crouching, covering himself with his hands, the guy reached for his shirt and scuttled away. Gómez heard him wrestling with his trousers at the foot of the stairs. Then he was gone.

Diego had turned his attention to the woman.

'Gabriela?'

She nodded, on her feet now, wiping her thighs with a scrap of towel. Her Spanish was far too fast for Gómez to understand, a torrent of what sounded like oaths, but it was all too easy to guess where she was headed. A working girl needed a little privacy. People like her had a living to make. What the fuck was

Diego doing in a place like this? And how come men always had to hide behind guns?

Diego handed the automatic to Gómez then took a step forward, bunched his fist and drove it hard into her face. Her head jerked back with the impact and she screamed in pain, holding her head in her hands. Gómez blinked at the force and suddenness of the violence. Not a hint of a warning. No attempt to frighten the woman first. When her hands came away, blood was spouting from her ruined nose. Diego studied her a moment, muttered something Gómez didn't catch, then hit her again. This time she took the blow lower, just beneath her breasts, sinking to her knees, fighting for breath.

Diego wanted the gun. Gómez gave it to him. Diego pushed the woman back across the mattress then straddled her. He cocked the gun, held it inches in front of her face. He wanted to know about Francisca, about the gringo Donovan, about the car full of kids that had driven down from the States. When had they arrived? Where would he find them?

The woman shook her head. She didn't know. Leave me alone. Just let me breathe. An address, Diego insisted. I need an address. Again the shake of the head.

Diego sat back, easing his weight lower, waiting for the woman to recover. She was wiping her face with her hand, then looking at the blood. Once, Gómez thought, she would have been as beautiful as her sister. He remembered Francisca in the chaos of Donovan's house in Albuquerque. They had the same bone structure, the same sense of fullness, the same ease with themselves. Except this woman was running to fat and thanks to Diego she wouldn't trust a mirror for a while.

'It's off the Avenida de la Republica,' she muttered in Spanish. 'Calle de la Cera.'

'Number?'

'Twelve. Yellow door.'

'And your sister? Francisca?'

She stared up at Diego, exhausted by this sudden spasm of violence. One moment she'd been earning her living. Now this.

Diego asked again about Francisca. The gun was back in her face. She pushed it aside, a gesture of disgust.

'Gone,' she said. 'Yesterday.'

'Where?'

'I don't know.'

'With Donovan? With Frank?'

'*Sí.*'

She said she hated this man. She said he was no good for her sister, no good for the rest of the family. When Diego wanted to know why, she said he was a *puta*, fucked everyone.

'Like you?'

'No. I fuck for a living. For pleasure men give me money. This man takes everything, from everyone. Men, women, everyone.'

'You mean he's a thief?'

'*Sí.* A bad man. The worst. You find him . . .' she nodded at the gun, '. . . you shoot him. The man is a rat. Kill him. Shoot him down. You don't believe me? Ask my mother. Calle de la Cera. Yellow door.'

*

It took a while for Stefan to get his bearings. The journey from the village had seemed interminable. He'd lost count of the bends in the road, of the roar of the engine as the van climbed yet another hill, of the endless potholes that sent fresh spasms of pain through his ruined leg, of the sour reek of the exhaust fumes. Only hours ago, he'd felt himself reborn. Now, in ways too terrifying to contemplate, he was probably finished.

With dawn came a proper city. Through the single window at the back of the van, still wrapped in his blanket, Stefan glimpsed lampposts, trees, a wall of buildings on either side of the street, plants on balconies, billboards, advertisements, real life. The guards beside him were asleep, their bodies slumped against the sides of the van, their mouths open, their heads lolling as the driver slowed then picked up speed again. From the front of the van came occasional snatches of conversation. The German spoke fluent Spanish, and – from time to time – had the good manners to laugh at what might have been the other man's joke.

The attaché from Coruña, Stefan thought, and it turned out he was right. When the van finally came to a halt, and the driver had shaken the guards awake, he got out of the van and stepped round to the back. When the driver opened the rear doors he leaned in as the guards pulled Stefan into a sitting position.

'Von Klissburg.' He extended a gloved hand. 'Otto.'

Half expecting the obligatory *Heil Hitler*, Stefan didn't move. Had he been captured by the British, he'd have been obliged to offer nothing but his name, rank and number. Was that what he was now? A prisoner of war?

Far from it. The guards helped him across the paving stones, heading for a heavy wooden door between two shops. It was daylight by now, though still early, and across the road a man with a cartful of loaves had stopped briefly to watch. This was a respectable area, probably the middle of the city. There were tramlines sunk into the cobblestones and a glimpse of the sea at the end of the street. Seagulls, too, wheeling above the rooftops.

Stefan paused beside the door, grateful for the support of the guards, while the German looked for keys. One of the shops was a florist. The other sold confectionery. Stefan lingered, gazing at the nests of truffles, each one separately wrapped, each a work of art. He could taste them, roll them slowly round his mouth, anticipate the moment when the chocolate shell surrendered to his probing tongue and he at last found the sweetness inside. Eva, he thought.

Otto was holding the door open. A light was already on inside and a flight of stairs led upwards. The guards were strong. They carried Stefan up, grunting with the effort. At a sharp word from Otto, they even apologised when they missed a step.

Finally, they made it to the first floor. Stefan found himself in a reception area. The ceilings were high, lovely mouldings, fitted carpet underfoot. Otto led the way into another room down the corridor. More carpet, blue rather than red, and a single bed tucked against the wall. The window in the room as tall as the ceiling, still curtained against the daylight, and the bed had been turned down as if in expectation of Stefan's arrival. The guards settled him gently on the bed. Otto asked whether there was anything he wanted.

'Coffee, perhaps? Something to eat?'

Stefan shook his head, said no to both. Nothing made sense any more. Expecting, at the very least, a beating, he found himself treated like an honoured guest. He asked Otto whether this was Coruña.

'It is. You've been here before? Showing the flag maybe?'

'Never.'

'A pity. A handsome city. Wonderful beaches. The nicest people. Let's hope you enjoy it here.'

Enjoy it here? Stefan gazed at him in wonderment. There was no point in keeping anything back. This man obviously knew the whole story.

'How did you know where to find me? How did you know I was even alive?'

Otto shook his head. Later, he said. Once Stefan had rested a little. He dismissed the guards, then nodded down at the bed.

'Someone will call you at noon. *Schlafen Sie gut.*'

Stefan watched him leave the room. The last thing he heard before he got into bed was the sound of the key turning in the lock.

He awoke hours later, deeply confused. He could hear music from the adjoining room. Brahms. The slow movement from the First Piano Concerto. He lay back, aware now of the growl of traffic from the street outside the window. The window was still curtained but he could make out the rumble of a tram, the clank of its bell, and the more distant mew of seagulls. Then came Brahms again.

Early in the war, back for a rare week of leave, his mother had taken him to hear a live performance in the Hamburg's *Laeiszhalle*. The piano concerto was one of her favourite pieces and he'd loved it ever since, especially the second movement. The tease. The slow build. The resolution. So deft. So passionate. So *right*. Exquisite.

Back in the village, up by himself in the narrow bed listening to Eva on the keyboard downstairs, he'd once thought of asking her if she knew this piece, and maybe if she could play the piano part. At that point in what he liked to think of as his convalescence he'd never been bold enough to broach the subject, and afterwards his thoughts had been elsewhere, but now he regretted not sharing this piece with her. He lay back, letting the music wash over him, wondering how many phonograph discs it took to record the entire concerto, then there came the scrape of a key in a lock and the door opened.

It was Otto and a woman who looked Spanish. She was carrying a tray. Otto gestured for her to put the tray on the bedside table. Stefan could see a pot of coffee, a curl of steam, a plate piled high with pastries. He might have been in a hotel.

The woman left without a word. Otto perched himself on the end of Stefan's bed. He was wearing a suit now, beautifully tailored, and a red lapel pin with a tiny black swastika that Stefan recognised from one of the formal dinners he'd had to attend as a cadet in the naval training college at Flensburg. The guest of honour that night had been the Reich ambassador in London and he'd been wearing exactly the same pin. He'd come to tell the cadets about the mood in the Royal Navy. He'd attended a review at Spithead down on the Channel coast, miles of battleships and cruisers and other elements from the Home Fleet drawn up in perfect lines with thousands of officers and sailors lining the decks, saluting their king. He told the cadets he'd talked to some of these men. There was no appetite for war, he said. If the fighting came, the British would stand aside. How wrong he'd been.

'Foreign Office?' Stefan was still looking at the lapel pin.

'I'm a diplomat, yes. A diplomat by temperament and a diplomat by choice. If you're lucky in this war you find yourself far from Berlin. I was lucky. I *am* lucky. Drink the coffee. It gets cold so quickly.'

Stefan did his bidding. The coffee was delicious. He couldn't remember coffee like it.

'The beans come across from Brazil. We get them from the embassy in Lisbon. They're kind enough not to forget us. Eat, please.'

Stefan helped himself to a pastry. The brioche was still warm from the oven. He wanted to know about the music next door.

'Brahms . . . but you'll know that. Claudio Arrau at the keyboard. Maestro Furtwängler on the podium.'

Stefan felt the first prickles of alarm. This man seemed to know everything about him. He might have been there in Hamburg, in the *Laeiszhalle*. He might have been up on his feet the moment the performance had swept to its finale, the conductor's head bowed as the applause rolled over him. So how come his choice of music had been so perfect?

Asking him any kind of direct question would be far too crude. This man, he sensed, expected better. Instead, Stefan asked about the recording itself. By now, he expected a change of discs on the phonograph. They spun round at 78 rpm and barely lasted a single movement. They'd always taken a phonograph to sea and Stefan knew how irritating they could be. So why was the Brahms so seamless?

'You don't know?'

'I'm afraid not.'

'We call it a Magnetophon. The music comes on a reel of magnetic tape. The people at BASF developed it. The reproduction is faultless and you never have to bother with all those tiresome discs. I like to call it our secret weapon. If we take nothing else from this war then at least we take our Brahms.'

He seemed amused by the thought. Stefan nodded and helped himself to another pastry, a *pain au raisin*, better even than the version they served in the mess at Lorient. A silence had settled between them, peaceable, in no way threatening. Then Otto picked at a thread of wool from the foot of the blanket.

'I imagine you'll be wanting to know what we have in store for you.'

'Yes, please.'

'Word has gone to Berlin. That won't surprise you.'

'Word about what?'

'About your escape. The fact that you survived. If I talk of mixed reactions, I'm sure you'll understand. On the one hand your reputation is second to none. Even Doenitz sends his congratulations.'

Doenitz headed the German Navy. They called him *Onkel Karl*, 'The Lion'. As far as Stefan was concerned, the Lion was God.

'I'm honoured,' he said.

'Then have another pastry. Because the rest of the news is not so good.'

The SS, he said, had also been in touch. First in the matter of certain personnel and cargoes carried by the submarine. Second because the body of one of their senior officers had been recovered from the wreck.

'I happened to be there, *Herr Kapitän*. Sometimes these people like to make things up. On this occasion they didn't have to.'

Stefan sensed what was coming. He put his plate to one side. 'And?'

247

'We brought the dead officer here to Coruña. The Spanish are most accommodating in these situations. The doctor who performed the post-mortem confirmed that *Brigadeführer* Huber had been shot three times, once in the face and twice in the chest. His body must have spent some days inside the submarine before the wreck broke up. Only then did it come ashore.' He paused. 'To put it bluntly, *Herr Kapitän*, our friends from Prinz-Albrecht-Strasse think you may have a view about the good *Brigadeführer*'s fate.'

Stefan nodded. Prinz-Albrecht-Strasse housed the headquarters of the SS in Berlin. The torture chambers were in the basement.

'Are these SS people here? In Coruña?'

'Not yet.'

'They're coming?'

'Of course. And soon. It might pay you to cast your mind back. They're not as generous with pastries as I am.'

Stefan studied him, trying to gauge where this conversation was heading. Was his amiable host, with his faultless manners and impeccable taste in music, marking his card? Or was he after something more practical? Like a confession?

'I'll bear all that in mind,' Stefan said. 'I'm grateful.'

'Don't be. I ought to add something else. I think we can both anticipate two charges. One will be desertion, the other murder. If our friends believe you to be guilty of either, then the consequences will be fatal. The Spanish, as I've already said, can be deeply helpful in situations like these. They like to do these things out of the city. It's a thirty-minute drive. They use a couple of men with rifles. It can be very quick.' He smiled. 'And very final.'

Stefan was looking at the crumbs on the plate. Eva, he thought. Her lover Juan pinned in the headlights of some car or other. His war coming to an abrupt and bloody end. Was there a house of death here in Coruña? Somewhere they'd store the bodies? Was that where he'd end up? Would Eva pay her last respects?

Otto was asking him whether there was anything else he needed. To the best of his knowledge the people from Berlin would be here this afternoon. They'd spent the night in the embassy in Madrid. They might even be in the air again by now.

'How long have you known that I was alive?'

'I'm afraid I can't tell you.'

'But longer than . . .' Stefan shrugged, '. . . yesterday?'

'That would be a reasonable assumption.'

'So how did you know? Did someone betray me?'

'There are no secrets in this war, *Herr Kapitän*. If there were we might already be at peace.'

Stefan frowned. He had no idea what Otto meant but the shape of the next few hours was only too evident. Pastries first. Then the bill.

'Can you help me across there?' He was looking at the window.

'Of course. My pleasure.'

Otto helped him out of bed, and supported his weight as Stefan limped towards the window.

'You want me to open the curtains?'

'Yes, please.'

'Like the theatre, *ja*?' Otto smiled, and then parted the curtains in the middle while Stefan clung to the back of a nearby chair.

Outside, as Stefan had expected, the street was busy. What little he'd seen of Spain had told him that these were poor people but the women drifting from shop to shop looked well fed, even affluent. Some of them lingered a while, gazing at the mannequins in the shop window. An old man had a stall across the road and Stefan told himself he could smell the sweetness of the roasting chestnuts. Further away, two girls were playing for the crowds of shoppers. One had a violin, the other a mouth organ. Stefan felt his eyes filling with tears. It looked so ordinary down there, so inviting, so removed from the war and all the killing. Eva, he thought again. She deserves some of this.

He let go of the chair. He wanted to get closer. His fingers touched the cold glass. Then he became aware of Otto's presence behind him.

'The window is locked, *Herr Kapitän*,' he said softly, 'if you were thinking otherwise.'

14

Francisca's mother was a plump woman in her sixties with the face of a peasant and a biggish square of garden she clearly tended with fierce passion. The garden was at the back of the house. Diego and Gómez found her bent over a row of fat eggplants, digging out the weeds with her thick fingers. She had a scarf knotted tightly over a mass of greying hair and her hands were caked in soil when she turned round to inspect these two strangers who'd made their way round the side of the property.

Diego showed her his ID. She inspected it without visible interest.

'Gabriela?' She sounded tired.

'*Sí.*'

'Again?'

'*Sí.*'

Diego dismissed her daughter with a wave of his hand. This wasn't about her, he said. He wanted to know about Frank Donovan, about the gringo who'd stolen her other daughter.

The word 'stolen' put a smile on the old woman's face. For once she agreed with a policeman. Stolen was right. Stolen was exactly what this man had done. Not just stealing her daughter but other things, too.

'Like?'

'Like cars. Autos. He comes here maybe last year, maybe the year before. He steals cars. He knows how to do it. He steals cars and takes them back to the US. These cars have owners. And where do the owners come? They come to me. Because they know about the gringo who stole my daughter. And so I have much trouble, much, much trouble.'

'Your daughter says he was here, the gringo, yesterday.'

'He was. He stayed three days. Until yesterday. Then I tell him no more. No more trouble. I love those kids, Francisca's kids, but if they stay he stays. And so they go. All of them. Mother of God . . .' he crossed herself, leaving tiny brown smudges on the front of her dress.

'You know where they went?'

'No.'

'Which direction?'

'No.'

'He never mentioned other friends? Mexican friends? Places he might go? Find a bed for them all?'

'No. But he has money. So he doesn't need friends.'

This was interesting. Diego glanced at Gómez, then went back to the old woman.

'How much money?'

'Lots.' She made a dismissive gesture with her forefinger and her thumb.

'Pesos?'

'Dollars. US. This man is very rich. Maybe a millionaire. You know what he brings to our house? To our family? Nothing. I talk to Francisca about it. She says it's the same for her, the same for the kids. He keeps the money, buys them nothing.'

Diego asked to see inside the house.

'Why?'

'Because he may have left something.'

'He leaves nothing. He keeps everything.'

'You've looked?'

'Of course. *Nada*.'

It was the first time Gómez had seen Diego crack a smile. This guy loves the rougher side of human nature, he thought. Something at last they had in common.

The old woman took them into the house. It was cool inside and spotlessly clean. Gómez remembered the dump where they'd found her other daughter.

'Gabriela lives here?' he asked in halting Spanish.

'Sometimes. Sometimes not. The gringo and Francisca were in here.'

She showed them a room at the front of the property. It was the biggest room in the house. Two adults? Three kids? Bit of a squeeze but *no importa*.

The room was bare: a double bed, two mattresses on the floor, a tall wardrobe with double doors, a gold-framed picture of the Madonna tacked on the wall above the bed. Diego was searching the wardrobe. It was full of dresses.

'These are yours?'

The old woman ignored the question. Something had come back to her. Something maybe important. The gringo had talked about business. He had to go back, he'd said. He'd had to go back north.

'To the States?' Gómez thought that unlikely.

'To the north,' she repeated. 'Maybe more cars? I don't know. And something else, too. My poor Francisca. You know what she tells me? She tells me the gringo has other women.'

'She knows that?'

'She thinks that. She found a photograph. Horrible.'

'Describe it?'

The old woman didn't want to. After this sudden flurry of information, she'd buttoned her lip. She's ashamed, Gómez thought. And embarrassed.

'The photograph,' Diego said. 'Tell me about the photograph.'

She shook her head. It was God's business and God would settle the gringo's debts in his own good time.

'It's a woman,' Gómez said softly. 'Isn't it?'

She looked round at him. Then she nodded.

'Naked?'

'*Sí.*'

'Doing what?'

'Showing herself, *señor*. All of herself.' One hand flapped vaguely at her belly. 'And a big kiss.'

'For the camera?'

'For the gringo.'

*

The knock on Stefan's door came in the late afternoon. The door opened to reveal Otto. With a hint of regret, he announced that the delegation from Berlin had arrived. The word 'delegation' prompted Stefan to enquire further.

'How many?'

'Two.'

'Definitely SS?'

'SD.'

The SD was the *Sicherheitsdienst*, the intelligence branch of Himmler's vast organisation, SS people with nicer accents and broader minds.

'You think the passengers on my boat were SD, too? The *Brigadeführer*? The others?'

'I've no idea, *Herr Kapitän*. I suggest you ask.'

The visitors were waiting in an office down the corridor as Stefan limped in through the door. Otto had supplied Stefan with a set of clothes, including a handsome pair of slippers. The trousers were slightly too short and the shirt was tight across the chest but he was glad not to be facing these men still wrapped in a blanket.

'*Kapitän* Portisch?'

The older of the two men behind the desk waved him into the waiting chair. He was medium height, black hair carefully parted on the left. There was a deep weariness in his eyes though something close to a smile lurked around the fleshiness of his mouth. He looked like a businessman up against a tight deadline rather than a spy patrolling the ramparts of the Reich. To Stefan's surprise, he wasn't in uniform.

He didn't offer a name or a handshake or even a *Heil Hitler*. Neither did he bother to introduce his companion, a younger man who was evidently present to take notes. Otto left the office with the murmured promise of coffee, shutting the door behind him. The man behind the desk turned his attention to Stefan.

'You'll know why we're here, I imagine?'

'Yes.'

'Do you have anything to say? Anything that might be helpful?'

Stefan held the man's gaze. He realised he'd seen this face before, maybe a photo in a paper, maybe a glimpse in a newsreel. He was a big player in Berlin, tugged along in Himmler's boiling wake. Walter something? Stefan would settle for that.

'I was captain of U-boat number 2553,' he said. 'It was one of the new *Elektro* boats. I'm afraid these boats are shit. They don't work properly. This one killed my entire crew.'

'Except you, *Kapitän*. Would you care to explain that?'

Stefan pondered the question. Luck? Chance? A wave that came from heaven and spared him the fate of everyone else on the boat?

'I jumped,' he said. 'Into the dark.'

'And here you are.'

'Yes.'

'Alive.'

'Yes.'

'For now.'

Stefan nodded. When the next question came – were you the last off the submarine? – he nodded. Traditions die hard. It was his job to get the rest of the crew off first. Only then did he climb the ladder to the conning tower.

'Leaving no one else in the boat?'

'I didn't say that.'

'Then what do you mean?'

'I mean there was no one else alive down there.'

'Really? Then tell me more.'

Stefan detected a spark of amusement in the face across the table. Thus far the conversation was an artful *pas de deux*, orchestrated by this powerful apparatchik from Berlin with his lazy eyes and tapping fingers. Stefan had already decided that his best hope lay in telling the truth. Anything else would diminish him, if not in these men's eyes then certainly in his own.

'The boat was breaking up,' Stefan said. 'There was only myself and the *Brigadeführer* left.'

'Johann Huber?'

'Indeed.'

'So what happened?'

Stefan described the earlier incident with Huber pulling a gun on him. At that point Huber had wanted himself and his men off the submarine first. He'd presumed there were life rafts available, some means of getting away.

'Why did that matter?'

'Because it turned out he couldn't swim. There was a struggle. One of my men knocked him out. I took the gun.'

'And later? When everyone had gone?'

'He asked me to shoot him.'

'Rather than drown?'

'Yes.'

'So what did you do?'

'I said no, at first.'

'Why did you say that?'

'Because it wasn't my job to kill people like that. Not in cold blood.'

'But you've spent this war in a U-boat, *Kapitän*. You must have killed hundreds of people, maybe thousands.'

'That's true.'

'So what's the difference?'

'They were the enemy.'

'And Huber? You're telling me he was a friend?'

'He was a German. That made him a comrade.'

'I see.' He steepled his fingers and half closed his eyes. 'Huber came from München. He was a Bavarian. I doubt he ever learned to swim.'

Stefan shrugged. He didn't know what to say. The truth, he told himself. Just stick to the facts.

'We didn't have much time,' he said. 'The boat was rolling. If it went over, that was the end of both of us.'

'And so you killed him? Shot him?'

'I did.'

'And left him there?'

'Of course.'

'And what happened to the rest of Huber's men?'

'They got off earlier. In fact, I sent them out first.'

'I see.' He steepled his fingers again. 'So you were the last to leave?'

'Yes.'

Stefan described fighting his way up the ladder to the conning tower. The storm was beyond belief. He'd never seen waves like it.

'But you still jumped?'

'Of course. I had no choice.'

'And plainly survived.'

'Indeed. As you can see.'

'Which makes you very lucky, no?'

Stefan didn't answer. This, he knew, was the crux of the story. Somehow he'd clambered ashore, made it off the beach, scaled the cliff, stayed intact. What next?

'I suspect you found somewhere to shelter.'

'That's true.'

'You were injured but you were alive. You had no idea what had happened to the rest of your crew. You were still their *Kapitän*. You were still in uniform. You were still responsible for those men. Why didn't you try to find them? Help them? Do your duty?'

'I knew they were dead.'

'How?'

'People from the village told me.'

'When?'

'Later.'

'But later's no good, *Herr Kapitän*. I want to know why you did nothing when you got ashore.'

'I couldn't.' Stefan briefly touched his leg. 'I was badly injured.'

'But, even so, you could have summoned some official, the police maybe, asked them to contact us. You knew you were on a special mission. You knew there was a special consignment aboard. You *knew*. And yet you did nothing.'

'That's true.'

'Good. You admit it. So tell me why.'

This was the point of no return and both men knew it. This was the moment, deep down, that Stefan had been dreading for weeks. Duty demanded a certain course of action. And Stefan had done nothing. *Nichts*.

'I'd had enough,' he said at last. 'I was finished.'

'With what, *Herr Kapitän*?'

'With everything.' Stefan made a vague gesture with his right hand, all the more hopeless because it felt like an act of surrender. 'I was finished with the war, the regime, all the killing, all the dying, all the propaganda, all the lying, I'd had enough. If you think that's cowardice, you're probably right. If you're saying I should have done more for my men, for you, for the Reich, you're undoubtedly right. But I'd had enough. I fought the war from the first day. I did well. That's a matter of fact. Check my record. I served on three submarines. Lots of sinkings. They were the Happy Times. I loved them.'

'Of course, *Herr Kapitän*. Winning's easy. Everyone knows that. It's the years that follow that really matter. These doubts of yours? This . . .' he frowned, '. . . exhaustion? You think you're unique? You think you're the only one to suffer?'

'Not at all. We all suffered on that boat, all my crew. None of us believed in the war any more. We all knew that Hitler was a madman, that he'd take us all down, that there'd be nothing left. But I was the only survivor. So maybe that's why it was tougher.'

'You mean they were spared the decision? The decision you took? The decision to turn your back on it all?'

'Yes.'

'And if they'd survived, would they have done what you did?'

'I don't know. I doubt it.'

'Why?'

'Because I was lucky. I fell among strangers. And they were kind to me.'

'So we understand.' A look of puzzlement had settled on his face. 'And what about Huber? Do you think he'd lost faith in the war as well?'

'Of course he had.'

'How do you know?'

'Because he was on his way out. We were taking him to Lisbon. He could have been in South America by now. What does that tell you about his loyalties? About his faith in the Fatherland?'

'You think he was deserting?'

'Desertion is a big word.'

'Of course it is. Be honest, *Herr Kapitän*.'

'Then, yes, I do. The man was a deserter, an escapee. They all were.'

'And you?'

'Me? You want the truth?'

'Yes, please.'

'Then the answer's yes, again.'

'You're a deserter?'

'Yes.' Stefan smiled. 'And proud of it.'

There was silence. Then came a soft tap at the door. It was Otto. He was carrying a tray.

'Coffee,' he announced.

They took the coffee in silence. The younger of the two SD men did the pouring. Stefan noticed that his boss took three lumps of sugar. While he was waiting for a refill, he extended a hand across the desk.

'My name is Schellenberg,' he said. 'Walter Schellenberg.'

Stefan nodded, shook his hand, said nothing. Of course. Walter Schellenberg. The favoured man in Himmler's inner circle. The intelligence genius who was said to go riding with Admiral Canaris every morning the two of them happened to be in Berlin. Canaris had been an officer in the *Reichsmarine* in the thirties until Hitler made him head of the *Abwehr*, the Army's intelligence service. He'd been another regular visitor to the naval college at Flensburg.

Stefan was aware that Schellenberg was watching him. In

some ways, not entirely unpleasant, this exchange had been like an audition or a job interview, a careful establishment of the facts coupled with an equally careful appraisal of exactly how well *Kapitän* Portisch could handle himself. The suspicion that his life probably depended on the outcome wasn't lost on Stefan but so far the process had been far more agreeable than he'd ever expected. This man didn't answer to the normal SS stereotype. He was sophisticated. He was nimble. He radiated an effortless charm. He was no Huber.

Stefan wanted to ask him a question while the atmosphere was so relaxed.

'What did those men bring aboard?' he said. 'What were we taking to Lisbon?'

'You mean why were you risking your lives?'

'Yes.'

Schellenberg took a sip of coffee. Then he used the napkin on the tray to dab his mouth.

'The SS emptied most of the galleries in Berlin. I gather some of the better stuff ended up in your torpedo compartment, carefully boxed of course. Then there'd be silverware, jewellery, all the usual trinkets.'

'And this would end up where?'

'In a bank vault, I imagine. These weren't the kind of people to hang art on their walls. They needed bargaining power once they got to Lisbon. It was your job to deliver it.'

Stefan nodded, said nothing. The news about their precious cargo was much as he'd expected.

Schellenberg took another mouthful of coffee.

'Tell me about your lady friend,' he said. 'I understand her name is Eva.'

'That's true.'

'Did you know her before you came ashore?'

'Of course not.'

'Then this is a young relationship, no? A matter of weeks? Maybe less?'

'Yes.'

'And all the better for that? Passionate? Complete?'

Stefan wasn't sure about 'complete'. He assumed Schellenberg was asking whether or not they'd had sex. 'Complete' sounded impossibly coy.

'She means a great deal to me,' Stefan said. 'I don't want her to come to any harm.'

'You think we're that crude?' Schellenberg looked briefly pained. 'You really think we'd apply that kind of pressure?'

'I'd hope not. But I imagine that depends on what you might want.'

'From you, *Herr Kapitän*?'

'I assume so.'

'Then ask yourself this. You're me. You're sitting here behind this desk. Every man has his price and just now it's my job to establish yours. You've had a good war, a very good war. Your people in Berlin speak very highly of you. That's why you were selected for this mission. That's why you ended up with Huber. I think I understand what's happened since. You've lost faith in this war of ours. You no longer want to be part of it. This is a sentiment, dare I say, that's more widely shared than you might imagine. The only difference is that you found you could do something about it. Not because you plotted or ran away but because events put you in the house of this woman and she became something special to you. From where I'm sitting, *Herr Kapitän*, you owe a very great deal to that storm. Am I right?'

'Yes.' Stefan felt like applauding. Perfectly put, he thought.

'My colleague's name is Herr Erwin Busch.' Schellenberg nodded at the younger man beside him. 'He's here because I trust him and because he's exceptionally good at what he does. As it happens he also comes from Hamburg. I suspect you'll have much in common.'

Stefan wondered whether the introduction should be sealed with a handshake. So far, Busch hadn't moved. Then he put down his pencil and smiled.

'Wandsbeck,' he said. 'Hansa Schüle. Then the university.'

Stefan had had friends at the university, many of them. He asked Busch how old he was.

'Twenty-three.'

'We all look older, *Herr Kapitän*.' It was Schellenberg. 'Under that beard I happen to know you're only twenty-four.'

'You were in Hamburg when the raids came? When the city burned?' Stefan was still looking at Busch.

'No, thank God.'

'Your parents?'

'Survived,' Busch said. 'They're still alive.'

'And the rest of your family?'

'An uncle and an aunt died. They lived in Hammerbeck, down by the canals. They were lovely.' He paused. 'Where did you grow up?'

'Hammerbeck.'

'And?'

'All gone.'

'Dead?'

'Yes. Except my sister-in-law. She's paralysed for life.'

'I'm sorry.'

Stefan looked at him for a moment and then shrugged.

'It's happened to thousands. Tens of thousands. Hundreds of thousands. Millions if you include what's been happening in the east. And for what?'

There was a long silence. Herr Busch was looking at his pad. Then Schellenberg checked his watch and leaned forward over the desk.

'I have to be back in Berlin by tomorrow morning. My plane must leave by seven this evening. Young Erwin here has a proposal for you. If for whatever reason you decline this proposal, you will be shot tomorrow morning for desertion and for killing a senior member of the SS. The arrangements are already in hand. If you are happy to agree to this proposal, and if you play the role we have in mind for you, then the rest of your life will be your own.'

Schellenberg was on his feet now. Stefan gazed up at him. A proposal? A role? This was a major surprise.

'And Eva?' he said.

'Eva will be waiting for you.' He buttoned his jacket. 'Afterwards.'

15

Gómez and Diego drove back up the coast to Ensenada. Diego had been thinking hard about auto thefts. Donovan wasn't the only man in Mexico who'd spotted the booming US market for second-hand cars and there was now a regular supply of stolen vehicles making the journey north across the border. This latest wave of thefts hadn't so far attracted much interest from the authorities but recently, after political pressure, the police had got themselves organised. A special unit had been established and Diego knew someone who knew someone who was supplying regular fucks for the guy in charge. His name was Carlos and – to Gómez's deep satisfaction – he was based in Ciudad Juarez.

When they got to Ensenada, Diego dropped Gómez downtown. He'd go back to his office in the police station and make some calls. When Gómez asked when they'd next meet, Diego told him seven thirty. Same bar as last night.

It was nearly five o'clock. Gómez strolled towards the waterfront. He had a couple of hours to kill and after last night's drinking the cogs in his brain were finally meshing again. In Diego's place, he wasn't sure he'd have been quite so brutal with Francisca's sister but Mexican cops had always enjoyed a certain reputation and you couldn't argue with the results. Violence, like it or not, sometimes kicked open doors that would otherwise have stayed tight shut. No way would Gabriela have helped otherwise.

Twenty minutes later he was on the promenade watching kids swimming off a bunch of rocks. These had to be kids from the poorer side of town, lean brown bodies, a grin for the watching stranger, absolutely no fear. They splashed among the drift of rubbish, occasionally collapsing with a yell and then floating face down, playing dead. Winning the game depended on keeping your nerve. The one who could hold his breath the longest, not a flicker of movement, would be the champion. Neat, thought Gómez. Keeping your nerve among all the shit. Just like real life.

After some minutes, the sun on his face, Gómez became aware of another spectator. He was slim, carefully dressed – new-looking black chinos, scarlet waistcoat. It was hard to guess his age – late twenties? Early thirties? Older? – and there was just a hint of make-up on the smoothness of his face. He had a little dog on a lead, a white poodle, and the mutt looked as groomed as its owner. The kids obviously knew him. One shouted his name, Ramón, and spun round to wiggle his ass at him. The other kids laughed and started to do the same. Ramón acknowledged the chorus line with a lazy flutter of his hand. Painted nails. Five-dollar sunshades. The full rig.

Gómez had stepped back from the water and was about to leave when a jeep arrived. It was battered and dusty, dents in the bodywork, a long crack in the windshield. Once it might have belonged to the military but now it was occupied by a couple of guys with private business to transact. They were well-built, in shape, heavily muscled under the tight T-shirts. The guy behind the wheel had shaved his head, the other was wearing a black bandana. They parked the jeep and approached Ramón. There was no foreplay, no conversation, no warning push, just a savage flurry of violence – fists and heavy boots – that brought Ramón to his knees, his face wrecked, pleading for his life.

'*Maricón*,' one of them jeered, kicking him in the belly.

Ramón folded under the blow, the air whistling from his lungs, and he tried to protect his head with his hands while the dog yapped and barked and did his best to protect his master.

It was the dog that did it for Gómez. He walked across, taking his time. The guy with no hair saw him coming, warned his partner to stop. The two men turned round to confront Gómez. Their *barrio* Spanish was too fast for Hector to understand but he didn't need a translation. Stand back, *amigo*. Mind your own fucking business. Faggots deserve what they get.

Gómez shook his head. He'd never let any man intimidate him and he didn't intend to start now. With a jerk of his head back towards the jeep, he suggested they leave. One of them stepped forward, pushed Gómez in the chest. Ramón was still on his knees, staring at the blood on his hands, on his jeans, trickling across the sidewalk. He was crying.

'*Vete a la mierda*.' Fuck off.

Gómez and the driver were nose to nose. The guy's eyes were bloodshot and his breath stank.

'You smell worse than an animal,' Gómez said in English.

The guy understood. He took a tiny step back and swung at Gómez. The blow went nowhere. Gómez barely felt it. His big hand went out, his fingers locking on to the man's throat, his thumb and forefinger on the pressure points beneath his ears.

He began to squeeze. Hard. The guy's eyes were popping. He was struggling for breath. Then his *compadre* arrived, circling to get a clean kick at Gómez, but Gómez had been here before. He knew exactly how to use the driver as a shield, as a buffer, while all the time increasing the pressure on the man's neck, cutting off the supply of blood to his brain.

The driver was frightened now. Gómez could see it in his eyes. He hadn't been expecting this. So sudden, so practised, so efficient. Gómez looked at him, aware that his world was changing fast. First grey, then – all too suddenly – nothing but darkness. His head lolled back, a baby in Gómez's arms. Gómez let him fall to the sidewalk, hearing the crack of bone as his shaved skull hit the paving stones, then spun round. The other guy had the chance for a clean shot. Gómez took the blow on the side of his chin. His brain exploded, pain everywhere, then his vision cleared and he had time to duck the next swing. Off-balance, the guy was briefly vulnerable and Gómez helped himself. Two short jabs to the solar plexus, bam-bam, then a knee to his face as his body folded. Sprawled beside his partner, he began to throw up.

Gómez stepped back. He was breathing hard, way more than he should have been. Easy on the beer, he told himself. Maybe a little more exercise. Maybe even a proper workout. He was looking down at the guy with no hair, the one who'd attacked him first. He didn't appear to be moving. Then came a flurry of movement as a young woman came running along the promenade. She'd seen the fight. She'd come to help.

Gómez watched her as she went over to the body on the sidewalk. The man in the bandana was sitting up now, wiping vomit from his trousers, oblivious to everything else. Ramón was nursing his dog. Gómez knelt beside the woman. She was trying to find a pulse. Nothing. She put the back of her hand against the guy's open mouth. *Nada*. She looked up at Gómez and shook her head.

Gómez was suddenly aware that the kids in the water had fallen silent. He turned round to find them standing in the shallows, staring up at him. They'd seen the fight. They'd seen everything. They weren't smiling any more.

The one who had shown Ramón his backside slid his forefinger slowly across his scrawny throat. It was a question. When Gómez nodded he turned to the other kids.

'*Muerto*,' he said. Dead.

*

To Stefan's relief, Erwin Busch turned the second interview into a conversation. He had an easy style, a light touch. Not once did he refer to Schellenberg's parting threat of execution, should Stefan decline to co-operate with whatever plan they'd hatched. On the contrary, he seemed already to have assumed that Stefan would prefer to live rather than die, an assumption he coupled to the woman he'd left behind in the village by the sea.

'Otto has met your friend. We understand she speaks English.'

'She does. That's how we got by.'

'And afterwards? You'll learn Spanish?'

'I'd like to. If there is an afterwards.'

'There will be,' he said with a smile. 'You have my word.'

'You're the one making the decision?'

'No, you are. But the decision will be easy. Believe me.'

Stefan wanted details. He needed to find out exactly what

his role in this plan involved. Erwin nodded. He wanted to know whether Stefan ever made up stories as a kid. Stefan thought hard about the proposition. Finally, he said that he and his elder brother used to invent little plays at Christmastime, entertainments for their parents. When they were young, the plays were based on old fairy tales, the Brothers Grimm, and other books their mother used to read them. Later, once Hitler had come to power, they'd dream up little adventures with settings in the neighbourhood. The men in the brown shirts, he added, were always the losers, especially the local *Blockwart* who spied on all the families in the apartment buildings and reported them for minor breaches of regime discipline.

'We had that, too, in Wandsbeck,' Erwin said. 'The man was an oaf. Really stupid. No one took him seriously. Not at first.' He paused. 'Your father, especially, must have been pleased.'

'With what?'

'With your entertainments. I understand he had no time for the regime.'

It was true. Stefan's father had worked all his life in the shipyards. He loved American jazz and practised smoky riffs on his saxophone whenever he got the chance. His heart was with the workers and, at first, when the Nazis were producing thousands of jobs after the grim years of little food and a worthless currency, he'd reserved judgement about whatever might happen next. But then had come the huge rallies, and the bully boys, and the city-wide pogroms against the Jews, and after that he regarded Hitler as a virus, breeding a terrible disease that was turning Germany into a country run by gangsters.

'You're right,' Stefan said. 'My father hated the regime. How come you know so much about my family?'

'Because we made it our business to find out.'

'But they're dead. My mother, my father, Werner, all of them.'

'We ask around. It's not a hard thing to do. You were the golden boy in the neighbourhood. Iron Cross First Class? Not once but *twice*? People remember such things.'

Stefan wondered whether to feel flattered but decided the compliment was genuine. He liked this man. Under any other circumstances they'd be sitting in some bar by now, sharing a beer or two.

'Your plan,' Stefan said. 'Tell me about your plan.'

'Of course. I'm sorry. Let's go back to the entertainments.'

For reasons Stefan might one day understand, Erwin explained, they had to invent an addition to Stefan's family, and for this to happen, for this to be plausible, Stefan would have to do much of the work himself.

'Addition?' Stefan was lost. 'You mean someone who doesn't exist?'

'Not in your family, no.'

'But a real person?'

'Yes.'

'Like who?'

'His name's Solomon, Sol for short. In real life he's Jewish through and through but we're going to change some of that because in our version he's going to be only half-Jewish.'

'Why?'

'Because his mother was your mother. Which makes you his half-brother.'

'I see.' Stefan was fighting to keep track. 'And does he have a name, this person?'

'He does.'

'A real name? In real life?'

'Of course.'

'What is it?'

'Sol Fiedler.'

Erwin paused to let this development sink in. A half-brother Stefan had never met in his life. Was this some kind of fantasy?

'Yes. That's exactly what it is. Except you have to believe it. More importantly, you have to believe it so much that you can make other people believe it.'

'Like who?'

'Like Herr Schellenberg for a start. And then the British.'

'You're sending me to England?' Stefan was out of his depth.

'Yes.' Erwin nodded. 'If you agree to go.'

They stopped for more coffee. Erwin left the office, locking the door behind him. By the time he came back, Stefan had begun to sense the faintest thread of logic behind this extraordinary suggestion. They want me to take this story to the English, he told himself. Indeed, I *am* this story, or at least part of it. For whatever reason was beyond him but what mattered just now was Erwin. He was the key player in this drama and Stefan knew he had no option but to trust the man.

He watched him pouring the coffee. He wanted to know more about Sol Fiedler. How could he possibly fit into the cramped third-floor apartment that Stefan had always called home? How come their paths had never crossed?

'Remind me when your parents got married.' Erwin passed a coffee across the desk.

'Nineteen hundred and four, 13 July.'

'And Werner? Your brother?'

'He came after the war. September 1919.'

'A year before you.'

'Fourteen months.'

'So why so long before your parents had children?'

'I don't know. Maybe they preferred it that way. They had no money. They wanted to give any child the best. And they did.'

'Good. Excellent. But maybe there's another explanation. Your mother was working at the university, am I right?'

'Yes. She was a secretary in the mathematics department. She always thought she was worth more than Hammerbeck.'

'Excellent. So why did she marry your father?'

'Because she loved him. He was a handsome man. He played the saxophone. He was a wonderful dancer. And a thinker, too.'

'Of course. Good. But she wasn't happy, your mother. Not *really* happy the way a newly married young girl should be. Maybe it was having no money. Maybe it was living in Hammerbeck. In any event, her head was turned.'

'Who by?' Stefan felt a tiny prickle of anger.

'A man called Dr Moshe Fiedler. Also at the university.'

'This man exists?'

'No, not in real life. But that doesn't matter because the Nazis have destroyed all records of Jewish academics at the university. Thank God for our more fervent brethren, eh? Poor human beings but wonderfully thorough when it comes to the paperwork.'

Stefan relaxed a little. Nicely put, he thought.

'So what happened to my mother?'

'She had an affair with Dr Moshe. She became pregnant. She couldn't hide it from your father because he was a man who took precautions so there was no way the baby could have been his. You can imagine the tensions between them, the trust

your mother had abused, the way your father tried to cope. He even offered to keep the baby but your mother said no. She wanted a new start. She wanted their own child.'

'But the baby came?'

'Of course.'

'So what happened?'

'Moshe took the baby. He really wanted your mother, too, but she was never going to let that happen. She wanted both of them out of her life. Why? Because she was determined to stay with your father. And so Dr Fiedler went to Berlin where he found himself a job and a wife.'

'And the young one?'

'The wife was happy to adopt him. As it happened, she even liked his name.'

'Sol.'

'Yes.'

'Sol Fiedler.'

'Yes.'

Stefan nodded, trying to absorb the news. His mother having an affair? His mother having a *child*? Playing any part in a fiction like this felt like a betrayal.

'There's more?' he asked.

'I'm afraid so. It takes your father years – more than a decade – to forgive your mother and make the baby she wants. Like everyone else, he goes to war. I understand he was in the Army.'

'That's true.'

'The infantry. In the trenches.'

'Also true.'

'So he goes away for four years and comes back a different man. The marriage is at last repaired. Werner is born. You come along. You grow up. You get older. You become aware that there are tensions in the family. That everything might not be quite right between your mother and father. Werner may be having the same thoughts but maybe not. And you know why? Because he's not as sensitive as you, and not as observant.'

Despite himself, Stefan laughed.

'Did you ever meet my brother?'

'Sadly not.'

'You didn't have to. He was exactly the way you describe him. Very intelligent. Very generous. But blind. And often deaf.'

'Good. Excellent. You join the Navy. You go to Flensburg. You go to sea on the square rigger the *Horst Wessel*. The war is coming. You know that. But Hamburg isn't far away and every spare moment, you get home.'

'To see my mother?'

'Yes. Especially your mother. Because you sense something about her. Maybe an emptiness, an inner loneliness. Then one day you come back to find your mother in tears. Your father is at work in the shipyard. She's alone in the kitchen. She's just received a letter from Berlin. And you know who the letter comes from?'

'Sol Fiedler.'

'Exactly. Your half-brother. And so you ask about the letter, about why your mother is so upset, and in the end she tells you everything. About the affair she had before you were born, about the baby she gave back to the father and about the life this child has had since.'

Stefan, despite himself, was doing the sums. This had to be 1938, the year before the war began. By then, Sol Fiedler would be thirty-two.

'So what's he doing? This half-brother of mine?'

'He's working at the KWI.'

'The what?'

'The Kaiser Wilhelm Institute. He's a physicist first, a metallurgist second. In his field, he's brilliant. He's winning prizes, publishing papers, getting himself recognised, getting himself *noticed*.'

'All this is true? This is the real Sol Fiedler?'

'Yes. By now he's married. A woman called Marta from Budapest. Also Jewish. But something isn't quite right because he's got to know about his past, about his real mother, about the world he's left behind in Hamburg. And you know what he wants to do? Before he flees like all the other Jewish scientists with a little money to their name? The ones who could get a job in England? Or a new life in America?'

'He wants to meet my mother.'

'He does, Stefan. And he'll also want to meet *you*.'

Stefan nodded. It was the first time Erwin had used his Christian name and it seemed to put the whole relationship on a new footing. They were suddenly complicit, co-conspirators in a fiction that doubtless had a purpose and would – if Stefan agreed to play along – save his life.

Stefan swallowed the last of his coffee. It was cold. He wanted to know whether he could have a little time to think about what Erwin had said.

'You mean to make your mind up?' Erwin asked.

'Yes.'

'Then the answer's yes. Of course you can. Shall we say an hour?'

'That would be fine.'

Erwin got to his feet and put the empty cups on the tray. About to leave the office, he paused.

'A word of warning, Stefan. If you say yes, then you pick up the story where I left it. Sol has to come to Hamburg. You two have to meet. There has to be something more than friendship between you. There has to be real trust, real kinship. Because Sol will be writing you letters. From England. From America. And he will be telling you certain things that will turn out to be important.'

'He writes these letters to me?'

'He does.'

'So where are they?'

'They burned in the firestorm,' Erwin smiled down at him. 'Like everything else.'

*

Hector Gómez was arrested within minutes of leaving the waterfront. The dead man's accomplice limped to the main road and flagged down a passing police car. That was bad enough. Worse still, it turned out that both of them were off-duty police, administering a little recreational justice. They'd known exactly when and where to find Ramón, and they considered themselves obliged to punish the *maricón* for taking too close an interest in the kids in the water. Mexico's youth needed protection against the attentions of people like Ramón. And Ensenada's finest had been only too happy to oblige.

Gómez sat in the back of the police car, wedged between two cops. Both of them had seen the damage he'd inflicted on their colleagues and although there was doubtless a beating awaiting him at the police station, for now they were content to stare out of the window. Twice he asked them whether they were interested in taking witness statements – from the kids, for instance, or the woman who'd come running to help – but both times they'd ignored him.

At the police station, word of the incident had somehow preceded their arrival. Gómez, handcuffed, was escorted through the filthy tiled space inside the main door that served as an enquiry desk and hustled up four flights of steps. The top landing was lined with cops and plainclothes detectives on both sides. Most simply spat on him. A couple landed a blow or two. One tried to kick him. Head down, Gómez kept walking. Once they really started, he told himself, they'd need a locked bathroom, preferably soundproof.

The Bureau could be rough when required but he'd heard some terrible stories from south of the border. As well as a lavatory brimming with excrement, most of them featured an assortment of objects destined for various orifices. Gómez knew enough about interrogation techniques to expect an hour or so in a cell by himself, quietly contemplating the excitements to come. That way, you'd frighten yourself half to death before the questions even began.

It didn't happen. At the end of the corridor, Gómez found himself in a biggish office. Maps of the city papered one wall. The windows in the other offered a view of the mountains beyond the port. An officer sat behind the desk. Mexicans love uniforms but this guy, thought Hector, belonged in an opera: the enormous shoulder boards, the crisp olive shirt, the line of medals on the heavily buttoned jacket, plus the inevitable moustache.

'You killed one of our men, *señor*. Not good.'

'I intervened in a fight. They were beating another guy to death. There's a difference.'

'They were arresting him, *señor*. Because he'd become aggressive. Here in Mexico, we call that self-defence. The moment he stops resisting, we put him in a car and it's over.'

Gómez didn't bother taking the argument any further. He wanted no part in this charade.

The officer asked him for ID. Gómez said he wasn't carrying any.

'We understand you work for the US Army. Is that true?'

Gómez didn't reply. Diego, he thought. Diego's already on top of this.

'I'm American,' he admitted at last. 'And, yes, I work for the Army.'

'As what?'

'An investigator.'

'Where?'

'I'm afraid I can't answer that.'

'Why not?'

'I can't answer that either.' Gómez paused. 'We have a presence in Tijuana,' he said. 'A branch of the Foreign service. I need representation.'

'We can find you a lawyer.'

'Thank you.'

'A Mexican lawyer.'

'I'd prefer someone from the legation.'

'You don't trust us? You don't think we have the right to decide your representation? After you've killed one of our men?'

'He fell badly. Cracked his head.'

280

'His fault, then? Is that what you're saying?'

'I'll wait for the autopsy. As I'm sure you will.'

'That might not be wise.'

Gómez nodded, said nothing. Guys like these demanded the bended knee but they also respected people who could handle themselves.

The officer appeared to have lost interest in the conversation. He was reading one of a number of documents on his desk. At length the door opened, and a younger man appeared.

'Take him away.' The officer didn't even look at the newcomer.

Gómez got to his feet. He must have a buzzer, he thought. Probably under the desk. He's taken a good look at me. And now he'll come to some kind of decision.

The cells were in the basement, as filthy as everything else. There was a tiny window high in one wall that wouldn't open and a concrete plinth where a small man might be able to lie down. Gómez didn't even try. He sat on the plinth, his elbows on his knees, tracking a cockroach as it scurried across the cracked tiles. The place stank of sweat and urine and there was a puddle in the corner where someone had pissed. There was still daylight in the window, just, but within the hour the cell would be in darkness. No light. No water. No blanket. No bucket. Nothing.

Replaying the fight in his mind, Gómez thought suddenly of Agard Beaman. Was that why he'd done what he'd done? Was that why he'd gone to Ramón's defence? He didn't know but he guessed at the very least that the people upstairs would be carefully weighing what to do next. If they troubled themselves with the facts, and if they sensed any advantage in returning the gringo to his masters across the border, then it was just possible that they might let him go. Otherwise, he was in for a real taste of Mexican justice.

For longer than was healthy he thought about the rest of his life in a cell like this, or worse still in some overcrowded jail where every inmate demanded a piece of you. Places like that existed in the States, especially in the South, and he'd seen grown men – men for whom he had some respect – reduced to ghosts by their years inside. At length, he got to his feet and padded across to the door of the cell, meaning to hammer for attention, for water, for some acknowledgement that he still existed. Then he realised that this would be exactly what they wanted, evidence that he was cracking, that he was afraid. And so, in the thickening light, he returned to the plinth. In vain, he searched for the cockroach but, sensibly, it had gone.

16

Stefan wondered whether the bar down by the harbour was Schellenberg's idea. When Erwin returned to the office, Stefan had said yes to his plan. He'd play along with the story. In fact, he'd already had an idea or two of his own. Erwin had nodded his approval. Wise decision he'd said. And one that deserves a modest celebration. And so here they were, at the back of the bar, with two plainclothes men from the legation just a table away. Stefan knew they were armed because Erwin had told him so in the car on the way down. Any bid to escape, Erwin warned with a hint of regret, and he'd be shot.

Stefan had no intention of escaping. He could still barely walk. And so now, with plates of tapas on order and a beer at his elbow, Stefan eased his leg beneath the table and picked up the story of Sol Fiedler.

'I don't know what he looks like,' he said at once.

'Here.'

Stefan found himself gazing at a sheaf of photos. They showed a man with receding hair and a fondness for open-neck shirts. He looked far older than his years. He had a kind face, gentle eyes, and in three of the photos he had his arm round a plump woman in a check dress. She was smiling at the camera. Her smile was uncertain. All three photos had been taken in a kitchen. Huge refrigerator. Glimpses of cactus and bright sunshine through the nearby window.

Stefan turned the photo over. July 1944.

'This is Sol now?'

'Yes.'

'Where were they taken?'

'In America.'

'Does he like it there?'

'He loves it there.'

'And her?' Stefan nodded at the woman.

'Less so. I think she misses Budapest.'

'This is his wife? Marta?'

'Yes.'

'And you're in touch with these people?'

'Yes.'

'How?'

Erwin didn't answer. Despite the setting and the hospitality there were clearly limits to this conversation.

The tapas arrived. Stefan had always adored seafood. Huge gambas in a dressing spiced with cayenne and splinters of roasted garlic. Smaller clams tasting of lemons and the ocean. He reached for the basket of bread, took a swallow of beer, and then his eyes returned to the photos. He'd imagined someone bigger, more sure of himself, more commanding, but he could live with the real thing.

'He looks a nice man,' he said. 'Maybe one day we'll meet.'

Erwin said nothing. He was busy spearing one of the gambas. Then he wiped his mouth with the napkin.

'Sol Fiedler arrives in Hamburg,' he said. 'It's early 1939. How long is he staying?'

'Two weeks.' Stefan had thought this through. 'He says he has money. He says he's booked a room at the Atlantic Hotel in St Georg. The first time I meet him, he's invited me to the courtyard bar.'

'You've been inside the Atlantic?'

'Yes. A couple of times. Naval functions on both occasions.'

'So what happens with Sol? What do you make of him?'

Stefan was looking at the photos again, adjusting this story of his. An hour ago, he'd imagined they'd sunk a bottle of the hotel's excellent Gewürztraminer between them. Now he wasn't so sure. Sol Fiedler didn't look like a drinker.

'We have afternoon tea in the lounge,' he said. 'Just like the English.'

'And?'

'He tells me his story. I know most of it already from my mother but not about his plans to get out of Berlin.'

'You mean Germany.'

'Of course.'

'Do you ask him why?'

'I do. *Kristallnacht* happened everywhere. Berlin, Hamburg, all over. I was at sea at the time but my parents told me about it when I came back for Christmas.'

Kristallnacht. November the 9th 1938. Nazi thugs off the leash, looting and burning Jewish businesses and synagogues after the assassination of a German diplomat in Paris. Erwin, it turned out, had been in Hamburg at the time, a student at the university. Stefan was right. Thugs. *Untermenschen*.

'So how much does he tell you? Sol?'

'He says that he's been to get the permissions. He says it's tough. The regime will take everything they have, he and Marta, but he thinks it's worth it. Or, more precisely, he tells me he has no other choice. Friends of his are disappearing. Berlin is a big city but there's nowhere to hide.'

'Does he tell you where he's going?'

'To England.'

'To do what?'

'He doesn't say. When I ask him he says he doesn't have a job to go to. Just contacts.'

'And a reputation?'

'Yes. He's well-known in the field. Partly word of mouth but mainly because he's contributed a number of papers to various publications.'

'Is that an assumption on your part?'

'I'm afraid so.'

'Excellent. You're good at this. As we thought you might be.'

Stefan accepted the compliment with a nod. Something had occurred to him.

'Does Marta know about me?'

'No.'

'Really?'

'Yes. It's important she knows nothing. This is something he keeps to himself.'

'In case they check with her?'

'Of course. Here. Take a look at these.'

From the same envelope as the photos came a sheet of specialist scientific periodicals in which Sol Fiedler's work had appeared. Many of them had been published by the *Deutsche Physikalische Gesellschaft*. Stefan quickly scanned the list, then looked up.

'These are genuine?'

'Yes.'

He nodded. Strange, he thought. Grafting himself on to the life of someone so real.

'You need me to memorise them?'

'A couple maybe. You need to know enough about the man to sound credible but not too much. Otherwise you're going to sound coached.'

Coached. Perfect. Stefan sipped at his beer.

'So where does all this end? Who do I have to impress?'

'Convince would be a better word.'

'Convince, then. Are we still talking about the English?'

Erwin wouldn't answer. Instead, he wanted to know what kind of impression Sol made on him that afternoon they met at the Atlantic Hotel.

'He was older, obviously. I'm nineteen. He's going to be . . .' he frowned, looking at the photos, remembering Sol's year of birth, '. . . thirty-five. I'm surprised by that because he looks even older and maybe I'm expecting someone much younger, like Werner, my brother.'

'Do you like Sol?'

'I do, yes. He's very easy to talk to and he wants to be my friend.'

'Why's that?'

'I don't know. I'm asking myself the same question. Maybe he wants to tidy up the German end of his life before he leaves. We're half-brothers, stepbrothers, whatever.'

'So what do you talk about? Apart from Berlin?'

'Me. He wants to know what I'm up to. My mother has mentioned the Navy in a letter she wrote to him. He wants to find out more about that. He wants to know why I joined up, what it's like to be in a submarine, what will happen to me when war comes.'

'He thinks war's coming?'

'We both do. A short war, but a war nonetheless.'

'Against the English?'

'No. First of all against the Poles. Maybe then Hitler will stop.'

Erwin picked up one of the photos and studied it for a moment.

'He looks very Jewish, this new relative of yours. Are you aware of that?'

'Yes.'

'Does it make you feel uncomfortable?'

'At the hotel, you mean?'

'Yes.'

Stefan sat back in his chair, aware of the escorts watching them both. He hadn't thought about this. He tried to visualise himself and this middle-aged Jewish scientist in the courtyard bar, surrounded by men and women who were feasting on the regime. Erwin was right. For the first time he realised that the Atlantic Hotel was no place for the likes of Sol Fiedler.

'OK,' Stefan said. 'This is the way it really happened. I'm sitting in the Atlantic Hotel, just like I described, but you're right, it doesn't feel good and there's something else, too. The place costs a fortune. And whatever he says to the contrary, I know that Sol has no money because the Nazis were taking everything off the Jews. So why waste money you don't have? Why take the risk?'

'And the answer?'

'The answer is he's lying. He's not staying there at all.

He's staying at some fleapit place further out of town he can just about afford. But he wants to impress me and he wants something else, too. He's a stubborn man. He's a proud man. He wants to leave Germany with his head held high. And I like that. I like that a lot. The people at the other tables, the people watching us, don't frighten him. Not in the least. He's made his decision. He's got control of his life. He's turning his back on all this madness. He's determined to make a new start.'

'Just like you.'

Stefan acknowledged the point with the faintest smile.

'It must be in the genes,' he said. 'Maybe that's why I paid for the tea.'

*

They came for Gómez in the middle of the night. He was still sitting on the plinth, his eyes open, his huge hands knotted in his lap. Hearing the approach of footsteps in the corridor outside, he didn't move. Then came the clank of keys and a muttered curse before the door opened and a dim light threw the shadow of two men into the cell.

Gómez didn't resist. They gestured him to his feet, then handcuffed him. Only upstairs, heading for the street, did he ask where they were taking him. One of them spoke English, heavily accented but OK.

'Nice hotel,' he said. 'Not this pile of shit.'

A battered old van was waiting at the kerbside. Gómez clambered into the back. One of the escorts sat beside him, the other joined the driver in the front. The exhaust was blown on the van and they deafened one area after another as they headed out of town. At three in the morning there was no traffic. Gómez sat back, staring out of the window. An old man asleep on the sidewalk. A silhouette behind a curtain at a first-floor window. Cats prowling the shadows. Enjoy, Gómez told himself. This may be the last time you get to see the outside world for a while.

Finally, the driver slowed. It was a prison. It had to be. The looming bulk of the building behind high concrete walls topped with barbed wire. Armed soldiers at the gate. Some fucking hotel.

He was processed through a series of offices. Most of the staff were asleep. He gave his name and address and once caught sight of his passport in the hands of the guy who appeared to be in charge. He was comparing Gómez to his mugshot. Already he had a three-day growth of stubble. In a couple of months, he thought, I'll be unrecognisable.

'Lawyer?' he said. '*Abogado?*'

He might have been asking for a four-course meal. The guy behind the desk didn't even register the question. No shrug. No apology. No explanation. Nothing.

'You have water? *Agua?*'

Again, nothing. At length, a shouted command brought another man in from the neighbouring office. He was huge, bursting out of his Army fatigues. He stood behind Gómez's chair. Gómez could feel the heat radiating off his body. The guy behind the desk nodded at the corridor, muttered something Gómez didn't catch, then looked him full in the face. He, too, spoke English.

'Enjoy yourself, Señor Gómez,' he said. 'No one will be watching.'

Enjoy yourself? Gómez got to his feet, mystified. The guard made to push him towards the door but Gómez shook him off. Out in the corridor were two warders. They flanked Gómez as the guard led the way through a maze of badly lit passageways, past cell after cell. He was familiar with the soundtrack that went with a big prison at this time of night. The mutter of men talking to themselves. Sudden demented cries. A cackle of laughter as some lunatic warmed the chill of his cell with a private joke. Finally, they paused at a flight of steps. Another basement, thought Gómez. The first circle of hell.

At the bottom of the stairs, the corridor was in semi-darkness and there was a heavy smell of shit. Gómez could feel the greasiness of the stone slabs underfoot. At the end of the corridor, last door on the left, they stopped. The guard produced a bunch of keys, wrestled with the lock. Finally the door swung open. The guard stepped back, sweating in the half-darkness. He nodded into the cell.

'*Buenas noches. Que duermas bien,*' he said. Night, night. Sweet dreams. One of the warders laughed.

Gómez stepped into the cell and the door banged shut behind him. It was pitch-black. For a long moment, he could see nothing. Then he made out the shape of two plinths, one either side of the cell. He reached out and touched the walls. Flaking plaster, soaking wet. From the ceiling, hanging on a flex, was a single bulb, no switch. Then he became aware of a body humped on one of the plinths. He stared at the shape for a moment. Dead? Alive? Asleep? Watching? Waiting? He hadn't a clue.

'*Hola,*' he muttered. Nothing.

This was bad. This was worse than bad. These people could

do anything with him. For ever. He lowered himself on to the plinth. At least he could stretch his body full-length. He pillowed his head on his arms, closing his eyes, wondering whether sleep would ever come. Mercifully, it did.

Hours later, he awoke. The light was on above his head. He stared up at it, moved his head a little. Spanish names inches from his eye, scratched into the plaster. Felipe. Angel. Manuel. A roll-call of the damned. He rolled over, remembering the body on the other plinth, then froze. The face was puffy and swollen, thick lips, one eye half closed, scabs of blood above the other, but the smile was unmistakable. Ramón. The *maricón* whose life he'd saved.

*

After the bar, the escorts drove Stefan and Erwin back to the legation. On the upper floor was a room bigger than the rest. It appeared to be used for formal receptions. The ceilings were tall, with a big rose moulding around the chandelier, and there were thick gold curtains at the window. A framed photograph of the Führer hung over the ornate fireplace and another wall was dominated by a pair of crossed standards, complete with swastikas.

On a smallish table beside the window stood a decanter of something red, plus a couple of glasses. By now it was late, nearly midnight. They'd had more tapas at the harbourside bar and slowly the evening had taken a different direction. Stefan had evidently satisfied Erwin that he had the guile to invent this new presence in his life, to invest Sol Fiedler with all the tics and mannerisms that would make him real, to add light and shade to the bare bones of the rapidly ageing metallurgist in the photographs he'd seen. That had come as a surprise to Stefan, this slightly alarming ability to fabricate a story that had never happened, but what was even more of a shock was something that felt like a genuine rapport between himself and his guardian. He liked this young protégé of Schellenberg's. They had a great deal in common. And as the evening went on, the conversation ranged way beyond Sol Fiedler.

'You'd like some port?' Erwin had eased the glass stopper from the decanter. He poured two glasses. 'To peace,' he said.

No *Heil Hitler*. None of the usual Nazi gibberish. Just that. To peace.

If only, thought Stefan, lifting his glass. In the street, driving back, they'd been talking about the Jews again. As a kid back home in Hamburg, Jews had never really registered with Stefan. He knew Jews at school, even had the odd Jewish friend, kids he fooled around with in the summer when they swam in the canals, and it wasn't until he was fifteen that he realised that something he'd taken for granted had changed.

It was winter, snowing day after day, and the ice on the Alster thick enough for skating. A bunch of his friends had gone out on the ice. One of them was Jewish, obviously so, swarthy, plumper than the rest, and wobbly on his skates but always ready with a joke and a grin. Somehow he got detached from his mates and when he realised Daniel wasn't around, Stefan went looking for him. For a while he drew a blank. Then he spotted a figure sprawled on the ice.

It was Daniel. He was lying on his back, trying to struggle upright. His lower leg had been gashed in three places by skate blades and there was fresh blood against the whiteness of the ice.

At first, Daniel didn't want to talk about it. He was embarrassed. It was nothing. Just an accident. A couple of guys too busy or too careless to have seen him flat on his arse on the ice. But then, slowly, the real story came out.

How these men – much older, maybe even in their twenties – had seen him fall. How they'd circled him, taunted him, called him a fat kike. And how, before they sped off, they'd stamped on his legs with their skates until the blood flowed. Stefan had helped Daniel back to the shore, then back to his home in Wandsbeck. He'd respected Daniel's pleas not to mention the incident to his parents – both doctors – but what really stuck in his mind was something else. There had been hundreds of skaters on the ice that morning, and not one of them had stopped to help.

'Ugly,' Erwin had agreed in the car. 'We should have watched. We should have listened. All the clues were there. Instead we did nothing.'

'Because the times were good?'

'Of course they were. That was the whole point. Food in your belly. Nice uniforms. Whole countries falling over like skittles. Austria. The Sudetenland. The rest of Czechoslovakia. All ours for the asking. A tap on the door and in we went. Did the French make a fuss? No. Were the English going to stop us? *Nein*. And why? Because Hitler was a gangster of genius. He looked these people in the eye and he took their measure and then he helped himself. You knew it couldn't work but it did. You knew it shouldn't work but there it was. The spoils of war. Beg for something you get a kick in the teeth. Put a gun in someone's face, they'll give you anything. Never fails.'

'Until now.'

'*Ja*. Maybe.'

In the back of the car, Stefan had put Erwin's frankness down to the beer and the wine. They must have sunk a couple of bottles of Rioja between them. Now, he wasn't so sure. Maybe this, too, was part of the script. Either way, telling himself he had nothing to lose, he had to find out.

'You really think we'll get through this?' he asked. 'The British on the Rhine? Patton at Metz? Our people chased out of Brest? No more U-boat pens? Non-stop bombing at home? Entire cities wrecked? You really don't think it's over?'

'I know it's not.'

'You're serious?'

'I am. And you know why?' He was toying with his glass. 'Sol Fiedler.'

'How? How can that man make a difference?'

Erwin looked up. So far he'd been concentrating on the relationship between Stefan and this new half-brother who had stepped into his life. How they'd bonded. How they'd written to each other. How they'd kept in touch after Sol had made it to England, and then to the States. The letters had kept coming, full of domestic news from the Fiedlers' new home in Chicago until Pearl Harbor and America's abrupt entry into the war. After that, nothing.

'He went to a place in New Mexico,' Erwin said. 'Los Alamos. The people who work there call it the Hill.'

Stefan nodded. New Mexico was in the Southwest. Down near the border. That's all he knew.

'So what's he doing there? Sol?'

'They're building a bomb. An atomic bomb. A bomb like the world has never seen.'

Atomic bomb? Stefan had heard the phrase before. A weapon so secret no one dared talk about it. A weapon that came out of the same cupboard as the V-1 buzz bomb, and the V-2 rocket, and – God help us – the new *Elektro* subs.

'He's building a bomb? For the Americans?'

'He's one of hundreds of people, thousands of people, just like himself. This is what our leader calls Jewish science. People like Sol. Clever physicists. Men of genius. Men who've worked out what happens when you split the atom. Men we've frightened so badly that they've taken all their brains and their learning and their calculations and gone to join the enemy.'

'In Los Alamos.'

'*Ja*. On the Hill.'

Stefan reached for his glass. Bits of the puzzle were slowly slipping into focus.

'You're telling me we have this bomb?'

'Not quite. Not yet. But nearly.'

'And what will this bomb do?'

'It will wipe out whole cities. London? New York?' Erwin snapped his fingers. 'Gone.'

'Christ . . .' Stefan felt his blood icing. It wasn't clear how you'd get an atomic bomb to New York but he knew London because he'd been there as a naval cadet, and the thought of someone as psychotic as Hitler having access to a weapon like this was beyond his comprehension. 'Crazy,' he muttered. 'Insane.'

'I'm afraid you're right. But it's going to happen. The Americans have been ahead of us. They've been working with the British. But we're not far behind.'

'And Sol?'

'Sol helped make that possible. Without Sol, without that half-brother of yours, we wouldn't even be in the race.'

'He's been leaking secrets?'

'He has. Through Mexico. From there he has letters posted to ex-colleagues in Göttingen and Berlin. They're on the program. He knows what they want. His data has made all the difference.'

'You said not far behind. What does that mean?'

'It means months. At the most.'

'Months from what?'

'From testing it. And then using it.'

'And where is all this happening in Germany?'

'I can't tell you. Because I don't know.'

'And the Americans are even closer?'

'We think so, yes.'

'So they'll use it on us?'

'Yes. Unless they think we also have the bomb. In that case, no one pulls the trigger. And who knows? Maybe we're suddenly looking at peace.'

'On whose terms?'

'A very good question. At the moment we face unconditional surrender. You'll know that. They are Roosevelt's terms. Think about that. Unconditional. No ifs, no buts. We simply lay down our arms, open all the doors, and let these people in.'

'These people?'

'The Americans, the British . . .' Erwin looked briefly away, 'and the Russians.'

'Which is why we need the bomb.'

'Of course.'

'Which takes us back to Sol.'

Erwin nodded, and reached for the decanter. His capacity for alcohol, thought Stefan, is impressive. Maybe that's how he keeps the regime – the madness – at bay. By pickling his brains and his conscience in the name of a good night's sleep. And all paid for by the Reich. Neat.

Sol Fiedler. America.

Two years ago, before he became a *Kapitän*, Stefan had been serving as First Officer in another U-boat in what his *Kameraden* called the Great Turkey Shoot. *U-689* had been one of the VII Class: trusty, strong, dependable. They'd crossed the Atlantic and taken up station astride the shipping lanes in New York Bay. That first night they'd surfaced to await a target and Stefan remembered standing in the conning tower, dumbstruck by his introduction to the New World. Although war had come to America, there was no blackout. He could see cars on the coastal freeway, soaring hotels along the beach, funfairs, Ferris wheels, and further away the glow of the city itself reflected off the belly of the clouds. Now he described that moment to Erwin.

'It was so alive,' he said. 'So big. Everything was happening. Those people were naïve to keep the lights on. They had no idea what war was about. And there were so many of them. They were so *powerful*. How could we ever compete with a nation like that?'

Later in the voyage, they'd headed south to Cape Hatteras. Target after target went to the bottom, always silhouetted against the lights onshore. In all, they scored nine kills. The following year, a *Kapitän* with his own boat, Stefan had returned to the hunting grounds off the eastern seaboard. By now the Americans were beginning to catch up and the killing was tougher but they still returned to Lorient with a decent score. On the radio, President Roosevelt had described the Nazi U-boats as 'the rattlesnakes of the Atlantic' and so – a day away from Lorient – Stefan had surfaced at night and ordered one of the crew to paint a rattlesnake on the conning tower. Later the following day, back at last in Lorient, the boast had won an extra-loud cheer from welcome-home crowd.

'That was the Happy Time,' Stefan said. 'Before the tide turned.'

Erwin tipped his glass in salute. He seemed genuinely interested, genuinely impressed.

'You miss those days?'

'Yes. Of course. At sea you live in a world of your own. Your own rules, your own priorities. You depend on each other. You respect each other. And it has to be that way because otherwise you'll die. Often there isn't a Nazi among you, not a real carpet-eating crazy. You're just there to do your job, to do it well, to make it tough for the enemy, and to get back in one piece. That's why the last voyage went wrong from the start. Submariners are superstitious. We had strangers aboard, people we didn't much like. A lot of the crew thought we were cursed because of them and you know what? They were right.'

'That's why you hit the rocks? Killed the crew? Because of Huber and his little gang?'

'No. We hit the rocks because the boat was *Scheisse*. Because the design wasn't right. Because everything had been rushed. Because it was thrown together by people who didn't know what they were doing. In this war you can get away with a lot, believe me, but with engineering that bad, even the weather will find you out.' He paused a moment, reaching for the decanter.

'I just hope this bomb of yours has been thought through. Otherwise it's *Götterdämmerung* all over again . . .'

Stefan lifted his glass in a mock salute. Then another thought occurred to him, something else that didn't make much sense.

'This half-brother of mine,' he said, 'this brilliant scientist we drove out of Berlin. Why is he sending secrets back to a regime he hates?'

'The secrets aren't going to the regime. The data goes to people he trusts. Fellow scientists. Ex-colleagues.'

'But it's the same thing. Everyone bends the knee to the regime because they have to, because there's no choice unless you want to end up behind the wire.'

Erwin seemed to accept the point, one elegant finger circling the rim of his glass. Then he bent forward.

'It may not be that way,' he said softly.

'Why? How come?'

'Because there are people back in Germany who know the end is coming. People who know – at last – they have to act.'

'They tried,' Stefan pointed out. 'And they failed.' An Army officer called von Stauffenberg had orchestrated a plot to kill Hitler back in July. The Führer had survived, unlike Stauffenberg and his friends. He'd hung dozens of them from meat hooks in a cellar in Berlin, their slow deaths filmed in case anyone else had similar ideas.

Stefan pressed harder. 'Who are these people? Who do they look to?'

'Who do you think?'

'Himmler. Has to be. Am I right?'

Erwin said nothing but his silence was all too eloquent. Stefan knew that he was from the SD. The *Sicherheitsdienst* was part of Himmler's sprawling empire, led by the black-uniformed SS zealots who'd become a byword for terror across an entire continent. Huber, he thought, had been a fine specimen, so different in every respect from this urbane young Hamburger. For the first time he was glad he'd shot the bastard.

He tried one last time with Erwin. The regime was beginning to collapse from the inside. The people at the top would be jockeying for power. Goebbels. Bormann. Speer. Goering. Even *Onkel* Karl. Unthinkable, then, that the chicken farmer from some godforsaken Bavarian village, the pasty-faced apparatchik who'd crawled all the way up Hitler's arse and given him the private army of his dreams, wouldn't be in the running.

'It's Himmler, isn't it? Just say it. The man with the funny glasses. Little Heine.'

Erwin smiled softly, shook his head, refused to be drawn any further. Then the door opened and Stefan half turned in his chair to find Otto standing behind him. Despite the lateness of the hour, he was still fully dressed. He beamed down at them, like a father calling time on his precious children.

'Tomorrow we have much to do.' He tapped his watch. 'Time for bed, gentlemen.'

17

Gómez had never tasted soup like it. Grease blobs the size of dimes. The faintest hint of what might have been garlic. Tiny curls of onion. Plus grit at the bottom of the bowl that ground between his teeth. Only the fact that he was starving kept the spoon in his mouth.

Ramón watched him from the other plinth, just an arm's length away. He was naked from the waist up, a slender man-child with a swollen face and livid bruising around his rib cage where he'd so nearly been kicked to death. Mid-morning in the tiny cell, it was already hot, the air stifling. Up at ground level and higher it would be even worse, the sun beating in through windows that probably wouldn't open, prisoners panting like animals in the rankness of the air. Ramón spoke good English, certainly enough to want to make a friend of this big, Mexican-looking guy who'd probably saved his life.

'You from round here? Only I never saw you at all.'

'The States,' Gómez grunted, 'Land of the Free.'

'But you're Mexican up the line, right?'

'A generation back, yeah.'

'So you like it down here?'

'I love it. Great cuisine. Nice accommodation. Agreeable company. You want the rest of my soup?'

Ramón declined the offer with a bark of laughter. Two teeth missing, probably from yesterday. When Gómez asked why he hadn't soup, too, it turned out that he had a thing going with one of the warders. Yesterday evening, before Gómez's arrival, it had brought a bag of fries to the cell.

'And what did he get out of it? Let me guess.'

Ramón nodded, opening the wreckage of his mouth and blowing three fingers.

'In here?' Gómez was looking round at the cell.

'Yeah. You too if you want. Call it a thank you.'

Gómez shook his head. No more sexual favours, he said. No more blow jobs. Not while he was in residence.

'So what about the fries?'

'Fuck the fries.'

Ramón pouted. Gómez was trying to guess his age. Thirty? Forty? Older? The thing about faggots, they knew the moves to make to keep the score down. Easy on the booze. Don't eat too much. Stay in shape. Did this apply to Agard Beaman? Trouble was that nothing applied to Agard Beaman but just now he didn't even care to hazard a guess. With his life marking time for a while, maybe it was best to forget about the outside world.

'You from hereabouts?' It was Gómez's turn to ask.

'*Sí.*' Ramón grinned. 'Ensenada. My family come from inland, from the mountains. My father is dead, *muerto*, killed in a fight. My mother has chickens and a donkey. She calls the donkey by my father's name. Alvaro. I guess she knew a thing or two about him.'

Gómez laughed, in spite of himself. There was something naïve yet knowing about this career *maricón*. He remembered him hanging over the rail on the promenade watching the kids in the water. His delight in their bodies was undisguised, almost child like, and they – in turn – seemed happy to have him looking at them.

'You make a good living doing what you do?'

'Sure. I fuck only who I want to fuck. I'm very good. I only have clean clients. They pay me well. No one beats me up, not until yesterday. Sometimes they ask me to stay, pass me round their friends. I know lots of people who know lots of people. Sometimes that can help.'

'So what are you doing in here?'

'In here is only for today. And maybe tomorrow. Maybe they want us to spend a little time together, just to see what happens. It's a game they play. In this country everyone is a child, especially the men.'

'Nothing happens in this cell,' Gómez said. '*Nada*.'

'Sure. We know that but they never think nothing is for ever.'

'Would it make a difference? If something did happen?'

'It might.'

'How?'

'I don't know. Like I say, they are kids. One moment, one thing. Another, something else. They get bored very quickly. Don't despair.'

'You speak good English.'

'Of course. Many of my clients are Americans. They liked to be fucked in their own language. They say it helps.'

'And you get more money?'

'Of course. And in dollars, not pesos.'

Gómez nodded. At first, he'd assumed that Ramón was a plant or – at the very least – a rich joke at the gringo's expense. Now he was beginning to sense there might be a way he could use this man. The coy boasts about his clientele were probably true. The guy looked good underneath all the bruises and probably earned every cent these people spent on him.

'I need to talk to an American, someone with influence, or maybe a lawyer. Else a cop called Diego. You could make that happen?'

'Probably, yeah. This is Diego La Paz?'

'I dunno his second name. He has a sister called Yolanda. Tall guy. Thin. Shit complexion. Crazy hair.'

'I know this guy. He's OK.'

'What does that mean?'

'He's honest. Maybe too honest. But you're right . . .' he tapped his head. 'It's not just the hair. The guy's crazy inside, too.'

'So you can get to him?'

'I could try.'

'How?'

'The warder. The man with the fries. He has influence, lots of connections. Everyone in here knows him.'

'And the price?'

'He comes in here. We fuck. Then he goes. Ten minutes. Maybe five.'

'How do you get him to appear in the first place?'

'I shout. He knows my voice. It's like calling a dog. *No importa.*'

'Right . . .' Gómez nodded, wondering exactly how much

humiliation he was prepared to suffer to try and get himself out of this place.

'Would the guy mind if I stepped out there into the corridor? Gave you people a little privacy?'

'*No se*. I can ask him.' He frowned. 'What if he wants to fuck you, too?'

'Then the deal's off. He can go fuck himself.'

'Impossible.' The frown deepened, and Gómez sensed his professional pride was at stake. 'That's my job.'

*

Mid-morning in Coruña, Erwin took Stefan to the harbour. Otto had laid hands on a wheelchair and much to Stefan's embarrassment he was obliged to use it. Erwin did the pushing and the two escorts, as ever, stayed five steps behind in case Stefan abused his new freedoms. They were talking about Hamburg again, the way the city had never really taken to the Nazis, the street battles with the Communists from the dockyards. As a kid at school those times were exciting. They carried the promise of change, of some alternative to the tide of Nazi diktats from Berlin that were throttling the country to death.

After a while, it began to rain. By now, they were beneath the city walls, on the very edge of the water. Pedestrians were hurrying for shelter and Erwin headed back towards the main road. Otto had recommended a café a couple of streets away that served excellent coffee. Somehow they'd laid hands on one of the new espresso machines. They had pastries, too, in case Stefan was hungry.

The café was packed. The escorts stood against the back wall, engrossed in newspapers, while Erwin commandeered the one remaining table. Stefan stayed in the wheelchair, beginning to relax now. Pre-dawn, had he made a different decision, he'd already have faced a firing squad. As it was, he was now obliged to decide between *churros* with hot chocolate or tiny squares of apple tart. Thank God for Sol Fiedler, he thought.

It was Erwin who brought up Trévarez. He said he'd been there, enjoyed his stay, appreciated the cooking and the extensive grounds.

'This is recently?'

'July. I only stayed a couple of days but it was thoroughly enjoyable. Wonderful weather. Wonderful setting.'

'I agree. May I ask what you were doing there?'

'Enquiring about you.'

'Really?' Stefan didn't know whether to be irritated or flattered. Was there any corner of his life that these people hadn't explored?

'We needed a reliable *Kapitän* to get Huber and the rest of them down to Lisbon,' Erwin said. 'We had a short list of two. You were one of them.'

'And the other?'

'His boat went down in August. Bay of Biscay. And so the decision made itself. Still, these days there are always more questions to be asked.'

Stefan lost interest in his *churros*. Something in Erwin's expression told him to tread carefully.

'And Trévarez?' he asked.

'It was interesting.'

'Meaning what?'

307

Erwin invited him to choose another pastry from the trolley. He agreed the *churros* looked a bit tired. Stefan declined. Trévarez was a château in Brittany, a couple of hours' drive from the U-boat pens in Lorient. The Navy had commandeered the place to serve as a recreation centre for submarine crews resting up between voyages, and the prospect of a week or so of fresh food in the quiet of the Breton countryside was a welcome tonic after all the pressures at sea.

'You were there on four occasions, I think. Anything you remember in particular?'

Stefan hesitated. He knows, he thought. He's asked around and somebody's told him.

'Aurélie,' he said softly.

'Exactly so. French, I assume.'

'Of course.'

'I understand she worked in the vegetable garden.'

'Yes. And loved it. You met her?'

'Sadly not. Very pretty, from what I heard.'

'To me, yes.'

'Was this a serious affair? Forgive the question, Stefan, but I have to ask it.'

Stefan thought hard about exactly how much he was expected to divulge. A serious affair? No. Aurélie was married to a farmer in the village, an ox of a man twice her age. They had no children and evidently he gave her a good deal of licence. Stefan was by no means her only liaison among the visiting submariners and he knew it from the start because she'd told him so.

'We were good friends,' he said. 'We made each other laugh. She was also a woman and, believe me, that matters after fifty-five days at sea.'

'I'm sure. You made love from time to time?'

'Often. Time was limited. You seized the moment. *Carpe diem.*'

'Because tomorrow you might die?'

'Yes. Or the day after that. Or whenever. Every time I kissed that woman goodbye I assumed I'd never come back.'

'Did that make you a pessimist?'

'It made me lucky.'

'And she was pleased to see you again?'

'Always.'

'And it was always the same? You talked? You laughed? You made love?'

'Yes.'

'So . . .' he nodded. 'What did you talk *about*?'

This was the question Stefan had been expecting, no less offensive for being so obvious.

'We never discussed anything operational,' he said at once. 'Nothing about what we did, where we'd been, how we'd done.'

'I'm sure you didn't.' Erwin was laughing. 'I can't think of anything more dull.'

'So why the question?'

'I want to know what you *did* talk about. Intimate things? Family things? The English call it pillow talk.'

'You mean Sol, don't you?'

'Yes.'

'Then I don't understand. How could I talk about someone I didn't even know existed? That's impossible, isn't it?'

'Of course it is. I simply want to know whether you talked about everyone else in your family. Your parents. That brother of yours, Werner.'

'I expect I did, yes.'

'Anyone else?'

Stefan frowned, thinking back.

'A friend of mine from school,' he said. 'An older boy. Dieter Merz. He was always a hero of mine.'

'Really?'

'Yes. He joined the *Luftwaffe*. Flew against the Republicans down in Spain. He was part of the Condor Legion. We were all very jealous, him getting into action so soon. Before the war he was a display pilot, too, back in Germany. They even made a film about him.'

'I think I remember it,' Erwin was smiling. 'Little blond guy?'

'That's him.'

'And he's still alive, this Dieter?'

'I don't know. I doubt it.' Stefan was trying to remember exactly how he and Aurélie had passed their time together. 'We had friends in common,' he said at last, 'other members of the crew. Aurélie knew them all and so did I. That gave us a family of our own. Does that answer your question? Put that mind of yours to rest?'

Erwin winced slightly. Then he called for the bill. Only when they were outside, hurrying back through the rain towards the legation, did he explain further. They were under a shelter of the tree, with Stefan back in the wheelchair, waiting for the traffic to part.

'Your girlfriend turned out to be working for a local Resistance network,' Erwin said. 'It's likely that everything you said went straight back to the British.'

'Why would they be interested in me? In my family? My friends?'

'Because intelligence people are interested in everything. Every last scrap of information. And you're talking to someone who knows.'

'I see.'

'Soon you're going to be meeting these people. You'll have to be word perfect. They'll set you traps. First you have to spot them. Then you'll have to avoid them. Aurélie will be a trap. You should think about that. Ask yourself why you never talked about Sol. Be prepared.'

Stefan nodded. Erwin had spotted a gap in the traffic. Stefan was looking up at him.

'What happened to Aurélie?' he asked.

'We shot her. The farmer, too.'

*

It was a piercing whistle from Ramón that brought the warder to the cell. For once, shouting didn't work. The warder's name was Montoro. Gómez had never seen him before. He opened the door with some care as if it might be booby-trapped. He was younger than Gómez had expected, clean-shaven, and wouldn't have looked out of place in a respectable bar. Gómez could think of a number of women he knew who'd be only too happy to offer a man like this a perch in their lives.

Ramón was on his feet. He kissed the warder on the lips and then the two men conferred, head-to-head, a whispered conversation that Gómez didn't begin to understand. From time to time Montoro spared Gómez a cautious glance, checking him out. Ramón was nodding at the corridor. Then Montoro shook his head. His job was to keep prisoners behind locked

311

doors. No way was he having Gómez prowling around outside.

Ramón turned to Gómez. Maybe he'd like to take a little nap, face to the wall? Gómez wanted to say no. He wanted this creep out of the cell. He wanted the door shut and locked. He wanted to be back safe with a guy who knew the rules he'd set down.

Instead he asked about Diego. He knows the cop? He'll get him along for a conversation? Try and stir a little action?

'*Sí.*'

'You trust him to do that?'

'*Sí.*'

'And it happens today? This morning?'

'Today, maybe. First he has to find this man. He has to make arrangements. Patience.' Gómez was still sprawled full length on the plinth. 'You want to turn over? Shut your eyes?'

Gómez didn't but just now he could see no alternative. Ramón would never have been his favourite cellmate but at least the guy had pull. How else was he ever going to see the light of day?

'*Rápido,*' he growled. 'Yeah?'

*

Stefan spent the rest of the day behind a locked door in the room where he'd slept. Erwin had found him a handful of German magazines from the legation's library and he sat in an armchair beside the window, looking up from time to time to watch passers-by in the street below.

The fate of Aurélie had come as a shock, not just the realisation that she'd been working with the Resistance but the way Erwin had chosen to break the news about her death.

You aid the enemy, you pay the price. So brutally casual, so matter-of-fact. Two more lives snuffed out. For what?

At the roadside, he'd tried to push Erwin further. Who'd betrayed her? How had she died? But the young diplomat appeared to have lost interest. Herr Schellenberg in Berlin was expecting a progress report on the telephone by lunchtime. Later he and Stefan would meet again to go over the Sol Fiedler story one last time before Schellenberg returned to put Stefan to the test. Then, God willing, would come the moment when they'd agree the next step.

Erwin was back in the early evening, knocking on the bedroom door and letting himself in. He appeared to be pleased with the news from Berlin. Schellenberg, caught up in yet another crisis, was unable to leave Prinz-Albrecht-Strasse. The consensus was that Operation Finisterre was now a matter of some urgency, and that measures to get *Kapitän* Portisch into the hands of the British should be expedited. Erwin had explained the progress that he and Stefan had made over the last twenty-four hours and on this basis Schellenberg was happy – indeed relieved – not to have to make the arduous flight back to northern Spain.

'He trusts me.' Erwin was beaming. 'Which means he trusts you also.'

The fact that the plan now had an operational code name intrigued Stefan. Why Finisterre? Erwin said the code name had only just been changed.

'Beforehand it was called Operation Benjamin,' he said.

'Why?'

'Schellenberg had the ear of the Führer. He was young and he was clever and some of the old fighters, the Brownshirts, resented him. Hitler called him his Benjamin. Maybe that's why.'

'You said *had* the ear of the Führer.'

'I did.'

'No longer?'

Erwin didn't answer. He was sitting on the bed, his briefcase beside him. He explained to Stefan that tomorrow he would be given a change of clothing, stuff he could have acquired from Eva. Once he was in the hands of the British, down in Lisbon, he'd tell them he'd just spent two weeks at her house in the village under the care of the local doctor. The wound in his leg had healed and thankfully his tibia had turned out to be intact. He'd say he'd thought long and hard about the war, about what lay ahead, about the future of what remained of his precious country, and had decided that his duty lay in trying to contribute to peace as soon as possible. He was also in grave danger of being traced by the Germans and shot as a deserter.

'That's all true,' Stefan said.

'Of course. So you don't have to invent anything. Just tell them the way it's been.'

'Except here. With you.'

'Of course. We never happened. You were never arrested. You made your own way to Lisbon.'

'How? They're going to want to know.'

'I suggest you came by boat.'

'*Boat?*'

'Fishing boat.' Erwin opened his briefcase and slipped out a couple of photos. They showed a sturdy wooden smack on a mooring in a tiny harbour. A cloud of seagulls was massing over a figure working on the deck. The name of the boat, the *Santa Maria*, was clearly legible on the bow.

'This is the village where I stayed?' Stefan was staring at the photo.

'Yes. O Barquero. The fisherman's name is Santos. He owns the boat with his brother Federico.'

Another photo showed a man of uncertain age, weather-beaten, grizzled, bent over a pile of nets.

'Who took these photos?'

'Otto. When he was in the village organising the funeral.'

'You knew then? You knew I'd survived?'

'We'd heard rumours. We suspected it was possible.'

'So you were already planning all this? Operation Finisterre?'

'Yes.'

Stefan was looking at the photo of the boat again, trying to imagine what kind of speed it would make.

'Lisbon's way down south,' he said. 'You're talking at least two days.'

'We think three.'

'And how am I supposed to pay for it? The skipper will need money, a lot of money.'

'You gave him some of those gold coins.'

'You know about the coins?' Stefan had abandoned the photos.

'Yes.'

'Who told you?'

'Ignacio. The carpenter. That's how we knew where you were. Who was looking after you. What had happened. The man's in love with Eva. He went to the *Guardia*.'

'And they told you?'

'Yes.'

Stefan nodded. Betrayed, he thought, by the oaf who made

that hideous splint. He remembered the way the man had treated Eva, his brusqueness, his sense of ownership, of entitlement. I should have realised, Stefan told himself. I should have taken more notice.

Erwin told him to keep the photos until tomorrow, to memorise every detail of the fishing boat, to weave a story around the passage south, to come up with an account that would survive hours of probing.

'By the English, you mean?'

'Yes. Tomorrow, we'll get you down to Lisbon. That may take a while. Once you're there, you make your way to the British Embassy. We'll tell you how to find it. You'll be walking in from the street. You give them your name and your rank. Within an hour or so, if they're any good, they'll realise exactly what kind of fish they've landed. Not just a U-boat commander but someone who survived the wreck up north, someone charged with special responsibilities. Lisbon is full of spies. It's a kasbah, a souk. Everyone knows everyone else's business. What happened to your boat will be all over town. And now the sole survivor walks into the arms of the enemy. Sensational news. And big, big smiles at the British Embassy.'

'And Sol?' Stefan asked again. 'Do I tell them about Sol?'

'No. That comes afterwards. Your credentials alone will get you an interview. There are counter-intelligence people like me attached to the embassy. You'll be debriefed. They're buyers in the market. They'll check out the goods. They'll want operational data. Communication codes. Details about the *Elektro* boat.'

'So what do I say? How much do I tell them?'

'Tell them it's *Scheisse*. Tell them why it doesn't work. Tell them they've nothing to worry about.'

'And the codes? The four-rotor system?'

'Already changed.'

Erwin paused. This was an area they'd never discussed and he sensed the depth of Stefan's reluctance to divulge anything remotely useful. *Kapitän* Portsich had spent his entire career in the service scrupulously guarding every last detail of the way he and his men fought their war. Now this.

'The war's lost,' Erwin said. 'That's where this story begins and ends. You can tell them anything. It won't make any difference. Just as long as they pass you up the line.'

'To England?'

'Indeed. There are regular commercial flights three times a week. The spies use them all the time.'

'And what then?'

'Then you'll be in the lap of the professionals. They'll need to go over all the technical stuff with experts in the field. You should have no problem with that because it's authentic. Then they're going to want to know about your motivation. You're one of the top *Kapitän*s in the field. You're much decorated. So why are you doing this? Why are you handing over all this information?'

'Because technically I'm a deserter. Because I've had enough of the war. Because I want out.'

'Exactly. But something else, too.'

'Eva?'

'Exactly. You want to be with her. But you don't want to live under the threat of being caught as a deserter. Which means bringing her to England.'

'They'd do that?'

'Only if you make it a condition of telling them about everything else.'

'And if they say yes, should I trust them?'

'Probably not. But it certainly strengthens your motivation, and that's important.'

Stefan turned to the window, eyeing the street below. Would Eva really leave her father? Would she want to come to England? His last glimpse of her face in the kitchen as he was hustled towards the door told him she would but he didn't know for sure and, worse still, there was no way he could find out.

Erwin seemed to sense his indecision. His voice had softened.

'We're in contact with Eva,' he said.

'How? Why?'

'We arranged for her to be taken into custody the night you were arrested. Her father, too. She's safe. They both are. And well looked after. She sends you kisses, incidentally.'

Stefan didn't know what to say. The implications were all too clear. He turned on Erwin. After everything they'd built together over the last twenty-four hours, beneath all the gossip about their days in Hamburg, this man was just like the rest of them. Ambitious. Ruthless. Hard as iron.

'You've taken her hostage,' he said. 'In case I have second thoughts.'

'On the contrary, Stefan, we've temporarily removed her from the scene. The last thing you need are witnesses to what happened the night you were arrested. The English will know where your boat went down. What happens to this story of yours if they check on Eva?'

'So how have you explained her absence?'

'We haven't. It remains a mystery. People in the village know that all of you have disappeared. They don't know why and they don't know how.'

'And the fisherman? Santos?'

'He's disappeared, too. Along with his boat. The same night you were arrested.'

'What happened? Where is he now?'

'Those are questions you don't need to ask.'

'Is he still alive?'

'I've no idea. Probably not. People die in wars all the time. It's a fact of life. That's what happens.'

Stefan held his gaze. He was beginning to dislike this man and Erwin knew it.

'Let's concentrate on Sol,' Erwin said. 'You're in England. You have some kind of deal to get Eva out of Spain. You've told them everything you know about operational matters. They're pleased with you because they've checked this stuff out and maybe they've been to O Barquero and they know that everything tallies with your account. That's when they start to trust you. That's when you mention Sol Fiedler. This will be the first time his name comes up. You have to remember this, Stefan. Counter-intelligence people are like dogs. They're trained to sniff out double agents, people – fugitives, refugees, deserters – pretending to be what they're not. They'll think you may be one of those. So before you mention Sol Fiedler, they need to be reasonably sure you're genuine.'

'*Reasonably* sure?'

'I'm afraid so. That's the best you can expect. Our world has no time for absolutes. One part of you always reserves judgement. It might be a tiny part, just that one last corner of your soul, but it's always there. Total belief? In our business there's no such thing.'

That one last corner of your soul.

Stefan stared at his hands. It made perfect sense. Go to the English. Convince them you're sincere. Share everything you know with them. And then, almost as an afterthought, tell them that Hitler is months away from blowing up half the world. Stefan looked up, voicing the thought.

'You don't know about the bomb.' Erwin was alarmed. 'You got that from me.'

'Of course. But tell me I'm wrong.'

'You're not.'

'Then it has to work, doesn't it? This thing we're doing? This warning I'm helping to pass on?'

Erwin nodded, said nothing. Then he leaned forward, his face suddenly inches from Stefan.

'Just feed in the information about Sol. That's all you have to do. Everything else is taken care of because the rest will be down to them. That's the way things work in our world. A detail here. Another detail there. An incident somewhere else. You have no idea how complex these things are. We're just a tiny part of it, believe me.'

'You mean me. You mean I'm just a tiny part of it.'

'If that's the way you prefer to see it.'

'But it's true isn't it? You've offered me a role. I've taken it. But the bigger picture? Where this whole thing might be heading?'

Stefan let the question hang between them. Erwin was on his feet. Enough, he seemed to be saying. He looked down at Stefan.

'At sea you had total command,' he said. 'Those days have gone. All you do is tell them about Sol. That's all we want you to do. It's not a big thing. Just tell them about Sol. Nothing else.'

'And this bomb of ours?'

'That's not your business. In real life, there's no way you'd ever get to find out about it. If you tell them about our bomb, the game's over.'

'Why?'

'Because they'll know you're a plant.'

*

They came for Gómez after the light had gone out. One of the two warders was Montoro, a nice touch. Gómez, who had no idea what was going on, half turned to Ramón in the darkness.

'*Adiós?*' It was a question.

'I hope so.'

Gómez felt for his hand, shook it.

'*Muchas gracias*,' he muttered. Ramón gave his hand a squeeze, said nothing.

They escorted Gómez back along the corridor, up the steps at the end. On the first floor was a line of doors. Montoro spoke no English. He stopped outside the last of the doors. A flurry of hand gestures indicated that someone was inside, waiting. Then he pushed the door open and stood to one side.

Expecting Diego, Gómez found himself looking at Yolanda. She was sitting at a table, flicking through Gómez's passport. She got to her feet, the concern obvious on her face.

'You OK? They beat you any?'

'No.'

'You're sure?'

'Yeah.'

Gómez heard the door shut behind him. Yolanda held her arms wide. Gómez didn't move.

'I stink,' he said.

'I know.'

She put her arms round him, held him for a long moment. Smelling someone as sweet as this was way beyond anything he'd expected.

'How come you're here?'

'Diego phoned me. Explained what had happened. You killed somebody? Did I hear that right?'

'You did.'

'That's foolish. Even the Mexicans notice.'

'He was a cop.'

'That's worse. You're lucky to be alive.'

He shrugged, then explained the way it had happened. In his view, most Medical Examiners would find a fracture in the guy's skull from where he'd cracked his head on the sidewalk but that would need a proper autopsy.

'Meaning?'

'They skip that stage. I'm there. I'm involved. A guy dies. They've got a cell waiting. Why make it complicated? Who's interested in justice?'

'You sound bitter.'

'I'm glad to see you, is all. Where do we go from here?'

'Back to the States.'

'Are you serious?' Gómez was staring at her. This just gets better, he thought.

She kissed him on the lips and then nodded at the door.

She had a car waiting out front. Best not to test Mexican hospitality any further. She gave Gómez his passport and they went downstairs together. The guy at the desk, rolling himself a cigarette, didn't even spare them a glance. Only when they were safe in the car, driving north towards Tijuana, did Yolanda break the silence.

'You hungry?'

'Starving.' Gómez jerked a thumb over his shoulder. 'A man could lose serious weight back there.'

They were out of Ensenada now. There was a roadside diner up ahead, just a shack beside the blacktop. Yolanda pulled over. It was late, gone midnight, and the place was empty except for a couple of solitary truckers, each at his own table. Yolanda ordered tacos and rice for Gómez, an enchilada for herself.

Gómez eyed her over the steaming plate. 'So how did you manage it? How did you get me out of there?'

'Diego phoned me yesterday, like I explained. Said you'd been caught up in an incident. No details. I phoned Agard.'

'Why?'

'That boy has connections. As you probably know. Good connections. At the very top.'

'We're talking First Lady?'

'I guess we are. Either way I get a call this afternoon, a voice I've never heard in my life, tells me to get to Ensenada, even gives me directions to the penitentiary. Happens I don't need them but it's a nice touch. I ask why I'm headed there and he tells me everything's been straightened out. I laugh and I ask how and the phone goes dead. Me? I do as I'm told.' She nodded at the plate. 'Taco any good?'

'Better than good.' Gómez was trying to figure things out. 'You're telling me I owe Beaman?'

'I guess you do. Mrs Roosevelt has the pull but Agard pressed the buttons. Turns out you're the one needs protection.'

'Very funny. And now?'

'Now I guess I get you home. Except one thing.' She was carrying a black leather bag. She opened it and peered in. Then she handed Gómez a brown envelope. No name. No address. Nothing.

'What's this?'

'Diego met me at the penitentiary. He asked me to give it to you. I have no idea what's inside but it came with a message. He doesn't want you to contact him again. Ever. I guess he's pissed about the cop you killed.'

Gómez nodded, then opened the envelope. Inside was a single sheet of paper. It contained an address. 23 Calle Maravillas. Ciudad Juarez.

'He said nothing else?'

'Nothing. I got the feeling he thought you'd know where all this fits.'

'All this? He's just given me an address.' He checked again.

'Some place you know?' Yolanda asked.

'Never heard of it.'

'And Ciudad Juarez?' She was looking at the address. 'Big city up by the border opposite El Paso?'

'Sure.' The auto scam, Gómez thought. Diego has made his phone calls, rousted a contact or two, and come up with this one solid lead. Quite where it might take Gómez was anyone's guess but one thing was for sure. No more Diego.

Gómez finished the tacos and wiped the plate clean. He

wanted to know whether he and Yolanda were expected at the border crossing into California, the Route 1 entry that would take them back to San Diego.

'I've no idea but something tells me you're not welcome here. We keep heading north, we're back in the States in a couple of hours.'

Gómez nodded. Nothing sounded sweeter.

'How about we head east,' he said, 'and hit Ciudad Juarez?'

PART FOUR

PART FOUR

18

Two days later, Stefan was on the outskirts of Lisbon. The journey south over nightmare roads had felt never-ending. A Spanish driver from the legation staff had done his best in the big Mercedes but some of the potholes, thought Stefan, could have swallowed a truck.

For hour after hour the road followed the coast, winding up and down the long escarpment overhanging the rocks below, then dropping to sea level for yet another of the sparkling *rias* that took them dozens of kilometres inland. Stefan sat in the back with Erwin, gazing at the lushness of the landscape and the poverty of most of the villages. Once they'd crossed the border into Portugal the lives of these peasant people seemed to get even tougher. Donkeys pulling ploughs over the red ochre soil. Semi-naked kids hauling buckets of water. Old women squatting in the shade, staring into nowhere. Neither war nor electricity had touched this landscape and at night darkness settled on the land like a shroud.

They reached Lisbon close to midday. The centre of the city overlooked the water, a sprawl of red-tiled roofs in the brightness of the sunshine. After the long journey south, Stefan was glad to be back among people, bustle, movement. Trolley trams rattled up and down the hills. Men in business suits conferred over tiny cups of coffee. A gypsy with a violin and a corner pitch begged for coins in the swirl of lunchtime passers-by.

Erwin evidently knew the city well. He directed the driver down to the waterfront, then headed west for several blocks. Stefan gazed at the forest of masts and the broad sweep of the river beyond. The driver brought the car to a halt. Traffic was light.

'Here . . .' Erwin was indicating a line of fishing boats alongside a quay. 'Santos dropped you before sunrise. There was no one about. You watched him putting to sea again. Maybe you waved. Up to you. But he's gone.'

'And the embassy?'

'A ten-minute walk. A stroll. Nothing.' He nodded inland, away from the road, and gave Stefan directions. 'You arrived with a handful of coins,' he said. 'Enough for a bowl of soup and a little bread. Times are hard in this city. There's not much to eat. You've walked around a little. Got the feel of the place. Maybe you've slept once the sun came up because the boat was uncomfortable. You found a park with benches. You won't remember the name or even where it is. Your leg still hurts. You take things slowly. There'll be people who speak German at the embassy and you'll be glad of that. Portuguese is a mystery. Even worse than Spanish.'

Stefan nodded, staring out at the fishing boats. This man had taken over his life and he felt resentment as well as helplessness. The way he'd organised the script, so meticulous, so much attention to detail, would doubtless serve some higher purpose but just now Stefan was glad that their relationship had come to an end. Only one question remained.

'How do I get in touch with Eva again?'

'When it's all over, you mean?'

'Yes.'

'You go back to the village. O Barquero. Or you ask the English to pick her up. That's where she'll be.'

'I have your word on that?'

'Of course. You don't trust me? You think this is all for nothing?'

Stefan didn't answer. His fingers had found the door handle. Erwin was looking at him, a smile on his face. He badly wanted Stefan to shake his hand. When Stefan opened the door, he tried to mask his disappointment.

'Take care.' Erwin put a hand on his arm. 'Good luck.'

Stefan limped away without a backward glance. He was wearing the clothes Erwin had supplied: faded blue overalls, frayed at the seams, pre-stained with engine grease that might have come from the boat, a pair of espadrilles that were falling apart, and a shapeless straw hat with a wide, floppy brim. Three days at sea, he should have picked up a tan. Thanks to the hat, his face above the growth of beard was still pale.

He began to cross the road, just another refugee alongside thousands of other incomers who'd slipped their moorings and ghosted west until there was nowhere left to go. According to Erwin, this city was full of people like him, washed up by a war that had taken everything but the clothes on their backs – Jews, Communists, POWs, deserters, men and women fleeing for their lives – and to find himself suddenly part of that community was the strangest feeling.

Safely across the road, he looked back but the Mercedes had gone. It was like a conjuring trick – here one minute, vanished the next – and the feeling of helplessness returned. He was briefly on his own at last, and that was a relief, but the last few weeks had put his life in the hands of strangers and he was left with an overwhelming sense of bewilderment he recognised from moments as a child when he stepped from the darkness of a Hamburg cinema back into the world outside. What was real and what wasn't? Who should he trust and who was going to hurt him? There'd been nothing simple about going to war in a submarine but these questions had never troubled him before because life at sea was black and white. Now, in this world of shadows, he had nothing to rely on but the most primitive instinct of all. Survival.

The embassy lay beyond a pair of green ornamental gates in a quiet, tree-lined street of grey cobblestones. It was a modest building, white stucco, two storeys, with circular windows on the top floor and a thicket of aerials sprouting from the roof. A pair of local policemen were stationed at the gate.

One of them stepped into the sunshine and gestured for Stefan's ID. Stefan shrugged and held his hands wide.

'*Nada*,' he said. I don't have any.

The two men conferred. They shook their heads. They waved him away. He didn't move. Then the first man took a closer look. Something about Stefan evidently impressed him. He turned to the gate and unlocked it. Then he escorted Stefan to the building's front door. The door was already open. A woman was on her knees inside, wiping clean the tiled wall. She stopped work as the visitors stepped past. She looked local, dark-skinned, blackened teeth in a wide smile. A desk lay beyond, dominated by a photograph on the wall behind. Stefan recognised the king and queen. George VI was German by ancestry, he thought.

One of us, one of our people. So what are we doing fighting this hideous war?

A woman appeared from nowhere. She was tall, not young. Black skirt, white blouse. She looked Stefan up and down, unsmiling, and then muttered something in Portuguese to the policeman. The policeman shook his head. She turned back to Stefan.

'Can I help you?' English this time.

Stefan removed his hat and asked to see the military attaché.

'Do you have an appointment?'

'No.'

'May I ask what brings you here?'

'My name is Stefan Portisch. I'm a *Kapitän* in the *Reichsmarine*. Until very recently I was in command of a U-boat.'

'You're a serving officer?'

'Yes.'

'I see.' She hesitated a moment. 'We normally expect a little more information.'

'Of course. You have a military attaché?'

'We do. He'll need to know the nature of your business.'

'Then I'll be happy to tell him.'

She nodded, rebuffed, and disappeared through a door at the end of the room. Stefan looked for somewhere to sit down. His leg had begun to throb again. Nerves, he told himself. Relax. Stay calm. You've survived far worse moments than this.

The woman was back minutes later. She signalled for Stefan to follow her and led the way up a flight of stairs. It took Stefan a while to get to the top. More pictures lined the corridor on the first floor. Hunting scenes deep in the countryside. A shooting party on a windswept moor. The woman asked him to wait for a moment while she disappeared into an office at the end of the corridor.

Stefan lingered beside an oil painting of the Thames. He'd been in this very scene as a naval cadet, showing the flag for the Reich. He recognised the Tower of London and the magnificent bridge behind it. The bridge had opened to admit his training vessel, and he and his crewmates had lined the decks, doffing their caps to a Royal Navy destroyer, moored in the tideway. Later, they'd played host to a long queue of visiting dignitaries and Stefan remembered circulating around the tiny mess room with an assortment of sausages on a silver tray. He thought he might have met an English admiral but he couldn't be sure.

'Mr Portisch? The lieutenant-commander will see you now.'

The woman held the door open. Stefan found himself in a small, comfortably furnished office with a view of a garden through the window. At the desk sat a man Stefan judged to be in his mid-thirties though it was impossible to be sure. He was medium height, not fat, not thin. Black hair grew in patches on the baldness of his skull and one side of his face was puckered with shiny pink scar tissue. The scar had altered the line of his mouth, making one corner droop, and when he got to his feet and extended a hand Stefan realised he'd been burned. His hands were like claws, more scar tissue, and the touch of flesh on flesh was no more than a gesture of courtesy.

'English or German?'

'I'm German.'

'I meant languages. Which would you prefer?'

Stefan said German. The strength of this man's voice – warm yet full of authority – took him by surprise. He'd been expecting a croak. Far from it.

'I understand you're a walk-in. No offence but we get lots of those. Absolutely happy to help but you'll know that time is one of life's rarer commodities, especially now. So what can I do for you?' Excellent German, perfectly accented.

Stefan had spent the last couple of days toying with a number of ways to launch this conversation but sensed it was hopeless to be hemmed in by any kind of script. Start with the obvious, he thought. And see where it leads.

'Until a couple of weeks ago, I was in command of U-boat number 2553.'

'One of the *Elektro* boats?'

'Yes.'

'The one that came to grief up in Galicia?'

'Yes.'

'Wicked coast. Can happen to anyone. I thought you all died?'

'They all did. Except me.'

'Good Lord.' The grimace may have been a smile. 'You need luck in situations like those and you're talking to an expert. Forty-eight souls went down in that wreck, am I right?'

'Yes.'

'And you're the forty-ninth?'

'Yes.'

'Then welcome again. Take a seat.' Another token handshake, over the desk this time.

Stefan settled back. He was on home turf. He was with someone who understood the ocean, understood what it was to take the war to sea. This might be easier than I'd thought, he told himself. Might be.

He explained about the grounding, about getting his crew

out, about finding himself alone with a senior SS officer who couldn't swim.

'He wanted you to save him?'

'He wanted me to shoot him.'

'Very SS. Take the bullet. Die for the Fatherland. So what did you do?'

'I did his bidding. No one argues with these people.'

'You shot him?'

'I did.'

A thin whistle escaped the slit of a mouth. It seemed to signal both surprise and approval.

'So what did that feel like? Killing the man?'

'Like nothing. You pull the trigger, bam-bam-bam, three shots, and he's gone. Later it didn't feel that way at all but at the time, as you might imagine, I had other things on my mind.'

He described getting ashore, lying up for the night, then finding himself at the mercy of a peasant farmer and his wife. Everything hurt. His leg wouldn't work. He had a gash the size of a *Blutwurst* in his thigh. They'd taken him into the village and left him in the hands of a doctor called Agustín.

'And the rest of the crew?'

'I never saw them again.'

'Did you know they were dead?'

'No, not then. I asked, of course, but no one knew.'

The military attaché nodded and reached for a pad. He held the pen in his fist like a primitive tool. Then he looked up again.

'You stayed in that village?'

'I did.'

'Did you make contact with anybody? The police, for instance? The mayor? Local officials?'

'No.'

'What about your crew?'

'I knew they were all dead. The doctor told me. Their coffins passed beneath my window.'

'But you still made no contact?'

'No.'

He nodded, another question on his lips. Then his eyebrows came together in a frown and he sat back.

'I'm afraid I have a confession to make,' he said.

'What's that?'

'I don't know the German for "desertion".'

*

Gómez and Yolanda, by mutual agreement, spent two days in a cheap hotel in Tijuana. They got up at lunchtime both days in time for coffee in a bar across the road and then lunch at a shack at the scruffy end of the beach where the fishermen mended their nets and the kids played games with an old mooring buoy they'd found in the shallows. In no hurry to move on, Gómez told Yolanda she'd make a fine therapist. He needed to get back on terms with being a proper man again and the knowledge that she was happy to ride along on this journey pleased him immensely.

They made love a great deal. To Gómez's immense relief, her appetite was at least the equal of his own. She introduced him to pleasures he'd never known before and he was duly grateful. On the second evening, at the back of a diner they'd adopted as their own, he wondered whether they ought to get married.

'You're supposed to propose to a girl.' She seemed amused.

'There's a script here. It includes roses and all kinds of pretty jewellery. A bended knee would be good. And more flowers. Plus a lifelong pledge that you ain't gonna do this stuff with any other woman.'

Gómez nodded.

'You want another beer?' he asked her.

'Sure. And if I get to say yes to the other question does that make me someone else?'

'Like who?'

'Like Mrs Gómez?'

Gómez ducked his head a moment. He loved this woman.

'You think I mean it?' he asked.

'I think you might.'

'And if I said I did, what then?'

'I'd say yes.' She took his hand and gave it a squeeze. 'Preferably a Bud, if it comes this far south.'

Later, back in the hotel room, they lay naked on the bed and picked at a bag of popcorn in lieu of a meal. Yolanda said it would be bad karma to get married in Mexico. They'd need formal ID, and formal ID just might put Gómez back in a prison cell.

'So we do it back in the States, yeah?' Gómez was staring up at the ceiling, a rare smile on his face. 'Somewhere in San Diego, maybe? Or Chicago? Or DC? Or any place else you fancy?'

'Sure, baby. But when?'

'Soon.'

'You're not answering my question. You mentioned Ciudad Juarez a couple of days back. What happens there that's so important my brother writes you little notes?'

'I dunno. That's the fun with being a cop. You get to find out.'

338

'You? Or we?'

'We if you wanna come along.'

'For the ride? Watch what happens?'

Gómez shook his head, fed her the last of the popcorn, licked his fingers, then looked her in the eye.

'Neither,' he said. 'I was thinking you were right.'

'About what?'

'Protection.'

*

Stefan spent nearly two hours with the military attaché in the British Embassy. Once he'd heard Stefan's account of what had happened to *U-2553*, he asked for a list of the five principal officers on board, together with their home towns. Stefan made the list himself, rank, Christian name, surname, bold capitals, and the Englishman glanced briefly through it before lifting the phone and summoning the woman Stefan had met earlier. He handed her the list and when she raised an eyebrow he simply nodded. Within the hour she was back. Another nod, from her this time. The list, and the embassy's latest walk-in, had evidently passed muster.

In the meantime, Stefan had been sharing everything he knew about operational protocols, code procedures, deployment schedules, attack patterns, maintenance intervals, plus the ever-lengthening list of reasons why the new electric subs were such a disappointment. It was a difficult face to read over the desk but Stefan sensed that the military attaché probably knew most of this stuff already. What interested him more was the issue of morale.

'We suspect all is not well with Uncle Karl's little tribe,' he said. 'Might we be right?'

Stefan nodded. The Allies had turned the corner last year, he said. Within a space of a single month – May 1943 – the advantage at sea had swung abruptly away from the U-boat packs. The convoys were better organised, better protected. Aircraft were appearing deep into the Atlantic, especially the new American four-engine Liberators, and it was unnerving for crews who'd only recently been so invisible to find themselves subject to attack after attack. After the D-Day landings, with the Americans pushing deep into Brittany, the situation became even worse. The approaches to the submariners' home ports had become suicide zones, heavily patrolled day and night. Nowhere in the Bay of Biscay was safe any more and orders to intercept incoming convoys in the Western Approaches turned into a death sentence.

'So how do the men feel?'

'Resigned.'

'And angry?'

'Not really. Not angry enough to do anything about it. We're like most fighting units. You're doing it for your *Kameraden*, for each other. The Reich is history. Just the mention of Hitler at sea is like dropping a fart. You don't do it. It smells bad. It upsets everyone.'

'So how do you get by?'

'You don't. It's nothing conscious. You know the odds are against you. You know it's getting more likely by the month, by the week, that you'll die but you never talk about it because death has become a given. Why? Because there's nothing else left. We've known that for a while now and it's probably the same for the men on the ground in the east. Barbarossa was a disaster, though no one ever has the guts to say so. You know how many men we lost at Stalingrad? Nearly a million. One of them happened to be my brother. And you know Goebbels' answer? *Totaler Krieg.*'

'Total war.'

'Exactly. More killing. More cities in ruins. More reasons for the Russians to eat us alive once they get to Berlin. That little cripple has a lot of questions to answer. They all do.'

The military attaché nodded. He'd folded his pad and returned it to the drawer. He understands, Stefan thought. He's been through it himself and he's probably drawn the same conclusions himself, though war tastes sweeter if you're winning.

'Can I ask you a question?' Stefan ventured. 'Do you mind?'

'Go ahead.'

'What happened to your face?'

'I got burned. I was a pilot on one of our aircraft carriers. HMS *Illustrious*. You may have heard of it.'

'Fairey Swordfish. Big old biplanes. You flew one of those?'

'I did.'

'At Taranto?'

'Indeed. Best night of my life. Pitch-black and half the Italian fleet in flames. You could feel the heat from fifteen hundred feet. Marvellous.'

'And you crashed?'

'No. We got back intact. Only lost two aircraft. No . . .' his fingers crabbed briefly over the wreckage of his face, '. . . this was a training accident some time afterwards. Got the approach wrong. Way too high. Banged it down far too hard, broke the undercarriage, ruptured the fuel feeds. They got me out, God knows how.'

'And the others?'

'The others survived, too. Not burned, thankfully, not like silly me. But they got a discharge nonetheless so it wasn't all bad news.'

'They were glad to be out of it?'

'Delighted. There were plans to fly the Swordfish against your pocket battleships. Short cut to an early grave, in my opinion. The Italians we could deal with. They didn't really want to fight. You lot were a different proposition.'

'Should I be flattered?'

'Absolutely not. You've caused nothing but trouble. The thirties were going so well, or so we all thought.'

'So where did you learn your German?'

'Oxford, for my sins. Know it at all? Dreaming spires? Pissed students? No women? Thank God the war came along, even if bad things happened.'

The face again. Touching it. Rueful, this time.

Stefan nodded. So far he hadn't mentioned what had developed back in O Barquero. One intimacy deserved another.

'There was a woman in the village who looked after me. Her name is Eva.'

'And?'

'We fell in love.'

'I see. Lucky old you. Is this why you've come? You're after some kind of trade?'

'Yes.' Stefan paused. 'I've been very frank,' he said. 'And I hope helpful.'

'There's more?'

342

'There is.'

'In what respect?'

'I mentioned the SS officer I killed. We were taking these people south. They came with a great deal of baggage, crates and crates of the stuff. The Germans seem to have recovered most of it from the wreck.'

'You're telling me you know what was inside those crates?'

'I'm telling you that I might be able to shed some light on these people. You keep few secrets aboard a submarine.'

It was a lie but – to Stefan at least – it sounded plausible. Anything to get him to the next stage, he thought. Passage to England and the chance to talk about the half-brother he never had.

The attaché wanted to know the price Stefan was putting on all this information. What did he really want?

'I need to make contact with Eva. I can't go back to that village. Neither can I stay here.'

The attaché looked amused. 'You most certainly can't. There are Germans everywhere.' He fluttered his claw of a hand towards the window. 'They've become an industry in this town. Anyone with intelligence about Allied shipping, the Germans pay them money, often good money, sometimes ludicrous money. And you know what happens? The locals make it up, pocket the money, and bugger off. Wonderful. You couldn't invent it.'

'The Germans know this?'

'Of course they do. They have quotas from Berlin, targets to meet, so they just pass all this stuff on. It's a gigantic fiddle and everyone knows it unless you're stuck behind a desk in Berlin trying to win the bloody war. That's why Lisbon's such a lovely posting. No one wants to leave. Ever.'

'Except me.'

'Except you.' The military attaché nodded. There was a calendar hanging on a nail behind his head. He peered round to consult it. Then he was back again. 'We have three flights a week to England. We also have a permanent booking on a limited number of seats. To be frank, some elements of what you've told me are beyond my pay grade and my betters would be upset if they didn't get a chance to meet you themselves.'

'And they're in England?'

'They are.' He slipped a drawer open and extracted a file. After a moment or two, his head came up. 'Today is Tuesday,' he said. 'We'll try and get you on the flying boat tomorrow morning.'

'As simple as that?'

'As simple as that. I advise you to take something half-decent to eat. You'll be staying with us tonight. I'll arrange for the kitchen to make you a little picnic. Hard-boiled eggs OK? Something in the fruit line?'

Stefan was touched. He offered a nod of thanks. These people attend to the smallest print, he thought. Erwin? This wrecked face across the desk? They're all the same. They think everything through. To the last detail. He mentioned Eva again.

'I need to know there's a future for us. Ideally in England.'

'I'm afraid I can give you no guarantees. I'm sure she's a lovely woman. What if she doesn't want to go?'

'Then that would be her decision and of course I'd respect it. I just need to know that you can get her out.'

'We can get anyone out. That's what this place is for.'

'Then you'll try?'

The military attaché studied him, then checked his watch before getting to his feet and extending his hand.

'We will, *Herr Kapitän*.' The grimace again. The smile. 'And that's a guarantee.'

*

Ciudad Juarez was a day's drive across Mexico. Gómez and Yolanda arrived in the early evening as the sun was setting over the black swell of the high sierra. Perched on the banks of the Rio Grande, the city had recently exploded thanks to the nearby border. This close to the States, money was pouring in from every source – most of them illegal, according to Diego – and the result was a frenzy of building. Diego had likened it to a cowboy town, everyone out to make a fortune, and motoring slowly towards the centre of the city Gómez could believe it. The downtown was painted in neon, a gaudy come-on for everything a man could ever desire, and for once Yolanda was moved to something that sounded to Gómez like disapproval.

'Pimp heaven,' she said, eyeing the street girls on the sidewalk.

Gómez found a motel down near the river. Across the Rio Grande lay El Paso. Yolanda wanted to know how long they'd be staying. She was standing at the grubby desk that served as reception, filling in the register.

'No idea. As long as it takes.' Gómez was looking at the guy behind the desk. He gave him the address from Diego. 'Ever heard of this street? Calle Maravillas?'

The guy behind the desk didn't even look up. Just shook his head. He wanted a deposit on the room, US dollars, else they'd have to find another place. Yolanda looked at Gómez. Gómez had nothing. Everything he'd been carrying had disappeared at the penitentiary except for his passport and a twenty-dollar note that he'd tucked into the waistband of his underpants and after Tijuana that was now done.

'You recommend any bars round here?'

'Take your pick.' The guy behind the desk nodded towards the door. 'We got plenty.'

Gómez waited while Yolanda checked out the room. Cleaner than she'd expected with hot water that worked. She left three dollars on the counter and took Gómez to the nearest bar. It was hideous, *maricónes* everywhere. The second was worse. A fight had just ended and a man was on his knees by the bar, holding his face, blood trickling through his fingers. Gómez studied him a moment then escorted Yolanda back on to the sidewalk. On the other side of the road, next to a strip club called The Hot Zone, was a roadside stall that sold beer and a mess of beans. Gómez ordered both. Twice. There was a sit-down area on the rubble behind the stall, battered chairs, no table.

Yolanda was gazing at the chair Gómez had pulled towards her with his foot. He had two plates of beans. Yolanda said she preferred to stand.

'Whatever. Care for some of this stuff? Only we need a little chilli sauce here.'

She went to the counter and spooned sauce on to both plates. The owner was sweating in the heat from the stove. He had a flat Indian face and a flower tattoo on the side of his neck. Gómez joined Yolanda at the counter.

'We're here to buy a car.' Gómez was looking at the owner. 'Any idea where to go?'

'What kind of car?'

'The kind of car that goes over that river and earns us a lot of money. *Comprende?*'

Gómez rubbed his fingers together. The Indian gave him a look.

'You have money?'

'We do.'

'US?'

'Yes.'

'Then maybe you call this person. He's a friend of mine. He does good business.'

He scribbled a name and a phone number on a scrap of paper, and handed it over.

'Call him tomorrow. Early's best.' He nodded at Gómez's empty plate. 'You want more beans?'

Later, in bed at the motel, Yolanda wanted to know more.

'You're serious? We're really here to buy a car?'

'We're here to find a guy called Frank Donovan. He's driving a lime-green Caddy. He has a pretty Mexican wife and three kids and the people I work for need to know a whole lot more about him.'

Coming from Gómez, this had the makings of a speech. Yolanda had never pressed him on his work before, though other conversations had given her ideas of her own.

'You're based in New Mexico, yeah?' She nodded at the window. 'Right there across the river.'

'Who says?'

'Agard. Some place near Santa Fe.'

'That's true.'

'Care to tell me more?'

'No. Except the Army pays my bills.'

'You're a soldier?'

'G-2. Counter-intelligence.'

'This guy Frank is some kind of spook?'

'He may be. Otherwise he's just another punk hit man.'

'You're telling me he's killed someone?'

'That's what the evidence says. Does that make him a bad man? Definitely. Are we going to find him? Yes, we are. Come here . . .'

He rolled over and kissed her. She held him at arm's length for a moment. She liked 'we'.

'Those beans were shit,' she murmured. 'You need someone who knows how to cook in your life.'

19

Stefan spent the night in a small, clean bedroom on the embassy's top floor. The window, barred on the outside, was open and he lay awake, alert to every sound. A dog barking in a nearby compound. Further away, a baby crying. The clatter of a late tram and the occasional parp-parp from shipping out in the estuary. Towards morning, fog rolled in from the sea, a blanket of clamminess settling on the city, and the temperature plunged. Stefan pulled the blankets a little tighter around himself, trying to imagine the coming days and weeks. By now it would be late autumn in England, he thought. The season of death.

He awoke again at eight, disturbed by a knock at the door. A maid left a tray of coffee on the table beneath the window. An accompanying note told him to be downstairs and ready to leave within the hour. Stefan swallowed the coffee and washed as best he could in the tiny sink. Inspecting his face in the mirror, he recognised a deep exhaustion in the hollows beneath his eyes. At sea, he thought, you expect the worst at any moment. At least he felt prepared.

A car from the embassy took him down to the flying boat terminal near the docks. There was no sign of the military attaché. The flying boat, a huge Boeing, had earlier arrived from Bathurst and refuelling was complete. Stefan was escorted along the wooden pontoon and handed over to a male steward. The Clipper service had once been a byword for luxury but most of the fittings had been stripped out and the cabin was full of military personnel. Many of them were still dozing after the long flight up from West Africa. Stefan had never flown in an aircraft like this before and, after the narrow confines of the Ju-52s that operated the daily shuttle from Brittany to Berlin, it felt enormous. I'm Jonah, he told himself. Sitting in the belly of the whale.

By late morning, after a problem with one of the engines had been resolved, they took off, slowly gaining altitude as the city dwindled beneath them. Stefan was still dressed in the clothes Erwin had given him in Coruña and his obviously German accent when the steward offered him a blanket attracted looks from the passengers around him. He was sitting by the window, the sun on his face, his mind a blank. Within minutes he was asleep.

Five hours later, the aircraft began to lose height and the steady throb of the engines diminished. For the last hour, awake again, Stefan had been staring at what he knew was the coast of northern France. St Nazaire was down there, and Lorient, and Brest, U-boat gateways to the happy hunting grounds of the deep Atlantic. Within a day or so, he'd be obliged to trawl his memory for the smallest detail from those wonderful days, cementing a bridge to the interrogation team that the military attaché had warned him to expect.

'They'll want to know you're real,' he'd said. 'They'll need to taste what it's like to have been in your position, to have your talents, your training, your expertise. You and I might think the fighting is nearly over but for these people the war never ends.'

Really? They were over the English Channel now, still droning north. The pilot had levelled off at a much lower altitude and Stefan could make out the white scribbles of wake towed by shipping heading south. He counted four of them, then spotted another. They're all making for the Normandy coast, Stefan thought, with supplies for the Allied armies pushing ever deeper towards the German frontier. Food, fuel, ammunition – material to bring the Fatherland to its knees.

In the Happy Time, Stefan had slipped through these waters, alert for the tell-tale thrum-thrum of enemy vessels. Peering through the periscope, or bent over his charts, had he ever expected to end up in a situation like this? Scuttling off to the enemy with a headful of secrets and a heartful of lies? Did he really believe he could outfox these people? Beat them at their own game? And if he failed, what then? He pondered the latter question for a moment or two and then dismissed it. There were situations in life that simply didn't repay too much thought, he told himself. Better to close his eyes again and try and sleep.

They landed on the vast expanse of harbour at Poole. England's south coast stretched away left and right, chalk-white cliffs in one direction, a long curve of sandy bay in the other. The clouds had gone now and the sun was out and as they taxied towards the quayside the only indication that a war was on was a uniformed naval officer waiting on the pontoon.

It turned out she'd come for *Kapitän* Portisch. She had a whispered conversation with the chief steward the moment the aircraft's door was opened. The steward handed over a brown foolscap envelope and moments later Stefan found himself helped on to the pontoon. The woman had the envelope under her arm. She extended the other hand in greeting. She was tall and blonde, handsome in the German style, and Stefan wondered whether the choice of escort had been deliberate.

'Lieutenant Mossman.' The smile was icy. 'I trust you had a good flight, *Herr Kapitän*.'

There was a car waiting on the quayside with a male driver at the wheel. They left the port area and drove through the town. After the emptiness of Spain and Portugal, even when they were out in the countryside, there were people everywhere. The villages looked shabby and rundown, none of the civic pride that Stefan remembered from pre-war Germany, and in the larger towns there were queues wherever you looked.

His escort wanted to know whether he'd been to England before. He said yes. He'd been to London as a naval cadet. They had stopped at a level crossing, waiting for the train to pass through. He nodded at a woman hurrying up the steps on the bridge across the railway line. She had something wrapped in newspaper in one hand and a basketful of kindling in the other.

'Do people go hungry here?' he asked.

'Not really. There's not a lot of anything but there's enough to go round. I believe it's worse in Germany.'

Stefan nodded. Barely a year ago, in Hamburg, he'd watched an old woman with barely a tooth in her head gnawing at a raw turnip.

'It's terrible in Germany,' he said.

'Because of the bombing?'

'The bombing doesn't help.'

'I expect not.' She was staring out of the window. 'We had the same problem with your submarines. That was the worst time. We nearly ran out of everything, which I imagine was rather the point.'

They spent the rest of the journey in silence, for which Stefan was grateful. He no longer trusted the kindness of strangers. Ignacio had betrayed him. Erwin had threatened him with the firing squad and then schooled him in lies which might still take his life. At least this woman was honest enough to leave her hostility undisguised.

It was dark by the time they reached the outskirts of London. Their destination turned out to be a sprawling red-brick property hidden behind a screen of trees. The grounds were extensive and Stefan glimpsed rolls of barbed wire on top of the surrounding brick wall as they paused at the gatehouse before the sentry waved them through. On either side of the drive were temporary huts that looked like barracks, each with a soldier posted at the door. The car came to a halt and Stefan stepped out into the damp chill, gazing up the house. With its rusting fire escape and peeling paintwork, it looked forbidding. It reminded him of an illustration in one of the books his father used to read him as a kid. Bad things happened here, he thought. Beware trolls.

His escort led the way into the house. It had the feel of a hospital, green paint on the walls, blackout curtains in the windows, a powerful smell of disinfectant, not a picture nor a plant anywhere.

A sergeant in Army uniform emerged from a room at the end of the corridor. He glanced at Stefan but the question was directed at Mossman.

'This is he?'

'It is.'

'Did he behave himself?'

'Impeccably.'

'Glad to hear it.'

He showed Stefan into a nearby office and told him to strip.

'Leave your kit on the desk. There's a towel on the chair there. Keep yourself decent.'

Stefan did what he was told. When the sergeant came back he followed him through a maze of corridors until he found himself in a bathroom. Four shower heads dripped water on to the cracked tiles.

'Barely lukewarm, I'm afraid. Problem with the boiler again. You'll need this.' He produced a tiny tablet of soap from his pocket. 'Don't hang about. We've lots to do.'

Stefan unknotted the towel and stepped under the nearest shower. The water was icy but he forced himself to stay there until his head and shoulders were numb with cold. The soap, unscented, made absolutely no difference. By the time the sergeant returned, he was towelled and pink.

'You want to shave that off?' The sergeant was looking at his beard.

'No, thank you.'

'That's an order, not a question.' He nodded at a line of washbasins in the corner and gave Stefan a pair of scissors and a razor. 'Take these as well.' He tossed a bundle of clothes across. 'I'm back in five minutes. You need to be dressed by then.'

Stefan did his best with the scissors and the razor but the blade was blunt and he ended up smooth shaven but bloody. He soaped his face one last time, pinking the water in the basin, then got dressed. Blue serge trousers. Cotton vest. Woollen socks. Army shirt. None of them fitted properly and the socks were badly in need of a wash. Stefan imagined the smell dogging him through the days to come. After the small luxuries of life at the German legation in Coruña, he at last felt what he'd become: a prisoner.

'Follow me, son.'

Stefan still had his espadrilles. He shuffled back out into the darkness and across the gravel towards the nearest of the huts. The sentry came to attention as the sergeant approached and threw Stefan a sidelong glance. Inside, the hut was bisected by a long corridor: bare boards on the floor, nothing on the walls between a succession of doors. Stefan counted the doors. There were twelve in all, each with a tiny window at eye level. The sergeant consulted his clipboard and paused towards the end of the corridor. The room was like a cell: bars at the single window, two beds, not much else except for a figure sprawled beneath a blanket on one of the beds. A mop of blond hair spilled across the pillow. He appeared to be asleep. The sergeant barely spared him a glance. He told Stefan his first session would be starting in half an hour. In the meantime he might like to meet his new friend.

'Does he have a name?' Stefan asked. The man still hadn't moved.

'I expect so. Ask him.' The sergeant took a final look round and left, slamming the door behind him. Stefan heard the key turning in the lock and sank on to the other bed. At length, his new companion yawned and turned over, blinking in the harshness of the overhead light.

'*Guten Abend*,' he muttered. 'What did they do to your face?'

*

Gómez was out early, leaving the motel before eight. There'd been a change of shift behind the reception desk and when he asked the woman whether she knew a street called Calle Maravillas she shook her head. If he'd leave the name she'd make enquiries later. When Gómez asked whether he could use the phone on the wall she said to go ahead. He still had the scrap of paper from the Indian with the beer stall across the road. He peered at the number and fed coins into the slot beneath the phone.

'*Sí?*' A gravel voice, abrupt, not unlike Gómez himself.

'I got your number from a friend. Who am I talking to?' Gómez knew already that lots of people in this city did business across the border and he assumed most of them would speak a little English. He was right.

'You want to know my name?'

'I do.'

'Who are you? Some kind of cop?'

'No. I want to buy a car. Am I talking to the right guy?'

There was a silence on the line. Gómez heard a muttered conversation and the hollow clang of metal against metal. Then the voice was back on the line.

'Casa Hernandez? You find it easy. *No hay problema.*'

He was right. The receptionist took Gómez out on to the sidewalk and pointed towards the river. First left. Two blocks. Then a right. Watch out for the dogs.

Gómez thanked her and set off. Casa Hernandez lay at the end of a street of single-storey properties, brick construction, finished in rough stucco. The stucco had once been painted

356

yellow but it had weathered badly and scabs of the stuff were falling off. Both windows were barred and there was a heavy chain on the iron gates that led to the scruffy area of wasteland that lay beside the house. The padlock on the chain looked new. A single tree in the middle of the wasteland threw a long shadow in the morning sun. A tyre hung from the lowest branch, swinging faintly in the breeze. No cars. And no sign of any dogs.

Gómez shook the gates. Yelled for attention. Nothing. After a while he gave up and tried tapping at the windows. Again, nothing. The house was empty. Across the road was another property, in even worse condition. He was about to knock on the door and ask where he might find the owners of the Casa Hernandez when he became aware of two figures in the middle of the road making their way towards him.

One of them had a pair of dogs on a leash. The dogs were barking already, the scent of a stranger. They were big dogs, ridgebacks, bred for hunting in the desert. The two men came to a stop in front of Gómez. He guessed they were older than they looked: black trousers, open sandals. The small one wore a leather waistcoat over the bareness of his chest. The other had a white Mountain Dew T-shirt smudged with grease. They both had the same flat Indian faces as the man at the stall the night before. Maybe brothers, Gómez thought. Best to keep business in the family.

'You're the guy on the phone?' This from Shortass.

'Yeah. Care to take those dogs someplace else?'

'You don't like dogs? They know that. They can smell it. Just makes it worse, not liking them.'

The conversation appeared to have ground to a halt. Gómez wanted to do business.

'You got cars?' he asked. 'Only I'd hate to waste your time.'

'We got cars.' Shortass again.

'They legal? Got all the paperwork? Ready to roll?'

'Sure. You want a car?'

'Yeah.'

'Where you want to take it?'

'Back home,' Gómez jerked a thumb towards the river.

'Cash?'

'No problem. US dollars OK?'

'US dollars is fine.'

'Anything special in mind?'

'Yeah.'

'Like what?'

'Like a Caddy. Stretched limousine would be good. Pre-war would be even better. Are we getting the picture here?'

'Sure. You gotta colour on that?'

'Pink?' Gómez frowned. 'Maybe lime-green? I'm getting married. It's a present. My woman, she loves all this Miami shit. Let's say lime-green. You can help me out here?'

It was far too obvious, and all three of them knew it. All Gómez wanted was a price. For the right money, most men will sell anything.

'You sure you want the car, *señor*?' Shortass again, obviously the boss.

'What else would I be wanting?'

'I dunno. I guess that's my question. You want the car, that's fine. You want the driver, that's maybe something different. Either way, we like to help. That's our business, helping, selling the right car at the right price, keeping people sweet, keeping folks happy, folks like you from across the border. Why don't you tell us a little more about yourself? You want something nice and cool to drink? Before the day gets real hot?'

He nodded at the house behind them, Casa Hernandez.

'You guys live there?'

'We do.'

'So where are the cars?'

'Someplace else.'

Gómez was weighing his options. There was the possibility of violence in the offing. He could smell it. But on the other hand these guys were at least a place to start. He was looking at the dogs. Without a firearm he was feeling deeply uncomfortable.

'They stay outside? The dogs?'

'Sure. They're yard dogs. No way do we ever have them in the house.'

Gómez was looking at the tyre hanging from the tree. He'd seen set-ups like this around slum properties on the South Side in Chicago. You buy your dog for protection. You want to work its jaws a little, get the mutt in shape. And so you hang an old tyre and train the dog to jump and clamp on. Get a little closer, and he'd be looking at teeth marks in the rubber and deeper gouges where the animals tried to shake the thing to pieces.

'OK.' Gómez nodded at the house. 'I could use a drink.'

Shortass produced a key and led the way to the door. His *compadre* dragged the dogs towards the padlocked gate. The dogs were going crazy again, looking round. Disappointment on legs, Gómez thought.

The inside of the house was cold after the warmth of the sidewalk. He stepped down on to a tiled floor. To his surprise, the place was clean, nicely furnished. A big refrigerator hummed in the kitchen area and there was even a vase of flowers in the space reserved for a leather sofa and a couple of chairs.

Shortass was pretending to occupy himself in the kitchen, busying about, doing nothing. He's waiting for his buddy, Gómez thought. And he was right.

'This drink of yours . . .' Gómez began. Then the door to the yard opened and the *compadre* stepped in. He was loading a shell into a shotgun. He snapped the barrel shut, then levelled it at Gómez's chest. From five yards he couldn't miss.

'I thought you guys preferred knives,' Gómez grunted.

'Guns are quicker.' Shortass again. 'Though we still have to clean the place afterwards.'

He told Gómez to put his hands in the air, then he patted him down. Both arms, neck area, torso, crutch, both legs. Impressive attention to detail.

The *compadre* was watching with interest.

'*Nada?*'

'*Nada.*' Shortass sounded disappointed.

'What are you guys expecting?' Gómez this time. 'You think I'm here to shoot you?'

'We don't know why you're here. Except you don't want to buy no lime-green Caddy.'

'You're sure about that?'

'Yeah.'

'You know where to find one?'

'Might do.'

'But it's gonna cost me, right?'

'Yeah. You want to find the owner? Big bucks.'

'How much?'

'A thousand.'

'*A thousand?* You're kidding. How many cars do I get to keep for that?'

Shortass shook his head. It felt like genuine regret though Gómez could read disappointment in his eyes. Shotguns frightened most men. Not this one.

'You're some kind of comedian now?' Shortass wondered. 'You figure we're not serious?'

'I'm sure you're serious but I have a problem with the money you want. A thousand is a joke. I could buy this place for a thousand and have change for the shitheap across the road. Why don't we start lower?'

'Like where?'

'Like a hundred.'

'A hundred is an insult. For a hundred you get nothing. For a hundred we might even shoot you.' He muttered something under his breath before conferring with his buddy. For a moment, Gómez anticipated violence but he was wrong.

'On your way, gringo.' Shortass nodded at the door to the street. 'Count yourself lucky. And don't fucking bother us again.'

20

The first session started at what Stefan judged to be late evening. There were no clocks that he could see and no one appeared to be wearing a watch. When he'd asked his new room-mate what this place was called he'd shrugged and said it had no name.

'The English call it the Centre,' he'd said. 'We call it *das Scheisshaus* because they just want to flush us away.'

Das Scheisshaus. Matelot slang for the toilet.

It was the sergeant who came to fetch him. They stumbled through the darkness outside, towards the looming shape of the house. The interrogation room was on the first floor. It was bigger than Stefan had expected and it had a bareness that was slightly intimidating: high ceilings, two windows shrouded in blackout cloth and a long oak table.

'Sit.'

The invitation had the force of an order. The sergeant had snapped a salute and disappeared. Two men sat behind the table, both in greatcoats. It was freezing.

Stefan settled on the single chair. The bigger of the two men was studying him with a frown that spoke of a deep impatience. He had a monocle in his right eye. His Brilliantined hair was swept back from a high forehead and the way he sat at the table – fingers tapping, shoulders hunched – suggested that this might be the end of a very long day.

'You will refer to me as Colonel,' he said. 'My colleague you will call Major. We will conduct this interview in German.'

His colleague was a smaller, rounder man. Unlike the colonel, he had a face made for the smaller courtesies. He offered Stefan a nod of welcome, even apologised for the temperature. The boiler again. The usual difficulties in getting hold of enough coal.

Stefan said nothing. Their German was fluent. They spoke the language with the same ease as the military attaché in Lisbon but in every other respect the contrast was obvious. Talking to the military attaché had been a pleasure. Sitting here, trembling with cold, was anything but. Already this felt like a court of law, with himself the accused and the colonel keen to bring matters to a head. He was leafing through a pile of notes. Stefan thought he recognised the brown foolscap envelope the steward had handed to Mossman on the pontoon at Poole. The colonel looked up.

'This voyage of yours,' he said. 'We don't seem to be able to find the boat.'

'It was wrecked. That's why I'm here.'

'The fishing boat, Mr Portisch. The one you say you took from O Barquero. It had a name, this boat?'

'The *Esmeralda*.'

'And the fisherman?'

'A man called Santos.'

'Describe him.'

'Thin. Dark complexion. Maybe forty. Maybe older. A tough man. At sea all his life.'

'Did you talk to him?'

'I couldn't. I don't speak Spanish. He didn't have any German, or even English.'

'Then how did you know he'd been at sea all his life?'

'Eva told me. Eva was at the house where I was staying.' Stefan nodded at the notes. 'I explained about Eva to your man at the embassy.'

'You paid this Santos?'

'I did.'

'How much?'

'Three gold coins. Probably more than he earns in a year.'

'So he'll be a rich man now? When we find him back in O Barquero?'

'He may not go back to the village.'

'How do you know? If you never talked to him?'

It was a good question, forcefully put. The colonel had dug a hole with contemptuous ease and Stefan had obliged him by toppling into it.

'I don't know, Colonel.' Stefan was trying to sound patient. 'I'm simply hazarding a guess.'

'What was the weather like? En route?'

'Calm.'

'And sunny?'

'Yes.'

'So why are you that colour? So white? So pale? Three days at sea, you'd be sunburned, turning brown.'

'I was resting up.' Stefan's hand found his leg. 'I was injured when I came ashore from the wreck. Lying down eases the pain.'

'There was a cabin?'

'Yes.'

'Bunks?'

'Yes.'

'How many?'

'Two.'

'And you stayed there all the time?'

'Most of the time.'

'For three whole days?'

'Yes.'

'Describe the cabin. Tell me what you could see from this bunk of yours.'

Stefan looked from one face to the other. He knew he was in trouble again and he cursed Erwin for his choice of transport south. A series of lifts on those crazy roads down the coast would have been so much easier, he thought. Stefan passed from hand to hand like a parcel.

'The cabin was very small,' he said. 'Very primitive.'

'Colour?'

'White. And dirty.'

'You could cook down there?'

'Of course.'

'How?'

Stefan hadn't a clue. He thought about the tiny galley on the submarine, about cooking facilities on a yacht he'd once helped crew on the Baltic. Nothing helped.

'It wasn't really cooking,' he said at last. 'We had bread. Cheese. Wine. Hard-boiled eggs. Onions. Fruit. Enough for three days.'

'You said you could cook down there.'

'I was wrong. You couldn't.'

'So why did you make it up?'

365

'I didn't make it up. I just got it wrong.'

The colonel nodded and glanced sideways at his fellow officer. The major was still bent over his pad. He hadn't stopped writing since the interview began.

'Tell me about this bunk again.' The colonel was back with Stefan. 'You had blankets?'

'Yes.'

'How many?'

'One.'

'What colour?'

'What *colour*?'

'Yes, Mr Portisch. Surely you must know. By your own account you spent three days lying under this blanket. Those same three days when you weren't up on deck enjoying the sunshine, enjoying the view. So I'll ask you the question again: what colour were the blankets?'

'Red.'

'Both of them?'

'Yes.'

'You told me one just now. You said one blanket. Am I right, Major?'

'Yes, sir.'

'Thank you.' He turned back to Stefan. 'So how many is it? One? Two? More? These things make a difference. It gets cold at sea, especially at night.'

'One.'

'One. Thank you. One red blanket. Make a note, Major. Ask the search party to check when they find the bloody boat.' His head came round again. 'Anything to add, Mr Portisch?'

'Yes.' Stefan was angry now, past caring whether this was

part of the softening-up process. 'I thought I was here to tell you about submarines, about that last voyage we made, about a war we're never going to win.'

'You're here to answer our questions, Mr Portisch, and I'd be obliged if you can keep your temper to yourself. In case it's escaped your notice, you're a prisoner. You have no rights. Only obligations. And just now they boil down to convincing us we can trust you. I don't believe for a moment that you came to Lisbon by boat. I think you're lying. I think you made it up. And if that proves to be the case, why should I believe anything else?'

Stefan didn't bother answering the question. He'd spent the last twenty-four hours rehearsing for this moment and already he'd failed. The simplest questions, the smallest details, were tripping him up. They were toying with him. Worse, they were making him look a fool.

'I came to Lisbon,' he said at length, 'because otherwise the Germans would have found me and shot me. Why? Because I'm a deserter. And because I killed a man whose life and reputation they appear to value. For me this is a bad end to a bad war. All I can do now is pray for an early peace. I know a great deal about my trade, about the submarine service. In my head I have a great deal of information that may be of service to you. You're welcome to all of it, every last detail. Yet all you can talk about are fucking *blankets*.'

'It's not just *why* you're here, *Herr Kapitän*.' The major this time. 'It's *how*. We have to take a look at you. We have to make our minds up. You'll understand that, I trust.'

'Of course. You're very welcome. One blanket. Red.'

'And the fishing boat? The *Esmeralda*? She went back to O Barquero?'

'I have no idea.'

'But we may be able to find her there? Or perhaps talk to someone about her?'

'I expect so.'

'Then rest assured that is what we'll do.' He sat back for a moment, nodding to himself, and Stefan wondered whether this phase of the interview was over. Far from it. The colonel took up the running, returning again and again to the voyage south. He wanted to know about the tides, the direction of the wind, whether or not there was a barometer on board, and most important of all the route the fisherman had plotted as he tracked south. Because Stefan was a fellow seaman, details like this would – at the very least – have been of some interest.

'He had charts? This fisherman fellow?'

'Yes.'

'Old? New?'

'Old. Well-used.'

'All the way down to Lisbon?'

'Yes.'

'He went there often? A voyage of four hundred miles? To go *fishing*?'

'Maybe the charts belonged to someone else. Maybe he borrowed them. Like I say, I was in no position to ask. I took a look at the charts, just like you'd expect me to. And, yes, they were old.'

'Coffee stains?'

'There was no coffee. Would I have liked coffee? Yes. Could he boil water? No. Did we drink unbrewed coffee? No. Therefore, no coffee stains.'

'Very logical, Mr Portisch. I congratulate you. You're getting better at this.'

The gruffness of the compliment took Stefan by surprise. Did he mean it? Was this the first flicker of warmth between them? A hint there might be more to this hard-faced martinet than volley after volley of impossible questions?

Stefan didn't know. Already, he felt exhausted. His brain, numb with cold, was ceasing to function. Ask me about submarines, he thought. Ask me why I turned my back on the war that night. Ask me about anything but a man I've never met aboard a boat I never set foot on.

Abruptly, to Stefan's enormous relief, the colonel changed tack. He had the list of officers Stefan had passed to the military attaché at the embassy in Lisbon. He was pleased to confirm that every name was accurate.

'I passed the test?'

'You did, Mr Portisch.'

'How did you check?'

'There are ways and means. The currency of that city is information. The right money buys anything.'

'You have a source,' Stefan suggested. 'Probably at the German Embassy. The names of the crew would be well known because our people have just buried them.'

'Your people?'

'My people.'

'But you're a deserter, Mr Portisch. They're not your people any more. You've turned your back on them. Personally I find that incomprehensible.'

'It shocks you?'

'I didn't say that. I live in the world of facts, Mr Portisch.

The facts suggest you've had a very good war. We've checked that, too. Yet here you are, only too happy to lay your trophies at our feet. Now why would that be? What would you have us believe?'

What would you have us believe?

Stefan blinked. This man compelled respect. In a single phrase, a single question, he'd skewered the essence of everything Stefan had been through since the moment he'd been dragged out of O Barquero.

What would you have us believe?

'Well?' The colonel wanted an answer. Reflections danced in his monocle.

'I'd have you believe that I mourn for my men, that I wouldn't be here if a single one of them was alive and needed me. I'd have you believe that my faith in this war has gone and that I'd do anything in my power to bring it to an early end. And I'd have you believe that a loss of this kind of faith leaves you in a place where no fighting man would ever want to be. Am I ashamed of what I've done? Of coming to you? Oddly enough, no. Do I think it might help? Yes. And am I left wondering who I really am? The answer, once again, has to be yes. For better or worse, I've made a decision. I know a great deal. As I say, I'm happy to share every particle of that knowledge and I suspect it's your job to make the most of it. All I can say is good luck, gentlemen. Help yourself.'

He sat back, happy at least that he'd been able to offer a rationale for what he'd done. Dishonourable, perhaps, but at least coherent. The colonel appeared to have come to the same conclusion. He gathered his papers and without even a nod of farewell, he left the room.

370

Stefan's gaze went to the major. When he enquired whether something warm to drink might be in order, Stefan said yes. The colonel's place would shortly be taken by another officer specialising in submarine warfare. And with him would come a mug of tea.

'Thank you,' Stefan said. And meant it.

*

Gómez met Yolanda back at the motel. She had news of the address Diego had left in the envelope. The woman at reception had phoned her husband. Her husband drove a cab and knew the city well. Calle Maravillas, according to him, lay out of town off the road that wound out towards the sierra. There were some nice properties out there and the area had become a playground for people who were making money from the war. She'd asked him if he happened to know who lived at the address but he'd told her he didn't.

'He'll drive us out there,' she said. 'If that's where you want to go next.'

Gómez said yes. The receptionist put another call through. The cab arrived at the motel fifteen minutes later. Yolanda sat in the front, making conversation in Spanish, while Gómez watched the roadside shacks begin to thin. The dusty brown rise of the sierra lay ahead. Gómez was checking left and right for a chance sighting of a lime-green Caddy. An automobile that colour should be easy to spot, and this morning's encounter with the Indian car dealers had suggested, at the very least, that the car was somewhere in Ciudad Juarez, but this was a city of a quarter of a million people and there were endless places to hide.

At length, the driver slowed for a turn. There were no street signs out here, no indication of where they were, but a quarter of a mile up a modest hill the rusting Buick came to a halt. They were looking at a bone-white hacienda-style property standing in maybe three acres of scrub. It was single-storey, much bigger than the other houses they'd just passed, and it looked brand new. Gómez caught sight of an interior courtyard through a tiled archway and there was a child's swing beside what appeared to be a sandpit. A cat was sprawled in the shade of a big acacia and the wind off the high sierra was stirring the fronds of a couple of palm trees. The place oozed money, Gómez thought. If you'd tired of the heat and the violence downtown, this is where you might pitch your tent.

Yolanda asked the driver to wait. She and Gómez pushed through the gate and walked through the dust to the front door. The door was barred with an ornamental grille. More fresh paint. Gómez reached through and knocked on the glass. He could hear nothing inside: no radio, no murmurs of conversation, no movement. He told Yolanda to go back to the cab. If anyone approached by car, the driver was to sound the horn twice. The last thing he wanted was another confrontation.

Yolanda gave him a look and told him to be careful. Then she was gone. Gómez skirted the house. At the back he found a tiled patio with a view of the sierra framed by yet more palm trees. Also a table for drinks and a couple of fancy chairs. There were two empty cups on the table and when he picked one up he caught the scent of coffee.

A big glass door led into the house. When he turned the handle and applied the gentlest pressure, it opened. He stepped inside, recognising the hum of an air-con unit. The big room was cold after the mid-morning heat outside and it took a second or two for his eyes to adjust to the gloom. This had to be a dining room. The big circular table looked as new as everything else and someone needed to clear up after breakfast. The smear of eggs on quality china. Crusts of toast pushed to the side of the plate. A jug of what must have been coffee. An American start to the day, he thought.

He froze on the tiled floor, hearing the faintest scuff from the depths of the house, then relaxed as a cat wandered in. It was a black cat. It looked him up and down then wound itself around his ankles.

'*Hola?*' He went to the door and called again. No response. Nothing except the ticking silence.

Back in the dining room he noticed a desk in the corner, away from the patio. There was a typewriter on the desk and a stack of what looked like correspondence beside it. He took a closer look. The machine was a Remington, a big thing, standard issue in offices across the States. The suicide note, he thought. Sol Fiedler's farewell to the job that had killed him.

Gómez found a box of foolscap paper in the desk drawer. He took a sheet and fed it into the roller. Then he typed across the keys, loud, clunky, and did it again with the caps lock down. Five lines of type, every character captured. He extracted the sheet and folded it into his jacket pocket. There was a waste-paper bin beside the desk, a couple of balled-up discards in the bottom. He fetched one out and smoothed it against the desk. It was an unfinished letter and he took that as well before pushing deeper into the house.

He was in the entrance hall now. A kid's tricycle lay beside the front door, together with a bucket and spade. A light summer

373

coat, adult this time, hung from a hook. On the other wall there
was a big oval mirror with notes pushed beneath the frame,
the kind of reminders busy people might leave when they were
in a hurry. He took one out, and read it in the throw of light
through the glass of the front door. The note was in German.
Was this some visitor, down from the States or across from
Europe? He'd no idea.

More doors led off the gleaming tiles of the hallway. He
tried the nearest. It was a kids' bedroom, two bunks, toys
everywhere. He went to the end of the hall, tried the far door.
Another bedroom, much bigger, the huge double bed unmade,
the sheets rumpled. He could smell perfume in the air, the smell
of serious money, and when he opened a drawer in the dressing
table it was full of sex toys. He gazed at them for a moment,
wondering what kind of woman needed three black dildos,
varying sizes, then slid the drawer closed again.

A woman's bag lay beside the bed. It was leather, new-
looking. He picked it up, emptied the contents on to the bed. A
handkerchief. A fold of dollar bills. A small, round mirror. A
bunch of cosmetic stuff. And a document wallet, leather again,
scuffed. He opened the wallet. Inside, were two documents.
One of them looked Mexican, perhaps a driving licence, no
photo. The other was unmistakable: the black German eagle
atop a swastika. The gothic script: *Deutsches Reich*. He felt
the texture of the cover between his fingers. Grey linen.

He opened it. On the left-hand side, in careful script,
a list of personal details. On the right, stamped on two
corners, a photo of a woman. He stared at it. She was three-
quarter profile, middle-aged, carefully coiffured hair, steady
gaze, undeniably beautiful. Her surname was Müller. Her

Christian name was Lara. She might have belonged in a movie magazine.

Gómez lingered a moment longer, then repacked the bag before slipping the ID into his pocket and making for the door. Only then did he become aware of the figure in the hall outside. She was wearing a dressing gown several sizes too big. Her feet were bare and the jet-black hair tumbled down over her shoulders. She was staring at Gómez. Donovan's woman, he thought. Francisca. From back in Santa Fe.

'What are you doing?' she asked. Not a trace of fear.

'I'm looking for your husband.'

'Frank?'

'Yes.'

'He's not here. And he's not my husband.'

'Where is he?'

'I don't know.' She nodded at the bed, at the dressing table, at the liberties Gómez had taken. 'You shouldn't be here. How can you just come in like this?'

Gómez didn't answer. He wanted to know about her kids. Were they with Frank?

'No. Lara has them. She let me sleep. You must go. Before she comes back.'

Gómez wondered whether she was lying. Then came the sound of a car horn from outside. Yolanda, he thought. And trouble in the offing.

He was still looking at Francisca. He told her he'd come to the front door, knocked, woken her up. She'd let him in. They'd talked.

'You're good with that?'

She shook her head.

'No.' She nodded at the bed again. 'I saw what I saw.'

'*Gracias*. Suit yourself.'

He pushed roughly past her. She smelled of recent sex. He wondered whether to search the other rooms in the house, to find the bedroom where she'd slept. Maybe Donovan was in there, listening to the murmur of conversation. He paused beside one of the rooms he hadn't checked. If he was right, what would he do with the man? Insist on a lengthy interview? Ask what he was doing in the house of a woman with a Nazi ID card and a taste for black sex toys?

'He's not here.' It was Francisca. She nodded at the door. It was already ajar. 'Open it. Take a look. There's no one here. Just me.'

Gómez opened the door. Another double bed. Another tangle of sheets. No Donovan.

'So where is he?'

'I just told you. I don't know. Please leave. It will be better.'

'For who?'

'For all of us. Especially you.'

Gómez held her gaze a moment longer, then opened the front door and stepped out into the blaze of sunshine. Half expecting a lime-green Cadillac, he found himself looking at a big Mercedes. Like everything else in this woman's life, it was black. A short, squat Mexican was opening the gate. At the wheel, behind dark glasses, was the woman he'd seen in the ID card. She was staring at him as he strode towards her. There were kids in the back, three little faces. No sign of Donovan.

Gómez was alongside the car now. The Mexican had a gun in his hand, a big automatic. Gómez gestured for the woman to open the window. Full lips. Unsmiling.

'I'm guessing you speak English,' he said.

'You guess right.' Just a hint of an accent. Impressive.

'My name's Gómez. I've come looking for Frank Donovan. Give him my best and tell him I'm at the Motel del Norte. Up by the river. You got that?'

He didn't wait for a reply. The Mexican was blocking his path back to the cab. The gun was levelled at Gómez's chest.

'Don't.' It was the woman. She was out of the car. She said something else in Spanish and the Mexican, with obvious reluctance, stepped aside.

Gómez didn't stop walking. Seconds later he was ducking into the back of the cab, hauling the door shut.

'Drive, *amigo*,' he grunted. 'We need to be out of here.'

21

Next morning, still dark, Stefan lay awake. Despite his best efforts he'd barely slept at all. Too cold, too uncomfortable, too far from home. Yesterday's interrogations had finally put him in the hands of an expert in submarine warfare and he'd willingly told the man everything that might conceivably have been useful. At the time, it had almost felt like a social conversation, two men who knew their business comparing notes, but the fact he'd been so open, so helpful, so *compliant*, must have troubled his conscience. Hence the sleepless night.

Now, barely dawn, he was back in front of the colonel and the major.

'Tell me about your leader, Mr Portisch.' This from the colonel.

'*Onkel* Karl?'

'*Tante* Adolf.'

Auntie Adolf? Stefan stared at the face across the table. Concentrate, he told himself. Think harder. This wasn't a cosy conversation about operational codes and the *Elektro* boats. This was a return to the world of make-believe. At all costs, he had to stay ahead of these people, especially the implacable colonel.

'*Tante* Adolf?' Stefan repeated. The sainted Führer recast as a woman? Never married? Never ate meat? Always did his best to resist the touch of flesh on flesh? Perfect, he thought. Auntie Adolf.

'What do you want to know?' he asked.

'I want to know what made you people follow that man. Hamburg was solid. It paid its way. It was a merchant city. It was full of business. Then the Austrian appears. The man with the mad eyes. Forgive me, Mr Portisch, but what made a boy like you, a youth like you, believe in a man like that?'

'You don't believe. You're young. You follow.'

'Same thing.'

'Not at all.'

They were back in the bareness of the big room on the first floor, all three of them. The blackout curtain had disappeared and it was, if anything, even colder. Grey fog at the windows. And a suspicion of ice where the condensation on the glass met the wooden frame.

'Explain.' It was an order. The colonel was still in his greatcoat. Had he slept at all? Stefan suspected not.

'I was thirteen,' he said. 'The regime was everywhere. It was like gravity. It was like the weather. You accepted it. It brought good things. The shipyards were busy. My father's job was secure. My mother had a little money to spend on sheet music. We laughed at the oafs in the uniforms. They knew nothing.'

'They knew everything, Mr Portisch. The world was theirs. I ask you the question again. Why him? Why Hitler?'

The question was put with some force, as if the colonel was trying to crack some deep historical riddle. What has any of this got to do with me? Stefan asked himself.

'Hitler came from nowhere,' he said. 'But he was different. You couldn't ignore the man. He was everywhere, even in Hamburg. He was all over the papers, all over the streets. He controlled everything. What they taught us in school, the special days you had to put the flags out, even what kind of music you listened to. That was our world. *Der Führer.* Hitler. There was nothing else.'

'The Communists?'

'The Communists fought to begin with but then they went quiet.'

'Would you describe your father as a Communist?'

'He was a socialist. He belonged to a union. He believed in the people.'

'But active? Am I right?'

'Certainly, yes.' Stefan remembered smoky evenings at the apartment in Hamburg, his father's mates gathered to debate the latest campaign. They'd raised their voices for fairer wages, shorter hours, better working conditions, but when they took to the streets it guaranteed nothing but violence. 'The Brownshirts broke the marches up,' he said. 'The regime was never very good at listening.'

'They beat your father?'

'He came back with a bloody nose, once, yes.'

'And you remember that?'

'Of course.'

'And what did it teach you?'

'It taught me these people would stop at nothing. They lied, too.'

'In what respect?'

'The party chiefs would come to town. Hitler himself came

once. There was a huge rally, a hundred thousand people, maybe more. It was like a festival. That's the trick they pulled. They made you believe you were on some kind of holiday. I even went myself. He promised us a new bridge over the Elbe. What we ended up with was rather different.'

'Yet you went along with all this nonsense. Kiel Olympics? Naval College? A berth in the *Reichsmarine*? Special training for the submarine service?'

Stefan nodded. He couldn't help but agree. This man wasn't even reading the notes in front of him. He seemed to have absorbed every detail of Stefan's career.

'I was a patriot,' he said wearily. 'We knew there was going to be fighting. Either you get involved or the fighting comes to you. You fight for the Fatherland. You fight for your crew. I never fought for the Führer.'

'But you were so *good* at it, Mr Portisch. That's my point. You had an aptitude, a gift, and that's what you put at the service of this clown.'

'Clown' triggered something deep in Stefan. He could think of a number of settings for Adolf Hitler but a circus wasn't one of them. This wasn't someone who'd ever make you laugh. Far from it.

'I signed up,' Stefan said simply. 'If you're asking whether I enjoyed it, then the answer is yes. Physically it was tough. I liked that. It made me feel good about myself. But it was a challenge in all kinds of other ways, as well. You're underwater for most of your working life. That's unnatural. That's not where you belong. So you had to make that work for yourself. It was a world apart. You had to understand it. You had to adapt. It was a world you made your own.'

'You and your crew.'

'Of course.'

'Men you fought alongside.'

'Yes.'

'Men you would have died for.'

'Yes.'

'Men you ended up betraying.'

Stefan stared at him, unblinking. 'My men were dead,' he said softly, 'and there was nothing else left. The clown had seen to that.'

The colonel rolled his eyes and got to his feet. He was leaving Stefan in the hands of the major. He promised he would return later to see whether his colleague had managed to get any further than this claptrap.

Stefan watched him depart, then turned to the major. This was a man who appeared to have none of the colonel's unbending aggression. He was soft-spoken, accommodating. He knew how to listen.

'The colonel has respect for brave men,' he said. 'He thinks you were brave. Indeed, he *knows* you were brave. What he can't account for is what happened at the end.'

'He thinks I'm a coward?'

'He thinks you were a deserter. In his book, that's even worse.'

'He's right. Technically, I was. I am. That's why I'm here. Another week or so in Spain and they would have caught me.'

'They?'

'The Spanish police. And they would have handed me over to the Germans. Think of it from my point of view. My men are dead. I want nothing more to do with the war. I've lost everything, absolutely everything. No family, no home, no past. All gone, erased, wiped out. You want me to tell you a little more about that?'

The major nodded, pulling his pad towards him. After nearly an hour, Stefan thought he'd done justice to his story and the major was looking at pages and pages of notes. About the early days of the war. About the Happy Time. About sitting in the cool blue light of the submarine and listening to the daily news broadcasts from Berlin. About beginning to suspect that the Führer's glorious plans for the Thousand Year Reich might have gone a little awry. Stalingrad. El Alamein. Parts of the homeland bombed into oblivion. Hamburg consumed by the flames. His brother Werner vanished, wiped out, disappeared. Much like everything else.

'So nothing left?' The major was flicking through his notes. 'No family at all? Have I got that right?'

Stefan nodded. His sister-in-law was still alive but would be helpless for the rest of her life. His grandparents, too, might still be working the farm but he couldn't be sure. Then he paused, frowning.

'One thing I never mentioned,' he said. 'I have a half-brother, a Jew called Sol Fiedler. And he had the good sense to get out in time.'

The major's head came up. He did his best to mask his interest but Stefan could see it in his eyes. At last, a spark of light in the gathering darkness, a tiny morsel to offer the colonel on his return.

'He's still alive, this half-brother of yours?'

'Yes, as far as I know.'

'And where might he be?'

'America.'

*

Back at the motel, Gómez went straight to the room. Yolanda had seen everything and so had the driver. The Mexican carrying the gun alarmed her.

'What is this?' She said. 'Who was that woman in the car?'

Gómez shook his head. He wasn't prepared to say. He wanted her to leave at once, head for the bridge across the Rio Grande, get herself back into the States.

'Why?'

Gómez ignored the question. He told her to find the FBI field office in El Paso.

'How do I do that?'

'Go to the regular police station. Give them my name. Ask them to make a call.' He wrote out a phone number from memory. 'This takes them to a guy called O'Flaherty. He's with the Bureau, too. Works out of DC. He knows all about this. In fact, he sent me.'

'I thought you said you were Army?'

'I am.'

'But you're telling me this guy O'Flaherty is FBI.'

'You're right. It's complex. Ride with the punches, eh? How much cash have you got?'

Yolanda stared at him a moment and then opened her purse and gave Gómez a wad of dollar notes. He counted them. Seventy-seven dollars.

'This is all you've got?'

'Yep.'

'You can get more across the border?'

'A little. Not much. You're cleaning me out here, baby.

And now you take my money, too.'

Her smile checked Gómez in his stride. He pulled her closer, kissed her.

'Tomorrow, I promise you.'

'Tomorrow what?'

'Tomorrow we get married. That OK with you?'

'Sure. But you're telling me you're staying here?'

'Yeah.'

'Why? Didn't you find the guy you were after? Wasn't he in the house?'

'No. But he'll come to me. I guarantee it.'

He produced three items from his jacket pocket. A couple were samples from the typewriter back at the house. He kept one and gave the other to Yolanda. She was staring at the third item.

'What's that?'

'A Nazi ID card. The woman's name is Lara Müller. You need to talk to O'Flaherty on the phone. Tell him to get his ass down to El Paso. Tell him to take a plane. He has to make it quick. Give him the ID and this other piece of paper. Tell him I can link Donovan to both the woman and the typewriter. That's all he needs to know.'

'Except you're going to meet this guy.'

'Sure.'

'And then what?'

Gómez shrugged, said he didn't know. He'd been sent to this shithole to find Donovan. The job was nearly done. Then he'd come north again.

'You're good with that?'

She wasn't. But it was obvious too that she was beginning to know this man.

'I guess I could say no.' She gazed down at the ID card. 'But would you ever fucking listen?'

Within minutes she'd gone. Gómez stretched full length on the bed. The border was a ten-minute drive away. Within the hour, she should be talking to O'Flaherty. O'Flaherty, in turn, would take the news to Hoover. A top atomic scientist was ferrying out the nation's secrets not to the Soviets but to the Nazis, an irresistible invitation for J. Edgar to batter down a few more doors in DC and lay claim to an acre or two of the Army's turf. How come these SOBs up on the Hill can't keep the genie in the bottle? How come the fucking place leaks like a sieve? What if our Nazi friends have stolen a march on Mr Oppenheimer? What happens if their bang turns out to be bigger than ours?

Gómez, who had no taste for power politics, tried to visualise the consequences of Yolanda's journey north. Hoover presumably had the ear of the President. That's where he'd be headed, to the very seat of power. It would be Roosevelt who'd have to weigh the odds, to call for specialist advice, to try and figure out quite how far the Nazis had got with their own bomb. On the Hill, they called it the Gadget but this little piece of whimsy was gonna fool no one. With their own Gadget, the Nazis could bring this war to an end, a possibility that would explain a great deal about their fanatic resistance. Hold on, guys. Another coupla months and London could be history.

Gómez wondered about the possibility, tried to imagine an entire city vaporised in a second or two, the way it happened in space fiction cartoons, then checked the door and returned to the bed. Something about the typewriter was troubling him but just now he had no idea why.

*

In London, at the Centre, it was nearly midday. The overnight fog had burned off and during a brief break Stefan had taken the chance to limp across the interrogation room and stretch his legs. It was sunny outside and from the window he could see the first fallen leaves beginning to carpet the grass below.

'Rain later, Mr Portisch. But I fancy the worst of the cold has gone.'

It was the colonel. He was back with his colleague and Stefan sensed at once that the major had briefed him about this latest development with their new charge. There was something different in his eyes, a hint of genuine curiosity, no less steely but definitely there.

'Interesting story,' he sat down. 'Tell me about your mother.'

'My *mother*?'

'Your mother. She'd had this affair. She was a married woman. I know it was years before you came along but did that surprise you? Shock you?'

'Surprise, definitely. I never thought she could be so emotional. She showed me Sol's letter. She was in tears.'

'What did the letter say?'

'It was very polite. Full of hesitation. This was someone who'd never met my mother despite being her son. The last thing he wanted to do was upset her.'

'So he failed.'

'Not at all. I think he touched a nerve. I think she'd felt so much guilt over the years, just letting him go like that, and suddenly here he was, a voice she'd never heard.'

'And your father? Wasn't he just a bit . . .' the colonel frowned, '. . . sensitive?'

'He knew nothing about my mother getting the letter. I was the only one she told.'

'How about Werner? Your brother?'

'He was in the *Wehrmacht*. He'd already joined up. He was away.'

'As you were.'

'That's right. But I was based at Kiel. That's just a couple of hours by train. I could get home regularly. And I was closer to my mother, too. Closer than Werner.'

'I see.' The colonel scribbled himself a note. 'Tell me about your father again.'

'I asked my mother what she was going to do about this Sol. She said it had been a long time ago. Things were very different now. We were a family. We were happy, secure.'

'And was that true?'

'Yes.'

'So?'

'She said she'd think about it and maybe make a decision. Which is what she did. By the next time I came home, she'd told my father. She'd also been in touch with Sol, and everything was arranged. My father knew that Sol and his wife were going to emigrate. They'd got the permissions. It was going to happen. My mother wouldn't be meeting Sol's father. She didn't want that, not after all those years, and neither did my dad.'

'Was Sol's father also in Berlin?'

'I've no idea. I never asked.'

'Really? I find that extraordinary. Why on earth not?'

'Because it felt disloyal to my parents, my father especially.

Sol? Yes, I wanted to meet him, to find out what he was like. My mother's one-time lover? No thank you.'

More scribbling. The colonel gave him a long, searching look.

'This letter of Sol's?'

'Gone. Along with everything else.' Stefan risked a small, private smile. 'Your fault, Colonel. Not mine.'

'You're blaming the firestorm?'

'Yes.'

'Neat.'

The word stopped Stefan in his tracks. Beware, he told himself. These people are past masters at sieving fact from fiction.

The colonel skipped forward in the story. The major had told him about that first meeting in the Atlantic Hotel, the way the two of them had bonded, the little *pas de deux* over the bill for afternoon tea.

'Do you recall how much it cost by any chance?'

'I do. Every last *Pfennig*.'

'How much was it?'

'One hundred and seventeen *Reichsmarks*. Half my weekly pay.'

Stefan watched the major writing the figure down. Thank God for Erwin, he thought. He'd made a phone call from Coruña, checking the figure out.

'And afterwards? You told my colleague you met again.'

'We did. I think Sol wanted me to believe that he was staying at the Atlantic but of course he couldn't afford the place. In fact, he couldn't afford any place. He had enough money for the train fare to Hamburg and back.'

'So what happened?'

'He stayed with a girlfriend of my mother. For nothing.'

'Her name, Mr Portisch?'

'Heidi.'

'Family name?'

'Brünner.'

'Address?'

'She lived in Hammerbeck. She was killed in the bombing, too. I can't remember the address.'

The colonel removed his monocle out and gave it a polish. 'You have a rare gift for erasing the evidence, Herr Portisch.' He replaced the monocle. 'One might find that troublesome.'

'Not me, Colonel. I didn't do that. Your people did.'

The colonel held his gaze for a moment, then returned to Sol Fiedler.

'This half-brother of yours was half Jewish. Yet this Heidi was happy to give him house room?'

'Of course.'

'Why of course?'

'Because she was my mother's best friend. And that made everything possible.'

Stefan marvelled at the smoothness of the lie. Heidi didn't exist but, airbrushed out of history by the English bombers, there was no way these men could ever be sure.

The colonel asked about subsequent meetings before Sol took the train back to Berlin.

'We met the following weekend when I had leave. We met on the Saturday afternoon and the Sunday morning.'

'You have an excellent memory.'

'That's because it had to be that way. The rest of the weekend I was on the train.'

'Exactly.'

'I don't understand.'

'It all fits,' the colonel said. 'Don't you understand? It all fits beautifully. In our line of business, Mr Portisch, we get to know about real life. Real life is messy. Very little of it fits. Unlike this little story of yours . . .' He gestured at his notes and tossed his pen down.

'You don't believe me?' Stefan was starting to lose his temper. 'You think I'd meet Sol on Saturday morning when I was supposed to be on the train? How would that be possible?'

'It wouldn't, Mr Portisch. Which I suppose is my point.' He looked up. 'So where did you go? Where did you take him?'

Stefan described the Saturday afternoon. This was before the war started. Germany was still at peace. They'd walked the canals of Hammerbeck. Fed the ducks on scraps of black bread. Afterwards, they'd gone into the city, and eaten at a cheap *Bierkeller* Stefan knew down by the Elbe. The major noted the name of the place. The colonel wanted to know what they'd talked about.

'Each other, but me mostly. Sol was like a second father. He was sixteen years older than me. That made a big difference. He wanted to know about my sailing, how I'd learned on the Alster with all the other kids, what the Olympics had been like, the races up in Kiel, and then he wanted to know about the Navy, and what I expected once the war came along.'

'And his own life? You asked him about that?'

'Of course.'

'And what did he tell you?'

'He told me about his wife. I got the impression they couldn't have children but that's not something I asked him. Maybe that's one of the reasons he wrote to my mother in the first place. To have someone much younger in his family.'

'And his work?'

'I didn't know anything about it. I got the impression he was clever, very clever. He said he was a scientist. He worked in a big institute in Berlin. That's all.'

'Weren't you curious? Did you want to find out more?'

'Not really. I was happy talking about my own life. He was so interested in everything I'd done. That doesn't happen very often.'

'And I understand he wrote to you. From America.'

'Yes. He wrote three or four times.'

'Which address?'

'To our flat. In Hammerbeck.'

'Why not to you direct? Wouldn't your mother have preferred that? Sparing your father's feelings?'

'Writing to me direct would have been foolish. The man was a Jew. And he'd gone over to the enemy.'

'This was when?'

' Nineteen forty. Nineteen forty-one.'

'But America wasn't the enemy. You weren't at war with them. Not until Pearl Harbor.'

'You don't think so?' Stefan was smiling now. 'You don't think we were sinking American shipping? Avoiding American patrols? Is that something you do to your friends?'

The colonel sat back in his chair, steepling his fingers. For once, thought Stefan, he's not sure about me. Maybe I'm lying. But maybe I'm not.

'And these letters from America? They've gone too? Up in smoke?'

'I'm afraid so.'

'What did they say?'

'Not very much. Sol was working in Chicago in some kind of lab. There were lots of other scientists from Europe and he knew some of them. He and his wife had found a place of their own. He loved America. There was so much of everything and no one knocking at your door at four in the morning. He felt safe. I think he was happy.'

'So much of everything? I understand there was rationing.'

'He told me they had everything they could ever want. Maybe rationing came in after Pearl Harbor. I don't know. I'm just answering your questions.'

'And after Pearl Harbor?'

'Nothing. The letters stopped.'

'And was he writing to anyone else at this time? To your knowledge?'

'Yes.'

'Who?'

'I don't know their names. I think they were colleagues from Berlin, scientists I expect. People he'd been working with. People he counted as friends.'

'On the same project?'

'I don't know. I imagine so.'

'And do you know what that project might have been?'

'I've no idea. He never said.'

'Never?'

'Never. I wish I could help you, Colonel, but . . .' Stefan shrugged, '. . . I'm afraid I can't.'

Gómez awoke to the sound of someone tapping at the door. It was the receptionist. She had a man on the phone for him. Gómez followed her down the corridor, rubbing the sleep from his eyes before checking his watch. Mid-afternoon.

'Gómez,' he grunted.

'This is Frank Donovan.' He sounded tense, nervous.

'Nice to hear you, Frank. Thanks for the call. We get to meet some place?'

'Tonight. This evening. You've got a pen?'

'Sure.' Gómez gestured for a pen. 'Shoot.'

Donovan gave him the name of a road down by the Rio Grande. It was like an industrial area, plenty of factories. He should be looking for an outfit called Fábrica Hortensia. They had a big fenced area out front. The gate would be open. Trucks parked up there sometimes. After dark, the place was deserted. Ten o'clock?

'Give me a clue here, Frank. What am I looking for?'

'Me.'

'In a vehicle?'

'Sure.'

'Like what?'

'Guess. Bring lots of money.' The line went dead.

*

Stefan was returned to his shared cell in the barracks in the early afternoon. By now his cellmate had volunteered a name. Hans-Dietrich Schwemmer. Recently of *U-452*. When Stefan stepped into the room, he was standing at the barred window, staring out. The moment the escort shut the door, he turned round and put his finger to his lips then gestured up at the ceiling.

Stefan followed his pointing finger then mimed bewilderment. What's going on? Hans had a scrap of paper and he had found a stub of pencil somewhere, which he held at the ready. He pointed to a single word he must have scrawled earlier, then nodded up towards the ceiling. *Mikro.* Microphone.

Stefan nodded, said he understood. The cell was wired for sound. Hans was back on his bed, hugging his knees. He was a small man, wiry, with a shock of blond hair and a deep scar that ran the length of one cheek. He told Stefan that his submarine had been forced to the surface after an attack by British corvettes working in pairs. Two of the crew had already died and a handful more were seriously injured. One of the corvettes had stopped to hoist them aboard and they'd spent an uncomfortable week at sea as the convoy wallowed towards Liverpool. Since then, he'd been here at *das Scheisshaus*, under interrogation.

Stefan knew about *U-452*. It was one of the old Type VII boats. A friend of his on the same voyage had been one of the men who hadn't made it. *U-452* had gone down more than a year ago. Spending all that time since in a place like this made no sense at all.

Hans wrote a question on the other side of the scrap of paper. *You're Kapitän Portisch?* Stefan nodded. Hans looked up at him for a moment. Then he was on his bare feet between the beds, his arm erect in the Hitler salute. Embarrassed, Stefan gestured for him to sit down. When Hans extended a hand, he shook it. Stefan wanted the pencil. *Was geht ab?* What's up? Hans put his hand over his heart, mimed a sad clown. He wanted to say sorry. Quite why, Stefan didn't know. Then came another scribbled message. *Ich bin hier um Sie zu sprechen zu bringen*. I'm here to make you talk.

Stefan nodded and settled on the other bed. He'd heard about this trick before. The British routinely planted prisoners like these alongside newcomers. They'd act as stool-pigeons, trying to open doors that had remained locked during formal interrogations, teasing out useful confidences. For all he knew, the Germans probably did the same. Trusting a fellow countryman, went the theory, often resulted in all kinds of windfall intelligence. The British called it 'pillow talk', and like everything else it went straight into a prisoner's dossier.

Stefan was trying to work out ways of turning this ruse to his own advantage. For a while, they swapped stories. Stefan saw no point in not talking about what had happened to *U-2553*. He described the night of the storm and how he'd been ordered to kill a senior SS officer. He talked about Eva, and her dying father. And then he mentioned the latest interview with the colonel.

'You know this man? The one with the monocle?'

'Sure. Be careful. That man knows everything.'

'Then why does he ask so many questions about my half-brother? Someone I haven't seen for more than five years?'

'He'll have a reason. He always does.'

'You think he'll tell me if I ask him next time?'

'I doubt it. Who is this person?'

Stefan explained about Sol Fiedler. He was a scientist. He was very clever. One day Stefan was going to get to America and track him down. Once the war was over they'd all be living in a different world.

'I agree, *Kapitän*. Next time round there won't be a war like this. Next time round we'll be able to blow each other up at the touch of a button.'

'You believe that?'

'I do. The Führer has plans. Everyone knows that.'

Stefan nodded, feeling a little jolt of pleasure that he'd managed to get the issue of a super-weapon on the tape. Not because he'd raised it himself but because it showed that he hadn't made the slightest connection in this regard to Sol Fiedler. Sol was his precious half-brother, so happily discovered, so briefly enjoyed. And that's as far as his interest extended.

He reached for the pencil again. How come you knew my name? This time, Hans didn't bother with the subterfuge.

'You're a legend, *Herr Kapitän*,' he said. 'It's a pleasure to have you here.'

*

Gómez walked the mile to the industrial zone. He'd shared the address with the woman behind reception who'd drawn him a map. The area, she said, was almost within sight of the river. The cheaper whores used it when they turned tricks in punters' cars. It offered reasonable privacy but little else. Gómez, who'd been wondering how Donovan had discovered this part of town, was amused. Whatever else happened tonight, he told himself, he wouldn't be the one getting screwed.

He set off after nine, walking slowly, taking it easy. There was little traffic around but downtown was less than easy on the eye: flat, desolate, a wasteland of cheap hotels, garish bars and drunken Indians. No wonder so many wetbacks risked the river and swam away to a better life.

He thought about Donovan. The guy would probably be armed. If he had any sense he'd also have someone else along, maybe hidden in the shadows, riding shotgun on this abrupt encounter. What was Gómez supposed to say? What kind of money would persuade Donovan to point his precious car north and volunteer for a conversation with the likes of O'Flaherty? If he said no, if it came to violence, if there was no alternative to knocking the man cold and shipping him over the border, would Gómez really emerge intact? This was a violent country. Donovan had almost certainly killed already. Adding Gómez to the score would be the work of a second.

He was in the industrial area now, long, low buildings, piles of building materials, a go-go economy catching its breath for the night. There were feral cats everywhere, tiny movements in the shadows, and a whisper of wind off the river. Further away, on the American side, he could hear the clank-clank of rolling stock in the marshalling yards, and the low, mournful blare of an approaching train.

He thought briefly about Yolanda. He'd trusted this woman on sight, ever since he'd met her in the Alexandria diner, and that had never happened to him in his life. She had presence and a sense of humour. She seemed to expect very little from other people and so obviously believed in making her own luck. She was also an angel in the sack, totally uninhibited, taking a raw pleasure from an extensive repertoire of tricks. He tried to imagine the impact she'd have on the FBI guys across the river, her face in theirs, Gómez's envoy from the madness back in Mexico. My man's taking care of it, she'd tell them. Better believe me.

Fábrica Hortensia. He'd arrived. Beyond the chain-link fence and the potholed parking area he could see the low rise of the factory itself. There were no lights burning, and no trucks. He walked on, careful now, wishing yet again that he had a weapon. This was no country to walk naked into an ambush. Moments later, he was at the main entrance. The gates, as promised, were open. He stepped inside, following what he took to be a pair of tyre tracks in the dust. No sign of the Caddy. Fifty yards took him to the factory. Not a factory at all but some kind of warehouse: sliding doors big enough to accommodate trucks, fatter tyre marks in the dust, the lingering stench of diesel oil and spent exhaust.

He paused in the darkness, on the balls of his feet, every nerve tuned to the next moment and the moment after that. Was Donovan late? Had he decided to nix the rendezvous? Or was this a set-up of some other kind? Gómez had no idea and no means of finding out except by looking. He followed the line of the building around the corner. Still no sign of life. A pile of discarded tyres lay beside the fence. He could hear the steady dripping of water. More cats. He walked on, hugging the shadow of the building until he reached the next corner. Very slowly, he peered round.

The fence was much closer here, ten yards from the back of the warehouse, and the strip of land formed a long alley disappearing into the darkness. At the end of the alley was a car, a big car. All Gómez could see was the back of it. It could be a Cadillac. Easily. One indicator was winking, on-off, on-off. Weird, he thought. Be very careful.

He approached slowly and as he did so he realised that the trunk was open. He was close now. There was no way of figuring out the colour, even with the splashes of orange from the indicator light, but it was definitely a Caddy. He paused, looking round, trying to plot the areas of opportunity, the spots he'd pick himself if he was here on bad business. Nothing obvious. Maybe nothing at all.

By the driver's door, he froze. He could see a body slumped sideways behind the wheel. Something dark was seeping slowly on to the long bench seat. With great care, he opened the door. There was a vanity light over the rear-view mirror. He glanced round again, checking for movement, for anything that might suggest a set-up, then he reached inside until his fingers found the switch on the light. One final check outside. What the hell. He flicked the switch.

It was Donovan. His face was resting against the squab of the seat and most of the back of his head had ceased to exist. The big shotgun lay beside him, inches from the limpness of his hand. No note, Gómez thought, turning the light off and closing the door. He removed his jacket, then his shirt, laying them carefully over the long hood. Then he walked round to the rear of the car and checked the trunk. It was empty. Back beside the car, he hauled Donovan's body out by the armpits and dragged him around to the open trunk.

Donovan was dressed in combat trousers and a T-shirt, now soaked in blood. Gómez got his breath back and then lifted Donovan's body and tipped it into the yawning trunk before returning for the shotgun. He lifted it carefully and laid it beside the body. In the darkness, fumbling in the back of the trunk, he found a couple of old towels. His chest and arms were covered in Donovan's blood and he did his best to wipe himself clean before slamming the trunk down and retrieving his shirt and jacket from the hood. The last thing he needed was a stop at the border.

The keys were still in the ignition. Dressed again, he quickly cleaned up the blood and brains on the upholstery and then fired up the big old engine. With the lights on, Gómez was glad to discover that he even had half a tank of gas. He slipped the car into gear, dipped the headlights and followed the alley round the building until he was out front. The gates were still open. He shook his head, not quite believing it. Moments later, he was back on the street, eyes on the rear-view mirror, waiting to be chased down. Again, as if by some miracle, nothing.

At the motel the woman was still behind the reception desk. Gómez had no need to revisit the room. When he asked for the check, the woman told him four dollars. He gave her a five and told her to keep the change.

'Where you going now?' She was looking at the Cadillac parked outside.

'Home,' he said.

The FBI office at El Paso was in a quiet downtown block beside a funeral parlour. The station chief was a long-term Bureau staffer by the name of Halliday. Gómez had never met him but knew the man had spent a busy decade trying to carve his private niche in J. Edgar Hoover's heart. Rumours of anything major about to break, and Richmond Halliday would be all over it. Tonight was no exception.

Lights were burning on the first floor when Gómez parked the Caddy across the street. He'd cruised slowly through the checkpoints on both sides of the border, attracting barely a glance from officials. Now he pressed the after-hours button beside the reinforced steel door. Did it a second time. Then a third. Finally the door opened. Gómez peered at the guy's ID. Richmond Halliday.

'Who are you?'

'Gómez.' The name didn't register. 'Lady called Yolanda? Guy called Raymond O'Flaherty? Any chance I can come in?'

'This is FBI property.'

'So am I, buddy.'

'Buddy' didn't sit well with Halliday, though at last he appeared to recognise Gómez's name.

'You the guy from Mexico?'

'I am. You've talked to O'Flaherty?'

Halliday didn't answer. His hand was out. He wanted ID.

'I haven't got any.'

'Everybody's got ID, Mr Gómez. No ID, *prohibida la entrada.*'

Gómez studied him for a long moment. Halliday looked like a bank clerk or an insurance broker: thin, pale, impatient, a study in self-importance.

'I need to know about O'Flaherty,' Gómez said slowly. 'I need to know that you have the documentation I sent across this morning. I need to be sure that you passed the word up the line. If O'Flaherty isn't on a plane already then someone hasn't done their job. And that, Mr Halliday, will have consequences.'

It was beginning to dawn on Halliday that this rough Hispanic on his precious doorstep might have friends in DC.

'He's due in tomorrow morning,' Halliday said. 'I'll be out at Biggs to meet him.' Biggs Army Airfield served the city of El Paso.

'You talked to him yourself?'

'I did.'

'And?'

'Like I say, he'll be with us tomorrow morning. We'll brief at eleven. According to O'Flaherty, Mr Hoover is taking a personal interest.'

'O'Flaherty's right. The lady who brought the documentation? Any idea where I find her?'

'The Super Chief. San Antonio Street. A couple of blocks and you're there.' He turned to go, then paused. 'This guy Donovan. Mr O'Flaherty needs to meet him. You'll make sure he's there?'

Gómez shook his head. It had been a long day.

'I can go one better.' He nodded at the Caddy across the street and then tossed Halliday the keys. 'Guy's in the trunk. Help yourself.'

PART FIVE

PART FIVE

22

The flight from Washington arrived early next morning. Gómez stood in the sunshine watching the silver DC-3 on final approach. Earlier, he'd seen Halliday and another agent in the cafeteria, heads down, deep in conversation. Neither men knew he was there.

The DC-3 taxied to a halt in front of the terminal buildings. Among the first passengers off Gómez recognised faces from the Hill, senior scientists who'd presumably been attending meetings in Washington. One of them, spotting him, raised a hand in greeting. Gómez didn't respond. Los Alamos was barely half a day away by car but already it felt like a different life.

O'Flaherty was one of the last passengers to make it down the steps. Gómez was glad to see that he'd once again ignored the Bureau's dress code. If Halliday was expecting a grey suit, white shirt and a quiet tie, he was in for a shock. For O'Flaherty's sake, Gómez hoped he was carrying ID.

Gómez intercepted him before he had a chance to get inside the terminal. Close up, O'Flaherty looked wrecked and he knew it. Two hours' sleep before riding the cab to National Airport, then a series of thunderstorms down the spine of the country before they left the Appalachians and flew into the hazy glare of the Deep South.

'There's somewhere we can talk?' O'Flaherty asked.

'The office is downtown.'

'I had somewhere closer in mind.'

'Is there a problem?'

'Hoover's involved. There's always a problem.'

Gómez was steering him towards the cafeteria. The door was blocked by Halliday. He was looking confused. He'd never met O'Flaherty and it showed. Gómez did the introductions. O'Flaherty led the way into the cafeteria and chose a table with a view of the apron outside. Halliday was looking at Gómez. He wanted to know a great deal more about the body in the trunk of the Cadillac.

O'Flaherty ignored the question. He pointed Halliday at the counter. He wanted coffee. Black. Halliday passed the request to his colleague. This was his turf and newcomers played by his rules. The three of them sat down. Now that coffee was coming, mention of a body had put a smile on O'Flaherty's face.

'Do we have a name?' he asked.

'Donovan,' Gómez said. 'I brought him back last night.'

'From Mexico?'

'Yeah.'

'You killed the guy?'

'I found him dead.'

Gómez described the circumstances: the parked Caddy, the open trunk, Donovan's body slumped at the wheel, a gun beside him.

O'Flaherty wanted to know whether anyone else had been around.

'Not that I saw.' Gómez shook his head.

'You think he killed himself?'

'I think it looked that way.'

'Then we'd need more.'

'Sure. If it was our jurisdiction.'

Halliday was following this as best he could. Confusion had given way to anger.

'There are procedures here,' he said. 'I have a conference room booked back at the office. Since when did we conduct sensitive business in public?'

O'Flaherty swapped glances with Gómez. The cafeteria was empty. The incoming passengers had gone in search of their bags. O'Flaherty turned to Halliday.

'You think we're going to the office?'

'Of course.' Halliday was itching to be on his feet.

'Then you're wrong.' He nodded at the DC-3 refuelling on the tarmac outside. 'We're booked on the return flight. Leaves in an hour.'

'We?'

'Me and Mr Gómez here. Mr Hoover's orders, buddy, not mine.'

*

There were two new faces at the table for Stefan's next session. The major was in charge. Of the colonel, to Stefan's relief, there was no sign. Overnight, he'd lain motionless in the narrow bed, trying to ease the ache in his leg. Hans, who was also carrying an injury, said that England was no place to get better in a hurry. Too damp. Too grey. Too depressing. What convalescents needed was warm sunshine and clean air, not fog thickened with so much smoke that it coiled in your lungs and made breathing something you'd try to avoid.

Stefan could only agree. His final glimpse of the Americas on the last of the transatlantic patrols had been dusk off the island of St Lucia when they'd surfaced to recharge the submarine's batteries. The horizon had been empty, the sea a lake of gold towards the west, and he remembered the smell of nutmeg and cloves carried by the offshore breeze from the low, dark swell of the island. One day, he'd told himself, I want to come back here. Preferably with a beautiful woman. And preferably for ever.

Now, he was listening to the major. He offered no clues about the newcomers except to imply that he was grateful for their time. They appeared to have been summoned at short notice and one of them – the younger man – was visibly exhausted. In conversation with the major before the interview began, he said he'd been on a train all night, every compartment packed, even the corridors full of sleeping soldiers.

The major invited the younger man to launch the interview. He had thinning sandy hair and what Stefan's mother had once described as an 'indoor face'. His voice was low, hesitant, and he didn't speak German. Stefan said it wouldn't be a problem. He'd do his best in English.

'I understand you know Sol Fiedler?' he said.

'I do. He's my half-brother.'

'What was he like?'

It was the bluntest of questions, full of disbelief, and Stefan frowned, pretending not to have fully understood, desperate to buy himself time. This man might be a scientist, he told himself. He might have worked alongside Sol. He might even have been his friend. Manchester was where Sol and Marta had stayed for a while before taking the boat to Canada, and coming from Manchester, thought Stefan, might explain this man's overnight train journey.

The newcomer produced a notebook, opened it, and then rephrased his question. He wanted Stefan to tell him what Sol Fiedler looked like. He wanted a physical description.

Stefan nodded. He was trying to visualise the photos Erwin had showed him, Sol and Marta together in their kitchen, presumably in America.

'He looked old,' he said. 'I knew he was thirty-six. That's what my mother told me. But he looked much older than that.'

'Older how?'

'Older up here.' Stefan touched his hair. 'And old in the way he behaved. He was a quiet man. He listened rather than talked. I liked that.'

'His hair was going grey? Is that what you mean?'

'No. Not when I met him. But it was getting . . . you know . . . thin.'

'Like mine?'

'Yes. Like yours.'

'Same colour?'

Stefan hesitated.It had been impossible to tell from the photos. He frowned, knowing whatever he guessed had to be a gamble.

'No,' he said.

His questioner nodded. Looking at the notebook, Stefan realised he had a list of prepared questions. He wondered whether he'd written them himself. Or maybe he'd sought the advice of someone else, like the major or the colonel. Trick questions. Questions to trap *Onkel* Karl's young *Kapitän* and turn his story inside out.

'Did he wear glasses?'

Sol was wearing glasses in the photos. Thick-looking glasses. The kind of glasses that suggested a long-standing problem.

'Yes,' Stefan said.

A tiny nod of approval from across the table. Stefan told himself he'd been right. This man had to be a fellow scientist, someone who'd known Sol personally. The thought had alarmed him at first but the deeper they got into this strange conversation the more he was beginning to enjoy it. It was a game. It was like chess. And the fact that he could hide behind his clumsy English was a definite advantage.

'Did he wear a ring?'

'Not that I can remember.'

'Did he smoke?'

'No. He had no money.'

'Had he ever smoked? Did you get that impression?'

'We never discussed it. There was no reason to. I don't smoke.'

'Did he tell you about his wife?'

'A little, yes.'

'What was her name?'

'Marta.'

'She was Jewish?'

'They both were. That was why they had to leave.'

'Children?'

'None.'

'Because?'

'Because . . .' Stefan shrugged, '. . . it wasn't happening.'

'Did you get the impression they were close?'

'Yes. Very.'

'Did he have a pet name for her?'

'I don't understand.'

'Something he'd call her in private?'

'I've no idea. I wasn't there when they were together. Before he came to Hamburg we'd never met before in our lives. He was a lot older than I was. He was very different from me. All we had in common was my mother, and that turned out to be enough, but we only met a couple of times. In some ways the man was a stranger – a nice stranger, a welcome stranger – but that's the way he stayed.'

'I see.' He turned the page. More questions. 'What did he tell you about his work?'

'Not much. I knew he was a scientist. I knew he was clever. We talked about me most of the time.'

'Did he ever describe the projects he was working on?'

'No.'

'And you didn't ask?'

'No. I was too full of myself. It was an exciting time.'

'And his colleagues? Back in Berlin? Did you get the impression he had good friends?'

'Yes.'

'Did he give you names?'

'No.'

Another nod. Then a sidelong glance at the major before turning back to Stefan. He wanted to know about the letters Sol had written from Chicago. The fact that he called him 'Sol' told Stefan he'd definitely known the man. Maybe he'd had letters himself. Maybe he'd even been over to see him. Careful, Stefan told himself. More traps.

'Was he happy over there?'

'I think so. That's the impression I got.'

'Where was he living?'

'In a place called Evanston.' Another detail from Erwin's briefing. 'He gave me the return address.'

'What was the house like?'

'Big enough for the two of them. And he told me it was an apartment, not a house.'

'Did they have cats? Or maybe a dog?'

'I've no idea. He never mentioned anything like that.'

'Did he talk about the snow?'

'The letters came in the summer. It didn't snow then.'

'Did he have a car? An automobile?'

'I don't know. He may have done.'

The exchange was developing into a fencing match, thrust, parry, and Stefan sensed that he was beginning to lose what little advantage he'd had. Too vague, too defensive, not enough detail. The older man at the table had the same impression.

'Forgive me, *Kapitän*.' There was a suspicion of a smile on his face. 'What *did* he talk about?'

'He talked about general things, about what a rich place America was, how different from Europe. And he wrote about his colleagues, too, how kind they were, how helpful. I think he must have loved what he was doing. He was certainly working very hard.'

'He said that? In so many words?'

'Yes. Long hours. Lots to do. Lots of problems to solve. But he wasn't complaining. I don't think he was that kind of person.'

'Did he ever send you photographs?'

'Yes. Once. There were only a few letters. Maybe three. But, yes, once there was a photo.'

The older man glanced at the scientist and then turned back to Stefan.

'A photo of what?'

'Of him and Marta.'

'And what was he wearing?'

'He had a jacket. And a shirt. She was wearing a dress.'

'And the background? What did you see there?'

'Nothing. They were in a kitchen. The refrigerator was huge.' He frowned. 'There was a window, too. You could see a cactus outside.'

*

Gómez and O'Flaherty were back in DC by nightfall. An FBI agent was waiting for them at National Airport. He drove them along beside the Potomac and then over the bridge to the Bureau's downtown headquarters. Expecting to meet Hoover, Gómez and O'Flaherty were taken to the office of Quinn Tamm, the Director's second-in-command. Hoover, it appeared, had been flown to Hot Springs down in Georgia where the President was enjoying a couple of days' rest. It was Tamm's job to debrief Gómez and try and figure out exactly where the developing investigation was headed.

The Assistant Director's office was, if anything, bigger than Hoover's. Tamm sat behind an enormous desk, surrounded by telephones. Behind him was a giant map of America covered by pins and lengths of cotton. Gómez had seen something similar in the Chicago field office. A talc overlay in blue indicated the nation's prime industrial cities while another in red highlighted concentrations of aliens deemed to be potential threats. The fact that these overlays coincided almost exactly was – on the face of it – testament to the Bureau's reach and efficiency, but both Gómez and O'Flaherty knew different. Far too much of the intelligence was bullshit – either planted by sources with private debts to settle, or pure invention by field agents with targets to meet. Now, though, they appeared to be confronting a threat of an entirely different order.

There was another man sitting to one side in the office, and Gómez quickly realised he was a Brit. Tamm didn't bother to introduce him but Gómez had seen photos of the man before. His name was Walter Bell, a bluff fiftysomething who served as liaison officer between London and Hoover's sprawling FBI empire.

Tamm wanted the bare bones of the story to date. Time, he kept emphasising, was tight. O'Flaherty gestured in Gómez's direction. This is the guy closest to the action, he said. Listen up.

Gómez began to lay out exactly what had happened. First the alleged suicide of Sol Fiedler, and all the doubts that attended it. Then the pressure from his Army G-2 colleagues on the Hill to throttle the enquiry at birth, ship the man out for burial and get on with the job in hand. The Gadget, he explained, trumped every other card. There were thousands of scientists on the Hill, marching in lockstep towards the biggest bang the world had ever known, and nothing – but nothing – was going to stand in their way. Certainly not Sol Fiedler.

'They told you to drop the enquiry?' Tamm was making notes. So was Walter Bell.

'They did.'

'And what did you do about that?'

'I carried on asking around. There was stuff that made no sense. Not to people like us.'

'Give me an example.'

Gómez explained about Fiedler's hatred of guns, about his passion for his wife, about his lack of enemies, and finally about the typed note found beside his body.

'There were anomalies in that note. Like how he addressed his wife. That made no sense either.'

'You think it was a plant?'

'Yes.'

'Like how?'

'Like it might have come from the guy who admitted lending Fiedler the automatic in the first place.'

Gómez told Tamm about Frank Donovan. The man who shot coyotes every Tuesday. The guy who called by Fiedler's house for coffee and jock talk about the Chicago Bears. The husband with a wife and three kids in Santa Fe who'd become – as far as Fiedler and his wife were concerned – a family friend.

'Except he wasn't? Is that what you're telling me?'

'Exactly, sir. I think he killed him. I think he planted the note. And both those facts would explain why he disappeared pretty soon afterwards.'

O'Flaherty intervened. Intelligence suggested that Donovan might well be over the border in Mexico. Gómez, he said, had been tasked to go down there and find him.

'And did you?' Tamm was still looking at Gómez.

'I did, sir. I traced his wife's family. I got on the right side of a local cop. In the end that took me back to Ciudad Jaurez.'

'You also killed a guy. Have I got that right?'

Gómez nodded. 'You know about that?'

'We do.'

'And should I be saying thank you? For getting me out?'

'Not to us, Mr Gómez. To be frank I have no idea how that happened. Except it involved the President's wife.'

'She has pull in Mexico?'

'Probably not. But the President does. So maybe he's the guy you should be buying a bunch of flowers.'

Gómez nodded, said nothing. The flowers would go to Yolanda, he thought. And maybe Agard Beaman.

'So you found Donovan?'

'I did, sir. I also traced his wife and kids. They were living in the house of a German woman called Lara Müller.'

'In Ciudad Juarez?'

'Yes.'

'She acts as a kind of honorary consul there, sir, representing German interests.' This from O'Flaherty again. 'She stays out of the States but we have a file on her. She's supposed to have the ear of certain elements in Berlin. Chiefly the Himmler organisation.'

'The SS?'

'Yes.' O'Flaherty looked at Gómez. 'Tell him about the typewriter.'

Gómez explained about the Remington he'd found at Müller's house. He'd brought back some text samples. O'Flaherty nodded.

'We had them flown up yesterday, sir,' he said. 'We've checked them out.'

'And?'

'Perfect match. The suicide note was typed on that machine. It was also in German.'

418

'So this woman – Müller – typed the note,' Tamm suggested. 'And Donovan pulled the trigger. Is that the story?'

'Yes, sir.'

'Why? Why would he do that?'

'Because Fiedler was feeding these people stuff from the Hill, atomic stuff, and for whatever reason he'd decided to stop. Maybe it was guilt. Maybe it was something else. Either way, he'd signed his own death sentence.'

'These people being the Nazis?'

'Yes, sir.'

Tamm made another note and then turned back to Gómez. 'So what did Donovan have to say?'

'Nothing, sir. By the time I found him, he was dead.'

He told Tamm about last night's rendezvous. The news that he'd left the corpse with Halliday appeared to amuse the Assistant Director.

'You think Donovan killed himself?'

'I have no idea. He may have done. It's possible. But I doubt it.'

'Do you doubt every suicide you happen across?'

Gómez didn't answer. Tamm glanced at O'Flaherty then he was back with Gómez.

'Tell me more about Fiedler. What kind of access did this man have down there in Los Alamos?'

'He worked in the metallurgical lab. He was part of the Tamper Group. Oppenheimer keeps the science to himself but I understand Fiedler was concentrating on the trigger mechanism for one of the bombs.'

'There's more than one?'

'There's two. Maybe more. Fiedler was working on the plutonium bomb.'

'So he'd know a great deal? Is that what you're telling me?'

'He'd know pretty much everything about the plutonium bomb and I'm guessing he'd know a whole lot of other stuff about the rest of the Project. The scientists down there are like kids in the candy store. They help themselves to everything.'

Tamm nodded, sat back.

'Shit,' he said softly.

'Exactly, sir.'

Gómez wondered whether he'd done the story justice. Tamm was looking at the Brit.

'Walter? What are you thinking? Not the Commies at all. Quite the reverse.'

Bell nodded. He complimented Gómez on tracing Donovan and making the link to the German woman. In his view, the war was by no means over. They were facing a madman who would stop at nothing to preserve what little was left of the Reich. If destroying London would buy him a peace treaty, then so be it.

Tamm didn't agree. 'He doesn't even have to do that, Walter. All he has to do is make us believe it's goddam possible.'

'You're right,' Bell glanced down at his notes. 'I talked to London an hour ago. It turns out we have a source of our own. I have no idea who or what it might be but it's important enough to warrant Guy's personal attention.'

'Guy?' Tamm looked lost.

'Guy Liddell. Director of Counter-Espionage. When he starts attending interviews, I'm guessing the shit's about to hit the fan.'

23

On Stefan's third day at the Centre he awoke to rain drumming at the window. For a moment or two he lay in the bunk, hopelessly confused, uncertain of his whereabouts, then the dream came back to him, perfect in every detail.

He'd been dreaming of his hero at school, Dieter Merz. In real life he knew from friends that Dieter had joined the *Luftwaffe* and ended up in a fighter squadron. These young pilots were the cream of the cream, combat-hardened in the Spanish Civil War, the very best of Goering's flying talent, which was no surprise because Dieter had always been someone truly special, a gifted athlete with the knack of meeting any challenge. Not just on the sports field. Not just on the ice of the Alster when winter came. But now in the air as well.

Stefan knew that Dieter had gone on to fly against the British once the French had been beaten. By now commanding a squadron of Messerschmidts, he'd personally accounted for thirteen Hurricanes and nearly as many Spitfires, but over the months that followed the clouds of war had slowly darkened until he'd found himself posted east to Russia. Had Dieter – like Werner – paid the price for Hitler's worst mistake?

Or was he still out there? Still aloft? With his crooked smile and god-like tangle of blond curls?

Stefan had no idea. All he knew for sure was that Dieter had returned to him in a dream. Easing himself out of a Messerschmidt 109. Dressed as a woman.

Now, fully conscious after the coldest of showers, Stefan trudged across the wet grass, accompanied by escorts on both sides. It was the first time he'd been handcuffed and the first time he'd warranted an extra guard. He didn't know whether this was a compliment or an abrupt turn for the worse, but either way he told himself to gather his wits, to shake off the dream, to keep his concentration. The only thing he knew for sure was that he was starving hungry.

'Is there anything we can get you, *Kapitän*?' Impeccable German.

The question came from the older of the two newcomers Stefan had met yesterday and this time he was alone in the big first-floor room. He was a stooped, rumpled figure, almost completely bald, someone you'd pass in the street without a second glance. Stefan judged his age at fifty-plus and there was something close to sadness in his eyes. His collar was a little too loose. His flesh had a pallor that spoke of snatched meals and insufficient sleep. He looked, if anything, slightly abandoned by life.

Stefan enquired how he should address his new host. The stranger across the table gave the question some thought.

'*Direktor*,' he said at last.

'Then I'd like some breakfast, please, *Herr Direktor*. Preferably with eggs.'

Both of the escorts were on sentry duty outside in the corridor.

The *Direktor* got to his feet and left the room. Within seconds he was back.

'They're going to be powdered, I'm afraid. That's all we've got.' He'd already settled back in his chair. He dismissed Stefan's thanks with a wave of his hand. Musician's fingers, Stefan thought. Long, delicate.

Stefan asked him whether the information he'd supplied so far had been helpful.

'The operational material was excellent. We had a full review yesterday. Most of it we were aware of already but there were elements that were new to us, especially with regard to the *Elektro* boats. We appreciate your candour, *Herr Kapitän*, even if we don't yet fully understand your motivation.'

'Is that what this is about? My motivation?' Stefan tried to bridge the gap between them with a smile.

'To be frank, yes. You've done something very unusual, *Kapitän*. That doesn't handicap you in any way. Indeed, in some respects it makes you all the more interesting. But in our world we're obliged to test everything. A fêted warrior like yourself turning his back on the Reich? Does that make you another Hess? Or should we be asking a different set of questions?'

Stefan acknowledged the point with a nod. Rudolf Hess had been at the very top of the regime when he'd stolen a plane and flown to Scotland to try and negotiate some kind of peace treaty. No one had heard of him since though the word in the Kernevel mess at Lorient was that the British had taken a good look and declared him clinically insane.

'You think I'm mad? Like Hess?'

'I think you've been through a terrifying experience.'

'You're talking about the storm? Losing my boat? My crew?'

'I'm talking about the war. With some people the pressure is cumulative. You refuse to deal with it, you dismiss it, you pretend it doesn't even exist, but it's there nonetheless, growing and growing. I've seen it with some of our own people, individuals I've known for years. Sane one minute, broken the next. And you don't have to be on the front line to crack. Am I making any kind of sense, *Kapitän*? Is this something you recognise?'

Stefan nodded. 'Broken' he recognised. It told him that this man must have been close to imploding himself.

'You're right,' Stefan admitted. 'War is like a virus. It eats away at you. You think you're immune and you're not. In the early years, you know nothing except victory. Targets hit, ships going down, flags and flowers when you get home. You think that's easy. You love it, the taste of it, the way people look at you in the street when you get home on leave. Later, when things go wrong, it starts to feel different. Maybe the victories were too soft. Maybe we had it too easy. Maybe we all fooled ourselves. Either way, you pay the price and maybe that's because you have to. We started this war for the wrong reasons but we were too blind and too greedy to realise it.'

'And too young?'

'Yes.'

'You're twenty-four. Am I right?'

'Yes.'

'How old do you feel?'

'Down there . . .' Stefan touched his leg, '. . . I feel like an old man. Up here . . .' his hand strayed to his head, 'I feel nothing.'

'And here?' The *Direktor* had covered his heart.

Stefan acknowledged the point with a smile. After being machine-gunned by the colonel, this man's touch was as light as a feather.

'In my heart, I know I'm lucky.'

'Why?'

'Because I survived. Because the storm didn't kill me. And because of what happened afterwards.'

'I imagine you're talking about Eva.'

'You're right. I am.'

'Eva Gironda.' For the first time, with the deftest touch, the *Direktor* had sprung a surprise and he knew it. 'You weren't aware of her family name?'

'No.'

'And now you're wondering how we found out?'

'Of course. I imagine you sent someone up there.'

'You're right. We did. We checked. Like we always check.'

'And?'

'She wasn't there. The house was locked.'

'Did you find her brother? Enrico? Or maybe the doctor? Agustín?'

'Yes. And in both cases we drew a blank. They didn't know where she'd gone. Very strange, *Kapitän*. And from your point of view, I imagine very unsettling.'

Stefan nodded, grateful for the figure at the door. Steam was curling from the tray. At a whispered word of command from the *Direktor*, the sentry unlocked Stefan's handcuffs. The toast was soggy and the scrambled eggs were the thinnest yellow but nothing, just now, could look sweeter.

'Do you mind?' Stefan gestured at the plate.

'Please. Go ahead.'

The *Direktor* watched him eating. When he'd finished, he asked the question again. Where had Eva gone?

'I have no idea. The last time I saw her was when I left the village.'

'On the fishing boat?'

'Yes.'

'Leaving was your idea?'

'Yes. We'd talked about it. She knew the police could pick me up at any time. And she agreed they'd probably hand me over to my own people. Germans don't like traitors.'

'Is that what you are?'

'In their eyes, yes. Otherwise we wouldn't be having a conversation like this.'

'And so you went?'

'Yes.'

'With regrets?'

'Immense regrets. You're right. The war broke me. She was the one who looked after what was left.'

'And put the bits back in working order?'

'Started to.' Stefan was staring at his empty plate. 'In Lisbon I asked the military attaché about her.'

'I know. He told us. You want her brought to England. That's partly why we went to find her.'

'You'd do that? You'd bring her back here?'

'If that's what you both want, it's certainly a possibility. But we need to be sure, *Herr Kapitän*.'

'About what?'

'About you.'

*

It was the phone that woke Gómez. The FBI had put him in a hotel for the night. He struggled upright, looking for his watch. Nearly nine o'clock.

'Gómez,' he grunted.

It was Yolanda. She'd got the number from O'Flaherty. She wanted to know whether he was up or not.

'The answer's no.'

'I woke you?'

'Yes.'

She said she was sorry. She was wondering whether they were still going to get married.

'For sure. Where are you?'

'Back home. San Diego. I was talking with Agard just now and he knows a Pentecostal church in Alexandria. Great music. Plus he wants to be your best man.'

'Beaman?' Gómez was awake now. 'You mean Agard Beaman?'

'The very same. He's disappointed because I guess he wanted you for himself but he thinks I'm the next best thing so he said yes.'

'To what?'

'To being your best buddy.' She was laughing now. 'How about next week? Only Agard needs time to work on his speech.'

Gómez was staring at the phone. Last night, leaving Tamm's office, he'd secured agreement to go back down to Los Alamos and fix a couple of loose ends before handing in his resignation. He'd have to route through Chicago. The next train left at twenty to eleven. Tight.

'Tell Agard I'll phone him,' he said. 'You thought of a dress yet?'

'No.'

'Good. Anything but white.'

*

It was nearly lunchtime before the *Direktor* returned to the subject of Eva. He and Stefan had taken a leisurely conversational stroll among the small print of Stefan's war. To Stefan's surprise, he didn't appear to be remotely interested in any of the hard, factual data that he'd always assumed to be the currency of this kind of exchange. On the contrary, he seemed to want to get a fix on what this talented young officer had expected from the Nazi regime, and how that expectation had survived what followed.

'It didn't,' Stefan told him. 'At sea we did what we were trained to do. It was our world. We were good. We got results. We trusted each other, relied on each other. It was the coming back that made us realise what had gone wrong.'

He described trips on leave back to Hamburg before the firestorm. He talked about visits to Admiral Doenitz's headquarters outside Berlin. He described long nights on trains, the company of strangers, how you learned to feel your way into a conversation without at first revealing what you really believed, and how quickly you realised that most people you met felt exactly the same way about the war as you did. That everything was going wrong. And that there was absolutely nothing to be done about it.

'A feeling of helplessness?'

'Exactly. Germany woke up one morning bound hand and foot by the Nazis, trussed like a turkey. And that was before the war when it didn't really matter. Later it mattered a lot but it was far too late. By then you knew there was nothing you could do. If you stepped out of line, they shot you. And that was if you were lucky. If you really stepped out line it could be far worse. They say it took the July plotters half the night to die.'

The *Direktor* wanted to know about the firestorm, about the night Stefan's entire past went up in flames. What did it feel like? Heading back to Hamburg the following month to find everything in ruins? Stefan did his best. Talking to this man was easy, a tribute to the way he listened.

'You had women when you came back from the sea?'

'Yes. Sometimes.'

Stefan talked about Trévarez, and Aurélie. The *Direktor* knew the name already.

'I understand she turned out to be working for us,' he said.

'That's right. She was with the Resistance. I didn't know at the time. The security people at Lorient only told me later.'

'Would it have made a difference?'

'Probably not. I didn't share any secrets with her. It was much simpler than that.'

'Did you tell her about Sol? Your mystery half-brother?'

'No.'

'Did that make him a secret?'

'No. He was just never part of the conversation. She talked about her husband a little. I mentioned my mother and father. My brother, too, and a friend called Dieter. But most of the time we were otherwise occupied.'

The *Direktor* nodded and made a note. Stefan was thinking about last night's dream. Dieter Merz dressed like a woman. Strange.

The *Direktor* looked up. He wanted to know whether Stefan had been involved with any other women during the war.

'A couple. One worked in a restaurant in Lorient. We met up once or twice. She'd been to Galicia. She knew the coastline. The other one I met during an air raid in Berlin. We were caught in the open. It was dark.' He shrugged. 'I didn't even know her name.'

The *Direktor* smiled. So many questions unasked.

'Eva is a Communist. Were you aware of that?'

'No.' Stefan blinked. 'How do you know?'

'She worked here in 1940. She was a photographer. We kept an eye on her. We had a file that went back to the Spanish Civil War.'

'She told me she was an anarchist then.'

'Her boyfriend was the anarchist. In Madrid she was reporting to a Russian called Sergei. I gather they rated her highly.' He smiled. 'A true believer.'

'And she stayed with them? In England?'

'That's not clear. I think we should assume she did.'

'But you don't know?'

'No, we don't. The Russians are masters of the dark arts. We'd like to think we have their measure but it isn't always true. The point I'm trying to make is this. You think you know someone and it turns out you don't. In your case that may be problematic.'

'You're talking about Eva? You're telling me not to trust her?'

'I'm exploring the notion of absolutes. She's stepped into your life. She took a risk in looking after you. She's putting you back together. You've fallen in love. On that journey, a man will do anything. On that journey, Stefan, you are utterly vulnerable. And you're talking to someone who knows.'

Stefan tried to mask his surprise. It was the first time he'd used Stefan's Christian name. The intimacy was so sudden, so unexpected. Vulnerable was right. Vulnerable was the key to everything.

'This has happened to you?'

'Not exactly. But it involved a woman, yes.' He studied Stefan for a long moment, refusing to go further. The silence stretched and stretched. Stefan began to feel uncomfortable.

'I'm sorry,' he said.

'Don't be. I don't need your compassion. I just want you to tell me the truth.'

'You think I'm lying?'

'I know you're lying. And what makes it worse is this. You've told yourself you're lying for the best possible reason. You're lying to see Eva again. To spend the rest of your lives together. To make a nest away from all this madness. But you know what? It will never happen. Not unless you tell us the truth. Think about that, Stefan. I have to fly to America tonight. We'll meet again once I'm back.'

24

Merricks couldn't believe it when Gómez said he was getting married. He'd been back on the Hill for a couple of hours having flown down from DC. Merricks had returned to the office to find him sitting behind the desk. Just like always.

'Name?' Merricks asked.

'Yolanda.'

'Photo?'

'It's in here.' Gómez tapped his head, then shaped an hour glass with his huge hands.

'Big?'

'Me-sized.'

'And this is a *woman*?'

'One of the best.'

'So how well do you know her?'

'Not at all. Which I guess makes it an adventure.'

Gómez asked about Marta Fiedler. Merricks said he hadn't seen her for a while but understood she was on the point of moving out.

'She's got friends back in Chicago. There's a queue of people after that apartment of hers and I guess she's sick of living with a ghost. Might be good if you happened by. She likes you.'

Gómez nodded. He had a visit in mind. Plus a couple of other questions for Merricks.

'Can't they wait?' Merricks gestured at the mountain of statements on his desk. Last week, there'd been a radiation accident in the metallurgical lab. There were rumours that it had been deliberate and with two guys in hospital in Santa Fe there was no way even Arthur Whyte could ignore it. Carelessness was one thing, deliberate intent quite another.

Gómez wanted to know how Whyte was shaping up.

'Just the same. Halfway up Oppie's ass. Oppie knows the schmuck did them a big favour when Fiedler died and Whyte ain't about to let him forget it. Groves is back in a couple of days. Whyte's called a departmental meeting. He says the general wants to get one or two things straight.'

'Like?'

'He won't say. If you put money on us being out of line you're looking at good odds. Ten to one says we're not doing the job properly. Sound familiar?'

It was late afternoon by the time Gómez made it to the Fiedlers' apartment. Marta's face brightened the moment she looked out of the window and saw Gómez making for the front door.

'I thought you'd gone for good.' She presented her face for a kiss. 'You promised to send me a postcard.'

'Did I?'

'Maybe I made that up. You want some coffee? Something to eat?'

Gómez said yes to both. She made him a sandwich in the kitchen, baloney on rye, while the kettle boiled on the hob. Gómez was relieved to find her so buoyant. This way, the next half-hour might be a whole lot easier than he'd anticipated.

'You've come for a reason,' she said.

'Always.'

'Care to tell me why?'

'It's about Sol.'

'Surprise me. You know what? He comes to see me sometimes, middle of the night, it's the damnedest thing. I'm lying there asleep and then I feel his presence in the room. He always used to get up around that time to visit the bathroom. A man of routine, my husband. Even now.'

'You talk?'

'We do. And always in German. There's another thing. He looks the way he looked when we first met. He was a little heavier then. America took the weight off him. Or maybe it was the work.'

'Is he happy?'

'To see me, you mean?' Her eyes were shiny. 'Always. *Meine Spatzling*. I love that man. I truly do.'

Gómez wanted to take her back a month. It was the weekend. They were both invited to go on a trek around the canyon.

'In Bandelier?'

'Yeah.'

'Sure I remember it. I had a problem with my leg but I told Sol he should go. He wasn't getting enough exercise. Those other ladies would take care of him. There was no one they liked better.'

'Why was that?'

434

'Because he was sweet and gentle. And because he made them laugh.'

Gómez wanted to know who'd organised the walk.

'Betty Kerekes. She organises everything. You want to speak with her? I have the address.'

She disappeared into the living room while Gómez finished the sandwich. He heard a drawer open. Then another. When Marta returned, she'd written the address on the back of an envelope. Gómez scanned it quickly. Ten minutes away on foot, he thought. He looked up. She was asking whether he'd had enough to eat.

'Plenty,' he said. 'I have to go.'

She tried to mask her disappointment and smiled gamely when he promised to call back over the next couple of days. Out in the hall, he paused. He gave her a peck on the forehead and held her for a moment.

'Mind if I ask one last question?'

'Go ahead.'

'Were you ever bothered by a coyote?'

'Here in this house?'

'Yes.'

'Never.'

Marta was frowning. Gómez told her not to worry. Then he nodded at the open door to the lounge.

'I guess it must get lonely,' he said.

'*Ja*. It does.' Her face was upturned to his. 'You ever see Frank at all? There's another man I enjoyed having around. It's like he's gone, too.'

Betty Kerekes turned out to be an American married to one of the Hungarian scientists. She was a big woman with two teenage kids and a face made for laughter. When Gómez offered her his ID, she asked what she'd done wrong.

'Nothing.'

'This is a social call? Only I have a goulash on the stove out back.'

Gómez explained about his visit to Marta. He needed to check on the last time Sol Fiedler had gone out to the canyon. Betty had been in charge that day.

'Sure. You're gonna arrest me for that?'

Gómez shook his head. He wanted to know how much Betty remembered of that day.

'Everything. It's all up here.' She tapped her head. 'Try me.'

'How many people went?'

'Three cars.' She was counting her fingers. 'About fifteen of us.'

'And you were there all afternoon?'

'Pretty much.'

'You walk together? Stay tight?'

'Always. House rules.'

'No stragglers?'

'No. We're like one of those Atlantic convoys. Always move at the pace of the slowest.' She paused, frowning. 'This is about poor Sol? Sol Fiedler?'

'It is.'

'He was the slowest, by far, and I guess pretty much the oldest so no one's blaming him. You want to see some pictures I took? Only Sol's in most of them.'

She pulled Gómez into the house but left the door open. Her kids were due back any moment. With luck, her husband might make it by nightfall. She was rummaging through a cardboard box on the floor. At last she laid hands on the photo she wanted.

'There. Second on the right.'

Gómez found himself looking at a group of walkers peering into the sun. They were mainly women and the grins on their faces suggested the walk was over. Sol Fiedler was in the front row, right beside Betty. At the back Gómez recognised Arthur Whyte's wife, her blonde hair neatly piled on top of her head.

'I just need to get this right,' Gómez said. 'You walked round the canyon? All of you?'

'We did.'

'And stayed in a group?'

'Sure.'

'And that group included Sol?'

'Yep. In fact he was with me the whole way round. He was telling me about the old days in Berlin and how sad he was that he and Marta had to leave in such a hurry. They had a little money before the Nazis stole it and they had plans, too. You know what's so sad about that man? He never left Berlin. Not once. That's how dedicated he was to his research. They wanted to see so much more of the country. Munich. The Black Forest. Hamburg. And now it's too late.'

Gómez nodded. He asked whether he could borrow the photo.

'Sure. Give it to Marta if you want.' She was staring down at the photo. 'You know what? That's probably the last shot anyone ever took of the guy.'

*

The *Direktor* was back from America by the weekend. For three days, Stefan had done nothing but lie on his bed and read. A package of books, all of them in German, had been delivered by one of the guards with no indication of where they might have come from, but Stefan detected the hand of his latest interrogator, not least because one of them contained a scrawled signature at the front that Stefan tried on Hans.

'Ever heard of Guy Liddell?'

'He's the boss. The big man.'

'You're sure?'

'*Ja.*'

Stefan was halfway through *Der Weg zurück* when he was summoned back to the house. It was late afternoon, not a cloud in the sky, and the temperature was beginning to drop.

The *Direktor* was waiting for him in the big upstairs room. He looked exhausted but did his best to summon a smile. Stefan thanked him for the books. He was reading the Remarque. It felt strange to have time to give a book the attention it deserved.

'What do you make of Tjaden? Might he be touching a nerve or two?'

Tjaden was the book's central character. He returned from the Great War to find a society he didn't recognise. Chaos and corruption everywhere and a deep pessimism that started to rot his soul.

'Not with me,' Stefan said. 'Not yet, anyway.'

'Glad to hear it.'

The *Direktor* wanted to talk about Sol Fiedler.

438

'Were you aware of the nature of his work in Berlin?'

'No.'

'He never discussed it?'

'Never. It would have been pointless. I'm a sailor not a scientist and he knew that.'

'Was there ever any suggestion on his part that this work might have been delicate?'

'Delicate how?'

'Delicate in terms of consequences, of outcomes?'

'Absolutely not.'

'No mention of a super-weapon?'

'No.'

'Not even when he got to America?'

'No.' Stefan frowned. 'Super-weapon?'

The *Direktor* took the subject no further. Instead, he asked Stefan for a frank assessment of where, exactly, his half-brother's loyalties lay.

'Not with the regime, obviously. He found the Nazis beyond his comprehension. They disgusted him. And they frightened him, too.'

'How about his colleagues?'

'I think that was probably different. My guess is that his loyalty was always to science. I think he sometimes worried that the science would fall into the wrong hands. He never had much time for politicians.'

'That's quite a sophisticated judgement.'

'On his part?'

'On yours, *Kapitän*. To be frank I'm having difficulty trying to understand exactly how well you really knew this man. You say you met over a single weekend.'

'Two weekends.'

'Two weekends. And after that there arrived a handful of letters.'

'Three, I think.'

'All of which have disappeared.'

'Yes.'

'So no corroboration. No photographs, for instance.'

'There were photos. My mother took some. I never mentioned that.'

'But I expect they've gone, too.'

'That's right.' Stefan nodded. 'In the firestorm.'

The *Direktor* shook his head and then got to his feet. Stefan wondered why he'd gone to the States, who he'd seen and what kind of light a couple of days of meetings and conversations might have thrown on this story of his.

'We need to be honest with each other.' The *Direktor* was standing by the window. 'As you may have guessed, I've been intimately involved with our country's counter-intelligence service for a number of years. From time to time our counterparts in the Reich mount operations against us. They send in agents. They often arrive by parachute. These people are always ill-prepared. They are very easy to pick up and when we exert a little pressure their stories fall apart. Why? Because of a lack of attention to detail. Speaking personally, I've always found that puzzling. Germans are famed for their practicality. For the way they put things together. But perhaps they restrict this talent to the objects they physically build. When it comes to my world, their failure is a failure of imagination. They can't make that leap.'

'You mean they can't lie.'

'Yes. To make a fiction work you need lots of lies and you need to be careful how you put them together. It's a talent that Herr Goebbels has but I'll wager he's the exception. When it becomes to deception, to crafting the lies that will keep you alive, your people are mere apprentices.'

Stefan was wondering how much of this he should take personally. The *Direktor* hadn't finished. He said there was one exception to the rule, a spymaster who'd survived the murderous chaos of Hitler's inner circle, identified the right patron and risen to the top of Himmler's SS empire. This man, he ventured, was an operator of genius. He was highly educated. He'd never been tainted by the rougher elements of the regime. He spoke a number of languages. And he had an extremely supple brain.

'Does he have a name, this person?'

'Yes. And I suspect you know him, Stefan. Or, at the very least, that you've met him. His name is Schellenberg. Walter Schellenberg. And you'll remember him, dare I suggest, because he's our kind of man. This story of yours has his fingerprints all over it. And that, I might add, is a compliment.'

Stefan knew he was in trouble. To his knowledge, he hadn't made a single mistake. He'd been fluent and plausible. He'd given these people exactly what he'd been fed in Coruña, in exactly the right doses, yet somehow the *Direktor* had seen through it all.

'Tell me more about the super-weapon,' Stefan said.

'I can't. Because I don't know.'

'You think Sol may be working on it?'

'Sol is dead.'

'Dead?'

'You should be taking that personally, Stefan. He's supposed to be a relative of yours.'

Stefan sat back, closed his eyes. Was this the moment he confessed all? He thought not.

'As you say, I barely knew him.' He did his best to muster an apologetic shrug.

*

General Groves arrived at Los Alamos a day early after a summons to Washington and an abrupt change to his schedule. Arthur Whyte, who'd been making elaborate plans for the general to address a smallish audience of hand-picked scientists, was caught off-balance. He'd detected a brewing crisis in a 06.00 a.m. phone conversation with one of the Manhattan Project team at the Pentagon, and he was never at his best in the face of uncertainty. All he knew for sure was that Groves was demanding a private conference the moment he arrived with just four named individuals: himself, Oppenheimer, Whyte and Gómez.

'Why you?'

Gómez was sitting in Whyte's office. He'd been half expecting a development like this but was impressed by the speed of events. Less than a week ago he'd been driving across the border with the body of a man in the trunk of a lime-green Caddy. Now, the most powerful players on the national stage were gathering to figure out the consequences.

'I asked you a question, Gómez. Something to hide here?'

'Nothing, sir.'

'How was the vacation?'

'Fine. Got to see a lot of places. Met a few new people. Glad to be back.'

Whyte didn't believe a word. His conversation with the Pentagon suggested a major breach of security on the Hill. It was deeply uncomfortable to receive this news so early in the morning and have nothing to say in response.

'You been talking to any Bureau people? Because Groves will want to know.'

'I have friends, buddies from way back. That's allowed.'

'So what do you talk about?'

'All kinds of stuff. Old times. Folks we know.' He shrugged. 'A man on vacation's entitled to a conversation or two.'

'This isn't helping, Gómez.'

'Helping who, sir?'

'Any of us. And that includes you. The FBI have no jurisdiction here, as you well know. That was the deal from the start and General Groves has fought like a lion to keep it intact. I happen to be one of the few people he's confided in. He's got Hoover running to the President behind his back and all kinds of other coons just waiting for us to fall flat on our fannies. You think that time has come, Gómez? You think that's what this is about?'

'I've no idea.'

'You're lying, Gómez.'

'Care to tell me why, sir?'

'Because this has to be about Fiedler. Am I right?'

Gómez said nothing. Rule one. Let silence sweat the perp.

'Talk to me, Gómez. Tell me I'm wrong. Fiedler was a basket case. The pressure had got to him. He'd figured what lies at the end of the line once this thing is operational and he couldn't live

443

with that kind of headline. Plus the guy was creeping around other women. Like my wife. You dispute any of that?'

'Plenty.'

'Like what? Like he couldn't cope with a million deaths?'

'He had misgivings. A lot of them do. That's why they sit around and try and figure out a way of keeping their conscience clean now they've pretty much done their work. Stage a demo for the Nips, for the Russians, for anyone who cares to watch. Show the world what's round the goddam corner. You're right. The guy had a conscience. That's what made him a human being. But that's not enough for him to put a gun to his head.'

'Says you.'

'Says the scene. I'm happy to go over it again but this time you have to listen.'

'You think I didn't last time?'

'I think you had other things on your mind. I'm a detective, Colonel. I deal in facts, evidence.'

'And me?'

'You deal in outcomes. There's a difference. And you know what that means? Sometimes it means ignoring the evidence, or maybe bending it a little.'

The two men stared at each other. Whyte was the first to blink.

'That's a serious accusation, Lieutenant. I had no idea you felt that way. This interview is terminated. I shall tell General Groves you weren't able to make it.'

'You can tell him what you like, sir. I plan on being there.'

'I'm not sure you heard me right, soldier. I'm ordering you to stand down. We'll discuss this later.' He nodded towards the door. 'On your way, son.'

444

General Groves arrived shortly after noon. Recognising the bulky figure in the back of the big Buick, officers snapped a salute as the limousine swept past. Then, from one of the more distant canyons, came the reverberating boom of yet another explosion. They'd been happening all morning, a sign, thought Gómez, that the program was slipping into top gear.

He was sitting in his office. He knew the location of the first of the general's meetings because Merricks had told him. Oppie's conference room, he'd said. Over in the Tech Area. Now, he lifted the phone. Oppie had two secretaries and Gómez knew them both. One owed him a couple of favours. The other, an older woman called Margery, was rumoured to have a secret passion for the Hill's taciturn Hispanic.

Gómez recognised her voice. He asked whether Groves had made it up to the office yet. She said no.

'When he asks, here's where you'll find me.'

'I thought you were off the list?'

'You thought wrong.'

The phone rang again within minutes. Marge again.

'Now would be good,' she said. 'How come the great man even knows your name?'

Gómez pulled a file from his drawer. He made his way across the site and flashed his ID to the sentry on the inner checkpoint. From here he could see the windows up in Oppie's office. The blinds were down in both of them. Marge met him in the corridor.

'What have you done to my favourite man?' She loathed Whyte as well.

'Speak truth unto power.' He shot her a rare smile. 'Never fails.'

The atmosphere in the conference room was icy. Groves, as usual, was sitting at the head of the table, flanked by Oppenheimer and Whyte. Oppenheimer was already on his second cigarette. Whyte was even paler than usual.

Groves returned Gómez's salute and waved him into the seat across from Whyte. Whyte had a file open in front of him. The case for the prosecution, thought Gómez. The file had Fiedler's name on the front.

Groves was asking about a contractor called Donovan. Whyte had some difficulty placing the name. Groves, a man not famed for patience, turned to Gómez.

'You can help us here, Lieutenant?'

'Sure. The guy turned up on Tuesdays. Drove up from Santa Fe. Shot coyotes.'

'So where did Fiedler figure in all this?'

'Fiedler became a friend. So did Marta. One of those chance meetings that might not have been what they seemed. Either way the guy Donovan began to drop by. Said he was a big Bears fan. Got Fiedler talking. Like I say, buddies.'

'You were the one who handled the incident?'

'I got the call, sir, yes. First responder.'

'And what did you think?'

'I thought I was looking at a dead man. The scene was picture-perfect: gun, note, weeping widow.'

'A suicide?'

'Might have been. In those situations, it pays to reserve judgement. On three fronts I had a problem. Number one, Fiedler hated guns of any kind. Number two, by his wife's account he hadn't appeared depressed. And number three, there was a major mistake in the note.'

He said he'd recovered the slug that had killed Fiedler and sent both the bullet and the weapon to Washington for forensic matching.

Whyte stirred. He said he'd never authorised the despatch. Knew it ran counter to Army rules. Gómez pointed out that the FBI ran the best forensics service in the country. He had contacts there. No place on earth was time so precious as up here on the Hill. Best get the thing done quickly.

Groves wanted to know about the match. He was looking at Gómez.

'Positive, sir.'

'And the gun?'

'The gun belonged to Donovan.'

'How do you know?'

'I asked him. He admitted lending it to Fiedler.'

'Why did Fiedler want a gun? When he hated the things?'

'They'd been bothered by a coyote. Fiedler wanted to shoot it.'

'Says who?'

'Donovan.'

'And Marta?'

'Marta says there never was a coyote. It never happened.'

'You put this to Donovan?'

'I couldn't, sir. By the time I checked it out, he'd left town.'

Groves shot Whyte a look. The rest of the story, thought Gómez, the general must know already. Not true.

'We have a problem here.' Groves was looking at Oppenheimer. 'The Bureau say they have evidence of a major security leak but they ain't telling me a thing. I have a fire to fight and all the damn buckets are empty. If we lose this one, Hoover will be all over us. I need to know what they know and I need to know it fast. Changing my schedule was a bitch but we're not leaving this room until I know exactly what's been going on here.' The huge head swung round. 'Any ideas, Colonel?'

'Fiedler killed himself, sir. No one knows what really happens inside a man's head but I can make a guess or two.'

'Go ahead.'

'He was out of love with the program.'

'We're all out of love with the program, Colonel Whyte. That's what it's there for, to drive us insane. You're telling me he killed himself because he couldn't keep up?'

'No, sir. I think there was an ethical component. He hated killing in principle. He couldn't bear the thought of all the blood we'd be spilling.'

'This is the guy that borrows the gun? To shoot the damn coyote?'

Whyte blinked. This was worse than any court of law. Much worse.

'There was something else as well, sir,' he said. 'Something more intimate.'

He described the afternoon Fiedler exposed himself to a woman in one of the caves in a nearby canyon. Afterwards, he'd tried to have an affair with her. When she'd threatened to tell his wife, Fiedler had panicked.

Whyte had at last got the general's attention. He was even making a note. Then his head came up.

'How come you know all this?'

'The woman was my wife, sir. She was deeply shocked.'

There was a silence round the table. Oppenheimer tapped ash into his saucer. Then Gómez opened his file and lifted out the photograph he'd got from Betty Kerekes.

'That incident never happened, sir. And I can prove it.'

Two hours later, at the other end of the afternoon, Gómez found himself alone with Oppenheimer. Groves, persuaded that Whyte and his wife had cooked up the story about Fiedler, had asked the colonel to make himself available later for a personal interview. With Whyte dismissed from the room, Gómez had briefed Groves and Oppenheimer about exactly what had happened down in Mexico. The news that Sol Fiedler had been ferrying nuclear secrets to the Nazis via Donovan and his lady friend in Ciudad Juarez had reduced even Groves to silence. Letting this stuff fall into the laps of the Soviets was bad enough. This was far worse.

Oppenheimer was in a reflective mood. One of the things Gómez was beginning to like about him was his refusal to panic. Behind the charm and the intensity that had become his trademarks, this man had nerves of steel. He also found time to ponder every aspect of whatever crisis came next until a resolution drifted into focus.

Now was no different. He'd known Sol Fiedler. The man wasn't a drinker, and neither was Oppenheimer, but they'd shared a glass or two together from time to time and prowled the ramparts of this strange new life on the Hill.

'I don't buy it,' he said. 'Sol hated the Nazis. There was no way he'd do anything to help them. Shipping stuff out to the Commies? Maybe. But even then it's beyond unlikely. That man loved America. He believed in what we were doing. Why would he ever want to murder our baby at birth? It makes no sense. None whatsoever.'

'Maybe Whyte was right about his conscience. Maybe he figured that a secret shared might let him sleep at night.'

'So how does that work? Imagine the Nazis are first past the finishing line. Say they drop their own Gadget on London. On Antwerp. How does that serve the cause of world peace?'

Gómez admitted he didn't know. Oppenheimer hadn't finished. He wanted to find out more about Donovan.

'Sure.' Gómez nodded. 'Another so-called suicide.'

'You don't think he killed himself?'

'It certainly looked that way but that doesn't mean he did it. There's always another question to ask.'

'*Cui bono*,' Oppenheimer said. 'Who stands to gain.'

'Exactly.'

Oppenheimer lit another cigarette from the butt of the old one. 'You're telling me Donovan had some kind of relationship with this German woman?'

'Yes.'

'Because she knew he had access up here on the Hill?'

'I'm guessing so.'

'So how did they meet?'

'He was running cars into the States from Mexico. Everything operated from Ciudad Juarez right there on the border. It's not a big city. Two gringos? It would be strange if they didn't meet some place, get to know each other. She's an attractive woman. He likes to play the stud. Plus she acts like a kind of consul so she's in constant touch with the regime back home.'

'And she's the one who wants Fiedler dead? Who types the note? Gets Donovan to pull the trigger? Then fake the whole scene?'

'Yes.' Gómez nodded.

'So why would she do that?'

'Because she wants us to believe that Fiedler has been leaking secrets.'

'Not she, buddy. Berlin. *Berlin* wants us to believe all this stuff.' Oppenheimer was frowning. 'But she makes mistakes. Like in the note. Like having Donovan lend him the gun.'

'Sure . . .' Gómez nodded, '. . . but maybe that was deliberate. Maybe that was a come-on. Maybe she was depending on someone like me to play the cop and sniff the air and follow the smoke upwind. What she wants, what she *needs*, is a solid link between Donovan and herself. Once that happens, she's got people like me and you believing what the Nazis want us to believe with only one problem left.'

'Donovan.'

'Exactly. He knows the suicide was faked.'

'So she has him killed.'

'Sure. Not a difficulty where she's living.'

Gómez sat back. In another life, he thought, Oppenheimer would have made a decent detective. Give the bag of evidence a shake and see what falls out. Then keep rearranging the pieces until you end up with the truth. Oppenheimer sucked smoke deep into his lungs, tipped his head back, and then expelled a thin blue plume towards the ceiling. Gómez, watching, sensed exactly where he was heading.

'There were no secrets,' Gómez said softly. 'The whole thing was a set-up.'

'Sure.' Oppenheimer nodded. 'All they need is for us to believe it *might* have happened. That's enough. *Might*. Catastrophe in the subjunctive. Never proven. Never one hundred per cent. But emphatically possible. Very neat. Very elegant.' He picked a shred of tobacco from his lower lip. 'Almost beautiful.'

25

Stefan was awoken in the middle of the night. This time he'd been dreaming about his mother. He was a child again, small, busy, inquisitive. They were on a tram into the middle of the city. His mother was trying to explain to the inspector why she hadn't bought a ticket. The man was unforgiving. He had a greying moustache. Every time he opened his mouth, he wanted more money. First one *Reichsmark*. Then ten. Then a hundred. His mother was crying. She had no money. Then the man's gaze settled on Stefan. 'Him,' he grunted. 'I'll take him.'

The *Direktor* was waiting for him in the main house. No handcuffs this time, and only a couple of blankets between Stefan and the intense cold. The escort lingered briefly at the door. The *Direktor* dismissed him with a wave of his hand.

'My apologies.' He turned back to Stefan. 'This is no time for civilised people to be talking to each other. Under any other circumstances, I'd have left this until the morning.'

'But you can't?'

'Alas, no. What I'm going to propose, Stefan, is in the nature of a deal, or perhaps an understanding. On your side, you must believe that I have the authority to make this thing happen. On my side, I have to believe that you're telling me the truth. Does that sound equitable to you?'

Equitable. Stefan frowned. Was anything fair in war?

'What do you want to know?' He asked.

'I want to know what really happened from the moment when you left your boat.'

'And me? What do I get?'

'Eva.'

'You know where she is?'

'We do.'

'How?'

The *Direktor* shook his head. Enough, he seemed to be saying. Trust me. Or face the consequences.

'And if I say no?'

'If you say no, then the matter will be out of my hands. What will happen to you, God alone knows. This isn't Prinz-Albrecht-Strasse but this country has an ugly side, believe me.'

Stefan enquired no further. He pulled the blankets more closely around himself. The silence stretched and stretched.

'I've turned my back on my own country once already,' he said at last. 'Maybe it pays to be consistent.'

'You consider yourself a traitor?'

'In some ways yes. In others, no. But deep down I'm not sure I care any more.'

'Is that a confession?'

'Yes.' Stefan forced a smile. 'Do you want the rest?'

*

It was Merricks who roused Gómez. He'd gone to bed early, exhausted by the events of the last week. Now Merricks had something urgent to tell him.

'A woman phoned for you. I'm guessing it was Yolanda.'

Gómez struggled upright in the narrow bed. It was a capital offence to impart any phone number on the Hill but he'd done it nonetheless.

'What did she want?'

'She wouldn't say. She sounded upset. She left a number. I said you'd phone back.'

Gómez dressed. The office was five minutes away. Merricks had left it unlocked. Gómez dialled the number, aware the call would be logged, but he no longer cared. Whyte was history. Marge said she'd found him in shock. The general had demanded he resign his commission, effective immediately. Marge had phoned his wife and asked her to come over but she said she was too busy. Nice people.

Yolanda picked up at once.

'It's Agard,' she said. She seemed to be choking on the phone. Gómez had never associated her with tears.

'What's happened?'

'He was attacked this evening. Two guys came to his apartment.'

'They beat him up?'

'Worse. Acid.'

'In his face?'

'Yeah. He managed to get to the Emergency Room. They did what they could.'

'You've seen him?'

'I just came back.'

'And?'

'It's horrible.' She started crying. 'You need to be with us, baby. You need to be away from that place.'

Gómez told her to try and stay calm. He'd get a flight tomorrow morning. His work on the Hill was done. He told her he loved her and put the phone down.

Arthur Whyte's wife was standing in the open doorway. She must have heard every word.

'Your work on the Hill?' she said. 'Is that what you call it? Wrecking a senior officer's career? Upsetting everything?'

Gómez studied her for a moment. The state of her make-up told him she'd been crying, too.

'A decent man died,' he said. 'Your husband just needs to find another job. One day you might understand the difference.'

*

Stefan was released from the Centre the following morning. A pretty woman in Royal Navy uniform drove him into central London. Bomb damage, light at first, got worse but nothing Stefan saw from the back of the car compared to what he'd seen in Hamburg.

The woman at the wheel hadn't introduced herself, neither did she answer when Stefan asked where they were going. The traffic was thickening now and behind the pile of sandbags he recognised the statue of the Duke of Wellington on horseback, one of the stopping points on the tour of the capital he'd taken as a naval cadet.

Hyde Park, he thought. Ducks on the water. Londoners lazing in the sun. And in the evening, a visit to a reception at a big house in a square somewhere near here. Back then Europe was still at peace, a fact of life it was all too easy to take for granted. Their hosts had made them very welcome, rich people, people who approved of the Reich.

The driver was slowing to make a turn. Two American airmen paused at the kerb and one of them blew her a kiss. She wasn't amused.

In the maze of streets off Piccadilly, the car finally came to a halt. The *Direktor* was waiting on the pavement. Summer seemed to have returned and he was sweating lightly in the hot sunshine. Stefan shook his outstretched hand and turned to thank the driver but the car had gone.

'This way, Stefan.'

It was a modest, three-storey house, Georgian, fine windows. The *Direktor* produced a key and stepped inside. There were fresh flowers in a cut-glass vase on a table in the wall and carpeted stairs led to the upper floors. The *Direktor* climbed the stairs slowly, turning to check that Stefan was able to manage on his injured leg. When they reached the top of the house, he paused to tender an apology.

'We had plans to install a lift before the war,' he said. 'If you've nothing else against your Leader, you might blame him for that.'

He showed Stefan into a bedroom. Everything was pink. Another apology.

'My youngest used to have this room. Girls love pink. Something else I've never got round to sorting out. At least you're spared the rocking horse and her army of bloody golliwogs.'

Stefan looked round. The *Direktor* clearly had children, and presumably a wife. He was tempted to enquire further but decided against it. After his week in the freezing cold at the Centre, the room felt warm and homely. Sunshine was streaming in through the window and when he stepped across to check the view he found himself looking down into a small garden. Directly below him was a woman sitting on a wooden bench, deep in a book. She was wearing a hat against the sun and, as he watched, she turned the page. Nice legs, he thought.

'Here. I had them typed up this morning.'

Stefan glanced round to find the *Direktor* offering him an envelope. Inside, he said, were the notes he'd made during their conversation in the small hours.

'Conversation? I thought I did all the talking?'

'You did but this is my version. I'd be obliged if you could check it for accuracy. Anything I've got wrong, please leave an indication in the margin.'

Stefan nodded. Of course, he said. My pleasure.

The *Direktor* offered a courtly little smile of thanks and said he'd be back later. To Stefan's surprise, he didn't lock the door. Stefan settled into an armchair at the foot of the bed. Opening the envelope, he shook the contents on to his lap. There were nine double-spaced sheets, immaculately typed, each page numbered.

The account was written in the first person, as if Stefan himself had dictated it, and as he began to read he could hear the sound of his own voice, hesitant at first, mumbling an apology for a misplaced fact or some other failure of memory, but then gaining in strength and confidence until he was in full flow, glad at last that it was so easy to get every detail exactly right.

He'd held nothing back. Eva. Agustín. The morning the villagers had buried his crew. The night the *Guardia* had come for him. Coruña. Otto. Erwin. And perhaps most important of all, the older man who'd also flown in from Berlin. At the *Direktor*'s prompting, Stefan had described him in great detail: the way he wore his hair, the fleshiness of his lips, how educated he'd seemed, and what a contrast he'd been to all the other SS people Stefan had ever met.

The *Direktor* had been delighted. Stefan might have been describing a close personal friend.

'That's Walter,' he'd said. 'Walter Schellenberg. You liked him?'

'I thought he was clever, And I suppose I must have trusted him.'

'Very wise. He's the best you've got.'

'Really? So why hasn't it worked?'

'Because we're better. And so, in some respects, are you.'

In the small hours, shivering under his blankets, Stefan hadn't known quite what to make of this remark, and reading through the transcription he could find no trace of it. Should he make a note, suggest a minor addition, or had this aside been something more personal, even intimate?

He read on, following his own journey south to Lisbon where Erwin had left him on the waterfront with nothing but a ten-minute limp between himself and the enemy's neat little embassy.

Enemy? He'd never used the term last night and it certainly didn't appear in the transcript but that, of course, was the way his generation had been schooled. War, they'd been taught, was unforgiving, pitiless, a struggle to the death. In war, you killed or you perished. There was nothing else on offer, no other means of securing your own survival. Either you released your torpedo, or pulled your trigger, or dropped your bomb, or the enemy would take that decision out of your hands. *Totaler Krieg*. Total war. It was the logic of the charnel house. It had led to countless deaths, untold disasters, but in some unfathomably obscene way it seemed to be necessary, even honourable. Your Führer expected no less. Kill for the Reich. And probably die in the process.

Nonsense.

Stefan took the *Direktor*'s pen and went through the account a second time, initialling each page. It felt like signing a contract and in a way he supposed it was. For nine pages of the truth, the *Direktor* had pledged to set him free. And here they were: checked, initialled and back in the envelope. Good, he thought. Sanity. At last.

Stefan got up and moved the chair closer to the window. Then he sat down again, his head tipped back, the sun full on his face. He was glad it was over. He closed his eyes. Within seconds, like a baby in this pinkest of rooms, he was asleep.

Later, he'd no idea when, he heard a soft tap at the door. The *Direktor*, he thought, as courteous as ever.

'*Kommen Sie*,' Stefan said.

The door opened. Still facing the window, Stefan's hand felt for the envelope.

'You got it right,' he said. 'Every last detail.'

'I did?' A woman's voice. Heavily accented.

Stefan froze, wondering whether this was some dream, whether he was still asleep, then he forced himself to look round. She had the hat in one hand, the book in the other, and she was smiling.

'Eva?' he said, lost again.

459

*

Gómez left the Hill without a backward glance. He'd said his goodbyes to the handful of people who'd ever mattered to him. Marta gave him a hug and wrote down the address of her friends in Chicago. She'd be staying with them for a while. If he found himself back home, he was always welcome to drop by. Merricks, for his part, slipped Gómez five dollars and told him to buy something cute for the kids when they happened along. Gómez hadn't once thought of having children but pocketed the bill just in case. For now, he told himself, Yolanda was plenty enough but real life could always take a man by surprise.

Arthur Whyte had been replaced by his sidekick, a thin, sardonic major with a nice line in wetback jokes. Gómez knew a little about his investigative record and had some respect for the man. In a final interview, just hours before Merricks was due to run him up to Albuquerque for the plane to DC, the major made Gómez sign a series of release forms that pledged him never to divulge a word about life on the Hill. Gómez's resignation had come as no surprise to G-2's new boss.

'Once a Fed, always a Fed. Am I right?'

Gómez hadn't answered but the ghost of a smile told the major he was on the money.

'You gonna step straight back into that old life? Same office? Same suit? Same fucking overtime?'

'No way.'

'You got something else in mind?'

'Yeah.'

'Care to tell me what?'

'No.'

460

They'd shaken hands and the major had accompanied Gómez to the door.

'Merricks tells me you're getting hitched.'

'Merricks is right.'

'Good lucky, buddy. Long life and happiness, yeah?' He'd nodded at the view from the nearby window. 'Let's hope the rest of this shit works out.'

Gómez had an hour to wait at the airport for the plane to DC. It was a military flight, booked solid, and he had the major to thank for his seat. The plane took off in the early afternoon, routed through Kansas City, and was easing on to the runway at National in the last glimmers of dusk.

A cab took Gómez to the hospital. Yolanda had phoned again with the details. Fourth floor. Big room at the end of the corridor. Gómez took it easy on the stairs. There were moments in life that deserved a little time, a little preparation, and this was one of them.

The ward took him by surprise. It was full of blacks, most of them old. Yolanda was sitting beside a bed at the far end. Gómez made his way across. She saw him in time to get to her feet and put her arms around him.

Gómez kissed her, told her everything was gonna be just fine. He couldn't see Beaman's face for bandages. Gómez settled on the side of the bed, reached for his hand, gave it a squeeze. Beaman had recognised his voice.

'Sonofabitch,' he whispered. 'You made it.'

'I did.'

'So what do you think?' One bony hand gestured at the wreckage of his face. 'You gonna take the job now? You gonna see I come to no more harm?'

Gómez stared at him for a long moment. He could feel the warmth of Yolanda's body beside him. Then he reached for Beaman's skinny hand and gave it a squeeze.

'You bet,' he said.

AFTERWARDS

General Leslie Groves sent a special mission into Europe in the wake of the advancing Allied armies. Code-named Alsos (*alsos* is the Greek for 'grove') it was tasked with finding out whether or not the Nazis had a viable atomic programme. In November 1944, weeks after Stefan Portisch's confession, it arrived in Strasbourg where detailed investigations convinced Lieutenant Colonel Boris Pash, the mission's leader, that 'Germany had no atomic bomb and was not likely to have one in any reasonable form'.

On 16 July 1945, scientists from the Manhattan Project tested the world's first atomic bomb at Alamogordo, New Mexico. The bomb was an implosion-detonated device with a plutonium core, the design on which Sol Fiedler had worked. The resulting explosion had a force of 20,000 tons of TNT and melted the desert sand. Within three weeks, two atomic bombs were dropped on the Japanese cities of Hiroshima and Nagasaki, killing nearly a quarter of a million people. Japan surrendered on 2 September 1945.

After the war, General Groves was appointed Chief of the Armed Forces Special Weapons Project, charged with controlling military aspects of America's nuclear programme. He left the Army in 1948 and died in 1970.

The war over, **Robert Oppenheimer** became a Chief Adviser to the US Atomic Energy Commission and lobbied vigorously to avert nuclear proliferation and an arms race with the Soviet Union. He died in 1967.

Edgar Hoover survived in office until he died of a heart attack in 1972. By then, as Director of the FBI, he'd served no fewer than eight US Presidents. Richard Nixon called Hoover 'one of the giants of American life'.

Walter Schellenberg acted as a covert envoy during the closing months of the war, trying to broker a peace between the Western powers and Germany. After the German surrender, he stood trial at Nuremberg and was sentenced to six years' imprisonment. After his release he moved to Switzerland before settling in Italy. He died penniless in Turin. Coco Chanel paid for the cost of his funeral.

Guy Liddell, in charge of counter-espionage at MI5, left the agency under a cloud in 1953 following the defection to the Soviet Union of his close friend Guy Burgess and went to work as a security adviser to the Atomic Energy Authority. He died of heart failure in 1958.

Hector Gómez married Yolanda in November 1944. They settled in Chicago where they looked after **Agard Beaman** and helped mastermind his successful campaign to become the representative for the city's First Congressional District. Despite his blindness, Beaman's was a leading voice in the struggle that led to the Civil Rights Act of 1964 which transformed race relations in the US. Gómez died of a heart attack in 1968. Yolanda, childless, never remarried.

Stefan Portisch and **Eva Gironda** returned to Spain in July 1945. Eva had inherited a half-share in her father's house after his death and they lived there until a third child necessitated a move to a larger property on the outskirts of the village. Eva died in 1963 after a long battle with ovarian cancer. Stefan was lost at sea while fishing offshore the following month. His body was never recovered.

A NOTE FROM THE AUTHOR

I've always been fascinated by the Second World War. My father flew in Beaufighters and fought in North Africa. My mum was working in London during the Blitz. Their experiences, plus the tidal wave of books that flooded out of that bottomless conflict, offered me a rich store of experiences, mercifully second-hand.

As a published writer, I was lured into crime fiction and wrote sixteen books powered by the same cast of characters. It taught me a great deal, but always, at the very back of my mind, I was aware that I'd ducked the really big challenge. What if I was to treat the Second World War as the biggest crime scene ever, narrow the focus to a handful of characters – some fictional, others not – and see what happened?

The result was *Finisterre*. My publisher, Nic Cheetham at Head of Zeus, liked it well enough to offer me a contract but wondered if I could turn this take on World War II into a series. The prospect of a recurring single character, heroic or otherwise, wasn't something I wanted to do. But the more I thought about it and the more deeply I read into the period, I realised that this global convulsion must have spawned an unimaginable wealth of untold stories as lives were torn apart and men and women faced challenges they could never otherwise have imagined. The potential buried in this tangle of threads might be fictional gold.

I had a notion, that – book by book – I could weave together a series from a loose cast of characters, taking a peripheral character from one book and casting them in a central role in another. Sol Fiedler, for instance, is found dead in the opening pages of *Finisterre*. But what of his life in pre-war Berlin? And as he and Marta faced persecution at the hands of an increasingly brutal regime? And how about Guy Liddell, the real-life MI5 spymaster charged with control of counter-espionage? Might he make a reappearance in one of the books to follow?

Thus was born the Spoils of War series. This notion, which I dubbed 'soft-linkage', is one of the structural elements of the Spoils of War, and has proved immensely fertile. Not least because most of these characters, deliberately or otherwise, found themselves lured into the treacherous swamplands of the intelligence world.

Stefan Portisch, of course, is the perfect example. Trapped by circumstances beyond his control, and threatened with a firing squad, he's forced to lie for a regime he's come to loathe. Likewise, in book two, *Aurore*, a young Quaker called Billy Angell becomes radicalised by the loss of a close friend, turns his back on his pacifist principles, and joins Bomber Command as a Wireless Operator. By surviving his first operational tour, he cheats almost certain death. But what follows, thanks to his recruitment by MI5, opens his eyes to a very different kind of terror. Fate and a mind-numbing despair turned Stefan Portisch into playing a role for which he had no taste, but in Billy's case he was an actor already – a career choice he will later come to regret.

After *Aurore*, there will be a third book in the series, *Estocada*. Set in 1938, when elements in Germany were organising a coup to kill Hitler, it pitches a young German fighter pilot – Dieter Merz – against an ex-Royal Marine put into play by MI5. His name is Tam Moncrieff. Both these characters have already appeared in *Aurore* and their first taste of the secret world will change their lives forever. Why? Because the business of war, and the business of spying, combine in ways that stretch mere warriors to breaking point.

Welcome to the Spoils of War.

About the author

GRAHAM HURLEY is the author of the acclaimed Faraday and Winter crime novels and an award-winning TV documentary maker. Two of the critically lauded series have been shortlisted for the Theakston's Old Peculier Award for Best Crime Novel. His French TV series, based on the Faraday and Winter novels, has won huge audiences. The first Spoils of War novel, *Finisterre*, was shortlisted for the Wilbur Smith Adventure Writing Prize. Graham now writes full-time and lives with his wife, Lin, in Exmouth.

www.grahamhurley.co.uk